Love to the Rescue

Kat Neil

Copyright © 2024 by Kat Neil

ISBN: 979-8-9905653-0-2

All rights reserved.

No part of this publication may be reproduced, distributed, or transmitted in any form or by any means, including photocopying, recording, or other electronic or mechanical methods, without the prior written permission of the publisher, except as permitted by U.S. copyright law. For permission requests, contact Kat Neil.

The story, all names, characters, and incidents portrayed in this production are fictitious. No identification with actual persons (living or deceased), places, buildings, and products is intended or should be inferred.

Cover Design by Wynter Designs

Editing by Indie Proofreading

Formatting by Indie Proofreading

For Darryl, Mason, and Maleyni. My loves.

Author's Note

This story and its contents are a work of fiction created from the author's imagination. Any resemblance to real people, places, or events is purely coincidental.

Trigger Warnings:
  - Fictional therapy sessions about grief and getting over the death of a loved one
  - Intimate, sexual scenes between the main male and female characters
  - Use of profanity
  - Detailed fire scenes

Contents

Chapter 1

Nicole

Nicole attempted to lift her weighty eyelids to no avail. She needed her surroundings to become familiar, to piece together her location. With legs sprawled across the park bench in a dreamlike state, she perceived the wailing sound of sirens growing louder, more intense and prominent. Consumed by a sense of disorientation and confusion, Nicole struggled to recall the purpose of her visit to the park. The sirens ceased. Nicole startled awake as she registered the sounds of car doors slamming, muffled voices becoming louder, and shuffling feet coming closer to her.

"Ma'am? Can you hear me?" a deep masculine voice asked.

Nicole opened her eyes to a blurred image. After several seconds, her vision became unbarred. Kneeling before her was the most stunning man she had ever laid eyes on. The mere sight of him quickened the pace of her heart. If Nicole didn't find a way to relax, her rapid heartbeat felt as if it could burst her chest wide open.

As his coffee brown eyes locked with Nicole's, the captivating man asked, "Are you able to share your name with me?"

Nicole's voice caught on a breath. "Nicole Graham," she replied.

"Well Ms. Graham, we're going to give you some oxygen and take some vitals, okay?"

Nicole could only nod her head in agreement.

Within seconds, the handsome man and a female emergency medical technician covered Nicole's nose and mouth with an oxygen mask. Her senses sharpened with each lungful of air, inhaling deep breaths in and out.

The shiny gold name tag hanging from Gale Hopper's shirt lapel shimmered as she grabbed the nearby black bag, pulling out a stethoscope.

"Davis? I'll listen to her heartbeat," Hopper said, blonde ponytail bobbing as she took a few steps to be on the other side of the bench, placing the cold diaphragm on Nicole's chest.

Davis? Was that the man's name? Nicole moved her head slightly, catching the sight of him as he placed the blood pressure cuff around her arm. A momentary pause seized her heart. His smooth russet brown complexion, closely cut dark brown hair, and tall, muscular frame became Nicole's sole concentration. Davis' fingers grazed her arm when he removed the blood pressure cuff, causing a tightening sensation in her stomach muscles.

"One twenty-eight over seventy-five," Davis called to Hopper, her eyebrows now raised by the reading.

"A little elevated. Her heart rate exceeds the normal range. We should take her in," Hopper suggested. "Is there anyone we can call Ms. Graham?" Hopper asked, gently touching Nicole's shoulder. "We want to take you in for observation."

It took a few seconds for the question to register in Nicole's mind before she could speak. She glanced at Hopper, standing close-by, holding her well-toned arms at her sides. "My brother. Levi Graham," Nicole answered in a soft tone.

"Where's your phone, ma'am?" Davis asked, staring into her eyes. For a brief moment, Nicole found herself captivated by his gaze.

"It should be in my side pants pocket," Nicole whispered, unable to move her arms to retrieve it.

Hopper extracted Nicole's phone from her pocket. "Can you open your phone and pull up your brother's number so we can call him?" Hopper asked, pointing the phone in Nicole's direction, its surface now displaying an image of Nicole's parents embracing one another, smiling into the screen.

Nicole inhaled a breath, now breathing easily with the oxygen mask. She lifted her weighted arm to reach for her phone. Once in her hand, she entered her code to unlock it and pulled up Levi's contact information. Hands trembling, she handed her phone to Hopper.

"Thank you! We'll call him and ask him to meet us at the hospital," Hopper said, walking a few feet away to make the call.

"We need to get you on the stretcher to transport you to the hospital, Ms. Graham," Davis said, looking down at her, giving her a warm smile. That smile had a mesmerizing effect on her Nicole thought.

Hopper walked over to Nicole's side and spoke. "Ms. Graham? I spoke with your brother and he'll meet us at the hospital."

Nicole nodded and gave Hopper a tight-lipped smile.

"Let's get her on the stretcher," Hopper commanded. "Stand back, Davis! I'll grab her upper body and you grab her legs, and then we'll move her onto the stretcher. On three! One, two, three!" Hopper tucked her arms under Nicole's armpits as Davis heaved her legs and moved her body. She sensed herself being elevated, almost weightless, as if being raised by angels, from the park bench to the waiting stretcher. The warmth of the sun heated her cheeks. The bright rays in her face, Nicole lifted her hands to shield her weary eyes from the piercing sunlight.

"Davis? Can you adjust the headrest so the sun isn't in her eyes?" Hopper asked.

Davis adjusted Nicole's headrest, then gave her a closed-mouth smile and pushed the stretcher into the back of the emergency vehicle. Butterflies were now flying around in her stomach. Here Nicole was, recovering from what she thought was a fainting spell, and the man standing at the foot of the stretcher occupied her thoughts. She found herself entranced by his attractiveness. She was unable to recall the last time she pondered a man in this way.

In a raspy voice, Nicole whispered, "Will I be okay?"

"You'll be just fine, Ms. Graham." Hopper moved around the well-equipped cabin, fluffing a pillow under Nicole's head, tucking the blanket under her legs, and monitoring her vitals. She then asked, "Do you remember what happened at the park?"

Nicole reflected for a second. What happened at the park? She remembered going for a run, sitting on the park bench, then everything went black. With a strained frown, Nicole replied in a hushed tone, "I only remember parts of the day."

Speaking with a compassionate demeanor, Hopper said, "Well, don't you worry. There's time for that later."

After what seemed like the briefest of moments, the emergency vehicle came to a stop. The door swung open and Davis unhooked the stretcher, pulling Nicole out of the ambulance. She studied Davis' effortless display of power as he maneuvered the heavy stretcher out of the ambulance.

"We can take it from here," a man in a white coat said. "Davis, we know it's your last day. Good luck, man!"

Nicole looked at Davis. Last day? What did that mean? Eager to discover his full name, she squinted to read the inscription on his name tag. Cameron Davis. An invisible force compelled her to look at him. He was a beautiful man. His defined cheekbones and almond-shaped eyes were exquisite. Experiencing an instant sense of connection when her eyes locked with his, heat spread through Nicole's entire body. If he touched her in this moment, she might torch his hand. Lying on a stretcher about to be rolled into the hospital, overwhelmed by vulnerability, she found herself incapable of maintaining her gaze.

Cameron's eyes were warm and forgiving. In a soft tone, flashing a million-dollar smile, he spoke directly to her. "Ms. Graham, take care of yourself now." Nicole shut her eyes, memorizing his face for later recollection. His infectious smile would forever leave an imprint on her brain.

Two men in white coats lifted Nicole from the ambulance stretcher onto a hospital rolling cot. They wheeled her through double hospital doors and into a waiting bed in the emergency room. A middle-aged nurse dressed in blue scrubs was waiting to attend to her.

"Hello, I'm Nurse Walker. We're going to draw some blood and run some tests, okay?"

Too exhausted to speak, Nicole nodded. Just as she lay her head back on the pillow, she saw Levi and her parents walking toward her bedside. Worry stretched across their faces, Nicole greeted them with a weary smile. She shut her eyes. Walter, Nicole's father, grabbed her hands and planted gentle kisses on her knuckles. Angst in his tone, Walter whispered, "We're here, little girl."

Levi studied his sister's face before asking, "Do you remember what happened? What were you doing this morning?"

A chill swept over her, leaving her cheeks tingling. Nicole turned her gaze away from her family, her head and body slowly rotating to face the plain white wall adjacent to her hospital bed. It was challenging to direct her eyes towards them. It has been almost two years. The park, her run, seeing Officer Stone. Him reminding her of Tyler. Tears now rolling down her cheek, Nicole put her face into her trembling hands and cried until there were no more tears.

Chapter 2

Cameron

T he thunderous sound of the fire alarm awoke Cameron out of a sunken sleep.

"Oh, shit!" he yelled, rushing to dress, as the guys on shift scrambled to reach their turnout gear.

"That alarm shakes me every time. Real shit," Cameron admitted to his work buddy, David Perry.

"You'll get used to it. EMT shifts are easy compared to a firefighter's schedule. It's only been a few months. Give yourself a break, Davis." Perry knew what it meant to get used to the grueling schedule of a firefighter. Perry had three young children at home and constantly felt sleep deprived with years on the job. He still hadn't gotten used to his own schedule. He wanted to help Cameron as much as he could.

Cameron knew Perry was right. He chose this career. He had to get used to long shifts and sleep deprivation.

"Cameron? You'd be afraid of your own shadow if you didn't know it was you," Jeff Nickelson barked.

"I should duct tape your mouth while you sleep. You wouldn't wake up being so annoying," Cameron barked back.

Dressed in turnout gear, headsets on and helmets in hand, the guys ran to the fire engine and moved to sit in their assigned seats. The guys were in expert hands with Captain Peter Garey at the wheel. Close to retirement, Garey only worked three days a week. They all missed his presence on his days off. No one had the wisdom, experience, or balls to call out orders at Station 12 like Garey. In control and always the incident commander, he swiftly arrived on each scene, assessed the situation, and made the calls to quickly put out fires and get back to the station without harm. It was Garey's strong work ethic and courageous actions that made him an excellent study and role model for Cameron. Lights flashing, sirens ringing, they raced down the main street, dodging cars that refused to merge right.

"What's the call?" Perry asked.

"Apartment complex fire. Three stories. Possible injuries. Cause unknown. This fire is vicious. Two other stations are en route," Garey announced.

Unsure of what would greet him upon arrival, Cameron took a deep breath and exhaled to release the coiled tension in his stomach. With seconds to turn it around, a surge of adrenaline and heightened alertness overcame him as they approached the burning building. The Los Angeles police department cleared the street, creating clear access for the truck's engine to open at full power. Sirens screaming, speeding down the street, bystanders looked to see the action. At the corner of the main and side streets of the fire location, they saw billowing clouds of smoke pouring into the sky, resembling spouting chimneys at a coal factory. Angry flames spit out of the three-story buildings with relentless force. Station 12 was the first company to arrive. As the truck came to a halt, Cameron, Perry, and Nickelson rushed off the truck and headed to its rear to grab the attack line. Garey leaped out and ran to inspect the front of the complex up close for his own assessment. Smoke surged upward, engulfing the night sky in a thick haze.

"We gotta act fast!" Garey shouted.

As residents and nosey onlookers stood across the street from the building, Cameron followed Garey, noting the location and intensity of the fire. Watching flames leap from broken windows, Cameron stood doing his own assessment of the inflamed dwellings, imagining what was waiting inside. Armed with courage and purpose, Garey and Lieutenant Victor Jackson charged to the building entry, Cameron, Perry, and Nickelson close behind them.

"We've got an engulfed fire on all three floors in at least two buildings!" Garey announced through the headset. "Nickelson, you're on the nozzle. Davis, back him up. Take the first building."

Nickelson, having a bit more experience than Cameron, took the lead with the hose line while Cameron trailed closely behind. Ignoring the intense heat, they entered the building. Blinding smoke seeped through Cameron's face shield. Blinking his eyes repeatedly, he pushed through the inflamed building, thankful for the SCBA, helping him breathe clean air. Adjusting to the constant presence of smoke and shadows in his surroundings would require some time.

"Hit it with a straight stream!" Garey commanded.

The powerful jets of water slashed through the darkness, covering the heart of the flames. Steam hissed, and swirls of smoke curled skyward, compromising the integrity of the walls. Puddles of water scattered the ground across the entire first floor. Unsalvageable belongings and charred furniture were the sole remaining evidence people lived in these spaces.

"Hey, Davis! Check that door. Are there flames on the other side?"

Nickelson asked.

As Cameron got closer to the door, he could feel the heat.

"I'm gonna open it, Nickelson, back me up with the hose," Cameron directed. Fortunately, the door opened inward, blocking flames inside, allowing Nickelson to spray water into the interior, reducing the intensity of the fire.

"Nickelson? Davis? Move to the second floor," Garey commanded. "All companies are on site and working on the second and third floor."

On the headset, Davis answered, "Yes, sir!"

"Nickelson? Do you see the stairwell?" Davis asked.

"Over here, Davis. Follow me. We gotta move quickly."

Amongst the thick smoke obscuring their vision, Cameron and Nickelson took careful steps up the stairwell, into the unknown. The sound of crackling flames and falling debris signaled the potential of an unstable foundation to the second floor. Nickelson scanned their surroundings for extreme heat and potential hazards using the thermal camera. With minimal heat against the door to the second floor, Nickelson opened it for them to enter the hallway. Filled with smoke, Cameron worked on one side, while Nickelson worked the other, calling out for trapped residents. Hearing no voices, Nickelson and Cameron entered each apartment, spraying streams of water to douse the flames. The guys, who had just finished spraying several apartments, were met with flames at the far end of the hallway.

"I'm sure those came from the 3rd floor. Let it rip, Nickelson!" Cameron shouted.

Heavy streams of water flooded the end of the hallway, lowering the flames to a hot billow of steam.

"Hey! Where'd you guys leave off? We'll help check each apartment," a firefighter from one of the other stations said, his partner right behind him.

"Start with 227. We'll resume in 228," Nickelson directed.

The loud beeping sound of Nickelson's thermal camera stopped the guys from where they stood.

"This apartment is live. We gotta go in blazing," Nickelson said matter-of-factly.

Nickelson kicked the door open, turning the water hose to full blast. Cameron held it steady, moving with Nickelson.

"Davis? Nickelson? There is a elderly woman and a baby in apartment 228. Get them out!" Garey demanded through the headset.

"I'll spray a path for you, Davis, while you search," Nickelson ordered. "Captain? Davis is searching for the old woman and baby," Nickelson reported on the headset.

Determination taking center stage, Cameron took in a deep breath from his oxygen supply and walked into what appeared to be a living room. Embers illuminated the space. The sudden escape of smoke from the kitchen stopped Cameron in his tracks. Moments afterward, the kitchen walls collapsed, spreading flames across the apartment floor, narrowly escaping Cameron's backside.

"Nickelson? Blast the kitchen," Cameron commanded, moving away from the flow of water coming his way.

Heavy streams of water reduced the raging kitchen fire, allowing Nickelson to focus on the apartment floor.

Cameron faced two doors, one to his left and one at the end of the hallway. Heavy smoke escaped the opening at the bottom of each closed door.

"Nickelson? Back me up," Cameron shouted.

With Nickelson behind him, Cameron opened the door to his left. Tiny flames spread over each piece of furniture in the room. With one coating of water, the flames were out. Cameron reached for the door handle to enter the main bedroom, but it wouldn't open. With a swift kick, the door escaped from its hinges. Clouds of smoke overtook the room. Armed with the hose, Nickelson was ready to spray.

"Hold the water!" Cameron commanded.

Using his flashlight, Cameron saw the woman lying in bed, looking like she was asleep. He spotted the crib tucked away in the room's corner.

"I found them!" he announced.

Without hesitation, his movements fluid and gentle, Cameron shook the woman awake.

"Ma'am? Can you hear me? The building's on fire. We must evacuate immediately." The woman sat up in her bed. Cameron jumped over to the crib and reached down to scoop up the baby. Reaching for the blanket in the crib, he covered the baby and carefully tucked it into his jacket.

"Ma'am? Can you walk?"

Coughing, the woman nodded. Cameron balanced the baby in one hand while guiding the woman with the other. They quickly left the apartment and headed toward the stairwell.

"The stairwell's now engulfed in flames," another firefighter said.

"How are we going to get out? I have the baby," Cameron said.

"Trail me," the firefighter directed.

Cameron felt the baby's breath on his skin. Thank God. The woman covered her mouth and nose with her pajama shirt and held onto Cameron. Nickelson followed behind the other firefighter, hose in hand, ready to spray. With a swift and forceful motion, the firefighter's booted foot kicked the stairwell door, Nickelson right behind him, spraying a pathway for Cameron, the woman, and the baby to exit the building. About halfway down the stairwell, Cameron missed a step, twisted his ankle, and landed on his ass.

"Davis? You alright?" Nickelson asked in a panic.

Before getting up, Cameron checked the baby, still feeling its breath on his skin. The grandmother now walked ahead of Cameron.

"The fire's moving from the upper floors. You gotta make a run for it," the other firefighter said.

Disregarding the intensified pain in his ankle, Cameron and the woman hurried down the remaining stairs, delivering the baby to the paramedics. Another team of emergency personnel greeted the woman and quickly guided her to the triage area. Lifting his shield, Cameron inhaled the cool air, shut his shield, and rushed back in to assist Nickelson. Moving in step, they doused the entire second floor while other firefighters contained the flames around the complex.

"Okay, guys! Looks like we're home free. Before we leave, let's make sure to extinguish all the embers."

The sizzling flames waned, smoke clearing, revealing the mass destruction. Nickelson, Perry, and Cameron were the last out from Station 12.

"Good teamwork, guys. Let's pack up and head out," Garey instructed.

One by one, each removed their helmet, inhaling the cool air.

"Anybody need oxygen?" a paramedic offered to each of the guys.

Shaking his head, Cameron looked up to the sky, mouthing thank you. His throbbing ankle needed ice. He was so grateful he made it out of the building.

"Hey, ma'am, you can't go past the rope. It's still an active fire!" Lieutenant Jackson yelled to the woman, ducking her body under the roped area and running in Cameron's direction. He felt someone run into his back and wrap their arms around him.

"Thank you! You saved my mother and baby. Thank you!" the woman said. "God bless you!"

Twisting himself out of the woman's embrace, Cameron studied the woman. "Ma'am? I was just doing my job."

Back at the station, Cameron and some guys wiped down the equipment and engine.

"Davis! In my office, now!" Captain Garey demanded.

The garage, loud with chatter, went suddenly silent. All eyes on Cameron, he shrugged his shoulders, dropped the rags he was using to clean the truck, and ran up the stairs into Garey's office, shutting the door behind him.

"Yes, sir?" Cameron said, fidgeting with his now sweaty hands.

"Davis? You did a fantastic job out there. I called you in to prepare you for what's ahead of you," Garey explained. "The press and media will make a big deal out of your heroic act. Saving an elderly woman and a baby doesn't go unnoticed. Especially saving a baby. Expect significant coverage for Station 12. I want you to understand the magnitude of your actions. Ready yourself for the flood of questions and interviews that are coming your way. I don't want this to distract you from your job. When we save someone, we celebrate for a minute, then prepare ourselves mentally for the next call. Can you handle yourself?" Garey probed.

Lips pursed, Cameron replied, "Yes, sir."

Showered, dressed in gray sweats and a gray hoodie with 'Los Angeles Firefighter' plastered across his chest, Cameron slung his black duffle bag over his right shoulder and opened the door to leave the station. Blinded by a flash of cameras in his face, a tall woman with olive skin and long, straight, brunette hair, dressed in a navy blue jacket with the Channel 5 logo on it, shoved a microphone in his face and asked, "Mr. Davis! How does it feel to be a local hero?"

Chapter 3

Nicole

Nicole marveled at the progress she had made, reflecting on how much she had grown since fainting in the park. The doctor prescribed rest and relaxation. Temporarily moving in with her parents had helped her heal, allowing her time to put things into perspective. Three home-cooked meals a day, daily linen changes, unlimited television watching on the big screen, and warm hugs from Mom and Dad were just what she needed. Now, it was time to embark on a new chapter in life's journey. Without Tyler. Since his death, she had only managed the bare minimum to live. Nicole met invitations to social gatherings with polite declines. If she was in the company of others, she would instinctively gravitate to the outskirts, silently observing the lively interactions while maintaining a comfortable distance. With Nicole's work being mostly independent, she could keep in-person interactions to a minimum. She didn't want to be around people. She limited communications with clients to Zoom meetings and phone calls. She didn't work to build her brand as a food stylist and writer on L.A.'s food scene. Since Tyler, Nicole had shut out the outside world, only allowing connection with family and a few close friends. She was forever thankful to her parents and Levi for keeping her refrigerator full and her house clean for the last eighteen months.

Going for a run in the park had seemed like the perfect choice that January morning. The urge to engage muscles, breathe in fresh air, and interact with people. However, her first actual day out, alone, had been detrimental to her healing. Erasing the memory of that day in the park was her goal. Getting over Tyler's death had been difficult for Nicole. How could she prevent triggers from initiating a descent into a downward spiral that felt nearly impossible to escape? The events of that day served as a stark reminder that certain situations had the power to elicit stress, leading to faintness, or worse. Was it the park? The run? The reminders? The memories?

Eyes closed, Nicole took in a breath, then exhaled. In her mind, she had returned to that day at the park. Reminiscent of the familiar scents of the freshly turned soil and patches of grass provoked a rush of nostalgia. The slight breeze swished through the trees as if whispering tales of her past. With her body unmoving on the bench, Nicole dreamingly allowed her mind to be transported to a specific memory. She and Tyler stopped in that same spot. She needed to catch her breath and rest. Tyler was always the stronger runner. The essence of that day lived within her. His teasing about her being a lightweight. Pulling Nicole to her feet so they could finish their run together.

It was the sudden piercing sound of sirens that prompted Nicole to scan her surroundings. Close to where she sat, under the towering tree with leaves vibrant and abundant, two black and white police cars parked on the grass. Heart racing, she watched one officer reach for his bully stick, the other slamming the car door. In what seemed like slow motion, the officers jogged towards her.

"Breathe, Nicole, just breathe," she whispered to herself, inhaling, feeling her lungs expand. Holding her breath momentarily, she then exhaled through her mouth, hoping in that moment the stress and abrupt anxiety would dissipate from her body. Studying the approaching officers, Nicole recognized one of them—Jim Stone. Tyler's fellow cadet in the police academy, partner on the streets, and best friend. Jim—tall, muscular, dark hair, chiseled face. Handsome. Seeing him triggered a wave of memories, transporting her back to the somber mood of Tyler's funeral. The services concluded, and the church was empty. She remained immobilized, unable to stand and walk out. Jim slowly approached, then sat beside her. He enveloped her in a lingering, firm embrace, reassuringly conveying the message everything would be okay. Jim's familiar voice pulled Nicole from her flashback.

"Ma'am. Good morning. It'll be safer if you get into your car," Jim suggested. "There's a situation on the basketball courts." Jim stopped in front of Nicole. His gaze held a mix of surprise and recognition. "Nicole? Is that you?"

Nicole froze. Rendered speechless, she found herself unable to utter a single word. Tilting her chin upward, towards Jim's face, their eyes briefly met. "Hello," Nicole whispered.

The corners of Jim's mouth turned upward in a soft, understated way. "I'd love to catch up with you, really learn how you're doing, but the situation on the courts is serious."

Nicole looked at Jim, softly inhaled, and said, "I'll leave then." She gave Jim a brief smile. He nodded and then raced toward the basketball courts.

The chiming of her phone alerting her of an incoming email broke her thoughts of that day. The reason behind her fainting remained unclear and elusive, not immediately apparent. Was it the park? She hadn't been there since Tyler. Or was it seeing Jim Stone? Did he trigger her blackout? Deep in her heart, Nicole was certain that Jim was the cause. Seeing him brought on overwhelming emotions that pronounced her shattered heart and profound loneliness. A sense of abandonment weighed heavily on her. It was Jim Stone. She was certain.

Before leaving her parents' house, Nicole gathered her courage and, with a firm resolve, announced their dismissal from the role of caring for her. She could shop, clean, and function without their help. Now facing the disarray in her living space, she stood resolute. Determined to embrace change, Nicole set out on a journey of renewal. With a heart full of courage, she readied herself for the abundance of good things that lay ahead. Synonymous with the month of April and the spirit of rejuvenation, she embraced the tradition of spring cleaning.

The clean scent of the laundry detergent now in the washing machine filled her nose as Nicole dumped the pile of darks into the washing machine. The pile of dirty dishes in the sink was chaotic and a testament to Nicole's recent inability to live in reality. Each dish had its own shape, size, and level of filth. Remnants of previous meals stuck to dinner plates and bowls. How could one person use so many dishes? Despite days of neglect, the sink was free of any crawling surprises. Liquid stained glasses, crust-layered silverware, and cooking utensils covered her entire granite countertop. The cluttered mess of dirty dishes emitted a faint, somewhat unpleasant odor. The pungent smell got stronger as she moved dishes out of the sink to fill it with scalding hot, soapy water and wash the dishes sparkly clean. Next, Nicole moved the toaster, air fryer, and mixer to wipe down all the counters with lemon-scented cleaner, disinfecting and sanitizing everything. Reaching under the sink for the gray bucket, Nicole filled it with water and floor cleaner, dipped the mop in the bucket, and splashed the mixture on the floor to scrub it clean. She then gathered old dust rags and sprayed lemon-scented all-purpose cleaner to polish the surface of every cabinet, table, bookshelf, hanging picture, television screen, figurine, and statue. Pulling towels off the racks, she swiftly piled them in the laundry room to be washed in the next load. With a scrub brush and abrasive cleaner, she scrubbed her guest bathroom squeaky and repeated these same actions in her ensuite bathroom.

As Nicole wiped the stream of glass cleaner that ran down her mirror, she admired her toned arms and the subtle contours of her physique. She swirled around, glaring at her stomach, hips, ass, and thighs in the mirror. Although she hadn't consistently exercised in months, she looked pretty good. Nicole's mind began to fill with thoughts of capturing the attention of a man, creating a cloud of contemplation that enveloped her. She knew she was attractive. Assertive in her self-worth, she recognized the abundance of qualities she could bring to a relationship. Could she love again? The question lingered in her head. Was her heart prepared to be filled with the love of another man? Could love be in her new chapter of life's journey? The mere thought of finding love overwhelmed Nicole, stirring emotions she wasn't prepared to feel.

"Focus, girl!" Nicole reminded herself. "This house won't clean itself."

Nicole went to her utility closet in the hallway and pulled out the vacuum cleaner. The repetitive push and pull of the machine across the sand-colored carpet lifted the dirt and debris, leaving a plush feeling under her feet. The unorganized desk in the spare room which doubled as her office needed attention. Feeling the ache in her arms and feet that hours of cleaning brought on, Nicole plopped onto her desk chair. In the middle of a pile of mail, a picture of Tyler and his parents caught her attention. She must have discovered it while in her whirl of sadness. Upon closer examination of the photo, the memory became vivid. "I remember this day. We were going to celebrate their 30th wedding anniversary," Nicole whispered.

"Memories of Tyler will live in your heart forever," Dr. Williamson had told Nicole during her recent therapy session.

The mere thought of stumbling upon a photo or reminder of Tyler could plunge her into a spiral of grief she couldn't control. Dr. Williamson suggested this very thought during last week's session. On her feet and with a mission in mind, Nicole painstakingly combed every room, drawer, and pile to gather all reminders of Tyler placing items on top of her entry table near the front door. She found sweatshirts, old deodorant, countless pictures, an Android phone charger, an electric razor, a half-empty box of old condoms, and a deflated basketball. She tossed the items into the forming pile. In the garage, Nicole reached for an empty plastic storage bin. Using a black Sharpie from her kitchen utility drawer, she labeled the bin. Memories of Tyler.

"That wasn't so bad," Nicole said out loud. She felt lighter, optimistic. Carrying the filled bin to the garage and finding it a special spot brought on a sense of accomplishment. The vibration of her phone and the incoming text message brought Nicole to a halt. She pulled her phone out of her sweatpants pocket and opened the locked screen to find a text from Edward.

Edward - Hey, beautiful! On Sunday, I'm going to the outlet mall to buy a few things. Wanna join me?

Nicole typed a response.

> **Nicole** - Hi, Edward. Sure… why not. When? Time?

Within seconds, Edward replied.

> **Edward** - I'll pick you up at 9 on Sunday morning.

> **Nicole** - Sounds good.

Nicole hadn't spent time with Edward in recent weeks. He had been her rock when Tyler died. He had assumed the role of looking after her wellbeing. He sent flowers, brought her food, kept her company when she didn't want to go out. He had a sense of what would make her smile and lift her spirits. He was a good guy. However, healing from her fainting spell and not allowing him to visit her at her parents' house gave Nicole a new perspective. Was it healthy to be around Edward, knowing he was a blessing and a curse? Feelings of anger towards Edward often troubled her. She became angry each time she saw Edward because he reminded her of Tyler. She often couldn't resist spending time with him for that very fact. It frequently became overwhelming. She hoped she could maintain their friendship for all he had done for her.

That evening, Aubrey breezed through Nicole's door, carrying a big brown bag that smelled of deliciousness in one hand and a bottle of wine in the other. "I thought some BBQ short ribs, garlic mashed potatoes, and collard greens would cheer you up."

"Did you bring cornbread?" Nicole couldn't eat collard greens without cornbread.

Aubrey nodded and smiled, showing all of her teeth. Nicole appreciated Aubrey's ability to make her feel better and was happy to have her around. When she had texted this morning, Nicole didn't know how to share what she was feeling. Aubrey, however, possessed a sixth sense for Nicole. She always knew when Nicole needed her. Best friends since tenth grade, they were inseparable. When you saw one, you saw the other. Now, as adults, not much had changed, other than their careers limiting their time together.

Nicole gathered two plates, spoons, and forks from the kitchen. Her appetite had not been consistent since Tyler died. For the first time in a while, her stomach rumbled with hunger, feeling she could really enjoy her food. Aubrey trailed right behind her, carrying two wine glasses and a wine bottle opener. Nicole piled food onto their plates while Aubrey filled their glasses with Cabernet Sauvignon. Now seated at the dining room table, Aubrey raised her glass for a toast.

"To you, Nicole. May future days be filled with prosperity and lots of dates."

"Dates, Aubrey? Really?" Nicole couldn't believe her best friend sometimes. They clinked their glasses and took a sip of their wine. Was Nicole ready to date? She would have to bring this up with Dr. Williamson.

"Dig in!" Aubrey ordered. The only sounds heard were the rhythmic chewing of the ladies as they enjoyed their meal. Aubrey broke their silence. "It's been almost two years since Tyler died, right? Don't you think it's time to get back out there? Do you want to be alone for the rest of your life?" Aubrey said adoringly.

After pondering Aubrey's questions for a few seconds before speaking, a thought dawned on Nicole. When was the last date Aubrey went on? It had been years since her breakup. "And are you dating, Ms. Aubrey?"

"I'm different. My restaurant is taking up my time. I love it, though.

You know that. When I get home, I just want to sleep. I can't even imagine putting on real clothes and makeup to go on a proper date. My chef's coat, black pants, and clogs are always on me. I've forgotten what it's like to feel pretty."

Nicole nodded. She grasped every word Aubrey said. Nicole knew she was an attractive woman. Sure, men hit on her, asked her out. She just hadn't been interested. The thought of the handsome EMT at the park entered her consciousness. Although their encounter had been months ago, for the first time in a while, she felt things within her she hadn't felt since Tyler. With just one look and his million-dollar smile, she had felt butterflies floating in her stomach.

Aubrey broke her train of thought. "What does your therapist recommend? Staying in this house is not healthy."

"She said I can honor Tyler's memory and still be happy with someone else, be happy in life you know?." But when I saw his partner in the park, it triggered me. It set me back. All I could think of at that moment was Tyler and the fact he's gone. Nicole put her head down, tears now rolling down her cheeks.

Nicole needed to finish her grandmother's cookbook that she had been working on. And, like Aubrey said, go on dates. She longed to experience a sense of beauty, attractiveness. Maybe she would find love again. Nicole owed it to herself to try.

"Nicole?" Aubrey called. "Nicole? I am talking to you."

"Aubrey, I'm sorry. I'm thinking about what you're saying. I have walked in slow motion since Tyler's death. He'd be so angry to know this is how I'm living now." Nicole knew better.

Aubrey stood and walked over to Nicole. "Then change it. Little by little, your confidence will grow. You're a beautiful woman. You're only twenty-nine years old. All the dreams you had with Tyler, you can find with someone else. You can love again."

"Do you really think I can pull it all back together?" Doubt crept in about her ability to begin anew.

Stomping her feet on the floor, Aubrey proclaimed, "I have all the confidence in you." Aubrey reached over to give Nicole a long, tight hug. Nicole was her best friend. They were like sisters. "I refuse to stand by and let my bestie waste away." Aubrey grabbed Nicole's cheeks and kissed her forehead. "There's too much life to live. Dreams to make happen. There's a man who will love you. Love you deeply, like you deserve. You possess strength and independence. You're the top food stylist in the industry. You have a book to finish."

"You're right, as usual. I have to at least try. I'll do better." Did Nicole believe the words she'd spoken? Living like this was not healthy.

For the rest of the night, Aubrey and Nicole discussed upcoming catering events and projects, getting Nicole out of her emotional rut.

Chapter 4

Nicole

Shaking off the grogginess she felt, Nicole indulged in a cup of coffee to revitalize herself before getting ready for the day. After a long hot shower, she dressed in blue jeans and a white t-shirt. She added a little pink blush and mascara, with lip gloss to her otherwise plain face, and was out the door. Feeling a surge of energy, Nicole wiggled in the driver's seat as the bass from the latest afro beats rumbled her car speakers. The store was only a fifteen minute drive. Her parents' vintage shop selling furniture, clothes, music, and art had been a staple in the Culver City neighborhood for many years. The nearby movie studios found the shop a few years back and since then her parents have had a thriving business. She and Levi were there on this day to help stock the floor. Sometimes, Nicole would find a gem of a piece and convince her parents it was a must have in her house, wardrobe, or music collection. The shipments were often a treasure hunt. You didn't always know what was coming in, but could always find gold. Record albums were her favorite. Her album collection was impressive. Especially for a twenty-nine-year-old. Her original hip hop albums were what she was proud of most.

"Hey, Mom? Dad? Where are you?" Nicole announced, unlocking the storefront door with her own key. Nicole heard movement and something dropping on the concrete floor near the rear of the store.

"Back here, honey," her dad yelled.

The layout of the store was different from the last time she had visited. At the front of the store, to the right, hung a sign that read vintage clothing. Colorful shirts, dresses, and pants hung from the lined racks. A mannequin placed at the foot of one rack wore a pastel yellow skirt suit. Oversized gold buttons adorned the short, boxy jacket. The skirt was cut straight and stopped above the knee. On the right, there was a mannequin dressed in belled, multi-colored pants and a white peasant blouse. To the left of the store stood partitions, filled with furniture from different eras, staged with coffee tables, figurines, and actual art hanging on the partitioned walls. To the back left of the store was now a sitting area, with shelves filled with books. There were crates of record albums lined across a wide wood table. A fresh case for jewelry sat in the middle of this area. A few stands hung necklaces and big hooped earrings, which sat on top of the case. In the back was a section for candles, incense, and soaps.

Impressed with the new look of the store, Nicole asked her dad, "What made you rearrange everything?"

Walter looked around and responded, "A producer from Sony came in and loved the store. Said it needed some rearranging to make it more appealing, but he would be back. He came back and brought two producer friends. They ordered some pieces for a project and stayed to suggest the new layout. They referred more friends, and four orders later, we made more this year than any other."

"Well, that's wonderful. How can I help?" Nicole was eager to get to business. She wanted to get over to the albums and flip through them.

"Hey, sis! You look great. How you feeling?" Levi questioned, one arm around Nicole's shoulders.

"I feel better than I have in a while, Levi. Thank you for asking." And Nicole meant it. She felt fantastic today. She wanted to keep this feeling as long as she could. No more days of slumming around the house feeling sorry for herself. She was making the promise to work hard to not disappear in life.

Jeannette admired her grown children, smiled, and said, "Okay, you two, can you unload whatever is in those boxes in the back and stack the stuff on this rolling bin? We'll find homes for everything soon."

Nicole and Levi began unboxing and removing merchandise. Nicole took in a quick glance of her brother. She sometimes forgot how handsome he was. Standing at six-foot-four, he dressed in jeans and a graphic tee, matching sneaks. The Scarface t-shirt couldn't contain his bulging biceps. With his neatly trimmed beard getting fuller and his perfectly laid soft, black wavy curls, Levi was the definition of handsome. He was a sweetheart and would make someone very happy one day. If he could get over his heartbreak. Now he was a serial dater. He wanted nothing serious. Was being a serial dater healthy? She knew she didn't want that for herself.

Levi looked over at his sister as she sorted record albums. "What you got going on later? You wanna have some dinner and catch up?"

Lately, Nicole and Levi hadn't spent much time together outside of his scheduled visits to help her around the house. They used to have a standing dinner date. They would go to the movies when Tyler was working. She would go to his house to cook and leave leftovers in his refrigerator. She missed her brother. She looked up from the cart of albums and smiled. "I would love that. Our usual spot?"

"Taco Palace!" Nicole and Levi spoke in unison.

After three and a half hours of work, they finished unpacking all the boxes and the bin was empty. Each item from the new stock found the perfect place on the showroom floor to showcase its uniqueness, and just like that, the store was ready for business on Monday.

Nicole left her car at her parents' shop and rode with Levi. She hopped out of his black SUV while he found a parking space. The restaurant was crowded, people standing outside, waiting for their names to be called to get a table. Nicole maneuvered through the folks who stood around the door and went inside to give her name to reserve a table.

"For two, the wait is only about fifteen minutes," the host said, handing Nicole a buzzer. "We'll buzz you when your table is ready."

Nicole thanked them with a smile.

With no open seats in the waiting area, Nicole made her way out of the restaurant to stand and wait for Levi. Rubbing her hands together, she generated heat by blowing her breath into her palms, trying to warm up from the shivering chill. Despite her being the older sibling, Levi acted like her big brother, making sure Nicole could depend on him. After her fainting episode, he checked on her daily, whether he visited her, brought her food, or called her to just tell her about his day.

Walking up to Nicole, putting his jacket over her shoulders, Levi asked, "How long is the wait?"

"Fifteen minutes," Nicole responded, pulling the jacket closed. As she was about to tell Levi about Aubrey catering for the city of Los Angeles, someone approached them.

"Levi? Hey!" A cute young woman with a stylish short haircut and light brown highlights said, walking up to him and planting a kiss on his cheek. Levi shifted his gaze from Nicole to the young woman.

"Hey, Suzette! How are you? You look good!" Levi said, with a look of surprise, but savoring the moment by sharing his flirtatious smile. The young woman's cheeks turned a blushing pink as Levi flashed a sexy grin that made her melt a little. Suzette looked at Nicole from head to toe and back up again. Then gave her a curt smile. Turning to Levi she said, "I'm sorry. I didn't realize you were on a date."

With irritation in his eyes, Levi responded, "Suzette, this is my sister, Nicole. Nicole? Suzette."

Embarrassment all over her face and an apology in her eyes, Suzette said, "Oh, I'm sorry. I thought you were his..."

"No, I'm his sister. Older sister. But thanks," Nicole smiled back. She loved moments like this. She and Levi were four years apart. They shared the same shaped eyes, button nose, and grin. Other than a difference in their skin tones, they were like twins. Since he was about eighteen, people thought they were a couple when they went out. Nicole got so much satisfaction from correcting the women who thought they were making her jealous with hugs, kisses on the cheek or mouth, sometimes stroking Levi's back or ass.

"You should call me, Levi, so we can reconnect," Suzette pleaded.

In a sultry, deep voice, Levi replied, "Sure thing, Suzette. I'll call you."

Just as he said his goodbyes, the buzzer went off, and Nicole grabbed Levi by the arm and led him into the restaurant. The host led them to their table and the two slid into their booth, sitting opposite of each other. Nicole and Levi peered through the extensive menu just as the server approached their table. "Can I get you two a drink from the bar?" the middle-aged senorita, dressed in her traditional Mexican peasant dress and apron, asked.

"Two margaritas—one regular, on the rocks with extra salt, and another blended, mango, please," Levi ordered. He knew what his sister liked and always took the lead to order for her. When he was about sixteen years old, he came to her and Aubrey to learn everything he needed to know about dating women. Levi learned chivalry from their dad. Nicole and Aubrey added some additional nuances, from food ordering to tips on pleasing a woman. He asked, so they had answered.

"So, big sister, tell me how things are going," Levi asked, hands resting on the table.

Nicole took in a breath before speaking. "I was having a hard time. Ever since I fainted and spent time at Mom and Dad's, I've been working hard to get my life back. You, Mom, and Dad helped so much. Coming back home and seeing everything for what it was sparked me to take control. My house is no longer in shambles. Next week, I'll get together with Carol to discuss my cookbook project. We'll work on the Los Angeles Food Magazine project. My upcoming deadlines for the small food magazine in San Diego are no longer scary. I'm giving myself a week to finish that. Aubrey has brought me in on a big project. I'm going to her gig for the City of Los Angeles in June. I feel good." Nicole couldn't believe her conversation, sounding confident, her words clear and convincing, even though she was rambling.

Levi looked into Nicole's eyes for a moment, then spoke. "I'm proud of you. I was worried. I hate to see my big sis hurting. Am I off the hook for Wednesdays and Saturdays now?"

With a chuckle, Nicole said, "Yes, no more Wednesday grocery shopping and Saturday cleanings at my house. I'm pulling it together." Feeling the vibration of her phone, Nicole retrieved it from her pocket, swiped the screen with her finger, and unlocked it to see a text from Edward.

Edward - Can I pick you up at 10 instead? Gotta run an errand for my mom before we head out.

Nicole - Sure.

Levi's curiosity getting the best of him, he peered over the table to look at Nicole's phone. He always thought he had the right to know who she talked to, spent time with. "Who's that?"

"Edward. We're going to the outlet tomorrow. He needs to pick up a few things and I'm going to look for a dress for the City of Los Angeles event." Nicole glared at her brother, knowing he would have something to say. Wait for it, she thought.

"What's going on between you two? Levi's eyes were now on fire.

"He's a good friend. I think he wants more, but that's weird. Me dating Tyler's cousin." Nicole shook her head. The very idea made her feel queasy.

"I'm not cool with him. Something about him is slimy," Levi confessed.

"Levi? Why do you think that?" Nicole didn't want to reveal how Edward's presence made her angry for reminding her of Tyler, but also comforted her, which she now realized was the reason she spent time with him.

"I've seen him out. He may be all smiles and charm, but he's not a nice dude. Watching him work a room of women, leaving with one but collecting numbers from several. He plays games, Nicole," Levi's admitted, jaw clenched and fists balled up on the table.

"Really? I don't see it." Edward had never revealed this side of himself. "He's always been a gentleman. I wouldn't tolerate it otherwise, Levi."

"I know business people that have had dealings with him. I've known him to over bill for his services. One of my buddies witnessed his interactions with an owner of a start up and it didn't end well." Levi's blood boiled just thinking Nicole spent time with him, even if it was only as friends.

"Well, that's good information to know. Thanks. I'll look for the signs." Nicole thought back to the last few times she spent with Edward. He was always mannerable, accommodated her needs and didn't push boundaries. At least she didn't think so.

"Just be careful. I don't like you spending time with him," Levi warned.

"I get it. Who's the older sibling, though?" Nicole said with a chuckle.

"You, but I'll always look after you," Levi said, relaxing his jaw, hands in his lap.

"I think I'm ready to date," Nicole blurted, thinking about the words that just escaped her mouth. Dating meant getting back to normal. Going on with her life. She was ready. Even if she had to force it. Dating would be good for her.

Jaws clenching again, Levi questioned, "But Edward?"

"Oh, no, Edward and I are not dating. No need to worry at all," Nicole explained.

The server arrived with their drinks and a basket of chips and salsa, placing them on the table. "Are you ready to order?" she asked.

Levi lowered his eyes at Nicole, then turned to the server. "My sister will have the fried whole fish, and I'll have the three enchilada combo—one cheese, two chicken."

"Okay, gracias!" the server answered, taking their menus.

"Levi? Have you heard from Elle?" Nicole knew with just the mention of her name, her brother's entire mood would shift. She wanted to know where he stood with his feelings. Where he stood with Elle. She knew Elle was the love of his life. He was heartbroken when her dad interfered in their relationship and made them break up.

Levi's eyes grew dark and sad. "No, I haven't. I think about her, though. I hope she's happy. I'm sure she's dating. It's been three years."

"Do you think you'll ever become serious with someone else?" Nicole wondered out loud.

"I'm sure I will. Haven't met the right person yet. I'm having fun, though." Levi's pearly whites shined through his devilish grin.

Thinking, Nicole concluded, "One day, we'll be happy and in love."

Levi stared through Nicole, as if in deep thought. Lips tight and jaw clenched, he replied, "I hope so, sis. I hope so for you. I'm not so sure for me. Elle still has my heart."

"I understand. I understand more than you know, little brother."

Chapter 5

Nicole

As Nicole stirred from sleep, a sense of agitation colored her waking moments. The previous night's dinner with Levi left Nicole restless. Tyler consumed her thoughts leaving her awake most of the night. Dressed in black running tights, a gray long sleeve dri-fit shirt, and matching running shoes, she was out the door. Instead of going to the park, she decided to run in her neighborhood. The hills around the corner from her house would wake her legs. Before she could think about what she was doing, her stride quickened into a jog. Nicole shared fleeting smiles and hello nods with kindred spirits out for a morning run. Laughter came from a small group of children chasing each other in their front yard.

Now in her stride, sweat rolled down Nicole's back. Feeling perspiration at her temples and across her forehead, she wiped her face with the back of her hand. Running toward her was a tall, thin man dressed in black on black running gear who ran alongside a woman in bright, fluorescent orange running tights. They smiled at one another and then at her.

"Good morning!" they said, carrying genuine warmth in their tone. Nicole responded with a nod. That simple greeting settled on Nicole's chest. Small connections like this created an extra layer of richness to the mental and emotional journey she was now on.

The rigid concrete pavement felt straining on her legs as she grew closer to the impending hill. She knew why she liked to run on a track, in the park, or even on grass. Rounding the corner, the approaching hill seemed larger, steeper than she remembered. With a deep breath, Nicole picked up her pace and began the incline to the top. As the incline grew steeper, Nicole took to focusing on the asphalt. With each step, she focused on the slight imperfections in the asphalt's installation. Varying shades of dark gray spread across the street. Flecks of ivory white microscopic pebbles mixed in with the ubiquitous material. Short of breath, breathing heavy, Nicole persevered, making it to the top of the hill. Bent over, hands on her knees, Nicole felt strong. Head now clear, she was ready for the day.

Shopping was therapeutic. Period! She couldn't remember the last time she ventured out to make a clothing purchase. A little retail therapy was a great way to unwind, to treat herself to something special. With Aubrey's big catering event for the City of Los Angeles being in late June, Nicole settled on looking for a dress to wear to that affair while shopping with Edward. That night would offer good food and networking opportunities, with the possibility of business connections that could lead to new contracts all while supporting her best friend. This event was shaping up to put a stamp in Aubrey's book for one of L.A.'s best chefs. Aubrey's

Eats, with plans to open Aubrey's Treats, ride or die was on her way to be culinary royalty.

Edward rang Nicole's doorbell at exactly 10am. Fastening the clasp on her large silver hoop earrings, she sauntered to the door, inhaled a deep breath, and opened her door.

"Good morning, sunshine! You look amazing!" Edward greeted, smiling from ear to ear.

"Thanks! Good morning to you! I'm ready. Let me grab my purse." Nicole grabbed her purse and keys from the dining room table and walked toward her door, stopping at the full-length mirror which sat against the wall. She didn't know what was so amazing about her ragged holey jeans, black ripped t-shirt, and white shell-toe Adidas sneakers. Maybe it was her ponytail?

"I stopped and got coffee and bagels for us. Rye is your favorite, right?" Edward's self-assuredness was palpable. Yes, it was her favorite. Why did this suddenly feel uncomfortable? He knew her favorite bagel?

"You know me so well," Nicole sarcastically said. Edward was always thoughtful. He remembered the little details about a person. He paid attention, took notice, made mental notes of things to use later. Nicole locked her front door and walked to Edward's black on black Mercedes sedan. Standing with the passenger side door open, Nicole tucked into the seat, putting on her seatbelt. Edward shut the door and jogged to the driver's side. The rich and inviting aroma of the freshly brewed coffee awakened Nicole's senses while the smell of toasted bagels made her stomach growl.

Checking the traffic app, Edward said matter-of-factly, "It's going to take us just under two hours to the outlet mall."

Nicole responded with a warm smile. "Is this my coffee?" she asked, noticing her name written on the side.

"Yes, and here's your bagel. Napkins are in the glove compartment." Edward was always prepared. Thinking back to her conversation with Levi, she wondered if he treated all of his dates with the same politeness. Did he remember the small things about them, ensuring they felt cared for and attended to? Instrumental jazz melodies flowed through the car's surround sound speakers, setting a smooth and soothing soundtrack for the drive. Nicole drank her coffee and ate her bagel in silence. Edward offered occasional glances in her direction, each accompanied by a warm and assuring smile. During the ride, Nicole checked emails on her phone and made notes to follow up on Monday.

"We're here," Edward announced as he pulled into a parking space in front of the Gucci store. "I figured we could start here. I need a new wallet. Maybe we can find something nice for you?"

This was new. Edward didn't usually offer to buy Nicole gifts. Nicole suddenly felt irritated by Edward's gesture. Maybe Levi was right. His words were in her head. Was there something slimy about Edward? She got out of the car. "No thanks, Edward. You don't need to buy me anything," she said as she scanned the nearby shops to see all the options for a dress for Aubrey's catering event. She then pointed to her left and said, "When you're done, you can meet me in Saint Laurent?"

Edward offered a sly grin and gave Nicole a wink. A nauseous feeling came over her at the thought of Edward hitting on her. The unexpected wink left her curious, suggesting she analyze his actions and gestures. Was his behavior playful teasing or a subtle sign of something more? She needed to closely observe his behavior.

Inside the store, Nicole headed straight for the clearance rack. Flipping through the rack, she found a beautiful, nude-colored jersey long sleeve gown. It was stunning. Eyeing the size of the dress, Nicole grabbed it and looked for a sales person. "Excuse me, ma'am, can I try this dress on?"

The sales woman appeared to be in her early twenties. Dressed in all black, a slick auburn ponytail and silver studded earrings, she turned and replied, "Yes, of course. Let me open a room for you. Do you want to look around some more?"

Shaking her head, Nicole answered, "No, thank you. I just want to try this dress on to see if it fits. It's perfect for an event I'll be attending in a few weeks." The dress, 100% viscose, had style, with a back keyhole and eye closure. The front of the dress was fitted with a flirty gown. Once on, it felt like a tight glove. Was it too tight? What did it look like? A reflective surface was absent in the dressing room which meant she had to leave the dressing room to see herself in the dress. Nicole carefully walked out and stepped onto the raised flooring in front of the wall to wall mirror. The dress hugged her upper body, arms, chest, and waistline, releasing to a shift bottom. The slit opened from the upper thigh, exposing her entire left leg. It was perfect.

Mouth dropped, Edward walked toward Nicole, applauded, then said, "You look bewitching. Elegant." His gaze traveled from her face, slowly down her body, and back up to offer a sizzling stare into her eyes. Nicole's face instantly heated with anger. What was that look? The intensity of his stare had crossed a line, and she couldn't shake off the discomfort it brought. Edward was definitely acting differently and she didn't like it.

The sales woman chimed in. "Oh, yes, this dress is perfect for you. Doesn't your wife look beautiful?"

Edward's mouth was ajar, then turned into a huge grin. Nicole's eyes darted at the sales woman, then said, "He's not my husband, nor am I his girlfriend. But thank you for the compliment. This dress is exquisite. I'll take it," she said, as she stepped down, heading back to her dressing room.

"I'll buy it for you. Where we going? I would love to take you anywhere in that dress," Edward pleaded.

"We aren't going anywhere, Edward. Thanks for the compliment, though. And I'll buy my dress." Nicole knew she could not give Edward the wrong impression. He had to understand what was happening here, or what was not happening. After changing into her clothes, she paid for the dress at the front counter, glowering at Edward, watching him wink at the saleswoman, flashing her a seductive smile. Rolling her eyes, she walked out, him following right behind her.

"I could've paid for the dress. You going to an event? Do you need a date, I mean escort?" Edward said, panting after Nicole.

"Yes, I'm going to an event. No, I don't need an escort. But thanks for asking. What other stores do you need to go to? I got what I came for," Nicole directly said. Nicole was annoyed and ready to leave. She hated the idea of people thinking she and Edward were a couple. They were just friends. Did he want that? He never suggested more than friendship. But today, his stares and wink made Nicole think otherwise. Edward was tall, skin a golden brown, clean shaven, and good looking. He was successful and thoughtful and had been a good friend, which were the makings of a love connection, but she would never see him as more than a friend. He was Tyler's cousin, and that was it.

Edward looked at Nicole with concern. "You look upset. Are you okay? Did I do something wrong?"

Like flipping a switch, he was back to being the Edward she knew. Thoughtful and catering to her. "No, Edward, you didn't. If you're done shopping, can we go please? I have work to do to get ready for Monday."

"We just got here. I wanted to go to a few more stores, take my favorite girl to lunch." Edward reached for Nicole's hand, but she pushed him away.

Now furious, Nicole blasted Edward by saying, "I'm not your favorite girl. We're not dating Edward. I don't know what you think this is. You were Tyler's cousin. I only see you as that. Nothing else. Please don't call me your girl."

With sadness in his eyes, Edward conceded. "I'll take you home."

The car ride home was silent. Body shifted toward the passenger car door, Nicole looked out the window the entire ride back to her house. She thought about conversations she had with Tyler. Him telling her he and Edward grew up like brothers. They went to the same schools, went on double dates, played on the varsity basketball and football teams in high school. He seemed to want all the same things Tyler wanted, including girls. Tyler shared countless stories of Edward trying to sabotage his relationships by making up lies. Some lies were detrimental to Tyler's reputation. Edward didn't care. He hated the attention Tyler used to get. How could Edward think they were dating? They only hung out. No hand holding, no candle lit dinners, no kissing. Only friendly hugs. Had she given him the wrong impression? Was she leading him on? She had to not make herself so available to him. She had to create distance between them. Nicole knew that meant one thing. Nicole knew it was time to start dating for real.

Chapter 6

Cameron

In the Sports Center Bar & Grill, every booth and table was occupied. Cameron searched the back of the bar looking for Myles, Terrell, Ryan, and Josh sitting in their usual spot. Knowing the bar's owner had its perks; she always reserved their favorite booth on big game days. Enormous screens hung from every angle, each televising their favorite matchups of the day. The big, dark brown leather cushioned booth could hold Cameron's six-foot-four frame, along with the guys who ranged from six feet to six-foot-seven in height.

"Hey! If it isn't Mr. Celebrity!" Josh said, a BBQ chicken wing hanging from his mouth.

"I'm not a celebrity." Cameron said as he slid into the booth. He knew his friends would heckle him about all the press he was getting over saving the baby and older woman from the burning building. "I was just doing my job. Hell, y'all would do it anyway, job or not." he said, reaching for a chicken wing, waving the server over to take his drink order.

"Hey there! Am I in the company of a famous man? You're getting more media buzz than your Laker buddy over there," Gina mocked, looking in Terrell's direction. "What can I get you?"

"Modelo, please! Light," Cameron requested.

"Make that a full round for each of us, please?" Myles asked.

Gina winked at Myles and nodded. "You got it."

"Man, I don't know how you do your job. You see all the emergencies—good, bad, dead. How do you sleep at night?" Terrell asked, always full of questions.

Fire trucks had fascinated Cameron since he was a little kid. He smiled, thinking about the memories he had of his grandfather taking him to the fire station. Papa's dream was to be a firefighter, but the Army was his best option out of high school. Rising in the ranks of the military became his career, and he lived a good life on his pension. So Papa shared his dream with his grandson. The massive fire truck, gleaming in the bright sunlight, had enamored Cameron. To his inexperienced eyes, the fire engine had been enormous, and he had wanted to explore every inch. The firefighters had pointed out the water tank, hoses, and the water pump. Cameron remembered falling on his butt when he held the turned on hose, pointed toward the pretend fire on the side of the station. He had filled coloring books with vivid shades of reds, oranges, and browns, mimicking fire scenes. At ten years old, the captain had stood behind him as he climbed the fire engine ladder to the top. In his dreams, Cameron fought fires alongside the men at the station. Being a college athlete and having the potential to play professional ball, didn't defer his dream of becoming a firefighter. He loved his job. Saving the baby from the building fire brought him celebrity status. Suddenly people recognized him on the street. Women came to the station to bring him dinner, desserts, and even bottles of wine with handwritten notes that included their addresses and phone numbers, all wanting a piece of his celebrity status. It was a bit much, and he didn't like the attention.

"Man, please tell me the honies are just throwing it at you, huh?" Ryan probed while sipping on his fresh bottle of beer. Crude thoughts about women lived rent free in his head.

"I can't pay attention to all of that. Firefighter groupies only want you for the status," Cameron responded, shaking his head.

"Exactly, and why not take advantage of that?" Myles said. "You aren't dating right now. The attention you're getting might be a good strategy to bring you back into the game."

Myles played his last game when he'd met Jessica. They've been serious since college. Myles now just listened to the guys' dating shenanigans.

With a frown and irritated stare, Cameron responded, "I'm good. And I haven't lost my game. I don't want back in. I gotta focus on my career." Cameron didn't have the time or energy to date.

"The baby thing should give you an enormous boost to your career, no?" Josh asked. On his way to make partner at his architect firm, he knew what it meant to stay immersed in work. It had its benefits and would pay off in the long run.

"Yeah, the city's giving me and some other guys in fire departments across the city recognition awards. It's a big event. I'll accept it and add it to my resume." The event would grant opportunities for networking and meeting influencers that could boost his career trajectory.

"You taking a date?" Terrell asked. His professional basketball career showered him with harems of women, and he could have anyone, anytime, anywhere. He was a good guy and would settle down, once the right woman came along. It was a good thing he could see through the gold diggers.

"Naw, going solo. I can't date right now. Gotta keep my nose clean and stay focused. Women are a distraction." Cameron couldn't risk hindrances that could steer his vision of being promoted earlier than most rookies.

"Dude, you gotta get some now and then, right?" Ryan added, lifting his buzzing phone from the table. "Excuse me. This one right here. I've been trying to take her out for weeks. Show time, boys!" Ryan shined a devilish grin. "I'll be back. After I arrange this setup–I mean hook up." Ryan, the forever player. It would be a snowy day in hell before he settled down.

Fist bumps, dozens of BBQ chicken wings, fries, and Modelo filled the rest of the afternoon. Cameron loved his boys. Close friends since college, the guys were the brothers he didn't have. He missed that comradery, banter, the brotherhood that came with male family members. The guys filled that void. Inseparable since meeting on USC's basketball court freshman year. Growing up, Cameron's grandfather pushed him to stay out of the streets, get good grades, and go to college. His mother worked late nights as a nurse, so his Papa made sure to pick Cameron up from school, give him a hot meal, and was in the house when his mom got home. Cameron would wake up many mornings to find his mom sleeping next to him, still in her nursing uniform. Patricia, knowing the streets were dangerous, was so afraid to lose him. The thought of losing him was too much for her to bear. Cameron's father, Tyrone, was the love of her life. Having died in a car accident when he was four years old, Cameron's grandfather was the male role model in his life. Patricia still lived in Cameron's childhood home, left to him and his mom when Papa died five years ago. Cameron wanted to succeed for him, already living his dream of being a firefighter.

Being away from the station, Cameron finally had time to spend time with his favorite girl and find something to wear to the upcoming event in his honor.

"Ma?" Cameron called, opening the front door to his childhood home.

"In here, son. I'm almost ready," Patricia called from her bedroom.

Not much had changed to the post-war, 1940s tract home, other than the additional bathroom added and upgrades to the kitchen, electricity box, and stucco walls. Cameron used his days off to fix things around the house, ensuring his mother's peace of mind about potential damages. His room was just as he had left it when he packed up and headed to his dorm room at USC. Papa's room was now an office and sitting room. The sound of his mom's voice broke Cameron's train of thought.

"Hey, baby! How's my handsome son?" Patricia asked, walking toward her son, arms stretched out for a hug.

Cameron gleamed seeing his mom. He often forgot how attractive she was. Cameron admired her radiant and warm olive skin, her long brown and gray hair that hung just past her shoulders, and her neat appearance. The matching stone colored leggings and sweatshirt flattered her toned physique. Her stark white leather sneakers gave Patricia a youthful look. Gathering her purse and keys to walk out the door, Patricia asked. "Do you know where you want to get your suit?"

"I figured we could go downtown. Terrell told me about a place all the ballers go to buy their suits," Camron replied.

"Okay. Terrell always looks nice when I see him. Let's go," Patricia said, closing and locking the front door.

Cameron drove downtown in half the time. The freeway had less traffic than usual. Finding a place to park could be hell, but the suit shop had plenty of spaces, and Cameron was glad for that.

"Hello! My name is Angelo. Can I help you?" The older salesperson said, greeting Cameron and his mom at the front of the store. Despite the worn brick concrete exterior of the store, the interior was well lit, with polished hardwood floors decorated with walls of photographs of men of varying sizes wearing different suits. Strategically placed mirrors hung throughout the store, allowing customers to view themselves in designer wear.

"Yes, Angelo. I need a suit for an event. Black, fitted, with a shirt and tie. Formal, but not like a tuxedo," Cameron explained.

In his thick Italian accent, dressed in slacks and a button-up shirt, measuring tape hung around his neck, Angelo replied, "Yes, let me show you our selection."

Angelo guided Cameron and his mom to the formal suit section of the store. Patricia left Cameron's side to rummage through the long racks of suits herself.

"Cameron, this one is nice. Do you like it?" Patricia called out, holding up a classic double-breasted suit jacket.

Cameron knew he didn't want to wear a classic suit. "Yes, that's nice. I want to try a few more trendy looks though, Ma." That suit looked like one his grandfather would have worn.

Angelo combed through the racks and selected a few suits and put them on a nearby empty small rolling rack.

"You can take these into the dressing room and see which one you like," Angelo directed.

With five selections to choose from, Cameron knew one of these would work. In the dressing room, he reached for the first pair of suit pants. The pants were too tight on his muscular thighs. Examining one of the suit jackets, he held it in front of him and stared into the mirror. The suit was a dark gray. He preferred black. Now in the third suit,

Cameron felt good, comfortable. The suit was modern, yet sophisticated. The fabric of the pants and jacket offered flexibility and comfort despite its solid fit. Pant legs covering his size thirteen feet, puddled on the floor.

"We can give you a custom fit." Angelo suggested. The one button well-fitted jacket fit complimented his broad shoulders. Cameron walked out of the dressing room to show his mom.

"Oh, Cameron, that suit is so perfect." Tears filled Patricia's eyes. Cameron was the spitting image of his father, standing taller than his dad was and with a more muscular build, he recognized the same jawline and million-dollar smile.

"Mom? Don't cry." He knew his mom got sentimental just looking at him, thinking about his dad.

"That one is it, son. Get that one," Patricia said into the handful of tissues she pulled from her purse.

"This one it is. Now let's go to lunch," Cameron decided.

The Italian Kitchen served delicious, authentic Italian food that was Patricia's favorite, and he loved to spoil her when they went out.

"Can I take your order?" the server asked.

"I'll have a glass of Bougrier Vouvray Chenin Blanc with the European seabass," Patricia ordered.

"And you, sir? What would you like?" the server asked, taking Patricia's menu.

"I'll have a glass of Chardonnay and Alfredo pasta with chicken."

The server took Cameron's menu. "Thank you! I'll be back with fresh bread and your salads."

Patricia placed the cloth napkin on her lap and smiled at Cameron. "So, are you taking a date to the event?"

Eyes closed for only a second, Cameron took in a breath. Why was everyone asking him that? Was he taking a date to the event? "No, I'm not taking a date. I want to fully appreciate and enjoy the moment. Dates are too much work."

"It's only early May. You have a month to find a date," Patricia pushed.

"Mom! I don't want to take a date. I'll be fine." Cameron said, wanting to end the date conversation.

"Well, I'll be happy when you find a nice girl and think about maybe getting married. I want grandchildren, you know." Patricia brought this up every time she had the opportunity.

Cameron wanted all those things. At thirty years old, he knew it would soon be time, but he wanted to make sure he found the right woman. A woman he could trust most importantly. "I want kids one day, Mom, but my current focus is solely on my career."

"Do you ever talk to Shannon?" Patricia asked, taking a sip of her wine. The mere mention of her name made Cameron's blood boil. He hated when his mom brought her up.

"No, not at all. Things didn't end well with Shannon. She's a good woman. Just not for me." Cameron wanted to keep things neutral. He hoped his response ended the prying about their breakup. His mother didn't need to know the betrayal he experienced at the end of his relationship with Shannon.

Giving Cameron an investigative stare, Patricia opened her mouth to speak, but hesitated. Then she spoke. "You have so many tendencies like your father. You aren't one to share your feelings, Cameron. You're often guarded and self-absorbed with your thoughts."

Cameron gave his mother an incredulous stare, waiting for her to continue.

"Communication was an issue for Tyrone, and I see it is in you. I thought Shannon was a nice girl. But after two years of dating, I figured you two could gauge if you're ready for marriage. But, y'all broke up. Your father and I only dated six months before we got married." Patricia paused and carefully considered her words before speaking again. "You'll meet someone, son."

Cameron was hopeful this would be the end of this conversation. The vein at his temple pulsed. "I'm not looking, Mom." Cameron wondered why his mother pushed dating. Why couldn't she take his word and leave the subject alone?

"Ms. White, at the hospital, has a daughter who can go with you to the event."

"Mom, I can find my own dates. Thank you." Cameron understood his mom's good intentions. He didn't want to be fixed up. If he needed a date, he would ask Ryan. However, he would have to do a background check on any women he suggested taking on a date. His women tended to be great looking, professional, but a little psycho.

After dropping his mom off at her house, Cameron decided to go for a run. When home, he combed through his mail and avoided turning on the television. He didn't want to see himself in another news story. The station's phone rang constantly with women requesting his personal contact information. Random pictures of naked women appeared in his Instagram feed, even though his account was private. Ryan had a blast getting to befriend those women.

Changed into Nike running pants and a dri-fit shirt, Cameron took the stairs to his condominium gym. Terrell's game would be on, and he wanted to just chill for the night, alone. Headphones blasting Tribe Called Quest, Cameron began with a brisk walk on the belt. He pushed the incline to ten and speed to six. With each pound of his feet on the treadmill, the stress of hearing Shannon's name evaporated. Thirty minutes later, dripping with sweat, Cameron lowered the incline to zero and the speed to three, then switched his music selection to Snoh Aalegra for his cool down. Back in his condo, Cameron showered and put on black sweats, his fire academy t-shirt, and pulled up Door Dash to order a pizza.

The Lakers weren't doing much tonight. They didn't have to. The Lakers against the Sacramento Kings were an easy win. Cameron stuffed six slices of pepperoni and cheese pizza into his stomach and put the rest in the refrigerator. His purchased DJ stand and turntable stared at him, waiting to be played. Cameron broke a sweat contemplating teaching himself how to spin records. The YouTube tutorial videos weren't helping him to learn how to use his equipment. First, build the record collection, he pondered. Second, learn by doing.

"DJ Cameron," he said in a sultry, deep voice. He sounded ridiculous. Part of the role, he believed. His new persona.

"DJ Cameron spinning on the one twos." He kind of liked his DJ voice.

Cameron was thrown out of his imaginary DJ set with the alert of a text message on his phone, Myles' name flashing on the screen.

Myles - Yo! Cam! Can you talk?

Cameron - Yo! Sure! Call me.

Within seconds, Cameron's phone rang.

"Hey, man, what's up?"

Cameron heard Myles take a deep breath, then said, "Man? I think I'm ready to get married?"

Cameron almost choked on his own saliva. "You what? Married? Are you sure?"

"Yeah, married. My girl, she's amazing. I listen to all the dating stories, glad I'm not part of that life. I love my girl, you know? I can't imagine being with anyone else." Cameron heard the sincerity in Myles' voice. He'd been off the scene since college, faithful to Jessica since the day they met. Cameron guessed it was time.

"Did you talk to the guys?" Cameron understood that some of their friends would have doubts. They were all single, not in serious relationships, and were twenty-nine, thirty, or thirty-one. Marrying was only an option for Myles.

"Naw, not yet. I wanted to talk to you first. You clearly have your sights set on your career. Even though you went through a bad breakup, you don't seem jaded. You seem the most level-headed one in our group," Myles confessed.

"Josh is level-headed. Why not talk to him? He's dating. This new girl has been around for a while. He ain't saying that's his girl yet, but it's getting close, right?" It's possible Cameron wasn't the ideal person to talk to Myles about this.

Cameron was aware that Myles was going to state his case. "Yeah, you're right. But I've known you the longest."

"What? Five minutes? We met on the court freshman year," Cameron said with a chuckle.

"Man, give me a break. I wanted to tell someone, and you were my first choice. I haven't even told my parents. Hers either," Myles admitted.

Cameron knew he had to change his perspective. He didn't want to discourage Myles. "Well, I think congratulations are in order then, man. Congratulations! If you're ready, then I'll support you. What can I do to help?"

Myles sighed into the phone. "I want you to be my best man."

"Really? Man, that's huge." Cameron took in a deep breath. He had never been a best man. Myles would be the first of his close friends to get married. "Of course I'll be your best man." Myles' heartfelt request touched Cameron.

"Thanks, man. I appreciate it. I guess I gotta go to her parents first, get a ring. Jessica has no clue."

A knock on Cameron's door startled him. "Keep me posted. I gotta go, man. Someone's at my door."

"Alright, man. We'll talk soon," Myles said and ended the call.

Cameron stood, tossed his phone on the couch, and walked to his door. He wasn't expecting any company. Who would show up unannounced? Peering through the peephole, he saw an unfamiliar woman dressed in a black trench coat.

"Yes, can I help you?" Cameron said through the door.

"Yes, I'm looking for Cameron Davis. I have a message for him?" the woman said.

Cameron wasn't expecting a message. She looked harmless. He knew how to handle his own. He opened the door.

He said, "Can I help you?"

Gazing at Cameron's entire form, the woman replied, "Yes, you can." She then revealed a black lacy lingerie set painted to her shapely physique as she opened her trench coat.

Without hesitation, Cameron held his hand up and demanded, "Oh, no ma'am, you gotta go. This is not what this is!"

The woman began frantically speaking. "I saw you on the news. You're a hero. You're so amazing, and I just had to come see you. Do you like what you see? I can be all yours." The woman moved closer, trying to cross Cameron's entrance into his condo.

Cameron extended his hand to prevent the woman from barging in. He shut the door, locking it behind him.

"Cameron, where did you go? I love you," the woman shouted from the hallway.

Cameron had not been acquainted with this woman. Who was she, and how did she find him? How did she find out where he lived? The news stories had to stop. First, women left messages at the station and were showing up at the firehouse. Women brought him food. They stocked his Instagram account with nude pictures. Now they showed up at his house. He was eagerly anticipating the event so when it was over he could solely focus on his career without the fanfare.

Chapter 7

Nicole

Nicole's bedroom window brimmed with a symphony of melodious bird chirping. She opened her eyes to her room, bright with sunlight peeking through the shutters. Nicole shot up, and in her morning raspy voice, asked herself, "What time is it?"

Her phone read 8:15 am. The act of hoisting the weight of her arms to stretch caught Nicole off guard with a sudden wave of wakefulness. Recollections of last night's early dinner date flashed through her mind. Richard, the accountant, steered the entire conversation to flatter his own experiences and the intricacies of accounting, leaving no room for Nicole to share anything about herself. He exhibited a slight excess of eagerness to delve into detailed descriptions of his financial record-keeping systems, shared the tax laws his clients bent, and then vividly described the impending audits that kept him awake at night. He checked his phone and said his calendar suggested they should arrange another date by 5pm on Monday. It concerned Nicole that he didn't ask about her career or her hobbies, favorite foods, her favorite music genre, nothing. He rambled on and on about numbers and spreadsheets. The food turned out to be the redeeming factor of the evening. The combination of Caesar salad with garlic and anchovy dressing made table side, filet mignon, and grilled asparagus resulted in a superior meal. The dinner reached its peak of excellence with the chocolate lava cake for dessert. Nicole knew that her mom's neighbor had good intentions, introducing her to her grandson. She had to remember these dates were to encourage her to socialize for the sole purpose of reintegrating herself back into the dating scene. Coffee with Darryl, the insurance guy. A movie and ice cream with Mason, the finance guy. All good-looking, nice men. Nicole just didn't have a strong enough connection to justify a second date with either of the men. She took pride in her growing dating experience, regaining her true self, increasing her confidence and her ability to perceive herself as a desirable woman. She was beginning to be open to finding a connection with someone.

"Nicole? You have homework," Dr. Williamson told her during their last therapy session. "This week, I want you to do something you haven't done in a while. Treat yourself. Splurge. Do you have something in mind?" she asked. Nicole didn't have an answer during the session, but today, she knew just how she would spend her time.

In an enthusiastic tone, Nicole squealed, "I'm going to The record parlor."

With each step, the memory of Nicole's strenuous run from the day before came flooding back. The stiffness in her legs conjured up thoughts of how demanding her workout had been. She gingerly stepped around her living room to her organized collection of albums, searching for a hidden gem within her vast record collection to listen to. She grabbed Anita Baker's Rapture album and shook the vinyl out of the jacket to place it on the record player, positioning the needle on the first song. As the melody and sultriness of the songstress engulfed her house, Nicole floated to the kitchen and poured a freshly brewed cup of coffee. With a gentle swivel of her hips to the beat, Nicole paused to place her cup on the coffee table before sinking into her plush couch. Scrolling through a local news app on her phone, a headline grabbed her attention. "Firefighter Saves Grandmother and Baby," she read aloud.

With a sense of curiosity, Nicole clicked on the firefighter story.

A raging three-story apartment complex fire threatened to tear through all structures, prompting a swift response from local firefighters. The fire erupted at about 10:15 p.m. Eyewitnesses reported the visibility of thick plumes of smoke and intense flames that could be seen from blocks away. Firefighters arrived on scene within minutes, engaging in a fierce battle against the voracious blaze with unwavering determination. Several ladder trucks were dispatched to battle the conflagration. It was assumed that all residents had left the building until Tracy Smith notified Captain Peter Garey that her mother and baby were still in the apartment. Without hesitation, firefighter Cameron Davis sprung into action, battling rising flames to locate the grandmother and infant, bringing both of them to the waiting paramedics. We are happy to report both grandmother and baby suffered no injuries thanks to Mr. Davis. His heroic actions will be recognized at the Los Angeles City Firefighters Night of Recognition being held later this month.

"Praise God, both are safe and the firefighter had the courage to go in and get them," Nicole murmured to herself. She sat in silence for a few seconds, working to recall where she had heard the name Cameron Davis. The photo in the article showed a man dressed in his firefighter uniform. Where had she seen this man? The magnetism and intensity of his eyes captured her attention. His beautiful smile stirred a sense of warmth and intimacy within Nicole. The article mentioned that Cameron Davis would receive recognition at the same event Aubrey was catering. They were going to be at the same affair. Nicole's intuition spoke to her senses. She needed to know this man. Should she stalk him at the event? That would be creepy. She knew that he must have garnered a lot of attention from the article. The sound of the needle scratching the inner core of the album interrupted Nicole's train of thought. The clock showed 11:30 am, and the day was passing. Time to do her homework.

An hour later, Nicole left the house, donning a fitted cotton black t-shirt dress, with a white beige and black flannel shirt tied around her waist, and Adidas white shell toe sneakers. Her full head of dark brown, spiral curls danced in the light breeze to her hip hop playlist. As she navigated the mid-afternoon traffic, the warm breeze warmed her cheeks through her open driver side window. Nicole pulled into the parking lot of the record store.

"Hmmm, nowhere to park," she mumbled, circling the lot. A silver hatchback left a space on the street and Nicole pulled into it.

Inside the record store, a sizable crowd gathered near the DJ booth. A mixture of jazz and hip hop spun from the turntables. Nicole walked over to the crowd and stood for a few minutes. She began to move her arm in the air, experiencing the energy of the fusion of brass, piano, and woodwind instruments with spoken word over base riddled beats. The music stopped and the crowd burst into applause, halting her dance moves.

"That was fun," a young girl with curly blond hair said, passing Nicole where she stood.

"That was insane," a young kid yelled to his friend.

Nicole left the dwindling crowd and strolled over to the hip hop section. She flipped through a rack of shirts, eyeing a black Run DMC top. The one she owned had seen better days.

"Size medium? Thank you," she mumbled to herself as she continued to browse through the hip hop t-shirt collection. Slick Rick and Queen Latifah t-shirts were added to her basket. As she riffled through the 80s and 90s record collection, a sense of familiarity washed over her. With each album she laid eyes on, she imagined her own record collection at home, knowing she had its identical one on her shelf. The recent addition to the store's collection was the twelve inch section of singles. She didn't remember this section the last time she was in the store. Nicole didn't have any twelve inch single song records in her collection. One twelve inch record, one song embodied grandeur. She plucked Method Man's, All I Need and Eric B. & Rakim's I Ain't No Joke, Prince's Purple Rain, and Marvin Gaye's Gotta Give It Up to add to her forming twelve inch collection. With the four twelve inch records and three t-shirts clutched in her hand, Nicole stood in line to pay for her items. She mentally scrolled through her hip hop playlists and reminded herself of the albums she didn't have. Creating a spreadsheet listing every album in her collection was the most valuable recommendation Levi had given her. Now, whenever she was out shopping for music, she knew what she had at home and what she could buy. Growing up, the rhythmic melodies and soulful rhymes of old school hip hop served as the soundtrack of her home. Her parents would often groove to their tunes, sharing their contagious smiles for the love of this genre of music. Both she and Levi were now dedicated fans of old school music, almost exclusively.

"Next," the sales woman called out. As Nicole put her items on the counter, she noticed a tall figure of a man also making a purchase. An intriguing fresh, aquatic scent with a hint of citrus wafted toward her, enticing Nicole to turn her gaze to its source. His gray sweats and navy blue long-sleeved ribbed cotton shirt hugged his body in all the right places. She couldn't help but notice the lines etching his face and the sparkle in his eyes strikingly resembled her own. She was sure they were about the same age.

Glancing at the register, the sales woman quoted, "$97.15 is your total, ma'am." Nicole reached into her black leather crossbody bag to pull out her debit card. The sales woman behind the counter began chatting with her co-worker, placing Nicole's bag of items behind the counter near her. The sales woman ringing up Mr. Smell Good reached for a similar bag to fill with his purchases and set it down behind the counter next to her bag.

"Here's your receipt and your purchases. Thank you for coming, and we hope to see you soon," the sales woman said, grabbing a bag in between her and her co-worker, handing it to Nicole.

"Thank you!" Nicole said, as she glanced at Mr. Smell Good. As Nicole was preparing to turn and exit the store, her stomach did somersaults just at the sight of him. Not moving, she stood and watched him leave the store and walk down the street. Her instinct whispered to her this may have been a missed opportunity to meet someone interesting.

After leaving the record store, Nicole stopped at her favorite smoothie shop nearby, got a banana, mango, and strawberry smoothie with a grilled cheese sandwich on sourdough bread, and drove the short distance home. Sitting at her table, enjoying her lunch, she heard her phone buzz with an incoming text message.

The Record Parlor - Hello Ms. Graham! This is Susan from the record store. We gave you the wrong bag. Can you please come back to our store when you have a moment? We apologize for the inconvenience this may cause. We will provide you with a store gift card for your troubles. We look forward to seeing you soon.

Nicole hadn't checked her bag. She assumed the bag she had contained her purchases. Inside the bag she had in her possession contained Run DMC's album titled Run DMC, Ready to Die by Notorious B.I.G., Straight Out of Compton by N.W.A., and Mary J. Blige's album, What's the 411? This stuff wasn't hers. Although the material was excellent, she already had these albums in her collection.

When Nicole arrived back at the record store, there weren't as many people mulling around as earlier. The DJ was gone. The Grease soundtrack played through the store speakers.

"Excuse me?" Nicole said to the saleswoman at the counter. "I received a text about me being given the wrong bag when I was here earlier."

"You must be the one who took my bag. I took yours. You have good taste in music," Mr. Smell Good said, looking as gorgeous as he did earlier in the day. The guy in the gray sweats and navy blue long-sleeved ribbed cotton shirt stood directly in front of her. Her stomach did that somersault thing again. He was really cute, she thought.

Grinning with unease, Nicole responded, "And you have my bag."

The sales woman who helped Nicole earlier looked at both of them with an apologetic expression and said, "We're so sorry for this mix up. Here is a $50 store credit for the both of you. Again, we apologize for this inconvenience."

"Thank you," they said in unison.

Nicole exchanged bags with the gorgeous man and introduced herself. "My name's Nicole Graham. Thank you for returning my bag. I'm happy to know I'll keep my purchases after this mix up."

"Cameron Davis!" he said. "Nice to meet you."

Nicole curiously asked, "Your name is familiar. Maybe we've met before?" It then dawned on her. The man was from the news article. In that split second, she had to decide if she was going to be a fan and seem like a creeper or play it off like she didn't know who this man really was.

"Um, I'm not sure," Cameron replied, considering Nicole.

Nicole and Cameron stood for a handful of seconds, looking at one another, smiling.

Nicole broke their awkward silence. She would not stand there and look silly, even though she knew exactly who Cameron Davis was. She was going to play it off. She knew she would run into him again in a few weeks. "Well, I have to go. It was nice meeting you, Cameron."

"It was nice meeting you, Nicole." he returned, then flashed her a million-dollar smile. He held his hand out to shake hers. Nicole grabbed his hand and gave it a firm handshake. The moment their hands made contact, she experienced a surge of electricity shoot up her arm and directly into her heart. They held their hands together for a few seconds. Nicole released her hand from his and admired his face for a few more milliseconds. They walked out of the store together, stopped for a second, gave each other one last glimpse, then walked in opposite directions.

Chapter 8

Cameron

After the strange woman dressed in lingerie showed up at Cameron's door, he bought a monster steel lock that included an extra bolt to secure the door from the inside. This padlock should keep unwanted women from entering his condo. The fear of an uninvited person entering his house had never crossed his mind. Dare he say he didn't trust women? Was trust the reason he hadn't dated in months? He hadn't been on a date since he and Shannon broke up. Toward the end of the relationship, Cameron just stopped talking. No matter his efforts, she was never happy. Shannon stopped laughing at his jokes. She returned his calls less and less. The naked chested man on her phone that wasn't him sealed his exit. He was done and gone. That was eight months ago. Was it time for Cameron to get back out into the dating world? Would dating and the possibility of a relationship interfere with his career? He wanted nothing to jeopardize his concentration. He did miss having a female around. He longed for a female body pressed against his. The subtle fragrance of a woman's presence, entangling his fingers in soft locks en framing a beautiful face. The sensation of running his touches up and down her soft body, the exchange of gentle, heartfelt kisses.

Reminiscing about yesterday's encounter at the record store, thinking about Nicole, Cameron couldn't shake off the curiosity of what if. Nicole! She was breathtaking. Why didn't he invite her for coffee? Maybe he should've asked her to go for a casual dinner. He had no familiarity with her at all but her striking smile, beautiful, thick, curly hair, her radiant warm honey colored skin that looked soft as butter reminded him of his missed opportunity.

"Why didn't I get her number? Fool! My dumbass didn't even appear interested. We had a moment. Damn!" Cameron couldn't wrap his mind around his own idiocy. He used to be on top of his game with beautiful women. He missed out on Nicole. How would he ever find her now? He snatched his phone from the kitchen counter and Googled her name. Nicole Graham. Her name was familiar too. The top of the search results linked her to food articles, photographs of diverse culinary delights, and an image of her and another woman associating them with an upcoming restaurant renovation and future re-opening. Nicole was entrenched in the Los Angeles food scene. He was certain it was the woman Cameron saw at the record store in the picture.

"So, she's a foodie of some sort," Cameron concluded, scrolling through the many articles Nicole had authored. He opened another link leading to an article in the Los Angeles Times. The headline read, Food Stylist Nicole Graham Named to Lead L.A. Eats. Cameron was impressed. She had insider knowledge about the culinary landscape in the city. Eyes shut, his mind ran through his mental Rolodex. He recognized Nicole from somewhere. Was she a friend of a friend? Was she the subject of a picture someone shared with him? Did he meet her at an event? He realized she was not someone Ryan dated. She was too sophisticated for his taste. He came up with nothing. No recollection of where he knew her name. After what felt like an eternity, he had an epiphany.

"The emergency call!" Nicole Graham was the woman who fainted in the park. He and Hopper drove her to the hospital. It was late January, before he started at Station 12.

"That was her?" Doubting himself, Cameron couldn't believe that was the same woman.

Was Nicole Graham from the park the same woman from the record store? She didn't look like that the day she fainted. He never picked up women at work. He was always the recipient of advances, never the initiator while on duty. That was one rule he adhered to, without hesitation. But had she looked as she did at the record store, he would have broken his cardinal rule.

"Nicole Graham!" he repeated.

Cameron could get Nicole's contact information. Ask Hopper to get her personal information from her file. It would be unethical to ask someone else to break code and release personal information. He couldn't do that even if he had access to her file himself. He missed out.

"Damn!" Cameron loudly said, slamming his hand on his couch.

Cameron's ringing phone snapped him out of his anger with himself. He picked up his phone and accepted Myles' incoming call.

"Hello?"

"Cam? You coming over or what? The guys are here, and we're getting ready to grill some meat." Myles asked.

"Right! Yeah, I'll be over. I needed to take care of a few things at home. I'm on my way. Do you want me to bring anything?" Cameron asked. He forgot all about the BBQ.

"Bring some sides, man. All we got is meat and bread," Myles demanded.

"Bet! I'll stop by Mama's Kitchen and pick up some potato salad and baked beans."

"Alright, cool! See you when you get here," Myles said, ending the call.

Cameron pulled his large black SUV into Myles' driveway, blocking him in. Grabbing the trays of food and walking into the backyard where the guys were lounging by the pool, he spotted Myles at the grill.

"Yo, Cam! Glad you could make it," Ryan said, sipping on his Modelo.

"I may be late, but I'll show up." The rest of the guys waved. Myles gestured his tongs in Cameron's direction, then turned his attention to the meat he was turning. Cameron took the food he brought into the house.

"Hey Cameron," Jessica greeted.

"Hey, Jessica!" Holding the trays in one hand, Cameron reached to give her a side hug. A ring missing from Jessica's left ring finger confirmed Myles hadn't proposed yet. He set the food on the kitchen counter and made a mental note to chat with Myles about his proposal plans.

Jessica pulled Cameron to the adjoining family room. "Meet some of my friends. Cameron, this is Rhonda, Trina, Carolyn, and Gee. Ladies, this is Cameron."

"Hey!" they all said in unison, a few waving, not taking their eyes away from the rerun episode of Martin playing on the big screen.

"Wait, aren't you the guy from the news? You're a firefighter huh?" Carolyn asked, her voice several octaves above normal.

"Yeah, that's me," Cameron admitted shyly. He got this almost everywhere he went.

"Oh, you cuter in person than on the news," Carolyn admitted. Approaching Cameron, checking him out.

"You can come save me," she said, licking her bottom lip and gazing into his eyes.

"Carolyn, slow down. Cameron's a good guy. He doesn't need you to pounce all over him," Jessica asserted. Cameron gave Carolyn one of his million dollar smiles.

"Ooh, and you got a pretty smile," Carolyn whined. "Okay, I'm done. Nice to meet you, Cameron," Carolyn said as she rejoined her friends in front of the television.

Cameron stood and observed the vibe in the house and decided he best go outside with the guys. "Jessica, I'm gonna head outside with the fellas." Cameron closed the sliding door behind him and reached into the ice chest to grab a beer.

"Yeah, you saw that crew in the house, huh?" Ryan asked with a sly grin.

"Yep! And no, thank you!" Cameron had thoughts of dating, but the women in the house were not his type. He couldn't shake his thoughts about Nicole Graham. The beautiful woman who got away.

"Man, I hear you. I'll give my new friend a call and ask her to bring some of her girlfriends over. What y'all think?" Ryan posed.

"Man, if you call more women over here, I'll have to explain to Jessica. This ain't no set up or match up gathering. Leave it alone." Myles just wanted to hang out with his boys. "Jessica just so happened to ask her girlfriends over. It wasn't the plan, but I just want peace."

"Well, I won't be staying long. This babe is it," Ryan said, holding up his phone adorning a photo of a woman dressed in a very short, revealing party dress. "I've been waiting for a call back from her for a while."

"Is there ever a day you don't think about a woman?" Josh asked.

"Nope! Cam, you want me to ask if she has a friend?" Ryan was just waiting to set him up. Cameron couldn't recall a time Ryan didn't talk about women or try to set the single guys up..

"NO! I'm good. Thanks!" Cameron wanted nothing to do with anyone who came near Ryan.

Terrell must not have been into the house yet. If the women were aware of his presence, everything would change, even if Cameron was interested in one of them. Wherever Terrell went, a diverse array of women seemed to gravitate toward him, drawn by his good looks and the notoriety of being a Laker. Before his five-game trip, Terrell simply wanted to enjoy time with his closest friends. Cameron walked over to the empty lounge chair under the shady tree and sat next to him.

"Josh? You didn't bring your lady friend?" Cameron asked. A woman he knew Josh was getting close to was obviously absent.

"Naw. I'm not sure about this one. She says she wants to date and then she doesn't want to date. We were on a good roll for a few weeks." Josh shrugged his shoulders as if questioning what was going on in his own dating life.

"She's not into you." Myles said. "If she was into you, you would know it and you wouldn't have to guess."

"You right, you right," Josh admitted.

Ryan, pushing send on a text message, asked, "Terrell, who is your flavor of the week?"

Terrell shook his head in response. "I'm just chillin', man. I'm not trying to get hooked in with anybody right now. I got my casuals on standby. No one to mention, though. Nothing serious. Women are clingy. They want to stake claim and demand a commitment. I don't have time for that. I just want to have fun right now. I'll be ready to settle down when I retire in a few years or when I meet the one."

Terrell wasn't the player type, despite his baller status. Cameron knew when his ball playing days ended, he would settle down and retire his dating card. All of his friends' dating stories made Cameron thankful he was single and focused on his career. Women were a distraction he wasn't ready for right now. Being in a relationship meant spending energy he didn't have at the moment. A flashback to Nicole's smile crossed his mind. Would she be different? She was different from the ladies in the house. She didn't have a ring on her finger. He assumed she was single. Cameron recognized the look. He could have sworn she was giving him an interested gaze. Some women were bold and would have asked him for his number.

"Damn!" Cameron said out loud, thinking about his missed opportunity.

"What, man?" Myles asked.

"Oh, just lost in thought." How long would Nicole Graham be on his mind?

"The meat's ready. Imma take this into the house and help Jessica set up everything so we can eat." Myles was already a family guy. He bought the house with her in mind. He was ready to tie the knot.

"Oh, bet," Terrell said, following Myles into the house.

Cameron, Ryan, and Josh all stood up and followed them into the kitchen.

"Look at these handsome men coming through the door!" Carolyn said at full volume.

"Oh, my God! Is that Terrell Brown of the Lakers?" Rhonda wondered out loud. Rhonda hadn't said a word all day, but Terrell caught her attention.

"Hello, everyone!" Terrell said, arms out, walking toward Jessica to give her a hug.

"We got barbecue chicken, hot links, turkey burgers and a large piece of salmon. Plus potato salad and baked beans. Dessert is on the dining room table. Drinks are in the ice chest outside, if you didn't already know. Help yourselves," Myles announced.

Cameron grabbed a plate and stood, waiting his turn in the food line. Myles walked up to him. Gathering close to Cameron's ear, he whispered, "I'm going to propose today here. Jessica's parents are on the way."

Cameron's eyes got big, mouth agape.

"Close your mouth, man! She has no clue, and I didn't tell the others, so say nothing. I wanted you to know," Myles said, looking nervous.

"I got you man, okay? You can do this!" Cameron was nervous for him. He would support his friend.

"So, Terrell, how do you think you'll fare in the playoffs?" Gee asked.

"We should be good if we stay injury free," Terrell responded.

"I think if your big guy stays injury free, you'll be good. You have a bench and at least two of you have a three pointer that's golden," Gee commented.

"You know basketball?" Terrell asked, giving Gee another glance.

Cameron was impressed. Few women could talk shop. Not in detail, anyway. He saw the familiar gleam in Terrell's eyes showing interest in Gee.

"Did you play, Gee? Terrell inquired, allowing his gaze to sweep over her from head to toe and up again. Gee was around six-foot-one and had a solid build. Hair pulled back in a neat long ponytail, dressed in fitted leggings, a Notre Dame Women's Basketball t-shirt and white leather *Nike* sneakers, she looked like a baller herself.

"Yeah, I played in college. Small forward. We made it to the elite eight in my junior year. I went to Notre Dame," Gee shared. "What college did you go to?" she asked.

"We all played with Myles at USC," Terrell answered.

"I thought I recognized you guys. I follow most college games, men and women. Even back when I played. Nice!" Gee proclaimed.

Cameron was halfway through his plate of food when his phone buzzed. He pulled it out of his pocket and noticed a text from Myles.

Myles - Come up to my room. I want to show you the ring.

Cameron - Right now?

Myles - Yes, right now!

Cameron looked up from his plate, surveying the room. Everyone was seated around the dining room table, at the kitchen table, or in the family room, having conversation and enjoying their food. Jessica was next to Carolyn, engrossed in a conversation about the upcoming season of The Bachelor. Terrell and Gee were next to one another, continuing their conversation about basketball. Cameron was certain Terrell would have her number by the end of the night. Women who had a deep understanding of sports had a special appeal to him. And she was cute. He knew his friend.

Cameron stood, took his plate to the kitchen, and found Josh plating seconds on his plate.

"Are you ready for your big night?" Josh asked.

"What big night?" Carolyn interrupted.

"Cameron's getting an award from the city for saving a baby from a fire," Josh explained.

"Do you need a date?" Carolyn asked, giving him a once over.

"No, I don't need a date. But thank you," Cameron politely responded.

"Well, if you change your mind, Jessica has my number," Carolyn said, giving Cameron a wink.

"Hey, what's your name again?" Carolyn asked, turning to Josh.

"Josh," he responded, giving his brilliant smile.

Cameron felt relieved as the attention shifted away from him. He slipped out of the room unnoticed and headed upstairs.

"Dude? What took you so long? Jessica's parents are outside waiting in the car," Myles blasted, perspiration beading on his forehead.

"You alright? You gonna make it?" Cameron asked, giving Myles a playful poke on his shoulder.

Myles reached into his dresser drawer and pulled out a deep blue velvet box. Hands shaking, he opened it to reveal the ring.

"Blue is Jessica's favorite color. What do you think?" Myles asked, holding the ring box in Cameron's face.

Cameron couldn't believe it. The ring made everything real. His best friend was going to propose to Jessica with a large solitaire diamond, the gem sitting in the center of a gold band. It shimmered under the recessed lighting in Myles' bedroom.

"This is gorgeous, man! Do you know what you're going to say?"

"I know I'll do better off the cuff. I've played this scene in my head for weeks. I get tripped up, so I stopped trying to rehearse my words."

Myles took the box, closed it, and put it in his pocket. "I'm going to text her parents to come into the house."

"Won't Jessica wonder why they're here?" Cameron wondered.

"They already know to say they came just to get some food." Myles wiped his forehead with his t-shirt collar. "Oh, can you film it please, for my parents?"

"Film the proposal? Man?" Cameron didn't like that much responsibility on his shoulders. As Myles' best man, he had to do it.

"Well? Then go do it!" Cameron said, reaching for Myles to pat him on his back, pulling him in for a bear hug.

Cameron made another plate and sat in the family room, placing his food on the side table to witness and film the proposal. He waved to Jessica's parents sitting on the couch next to their daughter.

Myles pulled Jessica from her seat, embraced her, burying his face in her neck.

"Myles? Are you okay?" Jessica asked in a shaky voice.

Myles pulled away from Jessica's embrace and held her hands before speaking.

"Jessica?" Myles spoke. His hands trembling, he took a deep breath and got down on one knee.

"Oh my God, he's going to propose!" Carolyn yelled. Everyone now on their feet, Cameron holding his phone to record everything, a tear running down Jessica's face, Myles took another deep breath, locked eyes with his soon to be fiancé, then spoke again.

"Jessica? There aren't enough words to express how much love I have for you. I have never ending gratitude rescue all the moments we've shared. We have laughed together, cried together, supported one another, and shared so many memories." Myles then reached into his pocket, producing the blue velvet ring box. With great anticipation, he opened it to reveal the engagement ring he had shown Cameron earlier.

"Please wear this ring as a symbol of my commitment to you and the life we'll share as husband and wife. Will you marry me?"

Jessica gazed at the ring, bringing her hand up to cover her opened mouth. Then a radiant smile spread across her face, revealing happiness as she took Myles' hands to bring him to his feet. Tears dropping, trailing lines of black mascara down her face, Jessica said, "Yes, I will marry you!" Drawing Myles into her, hands cupping his face, sharing a passionate kiss that only newly engaged couples shared.

Chapter 9

Nicole

The ocean side restaurant's charming and nostalgic ambiance created a sense of time suspension. On the waterfront, the eatery offered a unique dining experience reminiscent of a bygone era, with the option to dine inside overlooking the water. The large black umbrella proved ineffective in offering the much needed shade Nicole and Aubrey needed to work. This dining outlet was their office for the day. Aubrey had the tall order of updating the menu and transforming the place into a trendy hotspot. Nicole's expertise in food and decor would assist the much overdue makeover. For several minutes, Nicole and Aubrey reviewed the dated menu.

"I haven't seen a menu like this since my parents took me to dinner when I was like ten years old," Aubrey declared as she took her notebook out of her tote bag.

"Lobster with twice baked potato and steamed broccoli. Salad with green goddess dressing. Shrimp cocktail. Fried shrimp with butter noodles. I can't believe this. These dishes remind me of a restaurant I used to go to as a kid," Nicole observed.

"Do you remember the name of it?" Aubrey questioned.

"Steak and the Races. We used to go on Saturdays with my uncle and cousins. It was popular back in the day. I'm certain it's closed now." Nicole smiled at the memories flooding her thoughts. A large table filled with her loved ones chowing on steak, salad with green goddess dressing and shrimp cocktail, to name a few of her family's favorites. "What are your ideas for this place?"

Aubrey paused for a second, putting down the restaurant's original menu. "There needs to be more freshness. Lettuce greens with flavorful dressings. Exotic vegetables. Perhaps deep fried crab cakes or lobster mac and cheese bites, or smoked salmon sushi rolls. I'm also going to recommend he hire a pastry chef."

"This all sounds so amazing." Nicole was in awe at how Aubrey stayed up to date with all the food trends while running a restaurant of her own.

"Here is the food you ordered, Ms. Carroll," the server announced, setting five small plates on their table. Fried shrimp, a twice baked potato, iceberg lettuce with bacon and ranch dressing, bacon wrapped scallops, and butter basted rib eye steak.

"We have to taste what they are serving to judge whether we have to delete these staples from the menu," Aubrey remarked, as she perused the food in front of her.

Nicole and Aubrey took small bites from each plate. Nicole examined Aubrey's face, aware that she was already primed to offer fresher recommendations.

"The bread is warm, which means it's not fresh. The batter on the fried shrimp is too thick. The twice baked potato is overcooked. It's clear to me that the salad was dressed excessively and the bacon on the scallops is undercooked. The steak could use more seasoning."

With a slight chuckle, Nicole voiced, "I agree with all of that. Carol and I just finished photographing plates for a new restaurant that will open soon on the westside. They have a seafood section on their menu that's modern. We should go to their opening in two weeks for ideas."

Nicole and Aubrey could craft recipes based on the flavors in a dish, which made restaurant sampling so much fun. While the owner sought a revamped menu, Aubrey advocated for retaining the original culinary integrity customers had come to know and love over the years.

Unable to hold her news any longer, Nicole blurted. "Did I tell you I have a date tomorrow night?"

Aubrey stopped writing in her notebook and peered at Nicole. "No, you did not! Who with?"

"With a guy Carol knows." Nicole said, raising and lowering her eyebrows. Carol, Nicole's photographer, business partner, and friend, continued to parade potential dates her way. This guy piqued Nicole's interest, so Carol facilitated the exchange of personal information so the two could get acquainted.

"She's really trying to be the matchmaker these days. Does she have someone for me?" Aubrey was curious.

"Do you really want to date right now, Aubrey?" In the subtle nuances of their conversations and the quiet pauses between words, Nicole discerned a sentiment echoing within her friend's heart. A decision to embrace solitude rather than dance in the realms of romance for the time being. Aubrey wasn't over her last relationship.

"Absolutely not! But I do get lonely. It would be nice to have someone to call every now and again."

"His name is Eric. He's a photographer and travels with various artists on tour and takes pictures to sell to the different media outlets," Nicole shared.

"Really? That's interesting. Have you spoken to him yet?" Aubrey probed.

"We've texted. Carol sent me a photo. Let me show you." Nicole scrolled through her phone to pull up Eric's picture when she noticed an incoming text from Edward.

> **Edward** - Hey Nicole! Long time no talk to. All good? Would love to see you, take you to break-fast this weekend?

Nicole rolled her eyes in annoyance.

"What's that look for? Who texted you?" Aubrey wondered out loud.

With an irritated sigh, Nicole responded, "Edward."

"He will not leave you alone. After the trip to the outlet mall, I thought he'd give you some space." Nicole knew Aubrey was tired of Edward bothering her. Catching sight of him, spending time with him, did remind her of Tyler. Aubrey shared many times she wished she could wave a wand and make Edward disappear.

"He did for a while, but I think he's trying again." Nicole didn't understand why Edward wouldn't take the hint. It could be because of the mixed signals she gave him. Time with him likely equaled him, thinking she liked him. The only reason she saw Edward was because he reminded her of Tyler. She just wasn't interested in dating him. Nicole scrolled through her phone to find the picture of Eric. Edward could wait.

"What do you think?" Nicole asked, handing Aubrey her phone.

Aubrey stared at Eric's close cut, fair skin, dark round eyes, and warm smile. "He's nice looking." Taking one last glance before handing Nicole her phone.

"Eric and I spoke over text for a couple of days. He's thirty-one, divorced, with no children. He enjoys jazz music, quiet evenings at home, and is teaching himself how to paint. He'd like to find a special someone.

He knows it's hard because of his job. He meets lots of women on the road. However, he thinks they talk to him because they're trying to get to the artists," Nicole rambled.

"What are your thoughts on that? Women throwing themselves at him?" Aubrey wondered.

Nicole instantly pictured groupies clamoring for backstage access. "We're just going to dinner. Taking things slow is my approach. I'm excited, though."

"I can tell. You haven't talked much about your recent dates. I see the excitement in your eyes." Aubrey appeared to be lost in thought for a few moments. She then said, "The presence of a man can help you move on. You should go on lots of dates."

"Speaking of dates, Aubrey, the City of Los Angeles event is a big one. I don't need to bring a date, do I?"

"No, I want you to be an observer. I want this event to go well. I won't be able to leave the kitchen, so I need you to be my eyes and ears. I'd like to hear about people's opinions on the food. This could lead to catering for other city events," Aubrey said, wiggling her eyebrows at the thought of possibilities.

"I can do that," Nicole assured her friend.

For the rest of the afternoon, Nicole and Aubrey's conversation revolved around food, the restaurant aesthetics, and concepts for the grand reopening. Aubrey planned to pitch her ideas and create a compelling proposal to excite the owner.

The next morning, Nicole was up early, mapping out her run as she drove to the beach. Her timing was perfect. Finding the ideal middle ground, she arrived when it wasn't too early to be deserted, yet not too late to find it overly populated. The brilliant June sun heated her in its warm rays, while the moist, salty air blessed upon her sun-kissed complexion. With a playlist of gangsta rap bumping in her ear, Nicole began with a brisk walk to warm her muscles. Within ten minutes, Nicole ran at a rhythmic pace. With the sand stretched out alongside of her, the sparkling blue water extended as far as her eye could see. Waves crashed onto the shore, leaving the occasional pieces of seaweed behind. She passed sunbathers, people engrossed in a heated volleyball game, and fellow runners.

At the end of her run, Nicole stopped at a beachfront café to buy a drink to quench her parched throat. Now sitting on a nearby bench, soaking in a little more sun, sipping on a freshly squeezed large cup of a veggie blend of juice, she thought about her upcoming date. This date could be a good one. It could potentially lead to a second date. The idea of meeting a new man stirred mixed emotions within her. On the one hand, there was the fear of becoming acquainted with someone new, with all the uncertainty and vulnerability it brought. However, there was a need to move forward, embrace new experiences, and explore life's possibilities.

Approaching her house, Nicole spotted her brother's car parked in front. His SUV was empty. He didn't text to say he was coming by. Nicole hoped nothing was wrong. Whenever Levi arrived unannounced, she invariably experienced a flutter of nervousness in her stomach.

"Hello? Levi?" Nicole said, opening her front door, noticing her brother sitting on her couch.

"I saw Elle today," Levi uttered with a little breath.

"Oh? Where did you see her?"

"Of all places, at the grocery store. She was with," Levi sighed and took a deep breath, "her fiancé."

"Her fiancé? Really?" Nicole voiced in surprise.

Tears welled up in Levi's eyes. Nicole quickly sat on the couch and grabbed her brother and pulled him into her. "I know this is heartbreaking. I know you love her so much. It has been a few years since your breakup. Maybe it's time you move on. I mean, really move on."

Nicole gave Levi a tight squeeze. She gently rocked him back and forth, as if he were a young child, hoping this gesture would soothe his deeply hurting heart. Elle being engaged was devastating news. They were high school sweethearts, college sweethearts even, until her father broke them up. Levi's first love. A love he thought would be forever. "Honey, you'll get past this. You will. I promise," Nicole affirmed.

"Nicole, I still love her. I'm not sure if I can have the same level of love for anyone as I have for her." Levi released himself from Nicole's embrace and rested his head in his hands, unable to look Nicole in her eyes.

Nicole stroked his back, hoping to soothe his breaking heart. She reached for his face and gazed at his glossy eyes, her eyes reflecting her honest emotions. "I understand, Levi, but you have to try. You have to try to move on." Nicole was more aware of this than anyone. She knew what it meant to try to move on from lost love.

"If only you could have seen her expression, what her eyes were telling me. Her eyes said it all. She doesn't love that man. I'm sure she agreed to be engaged to him because her father said it was a good idea. She's still in love with me," Levi confidently stated.

"How do you know, Levi? Do you really know what is going on in Elle's life? When you looked into her eyes, maybe you saw what you wanted to see. She stopped communicating with you. You don't know how she really feels," Nicole said honestly.

"I'm conscious of the fact that I should set her free, but I can't. I'll always love Elle." Levi had a demeanor that suggested a need to cry, hinting that he was on the brink of tears.

Nicole was familiar with that expression. She understood the hurt her brother was experiencing. It's as if a profound sense of hopelessness engulfs you, leaving you at a loss of how to cope or manage the overwhelming emotion. They remained silent for a brief while, allowing the quiet to envelop the moment.

"Do you want some coffee or tea?" Nicole asked, knowing a hot beverage would calm his nerves.

Standing to his feet, Levi took in a deep breath and said, "No, thanks. I have to go home. I have groceries in the car. I love you, sis." Levi walked to the door, looking back at Nicole.

"I love you, too. Maybe we can have brunch tomorrow?" Nicole didn't want to leave him alone. She wanted to comfort Levi as he always comforted her. He had been by her side when Tyler passed. Despite his lingering, overbearing nature, his intentions were loving.

Levi looked down at his older sister with admiration. "Maybe."

"I can tell you all about my date tonight?" Nicole admitted, sounding giddy.

Levi stopped and turned to Nicole. "You have a date?"

"Yep! Now go, I have to get ready," she said, pushing her brother out the door.

Taking a glance at his watch, Levi said, "It's only 11:30."

"I'm aware. I want to take my time, relax, and do my hair. I'm meeting him at five."

Levi gave Nicole a stern look and said, "Okay... text me where you're going and his name."

Nicole watched her brother get into his SUV and drive away. She knew Levi seeing Elle was extremely hard for him. He wanted to marry Elle.

Now she was engaged to someone else. They were only twenty-five. Was twenty-five the marrying age? Levi said he was having fun. What did that mean, knowing he was unwilling to get serious with anyone? He didn't commit deeply or form long-lasting commitments with women since his breakup with Elle. Nicole understood the reasons why he never pursued serious relationships with anyone, recognizing the motivations that influenced his choices. He had not let go of Elle. She was well acquainted with the sensation. She was putting in considerable effort to move on from her feelings of losing Tyler. Moving on from loving him. Searching for the emotional closure that could deliver her from spiraling out of control again. Levi could see Elle. Perhaps not in the manner he desired, but she was alive. Tyler was dead. Nothing was going to bring him back. Nicole had no choice but to move on. She had to move on for her own sake, her health and wellbeing.

It had been a while since Nicole last picked out clothes for a date. Choosing an outfit for coffee and a movie was effortless. Dinner with the accountant had been simple. She wore a navy blue dress with silver strappy heels. Eric was taking her to a trendy restaurant on the first date. What do women wear to trendy restaurants? During their first phone call, Nicole greeted him with a hello and his deep baritone voice replied with a rich and melodic tone. They exchanged pleasantries about their day and the weather. After confirming their meeting time, they hung up. Nicole, out of practice, found their first conversation awkward. She wondered if they would have things in common.

Amidst the jumble of clothes thrown across her bed, Nicole eventually made her choice and settled on an off-the-shoulder black jersey dress that hit just above her knees. She paired the dress with a strappy fuchsia pink sandal and a matching bag. She included a silver necklace and earrings, which added the finishing touches to her outfit. The sound of Nicole's rumbling stomach served as a clear signal she was hungry. She grabbed string cheese, pretzels, and flavored water from the kitchen and switched on her chill playlist, flopping down onto her comfortable couch, ready to relax before her date. Eventually, she fell asleep and awoke to no music playing.

Nicole grabbed her phone. "Oh, no! It's 3:30," she shouted.

Nicole scrambled up and off the couch to hop into the shower. With no time to do her hair, she decided on a high bun. Butterflies swam in her stomach as she got ready for her date. Stepping out of the shower, Nicole pondered first impressions. Pictures can tell a story, depict an image in the likeness of the subject. However, meeting in person upped the stakes. She realized you only get one chance to create a positive first impression, and she was determined to make this one count. Not for Eric, but for herself. She yearned to regain a sense of normalcy and rediscover her self-worth as a desirable woman. Edward told her all the time she was beautiful. He tried to treat her to symbols of thoughtfulness and affections. She had been grateful for his kind gestures, which served as a reminder that she was indeed a beautiful woman. However, she always declined him. His recent behavior gave her reason. He was Tyler's cousin. Edward reminded her of Tyler. His good qualities and his presence made Nicole angry. The anger stemmed from the fact that Tyler was gone and wasn't coming back, and how Edward offered comfort was frustrating. Now he seemed to flirt, and that made her uncomfortable.

Nicole enhanced her makeup by applying a few coats of mascara, delicate shimmers of pink to her eyes and cheeks. Finally, she applied the fuchsia pink lipstick that elegantly complimented her full lips, finishing off her style with a touch of vibrancy and confidence. "Not bad, Nicole, not bad at all," she said, admiring herself in the full-length mirror.

Nicole left at 4:30, ensuring she would make it to the restaurant on time. The instrumental music blaring from her car speakers calmed her nervousness. As she pulled up to the restaurant to valet her car, she saw a tall, fair-complected man with a close haircut, dressed in black pants, nice shoes, and a black and white button-up, looking at his phone. Was that Eric? Nicole couldn't see his face. As she exited the car and walked to the curb, he lifted his head and revealed the likeness of the photo sent to her phone.

"Eric?" Nicole stepped toward him, extending her hand.

"Nicole?" Eric asked, grabbing her hand and giving it a firm handshake.

Nicole liked a firm handshake. They conveyed strength and assurance during introductions.

"It's so nice to meet you," Eric stated, gazing into Nicole's eyes.

"It's nice to meet you, too," she said, returning the gaze with a bright smile.

"Shall we go inside, get a table?" Eric suggested, using his hand to gently touch the middle of Nicole's back, guiding her to the door.

The restaurant was lively, with every available seat filled by diners, sipping on cocktails, enjoying their food.

"Reservation for two, Eric Beasley," he said to the hostess.

"Yes, Mr. Beasley, we have a table ready for you. This way, please,"

Eric led Nicole to follow the hostess, him close behind her. The restaurant décor predominantly incorporated shades of green, white, and rustic browns, with glass fixtures adding a touch of elegance and illumination to the ambiance.

"Here you are," the hostess said, placing the menus on the table, which was situated near a substantial water fixture placed at the center of the dining area. Eric extended the chair to Nicole, then settled into the one across from her.

Eyes surveying the menu, Eric shared, "I hear this place has delicious pan seared scallops in a garlic butter glaze."

"That sounds amazing," Nicole responded, scouring the selection of food choices herself.

The menu was not too large, consisting of five appetizers, eight entrees and three dessert choices. Nicole had her eye on the scallops with an assortment of greens and mushroom risotto.

"Have you made a selection?" Eric asked as he peeked over his menu, staring at Nicole with a slight smile.

"Yes, have you?" Nicole wanted to enjoy her meal, whether the date went well or not.

"I'll order the steak with mashed potatoes and vegetable medley," Eric stated.

The server approached their table. "Hello! Welcome! Can I start you with a glass of wine, drink from the bar, or water?"

"What wine would you recommend with the scallops," Nicole wondered.

"Well, you can have a glass of Chenin Blanc, Chardonnay, or Alsace Pinot Gris."

Nicole thought for a few seconds before she spoke. "I'll have a glass of Chenin Blanc. And water. Thank you."

"For you, sir?" the server asked.

"I'll have a gin and tonic and a glass of water, please," Eric ordered.

"I'll be back shortly with your drinks, and then I'll take your order," the server said, walking away.

Eric sat back in his chair, gazing at Nicole before he spoke. "May I say it's a pleasure to see you in person? Your picture doesn't do you justice. You are breathtakingly beautiful."

"Thank you, Eric! You're not so bad yourself," Nicole said, flashing him a broad grin.

"I must thank Carol for our introduction. Tell me, how was your day?" Eric said, folding his hands and placing them onto the table.

Nicole liked where this evening was going. "It was great, and yours?"

Eric flashed an exasperated expression on his face. "I have to admit, I worked most of the day. I edited some pictures that have to go out."

"Instead of working, I went for a run and ended up napping on my couch," Nicole said with a chuckle.

"There's nothing wrong with a nap. You're a runner?" Eric's eyes sparkled as he awaited Nicole's response.

"Wouldn't call myself a runner. Just someone who runs to get my blood flowing, wake up my muscles, you know?" Her muscles ached at that very moment.

"Yes, I do. Carol tells me you two work together. I know Carol commissions many types of projects. What do you two do together?" Eric asked.

"I'm a food stylist. I prepare and arrange food for cookbooks, magazines, advertisements and the like. Sometimes I'm contracted to decorate an establishment with photographs of their food. I also write about food. Carol's my photographer for all of my projects." Nicole was impressed with her own resume.

"Really? Can you cook?" Eric's eyebrows lifted in anticipation as he waited for her reply.

"Yes, I can. I have an eye for food combinations, color. I sometimes work as a consultant for menu development. By tasting, I can write recipes from scratch." Nicole thought to herself, when was the last time she had to explain her job?

"Wow! So, you style food for what magazines?" Eric leaned back in his chair, easing into their conversation.

Nicole ran down the list of her clients. Eric shared his roster of artists he worked with. Their discussion shifted towards more work related topics, becoming somewhat of a work conversation. She wasn't sure if their current topic of conversation was a sign they didn't have anything in common.

"Your drinks!" The server announced as he set them on the table. "Can I take your order?"

Nicole and Eric ordered their meals and continued talking about their work. He shared hilarious stories of fans doing any and everything to get him to take them backstage to meet the artists. She enjoyed his stories, relieved she didn't have to share more intimately personal things. When their food arrived, they were slow to eat, being engulfed in their conversation. Their work ignited a deep passion within both of them. At least their mutual passion for their careers was something they had in common. After their plates were cleaned, they mutually decided to indulge in a shared blondie dessert paired with a scoop of vanilla bean ice cream.

Nicole placed her hands over her stomach. "I don't know about you, Eric, but I'm really full."

"Me, too. I have an idea. Would you like to go dancing? There's a place nearby I've been to. We can work off some of our dinner," Eric offered.

"That sounds like fun. Of course, why not?" Nicole was feeling bold.

Eric paid the bill, and they walked to exit the restaurant, when they heard the sounds of commotion nearby. Nicole didn't pay much attention to it. She turned to Eric.

"If you don't mind, I'll drive my car to the club," Nicole said, handing her ticket to the valet guy.

"Of course. I understand. I parked just down the street. The club is about ten minutes from here. If you give me your phone, I'll punch in the name of the club so you can plug the directions into your navigation system?"

Nicole handed Eric her phone, watching as he typed the name of the club into the map app. His hands appeared strong, masculine in appearance, yet still well groomed and manicured. She questioned what the sensation of holding his hand would be. Perhaps she'd discover it at the club. The valet drove up with her car, got out, and waited for her to get in the driver's seat. Eric paid the valet. As he was going to close Nicole's door, a swarm of police cars stopped in front of the restaurant. Officers began to exit their cars, as a huge man literally carried a guy by his shirt, feet dangling, out of the restaurant.

Guns pointed at the man, the officers commanded, "Hands up!"

The huge man, obviously restaurant security, let go of the man he carried out. The man in question lifted his hands, not fully coherent, when four officers rushed him to the ground.

"What did I do? I didn't do anything," the man yelled.

An officer putting the man in handcuffs then said, "You are under arrest for attempted murder and conspiracy to commit murder. You have the right to remain silent. Anything you say has the potential to be used against you in a court of law. You have a right to an attorney."

At that moment, Nicole took a closer look. She recognized the voice. The officer handcuffing the man was Jim Stone. Nicole sat in her car, driver's side door ajar, in shock. Her mind raced with visions from the park, seeing him. Nicole had an immediate sensation of coldness and a light-headed feeling. Eric stood in front of Nicole, his countenance reflecting bewilderment.

"Eric, I'm so sorry, but I'm not going to be able to finish our date. Please forgive me. We can arrange another evening out soon, okay?" Nicole experienced a strong urge to drive away quickly and go home.

With a perplexed expression on his face, Eric asked, "Nicole, are you okay?"

Nicole's face was now ghostly. She could sense her skin becoming cold and clammy.

"I'm okay. I just... I just don't feel well," Nicole managed to say.

With concern in his tone, Eric wondered out loud, "Are you okay to drive?"

"Yes, I'll be fine." Nicole just wanted to be alone.

"Please text me when you get home, okay?" Eric urged.

"Sure," Nicole said with as much of a smile as she could muster, attempting to show she was fine. She then closed her door, put her car in drive, and slowly rolled away from the restaurant, looking at Eric standing where her car had just been, face displaying a look of confusion.

Nicole was unsure of her thoughts. The mere presence of those officers and seeing Jim Stone induced feelings of sickness in her. Was she going to have this kind of reaction every time she saw the police? With the sight of Jim Stone triggering her and rendering her unable to continue, how could she find a way to move forward? Hopefully, Dr. Williamson would be able to help her process what this was. She had to learn to manage her emotions. Nicole seemed to aimlessly drive, not having an idea where she was going. She seemed to forget her way home. A few seconds later, she realized she was on Edward's street. She parked in front of his house and just hugged the steering wheel of her car. Swiftly reaching for her phone, she messaged Edward.

Nicole - I'm parked outside your house. Can I come in?

A few minutes passed. Was Edward home? The living room light was turned on. His car was in the driveway. Nicole leaned back in her seat and closed her eyes. Seconds later, tears were streaming down her face.

Eyes now open, she noticed Edward running to her car door.

"Nicole? Are you okay?" he said, opening the door, grabbing her into an embrace that was all so familiar to her. She closed her eyes, and in the stillness, she sensed an invisible embrace, a reassurance that Tyler was right there beside her, even in that very moment. However, a few heartbeats later, Nicole recognized Edward's presence, and a surge of anger welled up within her, directed at his unmistakable self.

Now with an expression of indignation, Nicole quickly escaped Edward's grasp, realization setting in. She had to stop leaning on Edward when life got hard. He was not Tyler, and she had to resolve the fact that when she saw Edward, she saw Tyler.

Slowly stepping away from Edward, Nicole said in a hushed tone, "I'm sorry, but I have to leave. It was a mistake coming here."

"Nicole! Wait!" Edward implored, attempting to stop Nicole from getting into her car.

"Good night, Edward." Nicole said, closed her door, started the engine, and drove away.

Chapter 10

Cameron

Tonight was a night Cameron now longed to share with someone. He walked into his condo and into his room to lay his suit across his bed. After Myles proposed to Jessica at the BBQ, seeing Terrell hit it off with Gee and them exchanging phone numbers, he yearned to have a beautiful woman at his side. A woman who celebrated his achievement alongside him. But Cameron's reasons for not dating were clear. Despite his desires, his career came first. After Shannon, he wasn't sure if he could have faith in a relationship again. He recognized an attractive woman, but he understood looks weren't the only factor that mattered. He wanted someone who treated him with kindness, respect, and consideration. The women at the BBQ weren't his type. Terrell met someone who wasn't throwing herself at him, and his interest in Gee was rare. He hoped they would find a connection and begin dating. Cameron regretted not bringing his mother to this award night. She would love an evening like this, honoring her only son. Papa entered his thoughts, knowing that he would have loved to see his only grandson accept such an award.

Flashbacks of the night of the fire inundated his thoughts, replaying the harrowing scenes of running through the burning building in search of the older woman and baby and securing their safety. It was as if it was a rerun that was on repeat in his head. Firefighters were meant to leave work behind at the scene. Once you leave the scene, you move on. He contemplated whether he should have invited the baby's grandmother or mother for the event. Cameron's successful rescue had been his achievement, and he was confident that it would soon pave the way for a well-deserved promotion.

Cameron needed to relax. He had a couple of hours before the event.

While approaching the corner of his living room, Cameron acknowledged the beckoning of the turntables. To date, he had only admired the equipment. The steps were on replay.

"Step 1, compile your record collection." Cameron moved to where his vinyl albums were and took two from the stack.

"Step 2, pick two from a matching genre." He looked at the two he picked and put Sade back and chose De La Soul's Three Feet and Rising to go with the Great Adventures of Slick Rick.

"Step 3, cue up the first beat." Cameron turned his equipment on, placed each vinyl album on a turntable, and put on his headphones. He let *Buddy* begin playing. He then began to play Hey Young World, thinking he recognized a similar beat.

"Step 4, beat match the tracks." Cameron was certain this wasn't easy. He needed to make adjustments using the pitch shift to bring the tempo in line.

Overwhelmed by the next steps, which included blending the second track and using equalization, followed by adding sound effects and focusing on breakdowns, fading out the first track, and then scratching, Cameron realized he needed to take a class. He was incapable of teaching himself in one night, so he left everything where it was and showered for the awards ceremony.

Decorated with balloons, and signage, the entryway to the Museum of Art looked festive. Cameron followed the sparkling marble floors, which led to the enormous space roped off for the event. The room was filled with women adorned in elegant ball gowns and men dressed in dark suits and tuxedos, creating a sophisticated atmosphere.

"Mr. Davis?" a woman called from the registration table.

"Hello!" Cameron answered, stepping up to greet the woman.

"It's nice to see you this evening, Mr. Davis. You're assigned to table two, close to the stage."

A little confused, Cameron asked, "Thank you! Do I go to my table now?"

"Dinner will be served in less than fifteen minutes," the woman replied. "You can mingle for a few minutes."

Cameron gave the woman a nod and walked into the gigantic space, dressed in chandeliers, beautiful white lighting, and countless round tables. The band near the dance floor played smooth jazz, creating a melodic and mellow backdrop for the evening's festivities.

Cameron recognized Captain Gary walking toward him.

"Cameron, hey, man! Congratulations! I'm happy to see you win this award tonight," he said, grabbing Cameron's hand, giving him a hard pat on the back.

"Thank you Captain! I appreciate your words. I'm excited to be here."

"Let me introduce you to my wife. Linda, this is Cameron Davis, the young man I was telling you about."

With her hand extended, Linda said, "Hello Cameron. My husband has told me so much about you. And congratulations. What a heroic act you did," Linda complimented.

"Thank you. Just doing my job." Cameron sounded like a broken record, always telling others he was just doing his job when they paid him a compliment for his actions.

"I don't think we are at the same table, but let's grab a celebratory glass of champagne later this evening, okay?" Captain Gary offered, grabbing his wife's hand, leading her to greet other attendees.

Cameron shared greetings with fellow firefighters, their wives, and dates. He experienced the ping in his stomach, sensing a bit of loneliness without a date by his side. The lights dimmed, signaling everyone to find their table and have a seat for dinner. Cameron recognized he was assigned to sit with fellow award winners. He greeted his table mates and exchanged pleasantries as each one introduced themself. Although curious, Cameron didn't want to ask what each one did to earn an award. Each award winner would be introduced to everyone.

During dinner, the table was relatively quiet. Mumbles were heard by his table mates speaking to their dates. Cameron sat enjoying one of the best meals he had in a while. The dinners served at these functions were usually of mediocre quality. The night's dinner salad featured fresh greens, cherry tomatoes, cucumber, and shavings of Parmesan cheese, all elegantly dressed in a fragrant vinaigrette that stimulated his sense of flavor. The chicken and mashed potatoes were generously smothered in a flavorful brown gravy, expertly seasoned to perfection, served with long string beans. Tasting dessert, a delightful peach cobbler adorned with a dollop of what appeared to be freshly whipped cream, he realized the caterer wasn't just a skilled chef but also a culinary artist who possessed a profound knowledge of flavors. Cameron savored his last bite of his dessert as the lights lowered.

"Ladies and gentlemen, welcome to the Museum of Art and to the 21st annual Los Angeles Night of Awards. We honor our city's firefighters tonight for their heroic acts and contributions to our wonderful city," the announcer began. "Each year, we honor the selected individuals for their heroism, bravery, and commitment to their role as a firefighter."

The announcer continued with a history of the event, accompanied by a presentation of past award winners.

Beaming at the audience, the announcer said, "Without further ado, let's begin."

A big screen descended from the ceiling. Then, it flashed with news footage of the building fire Cameron had helped put out. To his surprise, there was footage of him carrying the baby out of the building, handing it to waiting paramedics. That scene faded and then displayed a picture of Cameron in his uniform. So captivated by the collection of footage, Cameron nearly missed the announcer calling his name. He stood, waved to everyone around the room, and walked from his table to the stage. Nervously, he began his prepared speech.

"Thank you! Thank you! Please take your seats. Ladies and gentlemen, esteemed colleagues. I stand before you this evening with a heart full of gratitude and humility. It is truly an honor to receive this award, but first I must express my profound thanks to every one of you, my colleagues, for your unwavering support and encouragement. Without your wisdom and service, I would not be standing here today. Your commitment to our shared goals is nothing short of inspiring. I also want to acknowledge the hard work and dedication of my colleagues who contributed to our collective success. It is your passion, innovation, and tireless efforts that have brought us here today. I share this award and it serves as a reminder of our shared commitment and the great things we can achieve when we work together. I am incredibly proud to be a part of this team. I accept this award with humility and pride, not for myself, but on behalf of the entire team. It is your dedication that deserves recognition. Together, we can achieve great things. Thank you!"

Waving to the crowd, Cameron stepped off the stage and returned to his table, with everyone congratulating him. He was filled with a sense of relief by taking the lead, which allowed him to unwind and enjoy the rest of the evening.

Once all the awards had been given out, the announcer proclaimed that the rest of the evening would be devoted to celebration, dancing, and fun. Cameron got up from his seat and searched for options to find a drink. At the bar, he laid eyes on the most stunning woman. Her long, nude colored gown had a slit in the front, exposing her beautiful, toned leg. Elegantly styled hair was adorned with an abundance of natural curls. She was breathtakingly captivating even. Her skin glistened with a gentle radiance, exuding a sense of softness and luminosity. He stepped up to the bar and looked in her direction.

"A glass of white wine please," she requested from the bartender.

The bartender set a napkin in front of the woman, then Cameron, and asked, "For you, sir?"

"An Old Fashioned, please," Cameron ordered.

Cameron experienced a flutter in his stomach merely from gazing at this woman.

"Oh, hey, you're Cameron Davis! Congratulations on your award," the woman said with a beautiful grin.

"Thank you, and you are?" Cameron asked, gazing into her brown eyes.

"My name's Nicole. Nicole Graham." Extending her hand for a handshake and he held onto it for a moment longer than the customary duration, a subtle yet meaningful gesture. He couldn't believe his fate. Nicole Graham was standing in front of him in all of her beautiful glory. He had to play it cool.

"Cameron Davis, but that's not news to you," he said, finally letting go of her hand.

"I've read stories about your heroic act. You're amazing and thank you. I know your family is proud and the mother of the baby is forever grateful," Nicole gushed.

"Thank you! Wait? You said your name is Nicole Graham? I remember you." Now he could reveal his recognition of her.

"You remember me?" Nicole asked with a look of wonderment.

"Here are your drinks," the bartender said, placing each drink on their perspective napkins.

"Thank you," Nicole said, reaching into her bag to pay for her drink he assumed..

"No, let me buy your drink. Please," Cameron requested.

Nicole flashed a grin, then said, "I should treat you."

"It's my pleasure." Giving Nicole his million-dollar smile. "Would you like to walk out to the patio with our drinks and get acquainted?" Cameron had to be smooth. He couldn't blow his chance with Nicole.

Nicole appeared to hesitate for a millisecond, then said, "Yes, that would be nice."

The night was clear, with stars sparkling in the sky, as they placed their drinks on the tall table.

"I hope you won't be embarrassed, but I went on a call some months ago in the park. I was one of the EMTs who transported you to the hospital," Cameron recalled. He had to come clean. She was stunning, and he wanted a chance with her.

"Yes, I'm embarrassed, but thank you. I guess you can say you saved me," Nicole said, cheeks warming as she looked at Cameron as she took a sip of her wine.

"And we met again at the record parlor. Our bags got mixed up," Cameron reminded Nicole. Did she remember him from the record store?

"I remember. Are you enjoying your vinyl albums?" Nodding in agreement, he saw the recognition in her gaze.

Cameron wanted to learn more about this woman. "Are you here with someone, an award recipient or guest?"

"No, I'm here with the head chef, who catered this event."

Cameron felt deflated hearing Nicole was with the chef. So much for getting to know her. "Really? Please give him my regards. The food was delicious. Especially the peach cobbler."

"I will share your regards with Aubrey. She and I are best friends and sometimes colleagues," Nicole said, correcting Cameron.

"Oh, my apologies. Please tell madam chef her meal was a highlight of the evening. Did you have anything to do with tonight's meal?" Cameron asked, relieved to learn Nicole wasn't accompanied with a date.

"No, only to sample. We're collaborating on a project, and she asked me to rate the peach cobbler. A recipe can change based on the quantity you make. Aubrey wanted to ensure the flavors were delightful, regardless of whether she made a small pan in her restaurant kitchen or a thousand mini pans." Cameron thought her in-depth explanation about catering for a large group was appealing.

Cameron let out a little chuckle and praised, "Well, it was delicious. So, are you a chef as well?" He asked this, knowing what Nicole did for a living, not revealing he Googled her.

"I'm a food stylist and writer. I create recipes, write about food and style food for photography, and I'm writing a cookbook."

Cameron remembered the extensive research he had conducted on her. To maintain the illusion of surprise regarding the information she shared, he had to act as if he had no prior knowledge. "Really? I don't think I have ever met a food stylist. What does it mean when you say you create recipes?" It intrigued Cameron.

"I can taste something and identify the ingredients, and create a recipe. Or, I research ingredients to formulate a recipe."

"I'm impressed. What an interesting job you have, Nicole. Oh, and I assume you are doing better?" Cameron asked as he sipped his Old Fashioned.

"Yes, thank you for asking. I was under a little stress, not taking good care of myself, when I fainted. I'm much better," Nicole shared.

On the patio overlooking the city sprinkled in white radiant light, Cameron and Nicole discussed the event. He could not discern or understand the emotions swirling within him. Just gazing at her evoked an emotion he struggled to comprehend or put into words. Cameron experienced an overwhelming desire to learn everything there was to know about Nicole Graham. It was the first time he'd experienced these emotions. He dated many women, had a few serious relationships, but this emotion was new, distinct.

"Nicole, do you mind if we exchange information? I'd like to get to know you better. How about lunch or dinner?" Cameron waited with bated breath for her response.

"That sounds like a good plan," she said with a grin.

They both reached for their phones, pulling up the new contact screen. Cameron handed his device to Nicole, and he took hers, typing in their information. Without saying a word, each took possession of their phones. Tilting her head, Nicole bashfully grinned at Cameron as she watched him access something in his phone.

"Did you get my text?" Cameron asked.

Nicole's phone pinged. She nodded.

Cameron glanced at Nicole before speaking. "I'm glad to see you in improved health. I apologize again if I embarrassed you. I'm happy we had time tonight to meet formally. You look absolutely stunning in that dress by the way." He inhaled a breath, then complimented, "You are captivating, Nicole Graham."

With that, Cameron reached for Nicole's hand and tenderly kissed it. As his lips made contact with her skin, he detected a surge of electricity coursing from his lips to his heart, a sensation that left him elated.

"I look forward to hearing from you, Cameron Davis." Nicole said softly.

They locked eyes, their gaze filled with a deep and unspoken connection. Cameron observed a twinkle in her eyes, as if they were engaged in a joyful dance of their own.

Cameron then said, "Yes, we'll connect soon." Flashing his million-dollar smile.

Chapter 11

Nicole

Nicole sat in the passenger seat of Aubrey's car, waving her arms out the window, the beat of Janet Jackson's 1990 R&B single Love Will Never Do (Without You) resonating deep within her soul. She swayed back and forth, singing the chorus at the top of her lungs. Aubrey glanced at her best friend, joyful to see her smiling.

Nicole giggled to herself, took a deep breath and squealed, "Cameron and I have been texting."

Mouth agape, Aubrey asked in a high-pitched tone, "Really? So, spill the details."

"Well, he sent me the first text right after we added our contact information into our phones. He said I looked beautiful. The next text came the morning after we met. It was so sweet. He greeted me with a good morning sunshine," Nicole recalled, closing her eyes and grinning ear to ear.

Aubrey gave Nicole a quick glance before turning back to focus on the road. "How did you respond?"

"I responded with a good morning and said I was doing well, with a smiley face emoji. I asked how he was."

"Are you going to give me the play-by-play? Seriously, Nicole? You guys have been texting. And? Where has the texting led?" Nicole knew Aubrey wanted her to get to the point. She saw Aubrey leering at her while at a stoplight, waiting for her response.

"Well? You're glowing." Aubrey said loudly. "Have you guys talked on the phone or only by text?"

"We talked the other night. Called me at 7:30 on the dot. Just like we arranged." Nicole was giddy.

"We like punctuality. Does he have a good phone voice?" Aubrey asked.

"Girl, yes! We stayed on the phone for hours. I learned he likes old school hip hop and R&B, too. He's a music lover like me. I haven't felt like this in a long time, Aubrey." Nicole sighed.

Aubrey grinned as she drove, asking, "What else did you learn about Cameron?"

"Well," Nicole said, clapping her hands together. Turning to face Aubrey, she continued. "His mother and grandfather raised him. His dad died in a car accident when he was four. He became a firefighter to make his grandfather proud. I told him my story."

"Did you tell him your whole story?" Aubrey wondered out loud.

"No. Only family stuff." Nicole wasn't ready to share her entire story. It was too soon. She didn't want Cameron to feel sorry for her or think it was weird to potentially date a woman who lost her boyfriend. She swallowed the sad feeling creeping up her throat. She allowed herself to envision Cameron and his sensuous voice. Her cheeks warmed at the mere thought of him, his million-dollar smile that was imprinted in her brain.

"Are you giddy, Nicole Graham?" Aubrey asked, seeing the red blush on her cheeks.

"You know, Aubrey, I think I am," Nicole admitted.

Nicole saw that Aubrey exuded a festive spirit in honor of her. Aubrey glanced at Nicole once more and saw her scrolling through her phone, rereading her text messages from Cameron. "Based on the expression on your face, you'd better go on a date with him soon, or you may explode with anticipation."

A few seconds passed, then Aubrey asked, "So, did you guys set a date? You know, to go out?"

"Yes, we did. We're going out later this week," Nicole admitted, giving Aubrey a cheesy grin.

"Really? When? What are you going to wear? It's July. A summer love," Aubrey said, laughing.

Nicole was going to share her outfit choices, but stopped as Aubrey pulled in front of Carol's studio. Carol stood by the store window, examining a set of photographic negatives, when they walked in.

"Hey, Carol!" Nicole announced as she opened the door, walking in with Aubrey right behind her.

"Hi, Carol!" Aubrey greeted, looking around Carol's designed photography studio. "Wow, the place looks great!"

Aubrey scanned the space and admired the larger-than-life photographs Carol took when working on her many assignments.

"Yes," Carol said. "I'm pleased with how these photos turned out."

Introduced by Food Magazine, coupled to work on a project, Carol and Nicole became fast friends. Now colleagues, they shared business and enjoyed each other's company. Carol acted as if she were a big sister to Nicole, sharing life experiences and offering her advice. Nicole styled the food and wrote the articles, and Carol took the pictures. They were a powerful pair. They continued to be grouped to work on food related projects locally and across the country.

"So, ladies, what are we doing today?" Carol asked, returning the negatives to the box.

"I would like to hire you for one of my projects," Aubrey said.

Aubrey stepped forward and spoke. "I'm working with the owner of Garston's, the restaurant in Malibu. Are you familiar with the popular place by the water? Or what used to be popular."

"Yes, I'm familiar with that place. It's been around for years. It's not as popular as it used to be. Nathan used to take me there when we were dating and he was trying to win me over. Now fifteen years of marriage, I'm lucky if he takes me to Chipotle," Carol said with a hearty laugh. "What are you doing over there?"

Aubrey took in a breath, winked at Nicole, and gave Carol a smile before speaking. "I've been commissioned to revamp the menu, make the restaurant trendy, and revitalize it to be the place to eat in Malibu. Decorating is not my thing, but the designer asked if I knew someone who could photograph the food. They want large photos of signature menu items hanging around the restaurant. Nicole has agreed to design the plates. You photograph everything so well. When I was asked if I knew anyone, I couldn't think of anyone else doing the job."

"Wow, that's huge. I'd love to do it. Thank you for including me in this." Carol was grateful for the opportunity.

"Great, I'll arrange a meeting with the owner and the three of us will talk numbers and draw up a contract."

Carol speculated for a moment before speaking. She looked at Nicole and Aubrey, then said, "You both came here to ask me that? We could've discussed this on the phone or on Zoom."

"I wanted an excuse to see you. We haven't talked much since my date with Eric," Nicole said.

"Oh yeah, Eric." Carol looked at Nicole for a second before she spoke. "What happened that night? He mentioned everything was going well. The two of you were going to go dancing. You walked outside, police were everywhere, and you abruptly told him you had to go. I was meaning to call you and ask you about it."

Nicole paused in contemplation for a moment. After the restaurant incident, she wasted no time and headed straight to Edward's house. He possessed the ability to provide solace during her moments of profound grief. However, it had been a mistake to seek his comfort. His lingering hug and the burying of his face in her neck was Nicole's reminder of the full extent of his fondness for her. Edward's hands roamed her back in a way that was improper. Nicole was so caught up in her own emotions, she didn't realize what he was doing at the time. It was the kiss on her neck that had brought her out of her daze. His response to her rejection was that he was comforting her. At that moment, Nicole got in her car and left his house. Sober from the night's wine she drank and no longer mourning over the sight of Jim Stone and the other police officers in action, she drove home, her anger simmering.

Releasing her recollection of Edward's touch, Nicole said, "When we walked out of the restaurant, police officers surrounded us prepared to arrest a man who was dining inside. The security guard carried him out and the officers rushed him. I later read in the paper that the man was on the FBI's most wanted list. They had been trailing him for months."

"Oh dear, I can only imagine how that made you feel," Carol said with a sigh.

"It triggered me. I didn't want Eric to think I was insane. I just left. We talked via text a few times. I've been busy and I know he's away for a while."

Nicole recalled the night she met Cameron. Something within her awakened. Something that was dormant, stagnant. The conversations she and Cameron shared ignited a sense of enthusiasm she hadn't experienced since Tyler was alive.

"Did Nicole tell you she has a date this week?" Aubrey revealed.

"No, she did not. Who is he, Nicole? I want to hear all about him," Carol said.

Right when Nicole took a seat on the couch in the waiting area, her phone buzzed with an incoming text from Cameron.

Cameron - Hey beautiful! I hope you're having an amazing day. You crossed my mind when I was listening to Michael Jackson's Rock with You.

Nicole - Hey yourself! And I LOVE that song!

Cameron - Yep! I'm at the station tonight, but I'd really like to talk to you later if that's ok?

Nicole - Sure, what time? You can talk at the station?

Cameron - If everything is done, we're just killing time, waiting for the next call. Maybe 8?

Nicole - 8 sounds good.

Cameron - Want to FaceTime?

Nicole - Ok

Nicole was beaming. Cameron not only checked in, he called her beautiful and arranged another phone call. A FaceTime call. Tonight.

"That must be Cameron texting you," Aubrey said, with a sly grin on her face.

"Yes, we're gonna talk on FaceTime tonight." Nicole grinned.

"Scheduled a phone conversation? Who does that? I like him already," Carol said.

Nicole and Aubrey left Carol's studio to grab an early dinner and work on the restaurant renovation. Laptops open, notebooks spread over the table, they were munching on french fries when Nicole's phone vibrated, almost bouncing off the table, with an incoming message. She swiped her phone to open the text from Cameron.

Cameron - Hey again!

Nicole - Hey! What's up?

Cameron - I've been thinking about our first date.

Nicole - Yeah? What about it?

Cameron - I know what you do. I'm guessing you like all types of food. What is your absolute favorite?

Nicole - Well…I like many things. My go-to, always Mexican food, if I can't decide on something.

Cameron - Mexican it is. I'll talk and see you tonight.

Nicole - Looking forward to it.

Nicole stared at the phone screen astonished. Cameron cared enough to ask her about favorite foods. He was very thoughtful.

"So, was that Cameron, again?" Aubrey asked with a whine.

"Yeah, he's planning our first date. He wanted to know my favorite foods."

"Mexican food!" Aubrey and Nicole said in unison, laughing out loud.

Nicole and Aubrey finished drafting plans for three menu options for the restaurant. They sent emails to set up meetings with Carol and the restaurant owner, and the decorator.

"Are there recipes we need to rewrite?" Nicole asked.

"No, I don't think so. I'm going to type these menus up and send them to the printer, so I'm ready for next week."

"Tell me if you need any help," Nicole offered.

"Nicole, I'm really happy for you. That you've met someone you have an interest in," Aubrey shared.

"I am, too. One of the best things I can do is move on. It's time." Nicole added one last thing to her to do list. She checked the time. "Oh, it's 7:15, can you take me home so I can get comfy for my call at 8?" Nicole wanted to at least freshen up and make herself look nice since she and Cameron were going to FaceTime.

Picking up their belongings, Nicole and Aubrey settled the bill and made their way to the car.

"It's cool you two are doing a video call, considering you have your first date coming up." Aubrey thought out loud.

"I suppose so. It'll remind me how handsome he is. Unless I imagined his attractiveness." Cameron's face was already committed to memory. She remembered how he looked. "How do I look this very minute?" Nicole asked, wondering if she even had time to freshen up.

"You look wonderful. When you get home, freshen up your face, smooth your hair down a bit and put on a V-neck tee. Oh, and some lip gloss," Aubrey recommended.

While driving, Nicole couldn't help but recall her last video call with a man. When Tyler was on duty, he always FaceTimed with her before she went to sleep. She held back the urge to cry. She reminded herself to ask the therapist how to manage and avoid being inundated by an unexpected moment of sadness. Aubrey pulled up in front of Nicole's house.

"Here you are, my dear," Aubrey said, putting her car in park, engine still running.

"Thank you for a productive day and good company. Call me tomorrow, okay?" Nicole said, gathering her things to get out of Aubrey's car.

Aubrey gleamed and said, "I will. And don't forget any details about your call tonight. I can't wait to hear about it."

Nicole stepped into her house, shut the front door, and leaned against it. Her watch said 7:48. She gathered her hair into a chic yet tousled bun, gently gave her cheeks a pinch and applied a dash of lip gloss. At exactly 8:00, Nicole's phone buzzed with an incoming FaceTime request. She inhaled a deep breath, brushed the free strands of hair behind her right ear and slid her finger over the accept call button. Cameron's face appeared on the screen.

Before Nicole said hello, she noticed Cameron catching his breath, before saying, "Hello, beautiful." Then flashed his million-dollar smile.

Chapter 12

Cameron

Cameron finished his shift at the fire station with a sense of euphoria. The station only received minor calls while he was on duty. A student at the nearby high school triggered the fire alarm. Thankfully, there were no flames, and no one was harmed. The office building a few blocks away had a person stuck in one of their elevators. Ms. Jenkins believed she detected the smell of smoke again. The guys proceeded with their obligatory task, but it proved fruitless. Cameron found it impossible to stop thinking about Nicole after their FaceTime conversation. She remained in his thoughts. Their conversation flowed the entire call, without interruption, as Cameron remained secluded in the compact vacant office at the fire station. He and Nicole shared a love for good food, career growth, and music. Both liking old school hip hop and R&B were rare. They shared a mutual admiration for a few artists, one being Chaka Khan. When he asked her favorite song by Chaka Khan, in unison, they said, Sweet Thing. Cameron made a note to remember that fact.

Indulging in lunch with his mom once a week was one of Cameron's preferred pastimes. With Patricia working extra hours and him working long shifts, it had been a while. Patricia and Ms. Thompson both waved in Cameron's direction as he parked and exited his SUV.

"Hello, lovely ladies! How are you this afternoon?" Cameron said, sounding very cheerful.

"Hi, Cameron. It's so good to see you. How've you been? How's your celebrity status?" Ms. Thompson asked.

"Ms. Thompson, I've been well. And I was just doing my job. I came to take my favorite girl to lunch," he replied.

"I'll be ready in a minute, son. You can wait for me in the house if you like?" Patricia suggested.

Cameron waved to his mom's neighbor. "Sure thing Ma. Take care, Ms. Thompson."

"You do the same, Cameron. Be safe out there," Ms. Thompson said, watching him go into the house.

Inside, Cameron plopped on the couch and turned the big screen television mounted on the wall to ESPN. The camera scanned the Lakers and Miami Heat summer league game. The score displayed a narrow point difference. The new Laker rookie stole the ball, dribbled down the court and passed it to another rookie for an easy layup.

"Wow, tied with thirty-four seconds left." This game was better than expected. Amid focusing on a Miami Heat rookie at the free throw line, Cameron's phone buzzed announcing an incoming text message.

Nicole - Hey! I enjoyed talking to you last night.

Cameron - Hey you! Talking to you was the high-light of my night. WYD

Nicole - Listening to music, working. You?

Cameron - Visiting my mom. I'm taking her to lunch and then I'll go home to clean up a bit. You wanna talk later?

Nicole - Yes. Text me when you are home.

Cameron - Most definitely.

Whether it be on text, over the phone, or on FaceTime, a magnetic connection seemed to hum between him and Nicole. Every topic they touched upon ignited a spark of enthusiasm within Cameron. He experienced a surge of energy and excitement he had never encountered with anyone else. Nicole possessed a refreshing and charismatic aura. He wanted to delve into her experiences, her dreams, and learn every layer of her being. Their first date was soon. Cameron's firm determination fueled his efforts to ensure their first date was natural and free of clumsy or bumbling moments. Cameron wouldn't see Nicole for a few days, but his anticipation and anxiety intertwined, leaving his stomach in knots.. He wished time would pass quickly.

"Son, why are you grinning at your phone?" Patricia quizzed, standing in her entryway, smiling at her son.

Cameron chuckled under his breath. "Ugh, no reason." Painting a mental image of Nicole's beautiful smile.

"You sure about that? I haven't seen that kind of smile in a while. Maybe since you and Shannon started dating."

"You may be right." The thought of Shannon, their relationship and how it ended, was not the same feeling he had in this moment.

"Are you ever going to share why the two of you broke up? You seemed happy," Patricia probed.

"I was, Mom, until I wasn't. We were happy for a while, then things changed. She changed." Cameron didn't enjoy talking about his relationship with Shannon. One day, he trusted Shannon and the next day he didn't. Couldn't.

"Oh? How did Shannon change?" Patricia pushed.

"Can we go get some food? I'm starving. I'll tell you the entire story in the car," Cameron pledged. He couldn't understand why his mom had to know everything. She couldn't fix anything. Not now. And he didn't want to fix his and Shannon's relationship. It had been almost a year since they broke up. Cameron was ready to give dating Nicole a go. He wanted to see where things went with her.

As Cameron and his mom drove to their favorite Thai restaurant, he thought of how best to share his feelings about his breakup. She didn't have to learn every detail. He thought for a moment and decided he would give her the abridged version. "Well, Mom? Shannon and I were happy at first. We were happy for about a year and a half. Then, I suspected she wasn't happy. Her time became unavailable. She dove into her work. I put in extra hours at work. And I didn't mind. The time we spent together wasn't the same. Our conversations felt burdensome. We would sit in silence for a good while before either of us spoke. We used to have friendly conversations. We could discuss anything. We stopped trying. We didn't put in the extra effort to spend quality time together and engage in activities we used to enjoy as a couple. So I ended the relationship. I realized that if I were to notice these signs at this moment, things could only worsen." He didn't want to tell his mother Shannon had cheated.

Patricia sat in silence for a few seconds before speaking, appearing to take in what Cameron shared. "In a relationship, effort and commitment are essential to its success. Change is inevitable, but as a couple, it's important to adapt and grow together. Maintaining open communication is crucial to ensure that you stay connected and don't drift apart." Cameron knew his mother only wanted happiness for him. He knew she didn't want him to stop trying. She clearly understood him, and open communication did not come naturally.

They walked into the restaurant in silence. Cameron had a deep familiarity with everything his mother shared. What he wouldn't communicate was that Shannon stopped trying. When they did arrange time together, she stayed glued to her phone, texting. That's when he saw the shirtless man on her screen. Dinner with girlfriends became more regular. Her weeknights remained busy. She didn't sleep over. When she did, she was cold and closed off. He recognized the signs of her unfaithfulness. He and his boys had countless discussions about cheating, the signs, and how a man feels when he's not the one. Cameron looked back on the night he phoned Shannon while driving to her house, planning a movie night with wine. She declined the invitation. That's when he understood it was time to call it quits. He didn't want to find out what he already suspected. The next morning, he called her to say he was done. Their relationship was over. She didn't fight the decision. Agreeing to his concerns, she concluded it was best not to be a couple. The truth always comes out. A few months after their breakup, Cameron ran into one of Shannon's friends in a coffee shop. They exchanged pleasantries. He asked how Shannon was doing. One friend said she was good, dating a guy she'd known for years, and they were happy. She shared they would likely get married. The confirmation of her "new" relationship before their breakup was all Cameron needed to confirm Shannon cheated. Now understanding the situation, it liberated him to start anew with someone else. That new person may be Nicole, and he was pining to find out.

"I'll show you to your table. Follow me, please," the hostess directed.

Cameron and Patricia walked in silence, sat down, and opened their menus.

"Mom, do you know what you want to order?" Cameron asked, eyeing the appetizers.

"Our usual please." Patricia closed her menu.

"Can I take your order?" the server asked.

"We'll have the lunch special for two please, and two Thai iced teas," he ordered.

The server collected their menus. "Thank you, sir. I'll bring your drinks shortly."

"Cameron, I'm going to the ladies' room. Be right back." Patricia stood and left the table.

"Sure," Cameron said, pulling out his phone to check his emails. Their food arrived shortly after his mother sat back down at the table.

Before Patricia could add more to the subject of Shannon and his breakup, Cameron blurted, "I met someone interesting recently," as his mother scooped a serving of chicken fried rice onto his plate.

Placing a piece of fish onto her plate Patricia asked, "Really? How'd you two meet?"

"Well, I actually went on a call and she was our patient. She fainted. I drove her to the hospital," Cameron recalled.

"You hit on a patient? Cameron, you know better than that." Patricia frowned.

"Mom, it wasn't like that. I didn't realize she was my patient until I saw her at the awards event. She recognized me from all the media stories and publicity I've been getting. We met a second time at the record parlor. The sales woman gave me her bag and Nicole got mine. We had to return to the store to collect our original purchases. She said I looked familiar but couldn't place who I was. It wasn't until I got home and Googled her, I realized she was the woman from the call. I thought I missed my opportunity, but we formally met at the City of Los Angeles event. We talked and exchanged information. We've been talking ever since that night. We're going on our first date tomorrow night."

"Well, I imagine she impressed you, considering you exchanged information. And you said her name is Nicole? What does Nicole do for a living?" Patricia's face brightened with curiosity.

"She's a food stylist. She writes food articles and recipes. She's also writing a book of her grandmother's recipes." Cameron was proud of Nicole and her work.

"That's impressive. I'd love to have a copy when it's published." Patricia said, taking a bite of her pad thai.

"Yeah, it's impressive." Cameron said contently. Among the women he encountered, none pursued a profession in a creative field. Her work was fascinating.

Patricia studied her son for a few seconds. He then revealed his genuine emotion at that very moment. "There's that smile again. The smile you flashed at the house. Were you two texting?"

"Yes, we were," Cameron said, stammering through his words, his cheeks warming with a telltale flush.

Patricia laughed under her breath and said, "If that's how you look and you haven't even gone on a date yet, I can't wait to see how you are after the date."

Cameron wondered about that, too. How would he look and feel after his first date with Nicole? He wasn't shy about dating. He was very straightforward. When interested in someone, he would strike up a conversation and ask her out based on their interaction. Nicole was special. Unable to put his finger on it, he sensed she was unlike anyone he ever dated. At the event, as their gazes locked, time seemed to stand still. It was as if an invisible thread bound their souls together, a silent understanding that transcended words. Wanting to explore their obvious connection, Cameron made reservations at the perfect restaurant.

Chapter 13

Nicole

Nicole and Carol had been working for a few hours on Los Angeles food magazine's yearly spread. Thousands of applicants competed for this prestigious contract. For the third year in a row, they beat out the more qualified writers and photographers. She enjoyed writing, especially about food. Her words floated off the page and into the imagination of her readers, flavoring their taste buds with wanting to taste the food she wrote about. Nicole and Carol's combined years of experience were the reason people put their trust in their collective work.

"Would you like to take a break, dear?" Carol asked, taking a swig from her bottled water.

"A break would be good, I guess," Nicole said with a sigh.

Nicole went to the back of the studio and sat at the farm table, snacking on her open bag of kettle popcorn. The wall in the room's corner grabbed her attention. The spider's legs crawled up the wall, reminding Nicole of that night when she huddled in the same crook of the room. That night she worked so hard to forget. She and Carol had a late night working. The constant ringing of her phone alerted her to stop what she was doing and answer the call. She remembered the words spoken to her like it all happened yesterday.

"Tyler's gone! Nicole, Tyler is gone, honey," his dad cried.

"What?" Nicole questioned. She was certain she didn't hear him right.

"He was on a call." Mr. James inhaled a deep breath, then continued, "A suspect shot him. He didn't make it to the hospital alive."

"Where is he?" Nicole asked.

"He's gone, baby, he's gone," Mr. James whispered, voice trembling.

Nicole heard Mr. James silently sobbing into the phone. Her device had slipped from her grasp and clattered onto the floor, as she let out piercing screams. In the room's corner, Carol found Nicole wailing. Silence replaced words as an overwhelming sense of grief overcame Nicole in an instant. Now beginning to tremble, tears flowed down her cheeks. She opened her mouth to speak, but no sound or words escaped. Carol, still confused, offered her utmost support, embracing Nicole to steady her trembling.

"Nicole? Do you want to call it a day or continue working?" Carol asked, pulling Nicole out of her flashback.

"Do you remember when I sat in that corner and just knew I was going to die?" Nicole asked, watching the spider now scamper along the baseboards.

Carol hadn't a clue what Nicole was saying. "What are you talking about, hun?"

"I was here when I learned Tyler had died."

"Oh yes, I remember. I remember that day. It was a long time ago, don't you think?" Carol understood it would be advantageous to shift the conversation.

Nicole carried that memory with her for months, only for it to resurface today. She found it amusing how the mind operated, conjuring up memories when she least expected it.

"I know that was likely one of the hardest things you ever had to do. Handling the disappointment of losing a man you envisioned a future with. You've grown and worked to get over him. You may be thinking you will never get over him, but you will," Carol said, rubbing Nicole's shoulder.

"You're right. My therapist said to cherish the flashbacks and work to move forward. However, this wasn't a good flashback." Nicole frowned.

"I'm so proud of you."

"Yeah, I'm putting in a significant amount of effort to shift my mindset. Sometimes I think I've cried my last tear. Sometimes the emotion still feels so raw. I'm optimistic these days." Nicole grinned at the possibility that Cameron may be the root of her sunniness.

"I'm happy for you. You've gone on dates. Your projects are going well," Carol reminded Nicole.

"Did I tell you I have a date tonight?" Nicole said proudly.

"With the firefighter? Tonight?" Carol asked in surprise.

"Yes!" Nicole said matter-of-factly.

Nicole recalled Cameron's last text. She pulled out her phone and opened the link to the restaurant they would go to that night. It was perfect. At least the images depicted the restaurant as flawless. Or was it the anticipation of seeing Cameron that was supreme?

"Look at you smiling, dear. I love it," Carol said, recognizing Nicole's excitement.

"I guess I'm pretty excited. What time is it?" Nicole asked. Judging by the fading sun now creating a shadow in front of the studio, she knew it was getting late.

Looking at her watch, Carol said, "3:45."

"Oh, Carol, I need to go. I'm meeting Cameron at 6:30, and I've got to get ready." Nicole began gathering her things, putting them into her tote bag.

"Have you decided on your outfit?" Carol wondered.

"Not a clue. Can we continue our work on Monday?" Nicole asked, knowing they needed to prepare for the photoshoot for the Malibu restaurant.

"Go have fun, dear. I'll clean up. And yes, Monday. Go," Carol said, waving her hands to get Nicole out the door.

Nicole gathered her keys and bag and headed to her car. While driving, she envisioned standing in front of her closet, flipping through the hangers and hangers of clothes, trying to identify the perfect outfit. Cameron said to dress L.A. trendy. In her mind, that signified a multitude of options.

Nicole's phone was buzzing with multiple text messages by the time she reached her driveway.

Aubrey - Hey girl! You ready for tonight? Call me if you need me.

Nicole loved Aubrey so much. She was always available to her.

Nicole - Hey girl! I'm just getting home to get ready. I'll text you a pic before I walk out the door.

Levi - Hey, sis! You good?

Nicole hadn't communicated with Levi in a few days.

Nicole - Yes! Very good!

Cameron texted Nicole the night before. She didn't expect another text before meeting him at the restaurant. But he did send one today. Opening the new text from him revealed a photo of a bouquet of flowers.

She wasn't sure why he sent her that picture. She replied.

> **Nicole** - Aww! The flowers are gorgeous. See you soon.

Nicole went into her closet and pulled out her favorite dark-colored pair of fitted jeans, a canary yellow sheer blouse with a matching tank top to wear underneath, and her gold strappy sandals. She laid out her big gold watch, gold necklace with her initial, and large gold hoop earrings. She dug through her closet for her gold purse and placed it next to her blouse to see the contrast between the blouse and accessories.

"Wow, this outfit is fire!" she said, admiring her efforts.

Out of the shower, a towel wrapped around her, Nicole pulled up Stevie Wonder's You are the Sunshine of My Life and tapped on her phone to start the song. It was a happy, uplifting, and cheery song. The lyrics resonated with her. Was love in the air? Did she want Cameron to be her sunshine? As Nicole added product to her damp hair, her phone buzzed with an incoming text.

> **Cameron** - Hey! Check your front porch...

"Check my front porch?" Nicole said in wonder.

Nicole put on her robe and looked out her front window.

"Are those the same flowers from the picture?" she asked in disbelief.

Greeted by an elegant display of fragrant English white roses mixed with white tulips, and green and purple orchids took her breath away. No one was in her front yard or in front of her house. Who delivered the flowers? She must have missed the notification that someone was near her door while she was in the shower. Nicole picked up the bouquet and brought it into the house.

"These are so gorgeous!" Nicole said, placing the bouquet on her dining room table. The card read,

Nicole! May tonight be as beautiful as you are. I'm looking forward to a delicious dinner and your company. Cameron xoxo

Nicole had never received such an exquisite bouquet. It wasn't her birthday. How did Cameron know where she lived? Was it scary he had found her address? After all, he was a firefighter, and it wasn't hard to find her.

Nicole completed her look by putting a shimmery gold gloss on her lips. She took out her phone, snapped a selfie for Aubrey, and sent it. With one last once over in the mirror, she was out the door, pleased that her unruly curly hair cooperated tonight.

Nicole eased her car to a stop in front of the restaurant, handing her keys to the waiting valet with a friendly nod. Before going inside, she checked her phone for any missed text messages.

Aubrey - Girl! You look hot! OMG! I hope you have an amazing evening and call me when you get home. I don't care what time it is.

Nicole - Thank you! I will. Smooches!

As Nicole entered the upscale Mexican restaurant, her eyes darted around the dimly lit room, searching for Cameron. She could see the refined charm and cultural richness of the eatery's décor. The interior was a tasteful blend of modern elegance and traditional elements. Deep terracotta walls adorned the entryway with intricate hand-painted murals telling stories of Mexican heritage.

"Can I help you, ma'am?" the hostess asked Nicole.

"Yes, I'm meeting someone. Cameron Davis?"

"Yes, ma'am. He asked me to show you to your table when you arrived. Follow me."

Nicole followed the young women. She was led into a different section of the restaurant. Warm ambient lighting bathed the dining area in a soft, golden glow. Tables were dressed in crisp, white linens, each adorned with a vibrant handwoven runner, polished silverware, and fine glassware. The hostess turned to Nicole, giving her a discreet smile, leading her to a cozy corner, away from the bustling main dining area. Nicole rounded the corner and spotted him. Cameron sat in a booth at the back left corner of the restaurant. Dressed in dark-colored jeans, a fitted, smoked gray button-up collared shirt, and stylish leather shoes. He stood when he recognized Nicole walking toward him.

"Mr. Davis, your guest," the hostess said and placed two menus on the table. "Enjoy."

Cameron stood to greet her. "Nicole Graham! It's a genuine pleasure to see you again, in person," Cameron said, reaching for her hand. He gave it a light squeeze, lingering there for a few seconds. Nicole felt a bolt of electricity move from her hand through her body and land in the center of her heart.

"It's nice to see you in person again, Cameron Davis." Nicole gave him an ear to ear grin. She detected his clean and boldly fragrant aroma. Their eyes locked, smiles mirroring the unspoken connection between them as they stood in silence, a moment of mutual appreciation. Cameron slowly let go of Nicole's hand, motioning her to take a seat.

"Cameron, I haven't been to this restaurant. You did well. I thought I had been to all the posh Mexican restaurants in town. I'm excited," Nicole said, wiggling in her seat to get comfortable.

"A colleague told me about this place. I've wanted to come. You gave me a reason to make a reservation." Cameron gave her a slight grin with a sparkle in his eyes.

"I wonder what's good here," Nicole said, picking up the menu and mulling over it.

"I hear the fried pescado is good. Also, the Mole Poblano is recommended. My colleague suggested getting the churros with the chocolate dipping sauce for dessert," Cameron shared.

"All of it sounds so delicious. Fried pescado is one of my favorites. It can be a little messy, though. I don't want greasy fingers to touch my blouse," Nicole shared shyly.

Cameron gave Nicole a sexy glance, then continued to preview the menu.

"I'm deciding on the chicken mole," Nicole decided.

"That sounds good. I'll get the chicken tamale and beef enchilada. Do you want a drink?" Cameron asked.

"Sure! It seems margaritas are in order, no?" Nicole suggested, wanting to calm her nervousness. A drink would be good for that.

Cameron peered over the menu and said, "Absolutely. Do you like guacamole?"

"Oh, yes," Nicole replied. Just as she and Cameron broke out in a soft laughter, their server came up to their table.

"Can I take your order? Interested in a drink from the bar? Water?"

Cameron smiled at Nicole, then said, "Water for the both of us, and this beautiful lady and I will have a blended margarita. And to start, we would like chips and guacamole."

"Do you know what you'd like to order?" the server asked.

"Yes, but we would like a few minutes before we place that order," Cameron stated.

"Thank you, I'll be back shortly with your drinks," the server said before walking away.

"I hope you don't mind me ordering for us," Cameron said, sitting back in the booth.

"No, not at all." Nicole admired that in a man. Someone who took charge. Discovering your preferences subtly, then making a deliberate effort to order what you like. She adjusted herself in her seat, accidentally brushing her knee against Cameron's.

"I'm so sorry, I..." Nicole felt so embarrassed.

"No need, Nicole. It's fine," Cameron assured her.

There was that smile again. He was going to win Nicole's heart with just his sparkling grin. Nicole recalled the last friendly date she had with Eric. She felt good about him, that is, until seeing the police outside the restaurant. Cameron was different. She struggled to put into words how distinct he was. She experienced these sensations when his gaze met hers or his touch grazed her skin. Thinking back to the day she fainted, just his gaze alone stirred a flutter of nervousness deep within her core. She ignored her feelings then, focusing on her own well-being. The last gaze they shared before leaving the store tugged at her heart. At the City of Los Angeles event, when their hands met, she felt a streak of electricity coursing from her fingertips straight to her heart. It happened again tonight.

"Did you work today?" Cameron inquired.

"I did. I was with my business colleague, Carol. She's the photographer I was telling you about. We were prepping for the photoshoot coming up at the restaurant in Malibu."

"Ahh yes, I remember you telling me about that project." Nicole had shared so much about her work. She appreciated what Cameron remembered.

"I lost track of time. I have to be honest, and rushed home to get ready to meet you. And the most unexpected thing happened. Someone left the most beautiful bouquet on my doorstep," Nicole said, giving Cameron a look from the top of her eyelids and a huge grin.

"I wonder who that was," Cameron said with a devilish grin.

"Thank you, Cameron, for the flowers. They're the most beautiful bouquet I've ever received." Nicole meant the gratitude she felt receiving flowers from Cameron. She received flowers from her family, even past boyfriends, but this bouquet was special. It seemed like someone had custom-made it specifically for her.

"It was my pleasure. We've been talking for the last few weeks. I've enjoyed our conversations. I thought it was a good way to begin our date." Nicole's heart melted right onto the table.

"Here you are," the server said as she set water glasses and margaritas on the table. The gentleman will arrive soon to prepare your guacamole. I'll come back in a bit to take your food order."

"Thank you!" Nicole and Cameron said in unison.

Both lifting their margarita glasses, Cameron toasted. "To tonight, and what I hope to be a future of strong friendship and more."

"Cheers!" they said in unison, Nicole gazing at Cameron beneath the hooded lids of her eyes.

Nicole let Cameron's words sink in. Friendship and more. What does that mean? She knew they were becoming friends. She appreciated he assumed nothing more. But she could feel Cameron wanted more. They shared a deep connection, considering the possibility of moving beyond friendship.

For the rest of dinner, Nicole and Cameron talked about careers, family, likes, dislikes, hobbies, and his recent celebrity status. They shared laughter and locked eyes during those fleeting moments of silence. When the dessert was eaten and the plates were cleared, Cameron extended his hand to reach for hers. Nicole felt the warmth of his hand, which sent a comforting sensation barreling through her body. They sat just like that for several seconds in silence.

"Here's the bill," the server said. "Take your time."

Nicole could see Cameron choosing his words carefully before he spoke. He squeezed her hand ever so slightly, then said, "This has been the best dinner with you, Nicole."

Nicole flashed a smile. "I agree. I can't remember when I had a better meal, or company."

"When can I see you again?" Cameron asked, his gaze burning into her soul.

"Soon. I'd really like that." Nicole felt her face warming, turning slightly red. They sat without moving, both hands now intertwined on top of the table.

"Shall we go?" Cameron asked hesitantly.

"If we must," Nicole said with a slight chuckle.

Cameron then took care of the bill. They stood, Nicole slowly walking away from the table, Cameron's hand rested on her lower back leading her to the front of the restaurant, then out to the valet. Nicole wished the night would never end. She wanted to continue the evening. But she used her better judgment and kept quiet. Cameron's large black on black SUV arrived first.

"I'm waiting for the lady's car to arrive before I get in," Cameron told the valet. Nicole's car stopped right behind his.

"Here's my car," Nicole said, looking up at Cameron.

Cameron grabbed Nicole's hands and brought them to his lips, landing a soft kiss on them. Nicole smiled, taking in the moment.

"Text me when you get home, Nicole, okay?" Cameron asked.

"I will." Nicole walked closer to Cameron and planted a gentle kiss on his cheek. "Thank you again for this lovely evening."

Nicole lingered for a few seconds before pulling her hands from Cameron, walking to her car. Sensing his gaze lingering on her, she felt the weight of his eyes as she slid into her car. Cameron blew a kiss to her as she drove off.

Chapter 14

Cameron

Cameron walked into the Japanese restaurant and found Myles at the sushi bar.

"What's up, man? How you been? Mr. Engaged." Cameron spoke as he approached Myles. The two slapped hands and Myles pulled Cameron into a hug.

"I'm good, man. You?" Myles said, smiling, happy to see his friend.

"Can't complain. Busy with work, you know? Same ole."

As they both sat down and examined the menu, Cameron was unable to overlook Myles' radiant happiness. He had a sparkle in his eyes. The server came over, took their orders, and quickly returned with their drinks.

"So, man, what's up?" Myles said, chewing on edamame.

Cameron looked down to gather his thoughts. Flashes of last night with Nicole brought a smile to his face. He couldn't recall ever experiencing a night quite like the one he spent with her. Not even his ex-girlfriend. Reminiscing their innocent touches and hand holding left him with a sense of elation. He thought back to her electrifying smile and infectious laughter. Nicole possessed a simple, yet undeniable, beauty. It defied any other description.

"Cameron? Why the sly grin? What you been up to, man?" Myles asked.

"Well, if you must know, I went out on a date last night?" Cameron admitted.

"A date? When was the last time you went on a date? Have you been on a date since you broke up with Shannon?" Myles asked, taking a sip of saki.

"No, I haven't. I didn't think I wanted to date anyone right now. Nicole entered my scene and I couldn't refuse the urge." Something about Nicole had made him set aside his diversion to dating; she was different.

The server arrived with their order, then asked, "Can I get you anything else for now?"

Myles responded, "No, we're good. Thank you."

"Nicole is her name? Okay. What do you know about her?" Myles wanted to know who this woman was who had his friend back on the scene.

Cameron looked at Myles, then down at his hands. "She's beautiful. She's a food stylist and writer."

"Okay? By the look on your face, you are already smitten. Did you sleep with her last night?" Myles asked directly.

"Man, no! I need to take my time with Nicole. Really romance her. And I want to. She seems to be the type that needs romancing. She's just so gorgeous. I want to treat her really well. I want to date her." This marked the first time Cameron experienced these emotions.

"Cam, I've never seen you glow like this over a woman in all the years we've known each other." Myles was shocked.

"Yeah, I think she's pretty special." In a daze-like state, Cameron smiled as he pushed his chopsticks around his sushi roll. Last night, Nicole had called him when she got home and their conversation stretched on for a full two hours. He couldn't understand how two people found so much to talk about. Cameron had never experienced such a profound connection with anyone he dated in the past.

Myles and Cameron chatted about work and Ryan's shenanigans while enjoying their meal. Just as Cameron paid the bill, his phone buzzed with an incoming text message.

Nicole - Hey! WYD

Cameron - Hey! Just finished lunch with a friend. What's up?

Cameron watched the three dots bounce under his sent text.

Nicole - Want to meet me for coffee?

Cameron couldn't believe his luck. He hadn't stopped thinking about Nicole since last night.

Cameron - Sure, where are you?

Cameron looked up from his phone to see Myles giving him an amused stare.

"It's Nicole, huh?" Myles asked with a chuckle.

"Yeah. I'm going to meet her for coffee."

"Right now? Wow. Okay. You go do that," Myles said, snickering at Cameron. "I'm happy to see you already happy, man."

"Thanks, man," Cameron said. "I appreciate that."

Cameron and Myles said their goodbyes, and he headed to his car to drive over to the coffee shop. It was a good sign, to get a text from Nicole inviting him to meet up. He couldn't stop wondering if he should stop and pick up a gift. Based on his Apple watch display, he only had enough time to drive there. Did this coffee invitation count as a date? Cameron entered the shop to find Nicole sitting by the window—laptop, papers, and books sprawled all around her. There she sat, hair in a messy high bun, dressed in a fitted white t-shirt, light gray jeans, and white sneakers. Today, she was a casual, effortless beauty. Gazing at Nicole while he walked toward her, he caught his breath, realizing he forgot to breathe in her presence. Cameron liked her style. When he saw her at the record store, she was stylishly casual. Of course, she was dressed up at the event, and he was certain she didn't walk around in the blouse she wore to dinner.

"Hey!" Cameron said as he approached Nicole.

"Hey, you!" Nicole stood to give Cameron a quick hug.

Their brief embrace was gentle and filled with warmth. Nicole's clean floral scent lingered in the air as he took a seat across from her.

"What are you working on?" Cameron asked.

"The same project I was telling you about. I needed some coffee. This is my second cup." Nicole said, her laughter filling the air.

"Wow, you like coffee, huh?" Cameron asked, noticing her almost empty mug.

"Yes, I do, and if you are wondering, it won't keep me from sleeping tonight," she added with a giggle.

Cameron flashed Nicole a mischievous grin and said, "Good to know." Resting his face on his hands, elbows on the table, he gazed into Nicole's eyes.

"What?" Nicole said, cheeks turning a soft pink.

"I was just thinking about how beautiful your eyes are," he admiringly commented.

"Really? No one has ever complimented me on my eyes," Nicole responded, lowering them for a brief second, then looked up at Cameron.

"I'm honored I'm the first, then. What kind of coffee would you like?" Cameron asked, standing to walk to the counter.

Nicole gave Cameron a brief smile. "Actually, I'm good, really."

"Oh, well, I'll get a cup and be right back. Do you want anything else?" Cameron stood, gazing at Nicole waiting for her response.

A quick flash of a smile crossed Nicole's lips, then she responded, "No, I'm good." Cameron walked to the counter to order a cup of coffee and a pastry. He could feel Nicole checking him out. This was not a bad day to be wearing his good fitting jeans and a tight graphic t-shirt. Returning to the table, he noticed Nicole had tidied away her papers and books. "Are you done working?"

"Yes, you're here now. I don't want to be rude. I invited you," Nicole said, giving Cameron a closed mouth grin.

"Yes, you did." And Cameron was so grateful. He couldn't wait to see her again.

Nicole tilted her head, smiling, then said, "Can I make a confession?"

"Sure," Cameron responded curiously.

"I wanted to thank you again for an amazing night last night. And I wanted to see you," Nicole boldly added.

"Really? Well, I'm glad you called. I wanted to see you, too." This woman couldn't be any more adorable. Cameron pushed down his excitement. He had to be cool.

They sat in quietude, eyes locked in a mutual, unspoken exchange. The server interrupted their moment by setting Cameron's coffee and pastry onto the table.

"Thank you," Cameron said to the server. They sat in silence as Cameron added sugar and cream to his coffee. He took a sip, then he spoke. "Nicole Graham?"

"Yes, Cameron Davis?" she said in a slow drawl.

"What do I need to do to take you on a second date?" Cameron asked without taking his eyes off of her.

"Just ask," Nicole responded, flashing a flirtatious smile.

Cameron and Nicole shared a laugh. He couldn't stop smiling at her. Everything about her was cute. For the next hour, the two of them talked. Nicole shared more detail about her grandmother and her cooking. Cameron shared he was teaching himself how to spin vinyl records.

"So, do you want to be a DJ in your spare time?" Nicole wondered.

"No, but if someone wants a DJ at the last minute or if I want to add a club atmosphere at my place, I can do it." An image filled his mind in that instant. Him at his turntable with a disco ball hanging from his ceiling with a red light illuminating his space. Would Nicole think he was creepy if she walked into his living room and saw that?

"That sounds like fun. What is your favorite music to spin?" Nicole asked, tucking a strand of hair behind her ear.

"You now know, I love old school hip hop, 80s and 90s R&B," Cameron confirmed.

"And you know I love old school hip hop, 80s and 90s R&B," Nicole reminded him.

"I know you like Chaka Khan, but who is your absolute favorite?" Cameron asked, wondering if he could guess her response.

"Sade, hands down." Nicole had no dispute about that.

"I like Sade, too! Anita Baker is a favorite. How did you develop a liking for that kind of music?" Cameron had no choice in his house. His grandfather and mother made sure he knew good music.

"My parents. That's all they played. Music they grew up to, partied to." Nicole smiled at the mention of her parents.

"My grandfather played that music. He was a lover of music too." Cameron had to grin at the thought of his grandfather blasting songs while he cleaned the house.

Nicole sat back in her chair with a revelation. "You know, we share a few things in common."

"Are you keeping a list?" Cameron asked.

Nicole tilted her head, then said, "Maybe? The more we converse, the more I discover our shared interests."

"That's a good thing, right?" Cameron asked, reaching for Nicole's hand that was resting on the table. He immediately sensed a rush of warmth coursing from his hand, spreading through his entire body. He needed to distract himself. He needed to control his impulse to kiss Nicole, determined to uphold his gentlemanly conduct.

"Would you like to share my pastry?" Cameron asked.

"Sure," Nicole responded, licking her lower lip.

Cameron ignored the sensuality of Nicole's lips and released his hand from hers to slide the plate of blueberry scone toward her. She was going to be the death of him for sure. Nicole's look was so stimulating. She reached for the scone and broke a small piece off and popped it into her mouth. Cameron found that simple action incredibly sexy. His thoughts circled around where to take Nicole on their next date. He needed to see her again, and soon.

For the next week, Cameron counted the days, hours, and minutes until he would see Nicole. He wanted to be in her presence, looking into her eyes. Since the coffee date, they texted daily, and on most nights, they video chatted until they were close to falling asleep. Most of the guys at the station had partners, and they would occasionally draw straws to decide who got the office for the night. It was difficult to have private conversations anywhere else. Ironically, to date, Cameron never had to get off the phone to go on a call.

Through conversation over breakfast one morning at the station, Cameron learned Perry's wife owned a paint and sip business. Each themed event hosted up to ten guests at different locations. The entrance fee to the event covered all materials, a selection of wine, and light snacks. After speaking with Carla, he reserved space for him and Nicole at the 80s themed event for next Friday. Cameron knew Nicole was an artist in her own right, but did she know how to paint? He didn't, but he planned to give 100% effort to create a masterpiece. Cameron thought it would be a good idea to give Nicole a heads up about how to dress for the night. Grabbing his phone off the kitchen counter, he opened the screen to send Nicole a text message, but saw she already sent him one.

Nicole - Hey! Where are we going tonight? I want to know how to dress.

Cameron - Hey! We're going to a paint and sip event, so dress comfortably and wear something you don't mind getting paint on.

Cameron watched the three bubbles dance on his screen. Within seconds, Nicole responded.

Nicole - Paint and sip? Really?

Cameron - Yep

Nicole - Ok, thanks. Looking forward to it.

Cameron - I'll see you there at 7?

Nicole - 6:50 smiley face. I want to get a good seat. LOL.

Cameron, I thought you wanted to be early to see me. Wink.

Nicole - That too.

Flirting with Nicole was seamless. He loved their text talk and flirting. Cameron was putting in an effort to conduct himself as a true gentleman. At the coffee shop, he gave Nicole a nice, tight, lingering hug. However, the thought of kissing her lingered in his thoughts. He wanted to gaze into her eyes, hold her face, and draw her in for a soft, tender kiss. But he knew it was best to wait. He sensed it would be wise to take things slowly. He planned to explore every facet of her personality and get to know her on a significant level. This was a departure from his approach in previous relationships. Nicole stood out. She was unique. Cameron experienced emotions that eluded a simple explanation. Her touch carried an electrifying sensation.

At 6:45pm, Cameron pulled into the parking lot of the industrial two story concrete building that housed several spaces people rented for short-term events. An event spiraled out of control one evening, leaving in its wake a dumpster fire that almost burned the entire building down. Not seeing Nicole's car, Cameron waited for her so they could walk in together. He checked his phone from his console to find a text.

Nicole - Running a little late. My ETA is 6:55.

Cameron picked up his phone to return her text.

> **Cameron** - I'm in the parking lot. I'll wait for you so we can walk in together.

To pass the time, Cameron started scrolling through Instagram when something caught his attention in a post. Shannon, his ex-girlfriend, was engaged. Why did he still follow her? We're engaged, the caption said, with Shannon holding up her left hand, flashing an engagement ring, shiny and new. She was marrying her ex boyfriend, now fiance. Shannon was engaged to the man she cheated with while still in a relationship with Cameron. His initial instinct was to be angry. Then he thought better.

"Good for her," Cameron said softly, realizing he genuinely didn't harbor any ill feelings towards her. He was over Shannon. He was over the hurt and humiliation he felt after finding out she had cheated on him with her ex. That meant they were meant to be, he guessed. He wasn't her person, and that was fine by him. It was interesting how you only realize someone isn't a good match for you once you're no longer together. Did he ever feel that for Shannon? Cameron heard a car pull into the parking space next to him. From the left corner of his eye, he saw Nicole's car. Cameron stepped out of his truck, locked the doors, and walked to Nicole's car, waiting for her to exit.

"Hey, handsome!" Nicole said, greeting Cameron with a soft kiss on his cheek.

"Hello, yourself. How do you make casual look so cute?" Cameron adored Nicole's choice of a pair of light colored baggy jeans and a fitted t-shirt that had the word smile written across the front.

"Well, I try," Nicole said with a giggle.

Nicole and Cameron walked into the suite, hand in hand, and discovered two couples sipping wine and exploring materials at their stations.

"Welcome, Cameron," Carla said, walking toward them. "And you must be Nicole. It's nice to meet you. I'm Carla Perry, Cameron's co-worker's wife," she said, holding out her hand.

"Hello, it's nice to meet you," Nicole said, giving Carla a firm handshake.

"I have you guys sitting here," Carla said, pointing to the two person station in the front row.

"Help yourself to a glass of wine. I have some light snacks set up over there," Carla said, pointing to the corner of the suite. There was an array of bottled wine, charcuterie boards filled with assorted cheeses, fruits, crackers, baguette slices, and sliced meats.

Cameron and Nicole grabbed a glass of wine and a small plate of snacks. A white canvas sat on an easel at each station, with an assortment of different colored paints, brushes in a range of sizes, cloth rags, and empty cups for water. Cameron observed the DJ playing music to the left of the art stations. His board, speakers, and computer stood alongside the crates of vinyl records.

"It's supposed to be an old school R&B theme tonight," Cameron said, between bites of cheese and crackers.

"Really? This should be really fun," Nicole said, moving her eyebrows expressively.

At 7:30, Carla announced they were going to get started. After sharing her resume and credentials with the group, she described how they were going to paint their own unique piece. She described how they would work in steps, and would give them options to consider when painting the focal point of their one-of-a-kind creations. The music selection started with The Emotions, Best of My Love. The DJ then blended in Michael Jackson's Off the Wall.

"Oh, Cameron, the music. I love this," Nicole said, swaying back and forth in her seat as she picked colors for her painting.

Cameron glanced at her for a moment, then said, "I'm glad you're enjoying yourself."

Carla guided the guests to first paint the background. Showing a cohesive aesthetic, she blended hues from the same family. Next, they were instructed to paint a scene, an object, or a person. Cameron and Nicole, now engrossed in their own paintings, began swaying to the music, singing each song's chorus. Occasionally, their eyes met, returning their gaze to their paintings, a silent understanding passing between them. By mid-evening, they were sitting near each other. Cameron's knee slightly brushed against Nicole's knee, later just resting there while they painted.

Carla ended the activity after what felt like hours. Their paintings were done.

With enthusiasm, Carla said, "Date and sign your masterpieces. You all are officially artists."

Cameron and Nicole walked away from the sink, drying their hands with paper towels, and stood to admire their work. "Wow, Nicole, you really are an artist," Cameron said in amazement. He noted the details in her bright red vase with what appeared to be droplets of water splashing out of it. The backdrop of the scene was shades of gray. Cameron couldn't shake the feeling that there was an undertone of sadness captured in her painting. He looked over at his painting. He, too, painted what looked to be a vase or bottle with shades of red, orange, and brown held inside. Cameron's painting wasn't as elaborate as Nicole's, but he took pride in his creation.

"I love the combination of red, orange, and brown," Carla said as she stood looking at their paintings. "Nicole? You're an artist in your own right. Your shadings are perfect."

"Thank you, Carla. I guess I'm an artist of sorts," Nicole responded with a proud nod.

"Well, be careful loading your paintings in the car. They aren't quite dry. Cameron, it's always a pleasure to see you," Carla said, reaching in for a quick hug. "Nicole, it was a delight to meet you. I hope to see you again."

"I do hope our paths cross again," Nicole replied warmly.

Cameron and Nicole carefully loaded their paintings into their respective cars. He leaned up against his car, arms folded, gazing at Nicole. He was captivated, eyes fixed on her, even with splotches of paint all over her clothes.

"I had an amazing night, Cameron. Thank you so much for planning this date. I'll plan the next one," Nicole said, hands clasped together, moving closer to where Cameron stood.

"Oh, you will, huh?" Cameron said, arching his eyebrows.

Cameron took a step toward Nicole and reached for her hands. Even after painting, they kept their softness. He gently held her hands, pulling her left hand to his cheek, slowly turning to give it a gentle kiss. Nicole watched him for a moment before meeting his gaze. In a wordless exchange, they stood together, locking eyes. They existed in a realm of their own, detached from the outside world. Cameron released Nicole's hand and reached for her waist to pull her closer. He wanted to kiss her. He was overcome with curiosity about the sensation of her lips against his. Instead, he wrapped his arms around her in a warm embrace. Enjoying the intimacy they were sharing, he absorbed the aroma of Nicole, which intoxicated him, generating a sensation reminiscent of being slightly tipsy. Nicole nestled her face into the crook of Cameron's neck. After a few moments, he gently pulled away, leaving a tender kiss on her cheek.

"Call me when you get home?" Cameron said softly.

Eyes low, Nicole smiled, then looked at him. "Yes, I'll call you when I get home."

Nicole slowly pulled away from Cameron and walked to the driver's side of her car, gave him one last smile, and got in. Cameron stood there, deeply engrossed as he watched her drive away, enamored by her charm and yearning to hold her all night.

Chapter 15

Nicole

Nicole woke up, night shirt drenched in sweat. Was she getting sick? Her head didn't feel warm. Her throat wasn't scratchy. Half asleep, Nicole pushed her feet to the floor, the cold tile cooling the tops of her toes. She sat there for several seconds, allowing the chill to permeate her entire frame. The coolness worked its way through her, regulating her body temperature to a degree that felt normal. In the bathroom, her image was scary. Makeup smeared down her eyes. Nicole speculated it might have been a bad dream, which caused her to wake up in a sweat. Guilt overcame her just thinking about bad dreams. Nightmares about Tyler resurfaced, leading Nicole back to a sense of guilt. Bad dreams made her consider Tyler circling back to a sense of remorse.

Turning on the faucet and dabbing cool water on her face sent a surge of wakefulness through her. "Why do I feel guilty?" Nicole whispered. Her night with Cameron had been amazing. She made a mental note to bring up her feelings of guilt during her next therapy session with Dr. Williamson. After Nicole brushed her teeth, washed her face and changed into running clothes, she did something she now thought she was ready for. She hopped in her car, headed to the park, and started a long run. Despite dreams of Tyler, the possibility of tears, sad memories or even a dramatic scene, she was determined to get through her run.

Amidst the serene beauty of the park, Nicole navigated the winding paths, each step echoing the rhythm of her heavy heart. The vibrant hues of the surroundings appeared muted as she pushed through the lingering grief in the air. She allowed the tears to fall. Memories of Tyler flashed before her eyes. Each stride felt like a battle against the weight of sorrow in her heart. Yet, with each passing lap of the park, a quiet strength emerged. The pulsing pounding of her feet became a cathartic tempo, a tribute to her lost love. Nicole channeled the pain into each step, transforming grief into determination. She embraced the healing power of the park surroundings. The unspoken empathy of the flowers and trees gave her solace.

An hour later, drenched in sweat, Nicole applauded herself for not only finishing her run, but arriving on the other side of her grief, embracing her newfound sense of inner strength and peace. Nicole sat on the same bench she fainted on months ago, catching her breath. She felt her phone buzz with an incoming text message.

Levi - Hey! Are you still coming to help me paint?

Forgetting her promise to Levi, she realized she was late. She typed a response.

Nicole - Yes. I'll be there in an hour.

Nicole drove home without incident, showered, threw on some old gray sweatpants, a pink t-shirt, and zip up jacket, then headed to Levi's house. He only lived five minutes from her. They were close. Why not live near one another? He wanted to keep an eye on her. Nicole knew that. Him being the overprotective little brother made him make decisions like that. Buy a house within a mile radius of his sister.

"Levi, I'm outside! Come open the door." Nicole yelled. Even though she forgot her key, she would not bang on his door another minute. She knew what she was getting him for Christmas. The Ring, so he knew when she arrived.

"Hey, come on in," Levi said, out of breath from running to open the door.

"Wow, Levi, you've been working on this place. Everything's coming together," Nicole said, noticing the upgrades he made to his home. Levi purchased his fixer home a few months ago, having painted the exterior and landscaped the front yard. Their mother helped him pick colors for his living room and dining area. She ordered his furniture and helped him style the large room right off the front door. Down the short hall led to an open kitchen and family room. The family room was painted and the big screen television hung on the wall.

Seeing that there was nowhere to sit, Nicole asked, "When's your couch coming?"

"Mom said it should be any day. I can't wait to lounge on it and watch the game," Levi said, rubbing his hands together.

The kitchen wasn't finished. Even though the granite slabs and the stainless steel stove with built-in oven were installed, the refurbished cabinets needed fixtures. Nicole and Levi were painting the kitchen walls prior to installing the twelve inch back guard.

"This shouldn't take us too long, right?" Nicole wondered out loud.

"Why? You got somewhere to go?" Levi asked, irritation etched across his face, leaving no room for ambiguity.

"No, just asking." Nicole knew in that instant it was brother sister time. She smiled to herself as she turned away to inspect the painting supplies sprawled across the counters.

Levi returned to the room, carrying paint and gloves for Nicole. Seconds later, the Love and Basketball soundtrack played through the nearby speaker.

"Aw, this is a good one, Levi," Nicole said, bobbing her head to I Want to be Your Man, by Roger.

"I knew you would like it." Levi chuckled.

Both dipped their paint brushes in soft eggshell white paint; Nicole went left in the kitchen, while Levi went right. There was something calming about applying strokes of paint to a wall. Nicole felt the stress of her earlier run melt away. Each layer of paint transformed the wall from one color to another, and within minutes, they gave the room fresh energy. The interior of Nicole's house hadn't been painted since Tyler. Wanting fresh energy in the inside of her house, she knew she would bring that into her house by changing the color of her home interior. Glancing over at Levi, she observed her little brother painting the walls on his side of the room. And Levi would help her. The buzz of Nicole's phone derailed her train of thought. Taking hold of her phone, Aubrey's face on the screen brought a smile to her face.

"Hey, girl!"

"Hey, yourself. So, why haven't I heard from you in the last few days? What have you been up to?" Aubrey knew Nicole was holding back the juicy information. It wasn't like her to not check in with Aubrey daily, even if only by text message.

"Well, Carol and I are ready to schedule time so you can bring in your dishes for the Malibu restaurant." Nicole knew Aubrey was not calling about work.

"Girl? I'm not talking about work. Cameron? The man you've been seeing?"

"Oh, Cameron, he's great," Nicole answered, face heating just by the mention of his name.

"Oh, yeah, spill, girl. What's the tea?" Nicole visualized Aubrey with her hands on her hips waiting for a response.

"Last night, I met him at a paint and sip event. It was really fun. His colleague's wife is an artist, and it was her event. You should see my painting. It's pretty cool."

"Cameron planned a good date. That's a plus. Did you do anything after the date?"

"We stood in the parking lot for a bit, holding hands. He gave me the best hug." The thought of Cameron's hug heated Nicole's cheeks.

"A hug? That's it?"

"Yes, this pace is nice, Aubrey. I don't need to rush anything."

"Then you went home alone?" Nicole knew Aubrey wanted her to get back in the saddle, get her groove back.

"Yes, we chatted for hours on the phone though. We have great conversations, you know."

"Yes, I know. When are you planning to go out again?"

"It's my turn to plan something. I saw something on Instagram I wanted to try. It was for a food crawl. I'd like to bring Cameron along to experience that." Nicole wanted Cameron to share her world filled with good food.

"Oh, that's a good one. When? I wouldn't mind going on that, but you're planning a date with Cameron for just the two of you, right?." Aubrey wasn't dating and Nicole knew that. Did she want to go too?

"Next Saturday." Not soon enough, Nicole thought.

"You won't see him until then?" A whole additional week without seeing Cameron seemed like an eternity.

"No, he has a four day shift. It's okay. I was hoping Carol and I could get you in the studio with your food to photograph."

"That'll be good. Let's plan for Wednesday. The owner gave the green light on the menu, so I'll pick the food I want to photograph for the walls in the restaurant. Where are you?" Aubrey asked, hearing music in the background.

"At Levi's helping him paint his kitchen. His place is looking good."

"Tell him dinner is on me when everything is done."

"He'll love that." Nicole glanced at her brother, eyeing her with suspension.

Nicole finished the call with Aubrey and returned to her painting. She glanced over at Levi and caught him glaring at her.

With an inquisitive but cautious look on his face, Levi inquired, "Nicole? Who's Cameron?"

"He's my new friend. We've gone out a few times. What's behind the look on your face?" Nicole was ready for Levi's interrogation.

"My sister is dating and didn't tell me?" Levi flashed Nicole a pained expression of not knowing this new fact.

"I didn't want to mention him yet. It's a new relationship." The last thing Nicole wanted to do was bring a man into her family's aura and it be a fleeting romance.

"And how did you two meet?" Levi wanted all the details on the new guy.

"That is a story for sure." Nicole thought about how she would explain the way she and Cameron met. They stopped painting, grabbed bottles of water while she shared the entire story of how she and Cameron met. Butterflies danced in her stomach as she spoke of him, a fluttering sensation betraying the excitement within. Heat tinged her cheeks as she recounted the details of their first date, the memories evoking a warm blush of worthy nostalgia.

"He sounds like a good guy. When do I get to meet him?" Levi asked as he gazed at his sister.

"You will, when it's time." Nicole wanted to be sure she and Cameron solidified their relationship before bringing him around to meet her family.

Levi gave his sister a good loving stare. He couldn't bear to see his sister hurt again. The thought of it would shatter his heart again.

"Will you help me paint the inside of my house, Levi? It's time for a change. Fresh paint, new vibe, new memories, you know?" Nicole wanted new energy in her house.

"Yes, I know. Of course." Levi would do anything for his sister.

The next week was busy. Wednesday came and although it was a long day, she and Carol took amazing photos of Aubrey's food. Carol sent the proofs to be printed and blown up on canvas. They would mount the photos on the newly decorated walls of the Malibu restaurant. Thursday, Nicole had to devote her attention to the article she was writing for the new food magazine the grub network was launching. Video chatting with Cameron from her bed was Nicole's highlight at the end of each day. By Friday night, anxiety and elation consumed her. She wanted to see him. She wanted to be in his company. She longed to sense the touch of his lips on her cheek as she held his hand. Curiosity sparked as Nicole wondered what it would be like to kiss Cameron. Maybe she would kiss him on their upcoming date. The mere thought of them kissing sent a flush of heat whisking through her body.

On Saturday morning, Nicole took time to tidy up her house. It wasn't dirty. But, since Cameron was picking her up, she wanted to make a good impression. She prioritized the bathrooms, followed by dusting all surfaces, and concluded with vacuuming and mopping the kitchen floor. Surveying her work, Nicole realized the space needed brightening up. Nicole grabbed her keys and headed to the market for floral bouquets to place in the living room and kitchen. Adding wine and snacks to her list, she ensured the house was well-stocked.

As Nicole pulled into her driveway from the store, her phone buzzed with an incoming text.

Edward - Hey Nicole! How are you?

Nicole knew she should respond to Edward. The last time they saw one another, she knew she sent him mixed messages.

Nicole - Hey! I'm good. You?

Within seconds, Nicole could see the three dots moving on the screen, showing Edward was responding to her text.

Edward - I'm good. It'd be great to see you.

Nicole - I have plans tonight, but thanks.

Edward - Really? Ok. Can I call you tomorrow?

Nicole - That's fine Edward. No expectations.

Edward - Right

Edward had looked after her since Tyler's death. After the night she showed up at his house, she understood her connection to Edward. He reminded her of Tyler. When she saw Edward, she saw Tyler. That made her angry. The constant reminder of Tyler's absence through Edward's presence fueled her annoyance. Yet, up until recently, Edward brought her comfort because of the remembrance of Tyler. She had to release Tyler from her heart. When she untethered her feelings for Tyler, once and for all, she could no longer encourage Edward's presence in her world.

Cameron was arriving at 4pm. Nicole had just enough time to shower and change into a pair of ankle jeans, a black blouse, and black leather flats. As Nicole fluffed her curly hair and applied tinted gloss, thoughts of Cameron and his beautiful tall frame, his firm hands holding hers, confirmed her attraction to him. During her most recent therapy session, Dr. Williamson conveyed to her it was common to have a sense of guilt regarding dating someone new when you lost a partner you were not ready to say goodbye to. There was no closure. Dr. Williamson thought it would be a good idea to hold a ceremony to close that chapter of her life. Aubrey also thought it was a good idea and offered to help Nicole with the ritual of writing thoughts on pieces of paper, placing them in a fire pit, saying closing words, and lighting those thoughts on fire. Nicole needed to attempt to move on from that chapter of her life. Did she deserve love again? Was she able to overcome her fear and love again? Was Cameron the one to love? Her fears wanted to push him away. However, the magnetic pull toward him seemed unbreakable. Better yet, she needed to release those feelings. She really wanted to make things work with Cameron.

The ring of the doorbell pulled Nicole out of her thoughts. She took one last glance at herself. Satisfied with what she saw, she took in a deep breath and opened her front door. Nervous excitement filled her with just the sight of Cameron. He was so beautiful. His beige shirt hugged his pecs and biceps. His navy jeans hugged his hips in a delicious way and clung to his nicely shaped ass. Nicole's breath caught as her gaze swept over him.

"Hi!" Cameron greeted, flashing his million-dollar smile.

"Hi! Come in," Nicole said, opening her door wide enough for Cameron to walk inside.

Cameron looked around and admired Nicole's choreographed living room, filled with a soft beige couch, fluffy matching pillows, a side table with what appeared to be a hand sculpted lamp, a coffee table with trinkets strategically placed, and beautiful African artwork hanging on the walls.

"Take a seat on the couch. We have a few minutes until our reservation and it's nearby. Would you like a glass of wine?" Nicole offered.

"Sure, small glass. I'm driving. Remember?" Cameron said teasingly.

"Yes. I remember. Did you have trouble finding the place?" Nicole standing in front of Cameron.

"No, not at all. Actually, my good friend is close to here. Maybe you'll meet him one day," Cameron said, looking at Nicole with sincere intent.

"I love the neighborhood. I've lived here for almost four years. It needed some work, so I got it for a good price. My dad and brother helped me fix it up." Nicole wouldn't mention Tyler helped as well. She believed it was in her best interest to keep that information to herself. At least for now.

"You did a great job. I'm not sure what it looked like before, but it's really nice."

"I'm thinking of repainting the entire interior. New color, fresh paint, new vibe, you know." She hoped there weren't undertones of a need to create a new vibe.

"Okay. If you want to repaint, I can help. We do all kinds of things at the firehouse, including home improvements. I've become skilled with my hands." Just as Cameron said it, Nicole noticed the flush in his cheeks.

"I just might have to take you up on that offer," Nicole said, her stare lingering for a second, before handing Cameron his filled wine glass.

"Please excuse my manners. I should've asked if you needed help with anything," Cameron said, as he grabbed filled wine glasses and placed them on the coffee table. He then noticed coasters in the center and pulled two out and replaced the wine glasses on them. They were both standing. Cameron extended his arms for Nicole to step into a hug. She obliged and surrendered to Cameron's affectionate embrace. His clean, yet woodsy scent tickled her nose. She loved the way he smelled. They stood entwined in a hug, lingering for a few seconds, only pulling away slightly. It seemed as though his lips singed her cheek with that kiss. The kind of burn Nicole wanted to feel all over her body.

Cameron found a parking spot at the corner of the row they would walk to visit a total of six restaurants. Each restaurant hosted a different theme.

"You ready? I'm hungry," Nicole asked, knowing what was in their dining future.

"Yes, let's go," Cameron said, reaching for Nicole's hand as he was a few steps ahead of her. Without hesitation, she grabbed it and held tight.

The crawl began at a Mediterranean tapas bar. They welcomed Nicole and Cameron with a burst of flavors in the small plates of hummus, tzatziki, falafel and stuffed grape leaves. They paired the delicious samples with shot glasses of sparkling wine.

"Do we toast?" Nicole asked, holding up her shot glass.

"I'm driving and I have to work tomorrow, so I'll drink water, but we can make a toast," Cameron said, holding up his glass.

"To a wonderful evening of great food, and to the fact I wore comfortable shoes," Nicole said with a giggle.

"To our wonderful evening," Cameron said in a low whisper. With a touch between glasses, they sipped their beverages and indulged in the display in front of them.

Two doors down from the Mediterranean tapas bar was a Japanese sushi lounge. A sushi chef described the art of sushi and sashimi. He then prepared a variety of creative rolls featuring fresh fish served with small glasses of sake.

Swallowing a mouthful of a sushi roll, Nicole spoke. "Cameron? I wish you were drinking with me. The cocktail pairings make each bite sparkle."

"Oh yeah? Well, I'll watch you sparkle for now," Cameron said, giving Nicole a wink.

The fragrance of Indian street food welcomed Nicole and Cameron as they walked out of the sushi lounge. Spice Route Adventure provided samples of chaats, pakoras, and kebabs.

"This is amazing," Cameron said, chewing the last piece of chicken kebab.

All Nicole could do was nod. With mouths full of delicious food, there wasn't much time for talking. The tour continued with a stop at an Italian trattoria where Nicole and Cameron sampled handcrafted pasta topped with rich sauces, paired with red wine. The Vietnamese Pho House served bowls of steaming pho, fragrant with herbs and spices, offering a comforting and aromatic interlude. They chatted while enjoying the communal dining experience before their last stop.

"So, are you enjoying yourself, Cameron?" Nicole asked, taking a spoonful of her pho.

"I've experienced nothing like this. All the food has been amazing. The next time we do this, I'll be drinking," Cameron responded, glaring into Nicole's slightly glossy eyes. "We'll take an Uber."

"Hanging with you, Cameron Davis, is a lot of fun," Nicole admitted, placing her head on Cameron's shoulder.

"Well, Nicole Graham, I can say the same about you." Cameron leaned into Nicole, feeling the warmth of her body next to his.

Nicole smiled and slowly closed her eyes, reaching for Cameron's hand. She felt the heat radiating from her hand to his as she intertwined their fingers. Nicole noticed him shift his head towards hers. Her heart was filled with so much warmth. She wasn't sure it was Cameron or the drinks she had along the tour. Nicole was certain that she liked Cameron, and she wanted to continue to date him.

The French Patisserie was the last stop on the food crawl. Dessert took center stage when the owner brought out a tray of exquisite pastries, tarts and macaroons, accompanied by brewed coffee and tea.

"Coffee!" Nicole said as she grabbed a cup, held it in her cooling hands, then took a deep sip, hoping it would help the slight buzz she was feeling from the sake and wine she drank.

"Are you good?" Cameron asked, chuckling.

"I'm good, alright," Nicole said, laughing out loud.

The slow walk to Cameron's car is what Nicole needed after indulging in all the delicious food. Cameron graduated from holding Nicole's hand to having his arm around her shoulders. His snug embrace offered a comforting closeness. She wanted to stay there, in his arms. He opened her door and helped her into her seat. Despite the cup of coffee, she was experiencing the effects of the alcohol she had at each stop. They rode in a pleasant silence, only hearing the smooth jazz that played from Cameron's car speakers. Nicole was filled with pure bliss. There was something about this man that brought her a sense of tranquility. As they pulled into her driveway, a wave of sadness washed over her. Knowing Cameron's work obligations the following day, their evening was reaching its conclusion. Cameron turned off his engine and endearingly looked at Nicole.

"I have to work tomorrow afternoon. I need to go home," he said, grabbing Nicole's hand and kissing it.

"I know. I wish you could come in. Just for a bit." Nicole felt bold. She wanted Cameron in her arms again.

"If I come in, Nicole, I won't want to leave," Cameron said softly.

"Yeah, I don't think I would want you to leave," Nicole admitted.

"I had a wonderful time. I have a new appreciation for different cuisines," Cameron said with a slight chuckle.

"As you saw, I really enjoyed my food," Nicole said, rubbing her full stomach.

"I love a woman with a real appetite," Cameron said, lowering his eyes to gaze at Nicole's lips.

In that instant, Nicole dared herself to just jump in. "Cameron? Can I kiss you?" Not wanting to wait, she had to feel his lips on hers.

"Is this the wine talking or...?" Cameron asked. Nicole wanted to kiss him and the need wasn't influenced by the drinks she had consumed earlier.

Facing Cameron, Nicole whispered, "No, I really want to kiss you."

Cameron's eyes never left Nicole's as he took his seat belt off and twisted his tall frame to get closer. Nicole unlocked her seatbelt, twisting her body to move in on Cameron. With their faces barely an inch apart, Nicole could detect his minty breath brushing against her lips. She closed her eyes and moved to brush her lips over his. She held her position for a millisecond, then engaged in the kiss more deeply, parting her lips to take in his. Each touch of her lips on his was deliberate, exploring the contours of his mouth with delicate intimacy. Cameron slowly took control of their kiss, claiming her tongue. Their tongues engaged in a choreography of desire, an intricate dance that mirrored the intensity of their connection. Their bond, intense and magnetic, was palpable with each shared breath. The warmth and lingering pressure of their first kiss spoke volumes, igniting a subtle, yet passionate exchange of shared desire. Nicole wanted to kiss Cameron all night. Reluctantly, she pulled away, touching her forehead to his. Cameron took in a deep breath, holding his gaze in Nicole's eyes.

With an inhale of breath, Nicole sadly said, "Goodnight, Cameron."

"Goodnight, Nicole," he said, caressing her cheek with his hand.

Nicole stepped out of the car, no longer experiencing the effects of the wine. The tingling sensation was from the shared kiss, a delightful buzz that lingered on her lips. Their first kiss. The lingering kiss etched every detail into the fabric of her memory.

Chapter 16

Cameron

Last night's date with Nicole transcended any ordinary date Cameron had with any woman ever. Every moment seemed painted with hues of enchantment, each more captivating than the last. Their first kiss created a symphony of sensations. It left an indelible imprint of desire within Cameron. He was dating someone. In Nicole's presence, he found a refuge that was more comforting than anywhere else. It wasn't just the physical space they occupied, but the intangible warmth that wrapped around them like they've known each other for years. This was Cameron's first encounter with such strong affections for a woman. It was this that frightened him. What did all of this mean? Where was all of this going? The kiss he and Nicole shared was beyond amazing. It was soft, sensual, and yet left him wanting more. He wanted to kiss Nicole, deep, long, and hold her close to him. In his past relationships, things progressed at a normal pace. Attraction wasn't ever instant but grew. But with Nicole, it was immediate. It was instantaneous.

Cameron had been at the station for over a week. He looked forward to some days off. Separated by the inability to physically see each other,

Cameron and Nicole built a connection through phone conversations. Despite not being in the same room, they learned to interpret tone, laughter, and meaningful pauses. When they texted one another, they expressed ideas, dreams, and fears. Cameron looked forward to each text notification from Nicole with anticipation, a digital tap on his shoulder that signified the other. Free from physical distractions, they explored each other's true selves. Their communication revealed layers of character, quirks, passions, and vulnerabilities. Words had power, turning sentences into a dance that conveyed more than what meets the eye. Without the interference of being in each other's presence, the bond they forged through verbal communication created a unique intimacy, building a profound connection.

Thursday evening was slow. The station hadn't gotten a call all day. Cameron retreated to the empty office to have his nightly call with Nicole.

"Hey, gorgeous!" Cameron spoke when he heard Nicole say hello. Thinking about her beautiful face took his breath away. She was so darn cute.

"Hey, yourself. How was your day?" Nicole asked with a smile in her voice.

"Better now that we're talking." Seconds melted away, sharing breaths, a testament of the comfort they found in shared silence.

"I have our date all planned." Nicole said eagerly.

"What are we doing?" Cameron wished their date was sooner than later.

"It's a surprise, but I know you're going to love it." Nicole felt giddy just thinking about it.

"Okay, I trust you. Do I have to do anything, go shopping for an outfit?" He didn't want to be caught off guard.

"Cameron, you sound like me. No, just be yourself. Wear something comfortable. You always look nice, though."

"Yeah? You like the way I dress?" Cameron was fishing for compliments he gave generously to Nicole. He meant them, though.

"Yes," Nicole said matter-of-factly.

"You have me intrigued." Cameron was touched at the thought of a date being planned in his honor.

"Good. I promise you will love it." Nicole sounded very sure of herself.

The sound of Nicole's voice brought about a remarkable change in his mundane existence. Her voice was his lifeline of joy. He already missed her, even though they had only been apart for a little over a week.

On Saturday morning, Cameron woke up with a need to burn some uncontrollable energy. Dressed in black running pants, shoes, and a white Dri-fit shirt, he grabbed his headphones and keys and was out the door.

The gym was crowded at 7am on a Saturday. The heat of active bodies, moving muscles, and limbs washed over Cameron's face as he entered the exercise room. Sounds of drums and calypso music signaled the start of the day's Zumba class. The free weights section was full of young dudes flexing their muscles and pushing iron. The cardio area was relatively free. Cameron walked toward the free treadmill next to the floor to ceiling window. He could both exercise and immerse himself in the view of the busy streets while running. Music blaring in his ear, Cameron began with a light jog, then pushed the speed and incline up to find his pace. While he jogged on the treadmill and observed the cars moving around the city, his mind dwelled on Nicole's beautiful smile. This sensation towards this woman was completely foreign to him. He didn't even feel this way about his first girlfriend from high school. He may have loved his past girlfriends, but they didn't begin the way he and Nicole started. The corners of his mouth curled upward, revealing a subtle smile. A gentle flush crept up from the base of his neck, infusing warmth into his cheeks. Cameron was blushing at the mere thought of Nicole.

Forty-five minutes later, Cameron checked the treadmill display that stated he ran just over eight miles. Not bad, considering his thoughts were full of Nicole and not focused on what he was doing. Cameron, still wound up, went to the free weights to blow off steam. He worked his biceps, pecs, and back. He mentally reminded himself to work on his legs during his next workout, whether at the station or the gym.

It was 3pm and Nicole was ringing his doorbell to be buzzed up.

"Hello?" Cameron asked as he talked into the speaker.

"Hi! It's me. Are you ready to go?" Nicole asked.

"Yep! I will be right down."

Cameron thought it would have been nice to ask Nicole up to his condo. However, the place was a mess. He wanted his place to be spotless before he let her in. Soon, he would invite Nicole over for dinner. Cameron took a quick look in the mirror dressed in casual but fitted jeans, a fitted cobalt blue long sleeve, ribbed cotton shirt, and blue and white Nike shoes.

"Kinda styling man," he said out loud, pleased with his outfit.

As Cameron stepped out of the elevator, he noticed Nicole standing in front of his building.

"Wow," he caught himself saying. Nicole was breathtaking.

Nicole looked gorgeous dressed in fitted jeans, a V-neck white cotton t-shirt with gold accessories and gold strappy heeled sandals. Her curls tumbled past her shoulders, catching stray beams of sunlight.

"Hey, gorgeous," Cameron said, greeting Nicole.

"Hey yourself, handsome," Nicole's lips curved into a bright, infectious grin that shined as bright as the sun.

Nicole walked slowly toward Cameron, reaching her hands outward for a hug. As Cameron pulled her in, he caught a whiff of the floral, yet clean, scent of her perfume. She perceived a pleasant feeling of warmth and softness as she molded into him for an embrace. They stood in each other's arms for several seconds. Nicole pulled away first.

"Are you ready to go?" Nicole asked, looking up at Cameron.

"Anywhere with you. Where are we going?" He was curious. He didn't have a clue what they were doing. He was with her and that's all that mattered.

"A surprise. We'll make one stop and you'll do something I think you'll enjoy, and then we'll get some food. Sounds like a plan?" Nicole asked, giving Cameron an ear to ear smile.

"I'm going wherever you take me," Cameron said flirtatiously.

Nicole pulled up in front of The record parlor.

"What are we doing here?" Cameron asked in surprise.

"You'll see. Come on inside," Nicole grabbed Cameron's hand, leading him to the front counter of the store.

"Hi, we're here for the DJ lesson. I made a reservation–Nicole Graham?"

Cameron's gaze quickly turned to Nicole, sensing an electrifying jolt of shock. She paid attention and planned something so thoughtful, he almost lost his cool.

"Yes, we have you all set up. Follow me." The woman at the desk led Nicole and Cameron to the back of the store, where a young guy with a beard was behind his DJ equipment. In a brief exchange, Nicole caught the reflection of joy on Cameron's face.

"You did this for me?" Cameron asked, feeling a weight of sentiment.

"Yes! You've talked so much about wanting to learn how to DJ. I knew you had the equipment and you've been experimenting with it, watching videos, trying to teach yourself." Nicole reached for Cameron's hands, holding them in hers. "I thought it would be fun for you to take a thirty-minute lesson."

Cameron pulled her hands to his mouth, brushing gentle kisses across her knuckles. "What are you going to do?" He couldn't imagine what Nicole would do while he played with DJ equipment.

"I'm going to watch you," Nicole said matter-of-factly.

"I can't believe this. You're amazing," Cameron said, closing their distance to give her a quick kiss on her lips. He never experienced someone planning such a thoughtful date. Nicole paid attention and scheduled a lesson for him. She didn't look for any specific enjoyment for herself.

Ben, the DJ instructor, showed Cameron the pieces of equipment around the store. Cameron pointed out the equipment he had at home. They began the session with the basics, and Ben showed him basic moves prior to giving Cameron the opportunity to try the moves himself. Cameron glanced at Nicole, now sitting in a chair watching him. There she was, sitting with focused intensity, her gaze unwavering as she observed him.

Cameron walked over to Nicole after his lesson. "That was absolutely amazing, Nicole. Thank you!" he said, pulling her into a hug.

"I'm glad you enjoyed it. Do you think you got the hang of it?"

"No," Cameron said, chuckling at himself. "I'll come back and take a few more lessons. But now I have something to start with. I really didn't know what I was doing."

"Well, I'm happy you now have some direction. Are you hungry?"

Nicole asked.

"Yes, starving. Where're we going?" Cameron heard a low rumble coming from his stomach.

"A spot that has amazing rice bowls and excellent wine," Nicole responded, grabbing Cameron's hand, leading him out the store.

On the car ride to the restaurant, Cameron described his lesson and what he would practice tomorrow before beginning his workday. He rambled when he was excited, experiencing the same joy as a kid on Christmas morning. He talked the entire way. Nicole barely said a word. She gave her keys to the valet, then Cameron intertwined their hands as they walked into the eatery. Seated by a window, the sun dipped below the horizon, the sky transformed into a canvas painted with hues of pink, orange, and gold. The scenery, in its tranquility, promised an exquisite night.

"Everything looks so delicious. What do you recommend?" Cameron asked, letting Nicole continue to take the lead for the evening.

"I like the shrimp rice bowl. It has lots of veggies, grilled shrimp, and hibachi fried rice," Nicole described, licking her lips.

Cameron's breath caught for a second, watching Nicole. He wanted to be the one licking her lips. "That sounds amazing. I'll have that, too."

Over dinner, Cameron wanted to ask Nicole on another date. He wanted to do something big. Chaka Khan's concert would be in a few weeks. Cameron knew it was a little soon, but he wanted to take Nicole to see the legendary singer.

"Interested in seeing Chaka Khan together?" Cameron asked, terrified at the possibility of Nicole rejecting him.

Nicole didn't hesitate with a reaction. "Really? I love Chaka Khan, as you know. My parents would be jealous," Nicole said, laughing.

"She's performing in Vegas, though. How do you feel about that?"

Cameron asked nervously. He didn't want to seem too forward. "Vegas?" Cameron read the apprehension on Nicole's face.

"We can get separate rooms. I don't want you to feel I'm pushing anything on you. I just thought it would be fun. Escape LA and enjoy a few days in Vegas."

"Las Vegas, huh?" Nicole said, biting on her lip. Cameron could tell she was nervous with her response.

"Think about it. Okay?"

Lips curved into a hesitant smile, Nicole responded, "Sure. I'll think about it."

After dinner, Nicole drove to Cameron's building and parked in front. She shut off her engine and faced him with a warm smile.

"Thank you for this wonderful time. I'm so touched," Cameron peered into Nicole's eyes.

"You're welcome," Nicole said, eyes sparkling with joy.

They sat in silence for a few moments. Cameron grabbed Nicole's hand, stroking the back softly.

It was Cameron's turn to ask. "Can I kiss you?"

With certainty, Nicole nodded. "You can kiss me."

Cameron and Nicole closed the distance between them as they leaned in. He brushed his lips against Nicole's, kissing her lips lightly at first. Their kisses intensified, each touch a fervent expression of desire. The air in Nicole's car crackled with a heightened energy as their lips met with a newfound urgency. The softness of their initial kiss gave way to a more passionate dance of their tongues, a hypnotic pull drawing them closer. Cameron moved his hands to cradle Nicole's face, deepening the connection. Nicole let out a soft sigh as she moved closer to Cameron. In the silence between kisses, they gazed into each other's eyes, the unspoken language of longing and intimacy speaking volumes, creating a moment charged with raw, unbridled passion. Nicole placed her hands on Cameron's shoulders, pulling him in, her lips urgent on his, licking his bottom lip, giving it a slight tug. Cameron moaned, opening his mouth, deepening their kiss. Both experiencing a strong desire, their tongues intertwined in a fierce clash, asserting their presence and craving for more. She was the first to pull away.

Gasping for air, Nicole uttered, "Cameron?"

With a heavy sigh, Cameron said, "Nicole?"

"I would love to go see Chaka Khan with you in Vegas."

Chapter 17

Nicole

Aubrey sat cross-legged on Nicole's comfy couch, Nicole sitting next to her in her oversized soft chair.

"Aren't you nervous, going away with Cameron?" Aubrey asked, shocked. "You agreed to go away with Cameron for the weekend so soon into your relationship."

"No, I'm not. I feel I know him well enough to take this trip. Besides, we aren't sharing a room. I booked my own room at the hotel." Nicole wanted to be mature about this.

"This is a big step, don't you think?" Aubrey wondered. "You have only been dating him a couple of months."

"I like Cameron. And I feel he's into me. I have a feeling about him. I can't define it just yet, but I like it. I like the way he makes me feel. I like who I am when I'm around him." Nicole knew she had to be strong around Aubrey. She didn't want her to talk her out of going.

"Have the two of you slept together?" Aubrey glanced at Nicole with uncertainty. Nicole knew she would ask that question.

"No, we haven't." Nicole felt the time was close. Their kisses reawakened a long-lost desire in her. If she could get over the tinge of guilt she felt when she recalled their dates. During their moments of embrace or kiss, she didn't feel guilt. When she spent time with Cameron, he was the only one she thought about.

Aubrey paused briefly before speaking her mind. "That's a big step for you. You haven't been with anyone since Tyler."

"Tyler isn't coming back." Nicole had to be realistic and face this very fact. "I loved Tyler with all of my heart. I'll miss him always. However, I have to move forward. I don't want to be single forever. I want love in my life."

"I know you do. I just want you to be careful. I don't want you to get hurt." Aubrey moved closer to Nicole.

"Aubrey, you know I love you. I know you're looking out for my best interest. I promise I won't get hurt." Nicole had to plead her case. She really wanted to spend the weekend with Cameron.

Aubrey had to support Nicole in this. "Okay... I'm excited for you, though. You're stepping out of your comfort zone."

"I have to, Aubrey. I have to. I can say, though, Cameron makes it easy," Nicole admitted.

"You really like him, huh?" Nicole knew Aubrey could hear the excitement and fondness for Cameron in her voice.

Nicole took a deep breath before speaking. "I do."

"So, what outfits are you taking on the trip?" Aubrey jumped up and headed toward Nicole's room.

"I thought about wearing a dress for the concert. A pair of jeans and shorts, a few t-shirts, comfortable but cute shoes. Nothing too fancy," Nicole said, right behind Aubrey.

"And lingerie?" Aubrey said, raising her eyebrows.

"Well, I don't plan to sleep with Cameron. I'll pack cute bras and panty sets. How's that? I want to feel sexy at least." Nicole wanted to be prepared for anything.

"Do you get those feelings around Cameron?" Aubrey asked.

"What kind of feelings?" Nicole didn't know what Aubrey was talking about.

Aubrey asked, with arched eyebrows. "Desire, want, longing?"

"YES! The last time we went out, he kissed me. He gave me a deep, passionate kiss. I felt dampness between my legs, permeating my jeans. I hadn't experienced that sensation since Tyler died. My attraction to Cameron is clear now. I thought I would lose it, drop my panties right there in the car in front of his house," Nicole said, laughing.

"Girl! I'm guessing you didn't do that." Aubrey laughed out loud. By the look on her face Nicole was sure the image appeared in her head.

"No, but I felt the urge. It's been a while." It had been two years. Cameron made her tingle, feel alive on the inside. She felt desirable.

"We'll see if you last the weekend. With y'all being all over each other, I'll be surprised if you can resist each other." Aubrey knew her friend. "If you feel the hots for Cameron, it's only a matter of time."

After laying out all of her clothing options, Aubrey helped Nicole put her things into a suitcase. When Aubrey left, Nicole finished packing and closed all her windows and shutters, since she would be gone for a few days. For the first time, Nicole walked around her house and didn't feel Tyler's presence. She no longer sensed him in her house. She didn't long for him in the middle of the night. She didn't reach for him, or hug her pillow, wishing it was him. She no longer felt the ache for Tyler. Was she actually moving on? Was she ready for a new relationship? Nicole drew in a deep cleansing breath, fell back onto her bed facing upward, staring at the ceiling.

With a tear rolling down her cheek, Nicole thought out loud. "Tyler, you'll always be in my heart. Cameron's a good guy. I hope you're happy for me. I want to give this a try. I want to feel love again. I believe I can love Cameron," Nicole whispered, wiping her cheek. She believed her spoken words, although feeling some hesitation. The dreams of Tyler were out of her control. She didn't know when she would have one. The scene was always the same. Tyler and Nicole sat in a room, staring at one another.

Nicole must have dozed off because the next thing she heard was her phone buzzing with an incoming text.

Cameron - Hey gorgeous! You ready? I'm on my way to pick you up.

Grinning, Nicole typed in her response.

Nicole - Hey! Yes, I'm ready. Can't wait.

Nicole stared at her phone for a few seconds. She noticed the three dots bouncing, letting her know she would see an incoming text from Cameron soon.

Cameron - My ETA is about 15 minutes.

Nicole - See you soon.

Nicole sat for a few more minutes, thinking about her words she'd spoken earlier, before falling asleep. In an instant, an intangible weight lifted from her chest. The constriction that had gripped her heart like a vice seemed to dissolve, replaced by an airy lightness.

"Thank you, Tyler," Nicole said, looking up at the ceiling. She knew it was a sign. It was a sign from Tyler. It was time to move on.

Nicole moved her suitcase and tote bag from her bedroom just as Cameron rang her doorbell. She glanced at herself in the mirror near the front door. A subtle radiance emanated from her skin, catching the light that seemed to unveil an inner luminosity. It had been a while since she last saw that glow. It was Cameron. Smiling at her newly found lightness, Nicole opened her door to see him, flashing his million-dollar smile, hands in his pockets.

"Do you want to come in? Use the bathroom before we get on the road? Get some water or something?" Nicole asked. She wanted to be polite. However, she was ready to get on the highway. Cameron's scent, the sight of him in his gray sweat shorts and tight white t-shirt hugging his large, firm biceps, made her want to lead him straight to her bedroom, move with feline grace and pounce on him.

Cameron walked inside Nicole's house and shut the door. Giving her an intense gaze, he strolled toward her. Standing only inches away, Cameron placed his hands on her waist, pulling her into him. He looked into her eyes, paused, licked his lips, then kissed her, tugging on her lower lip before licking it. He breathed her in, his tongue entering Nicole's mouth, tasting a minty flavor on hers. Cameron pulled away, only to brush a tender trail of kisses from her mouth to her right ear.

He inhaled a breath, then said, "I'm ready now."

The kiss left Nicole speechless. She couldn't move, planted where she stood. Her face turned flush and warm.

In a low, hoarse tone, Nicole said, "Then let's go."

Nicole settled into her seat inside Cameron's SUV. The plush leather enveloped her back, providing comfort that induced a sense of snugness and coziness. Their estimated time of arrival in Vegas was five hours, fifteen minutes. On their calls, Nicole and Cameron talked nonstop. For the first twenty minutes, though, they rode in silence. It wasn't an awkward silence. It was a tranquil hush that settled between them. Recognizing the songs on the playlist as 80s and 90s R&B, her lips curved into a gentle smile. Nicole shifted silently in her seat just as Cameron reached for her hand.

"I hope you enjoy this playlist. I made it the other day for our ride," Cameron admitted.

Nicole's heart was instantly filled with gratitude at Cameron's thoughtfulness. "I love it. I know the words to every song that's played"

Nicole sat back in her seat and let out a pleasurable sigh. Cameron held her hand for several minutes before bringing it to his lips, brushing a tender soft kiss on her forehand. Nicole dreamingly tapped her foot to the soft melody of D'Angelo's Lady.

"You good, Cameron?" Nicole asked, knowing they had only spoken a little since the start of the car ride.

"Yep! You? Are you hungry?"

"No, I'm good. I may want something when we gas up, though." Nicole appreciated Cameron's attentiveness to her, making sure she was okay.

"In Barstow, there's a place with delicious greasy, cheesy burgers and fries. And milkshakes."

"Oh, that sounds fantastic." Nicole felt her stomach rumbling.

"The show is tomorrow night. I thought tonight we could have a quiet dinner in the hotel. Tomorrow, we can walk the strip, shop, and then head to the concert venue."

"I'm game for all of that." Nicole would be happy as long as she was with Cameron.

They spent the rest of the ride to Barstow enjoying the playlist, Nicole singing to Sade, Nothing can Come Between Us.

"This is one of my favorites by her," Cameron said, swaying to the music.

"I would give anything to see her in concert." Nicole could cross this idea off of her bucket list. "We can go together."

"I'll hold you to that," Cameron said, giving Nicole a wink.

Once in Barstow, Cameron gassed up his SUV. They got cheeseburgers, shared an order of large french fries, and sipped on chocolate milkshakes. When they got to the hotel, Nicole checked in and received a surprise when she learned that Cameron had paid for her room. She couldn't believe his generosity. She made a mental note to give him a thank you gift when they got back to Los Angeles. Their rooms were on the same floor, which made her foster a sense of closeness and security.

"I'm going to freshen up for dinner," Nicole said to Cameron as they stepped out of the elevator. "We're having dinner at six o'clock?"

"Yes, I'll come knock on your door at 5:45." Cameron took Nicole's hand and pulled her in for a kiss on the cheek, then whispered, "I'll see you soon."

Nicole could barely take in a breath as Cameron pulled away from her. She could only manage a subtle cure of her lips, betraying a quiet joy.

When Nicole got into her room, she flopped on the bed and began texting Aubrey.

> **Nicole** - Hey, girl! We're in Vegas. I'm in my room relaxing before we go down to dinner.

Nicole was checking her emails when she noticed Aubrey replied.

> **Aubrey** - Hey! How was the drive?

> **Nicole** - Cool. We stopped in Barstow and had the best burgers and shakes. We listened to music, held hands, and talked.

> **Aubrey** - Ok… I like him for you. Where are you going to have dinner?

> **Nicole** - The restaurant is here in the hotel. It's supposed to have good food and a jazz band.

> **Aubrey** - So… are you wearing the black dress we picked out?

As Nicole began typing a response to Aubrey, a text from Edward came in.

> **Edward** - Hey, Nicole… Long time no talk. I hope you're well. I was thinking maybe we could hang out. I can take you to dinner or something?

Despite Nicole's lack of interest in Edward, she found herself puzzled by his persistent attempts to be with her. She understood how his presence made her feel. His companionship was a blessing and a curse. He offered comfort because of his reminder of Tyler. Yet, he made Nicole angry for his reminder of Tyler. A reminder that Tyler was gone. Edward's continued pursuit remained elusive to her, leaving a sense of confusion. Wasn't her lack of interest clear? She would respond to his text and talk to him next week.

> **Nicole** - Hey, Edward. I'm out of town for the weekend. I'll touch base with you next week.

> **Edward** - Out of town? A pleasure trip? You and Aubrey?

> **Nicole** - I'll reach out to you next week.

Aubrey would be upset with Nicole if she knew Edward was still pursuing her. She had told Nicole if she didn't put him in his place, she would. Nicole had to respond to Aubrey's text.

Nicole and Aubrey exchanged a few more text messages before Nicole put her phone down to close her eyes and rest. Lids shut, she inhaled deeply–not just for air, but a moment of respite. The slow measured breath filled her lungs, a conscious effort to anchor herself in the present. Splashing water and voices of children drowned out the negative thoughts of Edward's constant persistence. Cameron and she were alone in Vegas. Cameron's presence lingered in the corridors of her thoughts, like ethereal visions playing across the canvas of her mind. His image materialized in a series of fleeting snapshots. Cameron's million-dollar smile, his laugh, his thoughtfulness, his kisses. The lingering sensation of his kisses played on her lips like a soft melody of one of their favorite songs. While she was daydreaming, the air conditioner in the room switched on. The gentle brush of air she felt against her lips felt like a ghost of Cameron's affection, a delightful haunting that sparked a symphony of desire.

It was the buzz of Nicole's phone that woke her from a deep sleep. Reaching for her phone on the nightstand, she noticed a text message from Cameron.

Cameron - Our dinner reservation got pushed to 6:30. I hope that's ok.

Nicole panicked, wondering the time. How long did she sleep? Her phone read 5:30.

Nicole - That's fine. Thanks for letting me know. See you soon.

Cameron - smiling emoji

Thank goodness Cameron texted her. Otherwise, she would've had to rush to get ready.

At promptly 6:20, Cameron knocked on Nicole's door. She gave herself an approving smile when she glanced at herself in the mirror. Dressed in a black, fitted, halter dress and high heel black strappy sandals, even she thought she looked sexy. She was thankful she had washed her hair and put it in a bun prior to the drive. With the added product, she had beautiful long curls hanging just past her shoulders.

"Hi," Nicole said, opening the door.

"Hello, WOW! You look amazing," Cameron said, mouth curving to display a huge smile.

"Thank you! Let me grab my purse."

As the elevator descended to the lobby, Cameron and Nicole's hands found solace in each other. Fingers interlocked, creating a tangible connection that exceeded the confines of the small space. When the elevator door opened, the couple waiting to enter the elevator recognized Nicole and Cameron weren't moving. It was the man clearing his throat that brought them out of their gaze.

"Sorry, excuse us," Cameron politely said to the gentleman.

As they exited the elevator, Nicole stood slightly behind Cameron, admiring how sexy he looked in black slacks and a baby blue, long-sleeved button-up with a black jacket. A palpable hush fell over the hotel lobby as they strolled through, an unspoken acknowledgment that all eyes had gravitated toward them.

Once seated at their table, Cameron ordered a bottle of wine for sharing, steak with fresh greens, and potatoes au gratin for Nicole, and the seafood pasta for himself. Conversation over dinner was light and flirty. Nicole was certain her cheeks had remained flushed with color after receiving the compliments from Cameron. They sat at the bar, ordered after dinner cocktails, and watched the band walk over to their instruments to begin their set. A rich melody of smooth jazz blanketed them, filling the air with the rich timbres of saxophone, piano, and subdued percussion. The music quickly became a soothing backdrop, casting a spell of relaxation.

Cameron set his now empty drink on the bar, took Nicole's hand, and asked, "Would you like to dance?"

Nicole took the last sip of her drink and responded, "I would love to."

Cameron led Nicole to the small dance floor and pulled her close, resting his right hand on the small of her back. Streaks of heat spread through Nicole's body, just from Cameron's resting hand. As the notes danced through the air, they swayed to the harmony, the timeless tunes wrapping around them like a comforting embrace. Nicole nestled her face in Cameron's neck, breathing in his clean, spicy scent. With a slight pull back, Cameron and Nicole locked eyes, their lips almost touching as he lowered his head. Cameron moved in to brush a soft kiss on Nicole's lips. Eyes closed, she smiled as he pulled away. Butterflies circled her stomach at the thought of Cameron and his kiss. He was nothing but dreamy.

After dancing, Cameron led Nicole back to the bar. "Do you want another drink?"

Feeling a buzz, Nicole responded, "No, I think I better stop drinking before I embarrass myself."

"Oh?" Cameron said, eyebrows arched upward, sporting a devilish grin. "That sounds like fun."

Giggling, Nicole said, "We should call it a night."

Cameron kissed Nicole on her cheek, put his arm around her shoulders, and slowly let her toward the elevator.

"Thank you for a beautiful evening, Cameron. The food was so delicious. The dancing was the perfect end of the evening."

"It was a perfect evening, huh?" Cameron smiled at Nicole, gazing into her eyes.

Nicole retrieved her room key and faced Cameron. "I would invite you in, but after the wine and drinks, I can't be responsible for what I may do." She flushed.

Cameron's head cocked to the side, his eyes shifting from the ground to her, asking, "Can we take our chances?"

Nicole felt the heat climb up her face and knew she was blushing. "Cameron, I want to. I really do." A desire, unrestrained and fervent, pulsed through Nicole as she entertained the thought of inviting Cameron in her room and to her bed. The allure of shared intimate moments and whispered exchanges echoed within the walls of her mind. His body was tall, firm, and muscular. The way his butt looked in his pants made her want him. The prospect danced in her head like a provocative whisper, kindling flames of anticipation of when they could be intimate.

Cameron pulled Nicole closer, lowered his head and brushed kisses across her jaw, down her neck, then brushed his lips against hers. She looked up at him, her breath catching in her throat. He drew her close again, this time pressing his body against hers, holding her at her hips, and kissed her hungrily. Nicole responded by playfully biting his bottom lip, then gliding her tongue into his mouth. Cameron opened his mouth to receive her tongue, the kiss intensifying in a heated dance of their longing for each other. Cameron pulled away, looking down the hallway, looking to see if anyone was watching them.

In a deep, velvety rich tone, Cameron spoke. "I want to kiss you, hold you, be close to you, Nicole."

Nicole could hear the yearning in his voice. "I want that, too, Cameron. I just need to wait a little while. Is that okay?" Thoughts of the last time she had sex flashed through her mind. It was with Tyler. Cameron was a sexy man, and Nicole wanted him as much as he wanted her. Was it guilt she was feeling at that moment, or fear?

Cameron took Nicole's hands and brought them to his lips, brushing soft kisses on each palm of her hands. "Of course, baby. I'm not going anywhere."

Cameron grabbed Nicole into a tight embrace and hugged her close, kissing her on her forehead. He pulled away, giving her one last kiss on the lips, and said goodnight.

As Nicole's eyes fluttered open, sunlight greeted her, casting a warm and golden glow across her hotel room. It was 7:30, according to the nightstand clock. She reminisced about last night. She had dreamed of Cameron–him coming into her room, them making out, and his hands all over her. As they removed their clothes, she was just enamored by his beautiful, tight, fit body. They reached for each other, entangled in a horizontal embrace. As Cameron adjusted his body to be on top of her, she woke up. That dream made Nicole realize she was ready, and she didn't know how much longer she could wait to have Cameron. She banished fear and guilt away. She wanted that man.

She reached for her phone to call Aubrey.

"Aubrey, oh my goodness, last night was amazing," Nicole screeched.

"Hello to you, Nicole. Did you? You didn't." Aubrey didn't think Nicole was ready to have sex with Cameron.

"No, I didn't, but I felt I could. I was tempted to, but a feeling of caution made me hesitate." Nicole recalled her feelings of guilt and fear overwhelming her.

"Nicole, honey, I know you're scared. You're human. You have feelings, needs. It looks like this man is really into you. He likes you," Aubrey rationalized. Nicole knew she was right.

"He told me he isn't going anywhere," Nicole cheered.

"Do you believe him?" Aubrey asked, wanting to get to the root of Nicole's hesitance.

Her voice was now at a normal level. "Yes, I do." Nicole truly trusted Cameron.

After a moment of contemplation, Aubrey spoke. "Follow your heart. Follow your desires. Cameron's safe. He seems to be what you want."

"I know. Aubrey, I guess I'm just scared. I'll confess, Tyler never crossed my mind last night. So I know it's ok. It's as if I bring thoughts of Tyler into my thoughts on purpose. Did I tell you before I agreed to come to Vegas? It was as if I got the okay from Tyler, like I released him. I agreed to come with no reservations." Nicole left out the part about her reoccurring dreams of Tyler.

"You're ready, Nicole. You'll be fine. Have fun, enjoy your time there. Enjoy Cameron. I gotta go to work this morning. Call me later? I love you, girl."

"I love you, too. Bye."

Feeling better, Nicole began texting Cameron.

Nicole - Good morning!

The three dots on the screen started moving after a few minutes.

Cameron - Good morning! WYD

Nicole - Thinking about last night.

Cameron - Any regrets?

Nicole - A little, but…

Cameron - I'm a patient man, Nicole. I'm really into you. I'm not going anywhere.

Nicole - Thank you.

Cameron - How about we get dressed and get some breakfast? I know another great spot. We can catch a movie or something. Then we can come back and get ready to see Chaka.

Nicole - I love that plan.

Chapter 18

Cameron

Cameron and Nicole headed to the guys' go-to breakfast diner in Vegas. Fluffy pancakes, crispy bacon, perfectly good scrambled eggs, and seasoned hash browns were the main staples of the place. Cameron's extensive knowledge of great places to eat amazed Nicole. He suspected she might consider him a food enthusiast. They wandered along the Las Vegas strip for the rest of the day, captivated by the sights and the lively people. The air was electric with the neon glow of colossal marquees, each competing for attention with a kaleidoscope of colors. The sidewalks were alive with a tapestry of diverse individuals. The giant LED screens flashed with advertisements. Elaborate fountains danced in front of iconic landmarks, and the architecture ranged from modern marvels to replicas of world-famous structures. Cameron even snapped a selfie with Nicole in front of the fake Elvis monument.

Being early September, daylight waned unexpectedly, a gradual descent of darkness taking over earlier than the usual hour. Heavy, dark gray clouds covered the sky. Just as they were about to reach the truck and head back to the hotel, buckets of water poured out of the sky, flooding the ground. Soaked, Nicole and Cameron sat in his SUV and tuned into the news radio for weather updates.

"Yes, ladies and gentlemen, we're experiencing a flash flood," the radio announcer said. "It's September, usually the end of the flooding rain season. We're experiencing a monsoon. The weather reports didn't detect this one. We thought we missed it this year. Warnings are for the entire city of Las Vegas. To ensure safety, authorities have implemented road closures and banned travel outside the city until further communication is shared. Be safe out there."

"Well, luckily we have our rooms and the hotel is only two blocks away," Cameron said, relieved to have accommodations.

Nicole studied her surroundings outside of the car. "I've seen nothing like this before."

Thankful for his big SUV, Cameron drove the two blocks to the hotel. The underground parking was closed, but he found a spot on the top floor. Now drenched, Cameron and Nicole jogged out of the rain into a very crowded lobby filled with soaked guests waiting to check in. While walking to the elevators, Cameron heard Nicole's phone buzzing nonstop. He watched her pull her phone out of her purse to find several missed calls and a few text messages from the hotel. He stood over her as she opened her phone screen to read the text.

Wynn Hotel - Ms. Graham. Please come to the front desk at your earliest convenience. We need to discuss your accommodations.

Nicole looked up from her phone and spoke. "Cameron? I need to go to the front desk. I received this text message," Nicole said, showing Cameron her screen.

"If you have a reservation, please stand in this line. The other lines are to accommodate guests without reservations," the man in the center of the lobby announced. The line for reservations was short, thank good-ness, Cameron thought. He wanted to go back to his room to remove his wet clothes. He believed Nicole wanted to do the same thing. They stepped up to the front desk.

"Hello. I received a text message saying I needed to come to discuss my accommodations," Nicole said with uncertainty.

"Name, please?" the front desk clerk asked.

"Nicole Graham."

With a questioning look on her face, the desk clerk said, "Yes, Ms. Graham. There was a technological glitch in our system and it has wiped your room's reservation. You no longer have your room for tonight."

"What do you mean? I stayed in my room last night. You have to find my reservation," Nicole pleaded.

The desk clerk tapped onto her computer keyboard for several sec-onds, then spoke. "Ms. Graham? I see the problem. Because your room was paid for under a Mr. Davis' credit card, who is also staying at this hotel, our system thought it was a double booking–reserved in error."

Cameron looked at Nicole, then said, "I'm Mr. Davis. How is that relevant? I paid for two rooms."

"Yes, Mr. Davis. I see that. Unfortunately, with the unexpected rush of people searching for accommodations due to the monsoon rain, management swiped the system to find available accommodations for unregistered guests."

"So, what am I supposed to do?" Nicole asked, becoming angry.

"We apologize for this error. We are prepared to offer you a future two-night stay at the Wynn Hotel for your inconvenience."

Nicole inhaled a deep breath. Cameron knew she was trying to find the words to not appear angry. This wasn't the desk clerk's fault. "I still have my personal belongings in the room."

"Yes, we'd appreciate it if you formally check out so we can reserve the room for another guest."

Cameron knew Nicole was seeing red. He knew what was going through her mind. What was she supposed to do? She didn't have a room to herself. Where was she supposed to stay? Just as Cameron saw she was about to show her unpleasant side, he spoke. "Ms. Graham will retrieve her belongings. Can you please send a confirmation email outlining her comped accommodations for a future stay? Thank you."

"Thank you, Mr. Davis. I've sent that email. Can I do anything else to assist you?" the clerk said with a smile.

"No, thank you." Cameron then grabbed Nicole by her waist and led her to the elevators without saying a word. Once inside, he pulled her close and said, "Nicole? I know this is not ideal. We can't leave. The roads are closed. I even wonder if they will cancel the concert. You can stay with me tonight."

Eyes bulged open, Nicole looked into Cameron's eyes and said in a low whisper, "I don't have a choice, do I?"

"No. I'm afraid not. I promise I'll be a gentleman. Please don't worry, okay?" Cameron assured Nicole, taking her into an embrace.

Cameron watched as sweat beads formed on Nicole's forehead, her eyes widening, looking around the hotel lobby. Despite her reluctance, Cameron knew she had to come to terms with sharing a room with him for the night. This was so unexpected. The flash flood canceling her room reservation and sharing a room with Cameron so early in their relationship was a lot to digest. They had been dating for a couple of months. Despite the twists of nerves in his stomach, he met this unexpected adversity with a firm resolve. They were going to be roommates for the night.

Belongings in tow, Nicole stepped inside the large room with an even larger king-sized bed. Cameron walked to the window and looked out-side in disbelief. The water rose along the streets as he witnessed the rain pouring from the sky. Nicole joined him at the window.

"I know this is not what we planned. We'll make the best of it," Cameron said, reaching for Nicole to give her a comforting bear hug.

"Yeah, I know. The saving grace in my mind is that my room will go to a traveler who didn't have a room and they now have refuge for the night." Nicole said. Cameron liked the fact that she was being realistic about the matter.

"That's good thinking," Cameron said, placing a kiss on Nicole's forehead.

Cameron and Nicole rummaged through their travel bags to find dry, comfy clothes to change into. Nicole went first to the bathroom, taking a quick hot shower, changing into a cute cotton lounge shorts with a matching V-neck t-shirt. Cameron went next, showering and changing into a pair of green sweat shorts and a plain black t-shirt.

"You look cute in your lounge wear," Cameron said, giving Nicole a thumbs up.

"Thanks. You, too." They stood for a few seconds, looking at one another. Cameron's phone buzzed on the nightstand. He grabbed it and felt another round of vibrations in his hand. The screen displayed flood warnings and closures of Vegas streets and roads out of town until further notice. He noticed an unread text message.

Legends Entertainment Group - Because of the unforeseen weather, tonight's concert hosting Ms. Chaka Khan is canceled. We will send you a message to notify you of this cancellation, and we will process a refund to the credit card you used to purchase the tickets within forty-eight hours. We apologize for this inconvenience.

Cameron glared at his phone, frowning.

Nicole asked, "What's wrong?"

"Well, for one, we already know the roads are closed. We're stuck here in Vegas until they open the roads," Cameron reminded Nicole.

"And?"

He threw his phone on the bed and stood with his hands on his hips. "The concert is canceled," Cameron said, flopping back onto the edge of the bed.

"Oh no! I was looking forward to seeing Chaka Khan. It figures, though, with the weather." Nicole moved to the edge of the bed and sat next to Cameron, placing her hand on his thigh.

"Me too, babe. I wanted to see Ms. Chaka," he said, placing his hand over hers.

"What should we do for the evening?" Nicole wondered out loud.

Cameron looked around the room to gather his thoughts. "Maybe we can watch a movie?"

"A movie?" Nicole's face lit up. "Okay."

"We can also order room service, listen to the rain," Cameron said, tapping Nicole on her shoulder.

Cameron couldn't help but smile at the thought of being with Nicole for the entire night. He was a man of his word. He was going to be a gentleman. It was going to be really hard, though. Nicole's lounge shorts and t-shirt showed more skin than he was comfortable with. The slight quiver in her gaze illustrated a nervous energy that showed in the depths of her eyes. Cameron knew she wasn't prepared to be alone with him all night, in the same room.

"Are you hungry?" Cameron asked, wanting Nicole to be comfortable.

Nicole rubbed her stomach, then spoke. "The breakfast was delicious and so filling, but I could eat."

"Let's look at the menu. Do you want some wine? We can get a bottle, maybe some appetizers. Or do you want a meal? Or I think we should get some champagne," Cameron suggested.

Nicole gave Cameron a puzzled stare. "Champagne? What are we celebrating?"

"We're celebrating this evening. We're safe, out of the storm, and we have each other's company." Cameron had to think about the positives.

"I like that. We're celebrating. Appetizers sound fun. Do they have a charcuterie board?" Nicole asked.

"They do. They also have BBQ chicken wings. Do you want a salad?"

"Veggies may be a good thing. Can we share the salad?" Nicole suggested.

Cameron placed their room service order, then turned on the television to see what movie services were available. With crossed legs, Nicole sat in the chair next to the bed, appearing unsure of what to do. Just as Cameron thought he figured out how to access Netflix on the television, a loud crack of thunder sounded off, rumbling their room causing the lights to flicker.

"Do hotels have generators?" Nicole wondered.

"They're supposed to. The hotels in California are required to have them. I have to remember we're in Vegas. I'm sure they're required to have them." Cameron continued to mess with the television.

Cameron saw a look of disappointment on Nicole's face as she stared at her phone. "You okay?"

"Yeah, just letting my friend know we're okay. What did you find on television?"

"Not much. You like romantic comedies, right?" Cameron wanted to be accommodating to Nicole given she wasn't totally comfortable staying with him for the night.

"Romantic comedies are my favorite," Nicole said, holding her hands up in the shape of a heart.

"We can watch Sixteen Candles. I've never seen it, but my mom watches it all the time," Cameron offered.

"That's one of my favorites. I've watched it many times with my mom. It's her favorite too. She said it was a very popular movie in the 80s."

"Sixteen Candles it is, then."

Cameron sat up in bed, propped with pillows against his back. He motioned for Nicole to join him. She transitioned from the chair to the bed, arranging extra pillows behind her to near Cameron.

"I don't bite, Nicole. You can come closer," Cameron teased.

Cameron saw a flush of color appear on Nicole's cheeks. He couldn't help but notice how nervous she was. Nicole edged closer to Cameron so their legs were touching. With both of their arms folded, they watched the opening credits of the movie. Cameron felt Nicole relax as the movie played, now leaning her head on his shoulder. By the end of the movie, they were arm in arm, laughing.

Nicole clapped at the ending, turning to Cameron with a huge grin on her face. "I just love that movie. Did you like it?"

"It was cute. Pretty good. You know, I would get you a birthday cake on your birthday." Cameron said, giving Nicole a flirtatious smile.

"Yeah, well, I'll hold you to that."

The knock on the door broke their glances at one another.

"Room service," the voice on the other side of the door said.

"Finally," Nicole said. "I'm starving now."

"Me, too!" Cameron admitted, getting up to open the room door.

The server rolled the table into the room, removed all the silver plate covers, and opened the bottle of champagne, placing it next to two tall flute glasses.

"Enjoy your evening," the server said before exiting the room.

Drinking champagne and enjoying their food, Cameron had an idea. Cameron reached into his bag and pulled out a rectangular block.

"Is that a speaker?" Nicole asked, swallowing her cheese and crackers, picking up a BBQ chicken wing.

"Yep. I always bring it on trips. I like to listen to music when I'm in the room."

"Really? What are we going to listen to?" Nicole curiously asked.

"I'll surprise you." Giving Nicole a sexy smile.

Cameron glanced at Nicole as she went into the bathroom likely to wash BBQ sauce off of her hands. When she exited the bathroom, Sweet Thing, by Chaka Khan blared through the speaker. Cameron held out his hand and reached for Nicole's.

"Dance with me? Instead of going to the concert, I suggest hosting a Chaka Khan concert right here in our room." He hoped Nicole liked this idea.

"Oh, Cameron, this is so sweet. I love it," Nicole said, flashing Cameron her sunbeam smile.

Cameron and Nicole held hands, standing only centimeters apart, swaying to the music. As he held Nicole, he figured the champagne kicked in, her muscles now relaxed, giving him a warm sensation all over his body. Cameron looked at Nicole with simmering heat kindling in the depths of his eyes. To him, she was the epitome of beauty. Singing to the song, Nicole slowly closed her eyes and moved her body to the music. Every sway, twist, and turn became an expression of the melody's grab. Cameron was mesmerized watching her. Her allure was undeniable. She moved with confidence, charisma, with a sensual presence. In her shorts, Cameron could see how toned her legs were. He noticed her sculpted arms the first time they went to dinner. Now holding her close, he felt Nicole's athletic, warm body against his. Sweet Thing ended with I Feel for You following. A more upbeat song. They pulled away from one another and began to actually dance.

"Nice moves, sir," Nicole said, complimenting Cameron's dancing.

"I try, I try." Cameron watched Nicole sway her hips to the music, raising her arms to clap above her head, exposing the skin just above her waistline. He yearned to touch her.

They were having so much fun. The slower tempo of Through the Fire made them stop dancing. This time, Nicole held her hands out for Cameron to come close to her. She pulled him into an embrace, wrapping her arms around his neck, his hands resting on her hips. Amidst wonderful music, food, and champagne, they swayed in a blissful haze. When My Funny Valentine began playing, Cameron was holding Nicole so close, no space between them, yearning to kiss her. They were in their private hotel room, not in the hotel hallway. He began to stroke her back with his hands. Nicole's hands moved up his chest and settled on his biceps. She stroked his arms with a feathering touch. Cameron closed his eyes, cherishing the moment. He kissed the skin behind her ear, slowly working his way down her face and to her neck, tickling it with his breath. Caressing her face, he gently stroked her lower lip with his thumb. His lips now scalded claimed hers. Nicole kissed back, pulling him closer to her, opening her mouth to invite him in, his tongue playing with hers. They both slowly walked toward the bed, with her stumbling back and falling, and Cameron landing on top of her. Pulling away, Cameron gazed down at Nicole, his eyes dark, looking for permission to push boundaries. They had never been so close. They never made out. He kissed her again, eagerly and with a hunger for more. The music stopped, hearing only the sounds of the rain hitting their window, giving

Cameron pause. Without saying a word, Cameron moved to turn the lights out. In the room's dimness, the sporadic flicker of lighting outside became the sole illuminating glow that showed on their faces.

Cameron laid on his side, close to Nicole, gazing into her eyes, using his fingertips to stroke her ankle, all the way up to her upper thigh. Nicole's skin felt ablaze under his touch.

Cameron's hands moved from her upper thigh to her exposed stomach. He drew circles on her stomach, his eyes locked on her dark, longing gaze. His hands crawled up her t-shirt, his thumb stopping at the base of her bra.

"Nicole?" Cameron said in a deep, throaty voice.

"Yes?" Nicole responded, swallowing hard, feeling like she was going to choke.

"I want to explore you. I want to take in every inch of you." Cameron waited. Wanting Nicole to give him permission.

Nicole shifted her body closer to him, likely feeling his hardness against her upper thigh. "I want you, too, Cameron. But—"

Cameron kissed Nicole more passionately, ravenousness with need, lust. She met his kiss and allowed her hands to go under his t-shirt to stroke his back. He didn't know how much longer he could endure her touch without sensing her, penetrating her. He sensed she wasn't ready, so he slowed his pace.

"It's getting late. We should sleep," Cameron said in a sexy whisper.

"Sleep? Okay. If you say so." Nicole seemed relieved at the suggestion of actually sleeping.

Cameron gave Nicole a kiss on her forehead and headed to the bathroom. The bathroom light was extra bright after being in the dark room. He brushed his teeth, splashed his face with cold water, and left the bathroom with an aching sensation in his groin. He wanted Nicole so badly.

She went in after him and brushed her teeth. She exited the bathroom with a face clean of makeup. Her skin was so smooth. She was glowing.

Dressed in a black t-shirt and black boxers, Cameron said, "This is how I sleep most nights. Are you okay with this?" Cameron asked, observing Nicole's quick intake of breath.

"I'm fine," Nicole said softly in a low tone, eyeing his broad shoulders, which tapered down to a trim waist and long, firm legs.

They got into bed in silence. Nicole facing Cameron.

"Thank you for another amazing night. This was so much fun."

"I enjoyed it, too. I guess you can say we had the next best thing to Chaka Khan in person." Cameron chuckled.

"It was perfect," Nicole said, giving Cameron a confident smile.

Nicole reached for Cameron and gave him a long, drawing kiss before saying good night. His last memory was of being nose to nose with Nicole, side by side, sharing breaths.

Chapter 19

Cameron

The flashing and vibration of Cameron's phone alerted him awake. Of all days to forget to turn off his phone alarm. Laying on his side, Cameron tried to roll onto his back, but something stopped his movement. Nicole was in his bed. Her body swaddled him. Her fruity scented curly hair engulfed Cameron. Her back flush against his chest, her soft thighs congealed to his, warm ass snuggled perfectly in his lap. He was suddenly aware of his and Nicole's proximity. His morning erection was now nestled against her butt cheeks. Memories of Nicole dancing to Chaka Khan's sultry voice, swaying her body around him, made his current situation unbearable. He reached to put his arms around her waist, inhaling her scent. Nicole shifted closer, her toned bottom wiggling against his dick.

"Nicole," Cameron softly growled in her ear.

Her hips stirred again, sliding along his length, now rock solid. Cameron flared his fingers on her pillow soft stomach, allowing his fingertips to tenderly graze her ribs. Cameron knew he was risking the words he promised. Yes, he was patient, but he was going to lose his mind if he didn't get to feel Nicole, explore her body, kiss her lips, taste her, feel her. As he pulled her closer, he heard her breath catch.

"Is this okay?" He whispered in her ear, planting a soft kiss against the nape of her neck. Holding his breath awaiting Nicole's answer, he slowly ran his fingers up her stomach, stopping at the brush of her bare breasts. She wasn't wearing a bra. Lord help him. His mind raced with possibilities.

"I thought I was dreaming," Nicole whispered as she gripped his forearm, pushing herself further into him. "But you're real. You're here, next to me," she whispered over her shoulder.

"I'm here, Nicole. I'm very real," Cameron said, teasing the shell of her ear with featherlike kisses. To his surprise, she began rubbing herself against his dick, then moving up and down against him.

"Nicole? If you keep this up, I'll for sure lose it. I won't be very gentlemanly," Cameron hissed.

"Maybe I don't want you to be," she whispered, turning to face Cameron.

Time froze as they lay facing one another. Their gaze into each other's eyes, a silent language, speaking their consent to surrender their bodies to one another.

Whispering in a low, silky voice, Cameron said, "I really like you, Nicole Graham."

Nicole whispered with blushing cheeks, "I like you, too, Cameron Davis."

Cameron seized her lips by the time his heart took another beat. He kissed her tenderly, drawing her close, caressing her back under her t-shirt. Nicole returned his kiss, reaching for his shirt, pulling it up, exposing his six-pack.

She pulled away, looking up to Cameron. "I want to see you," Nicole hummed.

Without saying a word, Cameron reached to pull his shirt over his head, tossing it onto the floor. Nicole's fingertips lightly stroked his pecs, using one finger to trail down to his stomach, stopping at his navel. He let out a sigh, feeling the warmth of her finger dipping near his boxers. He claimed Nicole's lips, sinking into another kiss, this one more deep and passionate. Shifting their bodies, so he was now on top of her, he praised Nicole with kisses across her jaw, down her neck, hands floating over her stomach, then slowly moved up to her breasts.

"Can I take this off?" Cameron asked, tugging on her t-shirt.

In a breathy tone, Nicole said, "Yes, please."

Cameron pulled Nicole's shirt up and over her head, exposing her breasts. Staring down at her, he spilled his hands to cup and knead them. His hands moved to her raised nipples, teasing them with a squeeze. Nicole let out a moan when he took a nipple into his mouth, slightly pulling, then licking it. He dove to kiss her deeply as his hands explored her entire body. Cameron traced his hand gently down the middle of her chest to her navel, planting a sensual kiss in that spot. Fingers tickling around the waistline of Nicole's shorts, he tugged them lower, exposing her hip bone.

"Can these go?" Cameron asked, pulling on her shorts.

Taking in a ragged breath, Nicole consented, "Yes."

Towering over her, Cameron took in the full sight of Nicole's beautiful naked body. His hand moved to the inside of her thighs and spread her legs. Smothering her upper thigh with shallow kisses, he began sprinkling soft touches upward, landing in the folds of her soft, wet pussy. He massaged her clit with his thumb, shifting his body to bury his face and mouth between her legs, to taste her. Nicole cried out as Cameron slowly tongued the inside of her, gently pulling on her clit. She let out a sensual weep, arching her back with each lick and suck. Feeling her body tense, he knew she was close. Her taste, sweet as sugar plums, drove him to near distraction.

"Cameron!" Nicole said with urgency. "I need you inside of me. Please. Now."

Cameron removed his boxers, then, on his knees, gazed at every inch of Nicole's sexy frame. She moved to set herself up on her elbows, scanning his handsome face, to his muscular chest, down to his beautiful, erect, and ready dick. With a devilish grin, she floated her hand against his swollen shaft. The pleasurable look on Cameron's face gave her permission to gently wrap her hand around his circumference. She lightly squeezed his girth, stroking him up and down. He then lowered his body, his dick now nudging her belly. Nicole answered his movement with a hint of a smile before speaking.

"I want you inside of me," Nicole hissed.

Cameron quickly reached for his wallet on the nightstand, taking out a condom.

Nicole announced in a whisper, "I haven't been with anyone for two years. I'm on the pill and was tested about three months ago during my routine exam."

"It's been a year since I've been with someone. I'm tested every six months. I'm clean," Cameron said, rolling on the condom.

With a wicked grin on his face, placing himself on top of Nicole, Cameron said, "We probably should have had this conversation before now."

Chuckling, Nicole said, "Yeah, but better late than never."

Cameron lowered himself onto Nicole, kissing her slowly, pressing inside her, gliding over the spot that made her almost spill over. Taking his cue, Nicole gripped her walls around his manhood. Their bodies entwined in a dance of passion, moving in unison, as if guided by an invisible force. Finally, skin on skin, conveyed a love poem of longing and fulfillment.

Cameron pulled away from Nicole's mouth, moving it to her breast. Still inside her, he flickered his tongue around her nipple, taking it into his mouth, then releasing it in one long pull so it stretched between his teeth.

"Cameron," Nicole sang, grabbing his face, pulling it to hers. She showered his face with soft kisses, hissing into him at the sensation of his long, deep stroke. Wanting more, he lifted his hips and her left leg and drove even deeper inside her. Cameron felt Nicole tightening around him, letting him know she was close.

"Nicole. I feel you, baby. You ready?" Cameron muttered.

Nicole struggled to form words. "Cameron. Yes, yes, yes."

Cameron pushed in and out with rapid motions.

"Nicole, come on, baby, let go." He pressed his mouth against hers, their tongues dancing to the rhythm of his strokes.

"Cameron. Baby." She groaned.

He felt her tighten around him, then shiver. Her moans and convulsions told him she was there. With one deep, long stroke, Cameron let go.

"Nicole," he cried, releasing into her.

The mutual surrender between them created an unparalleled connection, the most intimate exchange he had ever known. Time stood still, echoing the pleasure they both experienced, blurring all boundaries set by Cameron and Nicole as single, unattached people.

"Nicole?"

"Yeah?"

"I want us to be exclusive. I only want to be with you." Cameron needed this woman to be his.

With a smile in her voice, Nicole answered, "I want that, too."

Chapter 20

Nicole

The drive back to Los Angeles was blissful. Cameron and Nicole couldn't keep their hands off each other. The fear and guilt Nicole felt before this morning was not in their bed. Sex with Cameron was mind-blowing. They held their hands palm to palm for most of the drive. Nicole kissed Cameron on his cheek and held his arm. He reached over the console to kiss her soft, sensual lips. They stopped in Barstow for gas, then got food to eat during their drive. Nicole wanted to learn everything she didn't already know about Cameron. Including what happened during his past relationships. She was cognizant of the fact that he had a former girlfriend and their breakup was a year ago.

"Cameron?" Nicole was aware that after this morning, now was a good time to inquire about his previous relationship.

"Nicole?" He said, grabbing her hand and kissing it.

"If you don't mind me asking, what happened in your previous relationship? We talk about everything, but we haven't talked about that."

"Well?" Cameron cleared his throat. "We were together and then we weren't. I held a stronger belief about the seriousness of our relationship than she did. We grew apart. And it ended."

"Oh." Nicole wanted more details, but his tone told her that was all he was going to share.

"You?" Cameron asked. "What happened in your last relationship?"

Nicole inhaled an audible breath then said, "I was in a relationship for three years. Like you, I thought the relationship would last, but it didn't. Before you, I went on dates, but nothing serious." Nicole couldn't bring herself to say Tyler died. Killed on the job. This morning was so amazing. It didn't seem right to tell the whole truth. Not at this moment.

"Nicole, you okay?" Cameron saw a sudden flicker of sadness in her eyes.

Not realizing she was lost in her own thoughts, Nicole looked at Cameron with a devilish smile. "So, what are we doing, besides just getting started in this new relationship?"

"I think we're just getting started with something amazing," Cameron said with an assertion. He then reached over and gave Nicole a lingering kiss. The best he could do while driving.

Cameron was on shift for most of the next week. Nicole helped Aubrey prepare for the restaurant opening, which would be in two weeks. Typing out her grandmother's recipes brought Nicole a sensation of peace, which settled her desire to see Cameron. They talked every night on video chat. Butterflies swam in her stomach each time she waited for him to appear on camera. Her cheeks blushed when he greeted her with a "hello, beautiful." She heard the passion in his words. The wanting of her in his throaty tone when he described how he wanted to kiss her, feel her, touch her, hold her so close he could feel her heartbeat next to his. Her stomach did somersaults at the thought of him holding her. Seeing his face only made her miss him more. She yearned to feel his touch, his kisses. She wanted to be wrapped all around him. The warmth between her thighs, aching for him, was something she had never experienced. Recalling the morning in Vegas only made her hunger for his hands to be all over her, kissing every inch of her. She wanted to smother Cameron with kisses, run her tongue over his most sensual and sensitive areas, hear him groan with desire.

By Friday morning, Nicole was on pins and needles with anticipation, preparing for Cameron to come over. She spent the morning trying to work on her laptop. Cameron's face kept appearing on her screen, blowing her kisses, distracting her from writing the article that was due in a few days. Descriptive words of the delicious food she had when she visited the restaurant inside the new hotel in Santa Monica turned into soft porn, thinking about Cameron. By noon, Nicole had had enough of the multiple edits and called it a day. She could come back to this article on Sunday when Cameron had to go back to the station. The aroma of chocolate chip pound cake filled the kitchen. As she drizzled a sugar glaze down the cooled cake, Nicole imagined splashing Cameron's naked body with the icing, enjoying every minute it would take to lick him clean.

"Nicole, get it together," she whispered, fanning herself.

After showering and changing into a fitted black crop t-shirt and black cotton full legged pants, hair in a high bun, Nicole turned on her surround sound speakers and played her Sade playlist. Cameron wasn't expected for another ninety minutes. Just as Nicole dropped the first batch of chicken into the cast-iron skillet, she heard her phone buzz with an incoming text message.

> **Cameron** - I can't wait to see you. I'm leaving the station now and heading to your house. Can I shower there?

> **Nicole** - Oh, wow! Now? I just started dinner. Umm, ok, you can come over.

> **Cameron** - I hope I'm not being too aggressive. I want to see you.

> **Nicole** - I want to see you, too.

Cameron rang the doorbell thirty minutes later, dressed in sweats and a hoodie. God, he was sexy, Nicole thought as she greeted him with a quick kiss on his lips.

"Hi, beautiful. I would hug you, but I want to shower first. Is that okay?" Cameron said, flashing a questionable smile.

"Sure. The bathroom is down the hall and to your right. There are towels in the hall closet."

"My goodness, is that dinner I smell? Fried chicken?" Cameron said, inhaling the aroma filled room.

"Yep, I hope you like it." Nicole couldn't think of anyone who didn't like this southern classic.

"Fried chicken is one of my favorites. My grandfather made it best." Cameron grinned, ready to tease Nicole..

"Well, I hope I do him justice. Although I've been told I make it best," Nicole said, giving Cameron a wink.

Planting a kiss on Nicole's cheek, he said, "Be right back."

Twenty minutes later, Cameron stood in the doorway of Nicole's kitchen, dressed in black sweats that hung low on his hips and a black t-shirt. With his arms crossed, a pleasing smile on his face, Nicole could see Cameron watching her. "Hey, you! Dinner will be ready in about thirty minutes. Would you like a glass of wine?" Nicole offered.

"Yeah, but first..." Cameron gave Nicole a hug from behind. His arms wrapped around her waist, he lowered his head and brushed kisses along her neck. The lingering scent of his freshly showered skin filled her, making his proximity a sensory experience. She lay her head back against his chest and closed her eyes, enjoying his lips against her skin. Cameron shifted her body so they were facing one another. He gazed into her eyes, lifted her chin and planted a soft, yet intense, kiss on her lips. Feeling intense heat, Nicole pulled away before she combusted.

Cheeks flushed with heat from the kiss, Nicole said, "I want to finish cooking dinner. You keep that up and we won't eat."

Cameron knelt down to whisper in her ear, "That wouldn't be a bad thing. But I'm hungry, for food, too."

Nicole withdrew from their embrace, a playful smile tugging at the corners of her lips. Eyes filled with a mischievous glint met his, both erupting into laughter. Her heart skipped a beat as he flashed her his million-dollar smile.

Cameron sipped on a glass of wine and watched Nicole finish cooking. "Can I help you with anything?"

Nicole turned her head to glance over her shoulder and said, "No. I want to serve you. Relax."

"My upcoming four day shift is extra." Cameron admitted.

"Why work an extra shift?" Nicole knew this meant she wouldn't see Cameron for a week.

"For one, I'm helping David out. He's taking his wife on a mini-vacation. You remember her? She's the painter."

"That's nice of you. I have to admit. I'll miss you." Nicole couldn't hold how she felt. "I'll keep busy with work then."

"I'll miss you too, babe. We'll still talk every day. I wouldn't be able to stand it if we didn't do at least that," Cameron admitted.

"You want to help me with the plates?" Nicole asked, holding a filled salad bowl with arugula, shaved radishes, diced tomatoes, and carrots tossed in a light vinaigrette dressing.

"Sure," Cameron said, grabbing the platter of hot fried chicken and the enormous bowl of garlic mashed potatoes. "Your chicken is like an image out of a magazine. I can't wait to taste it."

"I hope you like it," Nicole said, knowing he would. Everyone loved her fried chicken.

"Are you sure you don't want to snap a picture? The puddles of butter on top of the garlic mashed potatoes and the colorful salad are picture worthy," Cameron said. "My stomach is growling, just taking in the savory scent of this meal."

Nicole watched Cameron take his first bite of his chicken breast. Eyes wide and dancing with pleasure, he said, "Nicole? This is better than my grandfather's fried chicken. I think I'm going to stuff myself."

Taking a bite of her chicken wing, Nicole responded, "I'm glad you like it."

"Where did you learn to cook?" Cameron asked, taking a bite of a fork full of potatoes.

"My grandmother. I always hung around her kitchen when I was little. She saw I had an interest and so she began showing me how to make things. What ingredient paired with what. Cooking became a hobby." Nicole grinned at the memory of cooking for her parents for the first time. Some things were over cooked, some things under cooked but they congratulated her on a great effort.

"Is that how you and your friend met? Cooking?" Cameron asked with a mouth full of salad.

"My friend Aubrey? No, we went to high school together. I guess you can say we bonded over food, then became inseparable. We've shared secrets, life long desires. We still do." Nicole surveyed the table. This meal would make Aubrey proud.

"Well, I'm a happy man to be eating this delicious meal."

Nicole and Cameron shared childhood food stories over the rest of their meal. Nicole was stopped mid sentence by her ringing phone. "Excuse me. Let me see who that is," she said, grabbing her phone from the kitchen counter. Levi's face flashed across her screen as she swiped to accept the call.

"Hi, Levi!"

"Hey, what you doing tonight? Come out with me to this new dinner and jazz spot."

"I can't, hun. Cameron's over for dinner."

"Cameron? Oh... Cameron! The new guy. What'd you cook?"

"Fried chicken, garlic mashed potatoes and a chocolate chip pound cake."

"Can I come get some?"

"No, you cannot. I will save you some. Maybe. Goodnight, Levi. Love you."

Cameron raised his eyes from his plate, his face showing confusion at the love you sentiment at the end of the call.

"My brother. I had to stop him from coming right now to get a plate." Nicole knew by the questioned expression on Cameron's face he had more questions.

"Your brother? Levi is his name?" Cameron asked.

"Yes. Levi, my younger brother, four years younger, to be exact." Nicole could never understand why the brother-sister relationship fascinated significant others.

"Are you two close?" Cameron wondered.

"Yes, very close." Levi was Nicole's other best friend. Cameron would have to be okay with that.

"I don't have siblings, but you know that already."

Nicole sensed Cameron was relieved to know the caller was her brother. Their relationship was new, so there was so much they needed to learn about one another. Was Cameron jealous? She knew he had nothing to worry about. She fell into bed with Cameron, with no thought of Tyler. This told her she had a strong fondness for him.

After dinner, Cameron helped Nicole put the food away and wash the dishes. She sliced pieces of cake and put them onto dessert plates. They walked into the living room with cake and a glass of dessert wine.

"Do you want to watch a movie or something?" Nicole asked.

"I enjoy sitting here, listening to music, and being close to you," Cameron said as he sat on the couch next to Nicole.

"Did you enjoy your meal?" Nicole asked, taking the first bite of cake.

"Did I enjoy my meal? That is the understatement of the day. I loved my meal. And I have to take some leftovers home," Cameron said, sipping his wine. "Thank you."

The sweet melody of the Love Jones soundtrack played as Nicole and Cameron finished their cake and a glass of wine.

"You know, this is another romantic movie I enjoyed," Nicole shared, stroking her fingers up and down Cameron's thigh.

Holding Nicole by the waist, drawing her in, caressing the curve of her face before responding, "Oh, yeah? I saw that movie. A good one. He made eggs for her the morning after. Do you want me to make you eggs in the morning?"

Nicole's eyes grew dark, lusting to feel his lips on hers, then said, "Does this mean you are staying over?"

"I wouldn't have it any other way, Ms. Graham," Cameron said, dipping his head to give her a heated kiss.

"Mr. Davis. I like the way you think." Nicole interlocked her fingers with Cameron and walked ahead, leading him into her bedroom. Glancing over her shoulder, she gave him a seductive smile. She stood in front of Cameron, his legs at the base of her bed. She lifted his t-shirt, pulling it over his head, and tossed it on the floor. She gave him a soft push, him landing on her crisp white super soft sheets and fluffed pillows.

"Your sheets feel amazing," Cameron said in a soft, sultry voice.

With a devilish grin, Nicole climbed on top of Cameron and straddled him.

His dark stare landed on hers. "God, you're beautiful."

Nicole didn't say a word. She knelt to kiss Cameron, long and deep. He reached for her shirt and pulled it over her head, cupping her breasts, as she moved her hips on him. Cameron's smile shone white as he unlocked her bra, then taking a nipple into his mouth. Heat rushed Nicole's face as she whimpered at the sensation of Cameron tugging on her tip before releasing it with a pop sound. She shifted her body to allow herself to tug his pants down his legs and off. She gazed down, smiling at his erection straining the fabric of his boxers.

"These have to go, too," Nicole demanded.

"Take them off," Cameron ordered.

Nicole seductively pulled his boxers down and licked her lips as she gave Cameron a wanting look. She then moved her attention to his crown, diving in to give it a succulent lick before taking him into her mouth. A hot, searing bolt of pleasure struck through her as she stroked him. Cameron let out a low growl as he wrapped his fingers in her hair. When Nicole felt him pulsing, she slowed her suck to run her tongue up and down his shaft.

"Baby? Come here," Cameron whispered as he pulled Nicole up to meet his gaze. Her smile coaxed him to touch her. He sat up and flipped Nicole onto her back, shimmering off her pants and lacy panties. He planted kisses on each inner thigh as he stroked her moist folds.

"You're all wet for me," Cameron whispered. "I'm going to take care of that."

"Cameron, please. I want to feel you." Nicole whimpered.

He drew in a sharp breath as need stabbed him. He slowly entered Nicole. With each stroke, Nicole relished in the sensation of Cameron moving inside of her. She wrapped her legs around his hips and took in all of him. Nicole pulled him in, panting as her release was near. "I'm coming, Cameron." The urge to burst was overwhelming. He kissed her mouth, taking the kiss deeper, overwhelmed by the sensation of being inside Nicole.

"Let's come together. Can we do that?" Cameron whispered in Nicole's ear as he thrusted in quickly, with an urgency that sent her over the edge. Seconds later, bodies damp with sweat, they both succumbed to their climax. Cameron's soulful eyes studied Nicole with an intensity that made her skin melt. They slowly rocked their hips in ecstasy, allowing their breathing to return to normal. They lay in that position for a while, in silence, listening to each other's heartbeats.

Cameron was the first to move, going into the bathroom to clean up. Nicole lay in her bed, staring up at the ceiling, succumbing to her feeling of pure bliss.

Nicole woke up to feel Cameron's arm around her, his fingertips lightly brushing over her stomach as he breathed. She could lie like this all day. The flashing of her phone on her nightstand broke her thoughts of last night and how amazing it was, making love to Cameron in her bed. They fit. She knew Aubrey was dying to know how it went last night. Nicole glanced over at Cameron. He looked so peaceful when he slept. She slowly slipped from under his arm, got out of bed, and headed to the bathroom. She dressed in a cotton nighty and matching rope, brushed her teeth and went into the kitchen to start some coffee. It was 7:30 in the morning. And why did Aubrey want to talk this early? She picked up her phone and dialed Aubrey back.

"Hi, Aubrey!"

"Don't 'hi' me, young lady. How was it? Spill it."

"Amazing! Just amazing!" Nicole thought she needed to find another word.

"Was the meal good? Of course it was. Why am I asking that? You can cook."

"Everything came out perfect. He loved it."

"Well, you learned from the best. I would like to think I had something to do with it, too."

"Of course you did."

Nicole shared the details of last night in a whisper when her doorbell rang.

"Aubrey, let me call you back. Someone's at my door."

Nicole hung up the phone, walked to her door, and looked out her window to see Edward standing on her porch. She didn't know what he was doing ringing her bell this early, unannounced. She opened the door to greet him when he pushed through the door.

"Hello to you, too, Edward. What are you doing here so early? You should've called."

"I've been trying to catch you for weeks. You don't return my calls and always tell me you're busy when I text you. What's up?" Edward had the nerve to be angry.

"What's up? What I do is none of your business. I don't have to answer you. Why are you acting so attached? We aren't together. We never were together. We're just friends. That's all we will be." Nicole's fists clenched at her sides, her jaw tightened at the audacity of Edward showing up, accusing her of nothing.

Edward stood for a few seconds, looking at Nicole with a longing look of hurt and confusion. "Who's SUV is parked in your driveway?"

"Mine!" Cameron said, standing in the archway connecting the living and dining room area to the hallway, bare chested, wearing gray sweatpants. Arms now crossed, Nicole turned to Cameron, then Edward, watching Cameron's jaw twitch. He was sexy when he was angry.

"Who are you?" Edward asked.

"You don't have the right to ask who he is, but since you want to know, Edward, this is Cameron, my boyfriend. Cameron, this is Edward."

Neither man gestured to shake hands. They glared at one another. Cameron walked to stand behind Nicole, hands resting on her shoulders.

"Edward, you need to leave. Cameron is my guest, and you came here without calling. You're out of line." Nicole was furious. She was sure steam was escaping her head.

Edward looked away, then down at the ground for a few seconds. He gave Cameron a once over, looked at Nicole, then left. Nicole closed the door and stared at it for a few seconds. She turned to Cameron and was about to speak when he asked, "Who is he to you?"

Chapter 21

Cameron

After Edward left, Nicole gave Cameron a crooked smile, grabbed his hand, and pulled him into the kitchen. For several minutes, neither of them said a word. Nicole grabbed two coffee mugs from the cabinet.

"Coffee?" Nicole asked.

"Sure," Cameron said in a soft voice.

Nicole sat cream and sugar on the table with their filled mugs. Before saying anything, she added a spoonful of sugar and some cream to her coffee. She saw Cameron giving her an indiscernible gaze as she sipped her coffee.

With her hand resting on top of Cameron's, a smile appeared on Nicole's face as she spoke. "I want to clarify that Edward is only a friend. Nothing else. He's always been a friend."

Lips drawn in a thin line, Cameron asked, "He just comes over, unannounced?"

"Yes, this isn't the first time. I believe he wants more than a friendship, but I'm not interested. Never have been."

Cameron saw the sincerity in Nicole's eyes. "Did you tell him this?"

"I tell him all the time."

"Nicole, I really like you. I think you know that. I don't want to interrupt anything you have going on with Edward." Cameron felt his unresolved issues surfacing. Cheating was not something he could stand. Not even from Nicole.

"There's nothing going on between us. I promise." Nicole began drawing circles on Cameron's hand.

Cameron needed to put his feelings on the line. "We've only dated a few months. I feel like I know you really well. Well, enough to admit when I said I didn't want to see anyone else but you, I meant it. I want us to be exclusive."

Nicole looked at Cameron with warm eyes, smiling from ear to ear. "We are exclusive. We sealed that fact in Vegas."

Cameron returned the warm smile, grabbing Nicole's hand, and kissed the inside of her palm. He looked at her again, this time standing, drawing her close to him. Their hands intertwined, hanging by their sides. Cameron reached down and gave Nicole a soft kiss. The kiss grew in intensity, one filled with passion and want. He pulled her by her hand and led her into her bedroom.

Late in the afternoon, Cameron left Nicole's house feeling full. Ignoring the morning's introduction to Edward, he made a point to only focus on enjoying his remaining time with Nicole before he had to leave to go to work. They ate delicious leftovers and spent the rest of the day in a haze of lovemaking. He waved goodbye to his girlfriend from his SUV and pulled out of her driveway. Cameron didn't want his trust issues to ruin what was just getting started. Nicole was beautiful, kind, and they fit. It happened quickly. Edward's presence wasn't a cause for argument, but clarity. Cameron repeated this to himself. He believed Nicole when she said Edward was only a friend.

Cameron's place seemed empty and cold compared to Nicole's house. He placed his delicious food she prepared for him in his refrigerator, suddenly feeling restless. A wave of appreciation came over him, thinking of her. He pulled his phone out of his pocket to send her a text.

Cameron - Hey! I miss you already.

Her phone must've been nearby. Her response came within seconds.

Nicole - Hey, you! I miss you, too. WYD

Cameron - Sitting on my couch. Thinking about you. WYD

Nicole - In the bathtub.

Cameron - Oh yeah? Can I join you? I left too soon.

He closed his eyes, envisioning being there with Nicole, splashing together in the hot, soapy water.

Nicole - I wish you were here.

Cameron - I'll dream of you tonight.

Nicole - You know what, I've never been inside of your place. I want to know where you sleep.

Cameron - We'll have to fix that.

Nicole - I can plan our next date if that is ok?

Cameron - Do we call them dates anymore?

Nicole - huh?

Cameron - Nicole? You're now my girlfriend.

Nicole - Yes, yes I am, huh? And you're my boyfriend. We sound like we're in high school. LOL!

Cameron - Like we're in high school, I'm dedicating this song to you.

Cameron - Luther Vandross If Only for One Night

A few minutes passed before Nicole responded.

Nicole - If only for one night? What if I want more?

Cameron - You can have all my nights, Nicole.

Cameron - My grandfather used to say this was grown folks' music. Music for the grown and sexy.

Nicole - We are grown and you are very sexy.

> **Nicole** - This song will forever remind me of you and your first dedication to me.

> **Nicole** - hang on, I'm going to get out of the bathtub

> **Cameron** - Can I watch?

Five minutes later, his phone was ringing with an incoming FaceTime request. When her face appeared on the screen, he took a deep sigh.

"Hello, beautiful."

"Hi!" Nicole was on his phone screen, under her covers, face lying on her pillow.

"You look cozy. You're in bed already."

"I am. I wish you were here. I smell you on my sheets."

"Is that right?" Cameron said, making a mental note to get Nicole in his bed so he could smell her scent on his sheets.

Yawning, Cameron said, "I wish I was there, too."

"We're both tired. We had a busy day," Nicole said with a wink. "My eyes are heavy, so I'm going to sleep, okay?"

"Goodnight, beautiful. We'll talk tomorrow?"

"Yes. Goodnight, Cameron."

Cameron went into his bedroom and flopped on his bed. Knowing he had to be at work soon. He looked up at the ceiling, replaying his time with Nicole. He knew in that instant he was falling.

Since Cameron wouldn't see Nicole until Saturday, he used his unusual Friday night off to catch up with his boys. Terrell was playing in Dallas, so they all agreed to meet at their usual gathering spot.

"What's up, man?" Josh said as he stood and pulled Cameron into a bear hug.

"Where've you been, man?" Ryan asked.

"Just working, spending time with Nicole," Cameron replied, trying not to blush.

"Nicole?" the guys said in unison.

"Who's Nicole, and why have you kept her a secret?" asked Ryan.

"No secret. We all know how it is at the start of relationships. You'll meet her soon."

"Cameron, in a new relationship. I never thought I would see this day. You were done with relationships after Shannon," Ryan commented.

"It didn't work out, so I chilled for a minute. But when I met Nicole, everything changed."

"I'm happy for you, man. I'll keep playing the field for now," Ryan said with a wink.

"Thanks, I'm happy, too." Cameron said, adoringly thinking of Nicole.

"Look at you, blushing," Josh said in shock.

Filled with joy, Cameron said, "She's pretty great. Enough about me, how are y'all doing? Did you order our usual?"

Cameron spent the rest of the night catching up with his friends. Terrell won his game and FaceTimed the guys from the locker room. Myles talked about wedding planning. Josh had become a partner at his architectural firm. Ryan, as always, was Ryan. Cameron enjoyed spending time with the guys, but he missed Nicole. Halfway through the evening, watching the game, his mind was wondering what Nicole was doing.

On Saturday, the plan was for Nicole to pick Cameron up at his house and drive to their 5pm reservation. Dressed and waiting on the couch,

Cameron felt nervous. He scanned his living room and kitchen area to make sure it was clean. He got up to check his bedroom when his phone rang. Nicole's face flashed on the screen.

"Hey, are you close by?"

"Hey. I ran into some traffic. Can you meet me downstairs? I won't have time to come up."

"I'll be right down."

Nicole and Cameron entered the escape room lobby seven minutes before five. While in line waiting to be checked in, Cameron noticed someone he didn't want to see in front of him and Nicole.

"Hey, Cameron," she said, glancing from him to Nicole and back at Cameron.

"Hey, Denise. How are you?" Cameron said, interlocking his hand with Nicole's.

"I'm good. It looks like you're doing well," Denise said, looking directly at Nicole as she spoke. "Who's your friend?"

"Denise, this is my girlfriend, Nicole. Nicole, this is Denise," Cameron said, feeling a rush of irritation storming through his body. He never cared for Denise.

"Nice to meet you," Nicole said, giving Denise a curt smile.

Denise gave Nicole a once over and smiled.

Denise bluntly asked, "Have you talked to Shannon? You know she's engaged, right?"

"Yes, I heard that. I hope she's happy." Cameron wanted this awkward conversation to be over.

"Well, you know—" Denise added. Before she could say anything else, the guy at the front signaled the line to move.

Giving Cameron and Nicole a smile that didn't reach her eyes, Denise said, "That's my cue to say goodbye. You two have fun."

"You, too." Cameron responded, waiting for Denise to get out of earshot.

"Who was that?" Nicole whispered in Cameron's ear.

Cameron said in a wicked tone, "That was my ex-girlfriend's nosey friend."

"Well, she wasn't too happy to see you with me," Nicole concluded.

"She can kick rocks." Cameron didn't want Nicole to be worried about Denise. She was all hot air.

Nicole curiously asked, "Your ex-girlfriend is engaged?"

"Yep." Cameron didn't want Nicole to detect his irritation over Shannon. He didn't want Nicole to pry into his and Shannon's relationship. Shannon cheated. That was the ultimate betrayal. He pushed thoughts of Shannon and Denise into the back of his mind. He was with his girl. Nicole. He pulled her close and whispered, "I'm happy we're together." Then gave a quick kiss on the lips.

"Next," the attendant directed.

Cameron and Nicole stepped up to the front counter.

"We have a five o'clock reservation. Cameron and Nicole," she shared.

"Yes, I see you on the list. There's only one room left at the moment. Do you care what the puzzle is?"

Nicole spoke up. "No, we don't care."

"Here is the scenario. You hijack an armored truck and drive it to a secret location. The authorities are aware of the stolen truck and are closing in on your location. You want to keep the millions hidden in the truck. Time is ticking, as you must extract the money before the cops find you. Do you have questions?"

"We got it," Nicole said excitedly.

The attendant led Cameron and Nicole into a room. At its center was an armored truck. "The money is inside the truck. Find the money by deciphering the clues on the truck walls. If you find the money, you are to exit the truck and announce you found it. If you find the money, you win the game. You have thirty minutes."

"Okay!" Cameron said.

"Good luck," the attendant said, exiting the room.

Cameron and Nicole scanned the truck for a starting point.

"Under the driver's side visor, there's a paper with a riddle on it. This may be the first clue," Nicole said, reaching to retrieve the note.

"Let me read it," Cameron said, standing over Nicole.

"Name three consecutive days without naming Wednesday, Friday, or Sunday. Record your answer into the walkie-talkie. If your answer is correct, the glove compartment will open, revealing your next clue."

"Cameron, what does this mean? Think. Three days in a row that are not Wednesday, Friday, or Sunday."

Five minutes passed before Cameron had an answer. "Three consecutive days have to be yesterday, today, and tomorrow."

Nicole grabbed the walkie-talkie and recorded the answer. Within one second, the glove compartment flew open, revealing what looked to be a box with a combination lock attached.

"Where are the clues to get the lock combination?" Nicole asked as she shuffled through the glove compartment. "Here is the clue," she said, holding up a black piece of paper with numbers written in white ink.

Cameron took the note and read it. "These numbers are bound in a progression when written. It may come into view. The rule they follow is in question. The next set of numbers in three will open the lock."

"Ok, 1, 4, 7, 11, 15, 19, 21. Do you see a pattern, babe?" Cameron asked.

"I was never good at math. Let me see." Nicole studied the numbers, looking up to the ceiling, mentally making calculations. "2, 6, 10? No, that's not it."

"Try 3, 10, and 4," Cameron suggested.

Nicole put in the three numbers Cameron suggested and pulled on the lock. "That pattern doesn't work. Do you have another pattern? How much time do we have? We have a couple more clues until we locate the money."

Nicole looked up at the digital timer, which read five minutes. "I think I got it. We have been trying to figure out the numbers between each one. We have to name the three numbers that come after 21. Enter 24, 27,and 31."

"It opened. You are a genius," Cameron said, reaching to kiss Nicole. "What's in the box?"

"It's a key. Where does the key go? What does it open?"

Cameron and Nicole turned to look toward the back of the truck. There were three tall lockers that stood in front of the back seat, with an envelope taped to the middle one.

"We just can't go around, huh?" Nicole wondered.

"No. It's likely we have to find which one we need to open. Opening the right one will lead us to the back of the truck."

Cameron opened the envelope to read the riddle. "In each locker is something deadly. Only one locker will give you entrance to the back seat where the money is hidden. Which locker do you open? If you select the wrong locker, the game is over. One locker is wired to set a gun off when it opens. Locker two will ignite an explosive once opened. Locker three will release death stalker scorpions who haven't eaten in 8 years. Which locker do you open?"

"What do you think, Cameron?" Nicole wondered. She knew you can't survive a gunshot or an explosive. "I say we take our chances with the scorpions."

Cameron looked at the clock. They had two minutes.

"Locker three it is." Cameron reached out and opened locker three to reveal the back seat of the truck.

"Where are the scorpions?" Nicole asked.

"The note taped inside says the scorpions only live about five years. They're dead." Cameron laughed.

"Let's go to the back and find the money," Nicole suggested, rushing to the back seat, feeling underneath for a bag or briefcase.

"Where's the money?" Cameron began feeling the walls around them for a clue. As he glanced upwards, he spotted a gray bag seamlessly blending with the truck's ceiling. "I found it."

Immediately upon touching the bag, Cameron set off sirens, and a booming voice made an announcement. "You have escaped the police and are now safe to keep the money. Congratulations."

"We won," Cameron said, reaching for Nicole to give her a hug. "That was really fun," Cameron said.

"Of course it was fun for you. You knew how to navigate the clues. My brain doesn't work like that," Nicole said with a chuckle.

"Are you hungry?" Cameron asked as they left the escape room building.

"Yes," Nicole said, eyes shining with wonder.

"Want a really good grilled cheese sandwich and a beer?" Cameron asked.

"That sounds amazing. Let me guess: you know a spot."

Nicole drove in silence to Cameron's condo. He knew something was on her mind. They enjoyed the escape room. Dinner was superb. She gripped the steering wheel of her car, an intense expression etched across her face. She turned to him at a stoplight.

"Cameron? Can I share an observation?" Here it comes. Cameron knew something was up.

"Sure," he anticipated her question. Denise. She was likely thinking about our exchange.

"The few words you and Denise exchanged were really cold. I know she isn't Shannon, but I get the feeling things didn't end well with your ex-girlfriend," Nicole calmly shared.

Cameron gave little detail about his and Shannon's relationship. The brief conversation was stiff and bordered on rude. Did he have to explain his history with Shannon? Revealing she cheated on him, which was the reason they broke up? The breakup may have caused him to develop trust issues. He didn't like to talk about it or anything else complex. Cameron knew he would have to say something at some point. It was only fair. He would have to communicate if he wanted his relationship with Nicole to work.

"No, my relationship with Shannon didn't end well. It was for the best. Shannon and I breaking up led me to be here with you. Our beginning has been wonderful, and I look forward to our future. Us is all that matters." Nicole's smile unveiled a sense of relief, mirroring the same sentiment. The start of their relationship has been amazing.

Cameron exited the car and waited for Nicole at the curb. Before she could step up to meet him, he reached for her, pulling her into him. He gently cupped her face, locking eyes with an intensity that spoke volumes. The kiss that followed was filled with purpose and passion, a deep connection conveyed through each deliberate and tender touch of their lips.

They walked arm in arm into Cameron's building, rode the elevator to his floor, then stood outside his door. Cameron inhaled a deep breath, then turned to Nicole and said, "Now, I'm a single guy who doesn't decorate or take time to make my place mirror Architecture Magazine, but it's me. Don't judge."

Nicole stepped in, mouth agape as she observed his living space. "Wow, Cameron, this place is amazing! I love the wall to wall windows that overlook the city. The view is breathtaking. The lights around the city make it so romantic."

"I bought this place when the building was brand new. I couldn't afford what the asking price would be today. It was an excellent investment. I'm glad you like it." Cameron felt proud Nicole liked his place. He hoped she would spend a lot of time there.

The living room was spacious, including a large sectional couch which backed a few of the large windows, a marble table and a big screen television mounted on the wall. His DJ equipment sat in the corner of one side of the space.

"Do you cook in this beautiful kitchen?" Nicole asked as she ran her hand over the white marble countertops.

"Very little. Although I was thinking of inviting you over for dinner."

"Were you going to cook for me?" Nicole asked, giving Cameron a shy grin.

"That's the plan," he said, having no idea what he would cook.

Nicole and Cameron settled on his couch, stuffed and mentally drained from using all that brainpower to escape the armored truck with the millions of dollars. Cameron moved closer to Nicole and put his arm around her, pulling her into a casual but sensual kiss.

"Did you enjoy tonight?" Cameron whispered.

"I did," Nicole said, giving him an alluring stare.

"I have a treat for you," Cameron said, getting up from the couch and moving toward his DJ equipment. Giddy in his step, he said, "I have a dedication." Cameron turned on the equipment and his laptop. "Let's see." Since his record collection was limited, Cameron scrolled through his playlists to find the perfect song. Nicole appeared to wait with bated breath until she heard the beginning sounds of Joy, by Blackstreet.

"Aw, Cameron, this is a good one. You dedicate this song to me?" Nicole stood and began swaying her hips to the tune. Cameron did something on his computer and then joined her to dance.

"I dedicate this entire playlist to you," Cameron said, bewitched.

Mesmerized, Nicole asked, "The whole playlist?"

Cameron pulled Nicole into him, hands holding her waist, now nibbling on her neck. Enraptured, he replied, "Yes."

They embraced while swaying to a few songs.

Suddenly pulling away from Nicole, Cameron signaled for her to follow him into the kitchen.

"I've got a surprise for you." He opened the refrigerator and pulled out a bottle of champagne, then got two flute glasses out of his cabinet.

Blown away, Nicole smiled and asked, "What are we celebrating this time?"

"Us," he said, as he pulled the cork out of the bottle, signaling a loud pop. He poured the sparkling liquid into their glasses, then handed Nicole hers. Cameron lifted his glass and said, "To Nicole, my new best friend, my new beautiful girlfriend, my baby."

Nicole smiled up at Cameron as they clicked their glasses. "I'm your baby?" she said in a low whisper.

"You are," Cameron confessed, setting his glass on the counter, drawing Nicole into a tender embrace.

Nicole didn't say a word. She stroked his face tenderly, then kissed him, urging his lips apart, sweeping her tongue into his mouth, shifting the kiss from persuasive to demanding. He saw in her eyes, she yearned for him to be even closer to her. But she gathered herself and broke away to gaze into his eyes. They moved to the couch. Cameron leaned into

Nicole, kissing her as his fingers slid down her now bare shoulders. Her mouth tasted of champagne and a hint of the slice of chocolate cake they shared. Nicole stripped down to only her matching midnight blue lacy bra and panties. She motioned to flip Cameron, so she was now on top of him. Lifting his shirt over his head, she then reached down for his belt buckle to undo the latch. She pulled on his jeans to shake them off. Nicole gazed at his body. She lowered herself to plant soft kisses around his collarbone, trailing to each pec, then down his sensitive trail leading to his erect penis. Entangling her fingers into the hem of his boxer briefs, she tugged them off. She climbed him, pressing her lips to his, nipping and tugging at his mouth with a boldness that surprised Cameron. She cupped his dick, swirling her hands around it.

"Nicole," he said in a throaty whisper.

Lowering her mouth to him, she circled his tip with her tongue before taking all of him in. Cameron hissed as she stroked him in one hand, mouth drawing him in and out.

"Baby. I need to get in you," Cameron said, pulling her off of him, flipping Nicole to her back.

"I like this bra and panty set, but it's got to go," he said, giving her a sexy stare.

Cameron pulled her panties off, then lifted her to unsnap her bra, releasing her beautiful breasts. He lowered himself to pull a nipple into his mouth, swirling his tongue around the tip, then moving to the other breast. He ran his hand down her stomach, landing on the apex of her thighs. Feeling the wetness of her sex, he yearned to sink into her.

"Cameron, hurry," Nicole murmured.

He gave Nicole a steamy gaze, then sank into her. The slow, rhythmic melody of each song emphasized the harmony of their bodies, synchronizing every gyration with the beat of the music. The sultry voices of each artist evoked a hot and seductive atmosphere, stirring up heightened desire. Bodies in sync, each poetic stroke brought overwhelming pleasure, bringing Nicole and Cameron to a mind shudder.

Lying on top of one another, Nicole caressing Cameron's back, she asked, "Promise me something?"

Cameron inhaled a breath before saying, "Anything, beautiful."

"We'll always let the music play."

Cameron smiled into her satiny skin and responded. "Only for you."

Chapter 22

Nicole

Nicole looked forward to meeting her parents at their favorite restaurant close to their store. The Chinese food was so delectable and heavenly. Their sautéed green beans with minced pork and shrimp, fried and smothered in a tangy, flavorful garlicky sauce were must-haves during each visit.

Nicole walked into the restaurant to find her parents sitting at a booth near the window. "Hi there," she said, kissing her mom and dad on their cheeks. "I'm starving. Did you order?"

"We sure did. We know what you like," Jeannette said, sliding a water glass toward Nicole. "You look great, baby. Your smile is shining."

"I've been meaning to ask you, how's your grandmother's cookbook coming along?" Walter asked.

"Well, I wrote out all the recipes. Now I'm organizing them into food categories."

With a questionable expression on his face, Walter asked, "What kind of categories?"

"Typically, people organize cookbooks for breakfast, lunch, and dinner, plus dessert. I want to be more unique. I haven't solidified each category, but I know they won't be your typical categories you see in a typical cookbook. Maybe by occasion? Sunrise breakfast, Sunday dinner, holiday meals. Something like that," Nicole eagerly and animatedly shared.

"That sounds wonderful. When do we get a taste test?" Walter asked, smacking his lips.

"I go into the kitchen and start cooking and taking notes, so I can write step by step, how to prepare the recipe, next month. I'm going to add recipes for cocktails and pairing recommendations to modernize the traditional foods highlighted in the book."

Just as Nicole's mom was going to ask what alcohol or drink paired with smothered pork chops, Levi slid into their booth.

"Hi, family," Levi said, waving his hands in the air to greet everyone.

Nicole reached over and squeezed her brother's shoulders, kissing him on the cheek.

"Did you order? I'm starving," Levi said, reaching for his mother's hand to kiss it.

"We did. All our favorites," Jeanette confirmed.

"So, Nicole, you were saying?" Walter asked, prompting Nicole to continue talking about the cookbook.

"You guys talking about Cameron?" Levi probed.

"Who's Cameron?" Walter and Jeannette needled.

Nicole glowered at her brother. Judging by the expression on Levi's face, he regretted posing that question.

Reluctantly, Nicole replied, "Cameron's my new boyfriend."

"Boyfriend?" Levi and parents said in chorus.

"Yes, my boyfriend." Nicole knew sharing this news, her having a boyfriend, was big. Levi and her parents nursed her from her deepest valley, grieving a lost love, to her warming heart, for Cameron.

"When did this all happen?" Walter pressed.

Nicole told her parents the story of how they met, when they started dating, and their exclusivity, which was weeks old.

"Well, we're happy that you found someone," Jeannette said, elated for her daughter.

"Me, too," Nicole said, flashing her rosy complexion.

Nicole didn't enjoy sleeping alone on Sundays now that she and Cameron spent so much time together on his off days. Either he stayed at her place or she at his. Cameron was unexpectedly called into work in the middle of the night because of an uncontrollable mountain fire. She lay awake for at least an hour before falling back to sleep. In her early morning slumber, Nicole dreamed of Tyler. The dream was incredibly vivid, almost like reality. She and Tyler were sitting in a room. He was next to her, then moved to get up from his seat, Nicole wrapping her arms around him, holding him, not letting him go, preventing him from walking out of the room. Tyler stood, his stare at Nicole was affectionate yet firm, a combination of love and seriousness. In this dream, Tyler actually stood up. Nicole tried to process what was happening in her subconscious mind. Why did she have this recurring dream about Tyler? She focused only on Cameron when they were together. She really liked him. Dr. Williamson told Nicole dreaming of a lost loved one during the grieving process was not uncommon. Her therapist's words remained lodged in her mind, unspoken and lingering.

"The image of Tyler is in your subconscious mind. His spirit is still with you. You're struggling to let him go. His being, your past, and love for him are a comfort for you. Your fear of letting him go overwhelms you. And so, you hold on to him," Dr. Williamson had said during their last session.

Nicole let Dr. Williamson's words sink in before speaking. "How do I release him? How do I let him go?"

The therapist observed Nicole briefly. "Work to reduce your fear. Let go of it and embrace your possibilities. Be comfortable with that. Letting him go, Nicole. Letting go of the fear you hold on to is the key to embracing a new love and life without Tyler."

"When I'm with Cameron, I don't feel fear. At least I don't think I do. I'm in the moment and genuinely want to be with him. But these thoughts enter my head when I sleep." Nicole wanted to process the concept of the fear she was sheltering and her struggle to let Tyler go.

Composed, Dr. Williamson had asked a question, "Did you tell Cameron about Tyler?"

Nicole had stared at Dr. Williamson, then turned to look out her window. "No. I don't want him to feel sorry for me, or pity me. I want Cameron to be with me because of me."

"I think you haven't told Cameron about Tyler out of fear. You are holding on to Tyler like a comfort blanket," Dr. William had said. She stared at her notebook for a moment and then spoke. "Release and let go of the fear in your subconscious mind to free yourself from Tyler. You'll embrace Cameron for who he is and for the happiness he can bring you, so you can move on."

Nicole knew all of Dr. Williamson's words to be true. She had to accept these words. What could Nicole do to release her fear of loving again? Was it the fear of loving again? Or was it the fear of loving Cameron and losing him? Was she in love with Cameron already? What would it look like, feel like, to release Tyler?

Work and the reopening of the Malibu restaurant on Thursday were a welcome distraction. Monday, Nicole focused on writing the restaurant blasts to post on all social media outlets, hopefully drawing interest for patrons to reserve their tables in the upcoming months. On Tuesday, she dedicated her time to finalizing her proposal, aiming to be chosen as the featured food stylist for the upcoming layout of premiere dishes from the chef of the year. On Wednesday, Nicole spent the day at the restaurant, adding the finishing touches to Aubrey's vision. Cameron's contact with Nicole was limited because of unstable internet access in the mountains. However, he managed to send a text letting her know he would be home Wednesday and would go to the restaurant reopening as planned.

Nicole was sitting at her dining room table organizing her grand-mother's recipes into themes when her doorbell rang. She wondered who could be dropping by without calling? Before she could reach the door, the person began knocking. Pulling back the curtain next to the door, she discovered Cameron, still in his gear.

Stunned, Nicole asked, "What are you doing here?" as she opened her front door to let Cameron in.

"Hello to you. I couldn't go home. I couldn't wait until tomorrow to see you."

Nicole's smile beamed upon seeing Cameron. She opened the door wide and watched him walk in and stop at her entryway. He dropped his gear and stripped down to his thermos. Eyes sparkling with excitement, Nicole rushed him and began kissing Cameron's face, then his lips. She didn't care that he reeked of smoke. She was so happy he was at her house and in her arms. Cameron suddenly pulled away from her.

"Babe, I need to shower. If we keep this up, I won't be able to separate myself from you. I can't stand myself. I don't know how you can stand me," Cameron said as he slowly began to pull her in the direction of her bathroom.

"Well, now that you said it, shower. Are you hungry?"

"Yes, I'm hungry. For you," he said, devouring every inch of her with his gaze.

"I mean, do you want to eat something? A sandwich, pasta, breakfast for dinner?" she asked, walking away from Cameron.

Starving for Nicole's affection, he said, "Whatever you want to feed me. I just want to be with you."

"A sandwich it is," Nicole said, kissing Cameron on his cheek.

Cameron took a shower and Nicole made chicken breast sandwiches on sourdough and homemade seasoned chips. Cameron sat at the table, hair still wet from his shower, and watched Nicole as she loaded his plate with the delicious food she made. Placing the prepared food on the table, Nicole fetched two beers. The two then sat and ate their late dinner while Cameron shared stories from the mountain fire. As he reached for more chips, Nicole noticed some burns on his right wrist and lower arm.

Nicole asked in alarm, "What happened to you?" as she gently reached out to brush his wounded area.

"Oh, this is nothing. I get lots of burns from the job. I forgot to wear my long thermal shirt on Monday. Give it a few days and the marks will vanish."

Nicole had a flashback to the day Tyler came over with a black eye. He told her the suspect caught him off guard. Tyler shared how he punched the guy in his eye and stomach, tackled him to the ground, flipped him over and pinned his hands together while his partner put the alleged offender in handcuffs. "It's part of the job," he'd told her.

"Babe, you okay? You look like you went somewhere else," Cameron asked as he put his hand over hers.

"Oh, no, I'm fine. Be careful, okay? I want you safe, always," was all

Nicole managed to say.

Cameron wiped his mouth with a napkin, stood, and walked over to Nicole, pulling her to her feet, drawing her into him. He then engulfed her in a warm hug. Reaching for her cheeks, he held her face to his so their noses were touching, and gazed into her eyes before kissing her. Nicole consumed his kisses that were salty from the chips but so luxurious. His tongue danced with hers before he moved his hands to cup her breasts. Their kiss intensified, becoming more urgent and passionate, as if he couldn't get enough of her. He lifted Nicole up, she straddling his hips, keeping their lips firmly pressed together, refusing to part. Their tongues remained entangled, moving their heads only to better position their mouths to be on one another. Still engaged in their kiss, Cameron walked Nicole to her bedroom. Nicole ended the kiss with a smack against his lips, then gasped for air. Without saying a word, Cameron gently placed Nicole across her bed, positioning his body over hers. He traced kisses on her neck, using his hand to lift her shirt as he ran his hand across her lacy pink bra. He then shifted his body to be on his side, giving him more access to Nicole's body. He gently kissed her navel, moving up to her upper stomach. Cameron reached behind Nicole to unhook her bra. He amusingly watched as her breasts spilled out of captivity and into his hands. A seductive gleam flowered his eyes before putting his mouth over one breast, moving his tongue playfully over one nipple, then the second one.

"Cameron? Please. Strip me naked," Nicole cried.

Without saying a word, he lifted her t-shirt over her head. He then moved to her shorts, tugging them away with his mouth. He spread her thighs, lifting one leg over his shoulder. Her sex pulsed as he massaged her clit before entering her with his fingers. Nicole rode his fingers until she was almost there. The entire room seemed to spin as she felt the most incredible pleasure imaginable.

"Baby, you're so wet," Cameron hissed in a low, husky tone. He removed his fingers, licking them to savor her sweet taste. Nicole quivered in anticipation, knowing what was coming. She then pulled Cameron, so he was on his back.

"I wanna ride you, Cam," Nicole hissed.

The urge to feel her slick heat on him nearly blew his mind. She straddled his hips while he fiddled with himself until he found her mound, pushing into her. She slowly began to ride him with a deliciousness that made her moan. Cameron watched as her breasts jiggled as she quickened her movements.

"Cameron, I don't know how long I can hold on," Nicole whispered.

"Hold on, baby," Cameron said as he flipped Nicole onto her back. "It's been forever. I missed you. We can take our time later. We need to come," he said as he pumped into her with quick thrusts.

"I'm coming, Cameron," Nicole panted.

"I'm almost there, baby," Cameron whispered.

Nicole slid her hands to his ass to cup his butt cheeks while he pushed inside her. Within seconds, they both exploded, satisfaction tearing through them like neither had ever felt.

Out of breath, Cameron spoke first. "Nicole, my God, you are going to be the death of me. I get so excited around you."

Nicole was speechless. She felt it, too, but her words were elusive, refusing to surface. She reached for Cameron and kissed him tenderly. She buried her head into his chest and inhaled his scent. He hugged her close and planted a kiss on her nose before she went into the bathroom to clean up. She gazed at her flushed face and mouthed, "Ditto", walking back to her bed and into Cameron's waiting arms.

Sleep came quickly for Cameron. Nicole knew he was exhausted. He had worked for three days with little sleep. She slowly removed his hand from her waist and slipped out of bed. Not being able to sleep, she put on a robe and began cleaning. After clearing the dining room table, washing the dishes, and sweeping the kitchen floor, she grabbed two water bottles and went back to her room. Nicole stood at the doorway to her room and watched Cameron sleeping. He was so masculine, strong, and beautiful. She knew she was lucky to have him in her life. If she ever got the chance to meet his ex-girlfriend, she would thank her. He was a true gift to her, and she hoped to express her gratitude someday.

Chapter 23

Nicole

The next morning, Cameron left to return home, tidy up, and get ready for the restaurant opening. Carol shared the news of them gaining the contract to shoot and write up the restaurants for the upcoming wine festival via text. With this news, Nicole spent her day in the studio, working with Carol to research each restaurant that would be at the event, aiming to gain an understanding of how to showcase the unique qualities of each food and wine offering.

"So, is Aubrey ready for tonight?" Carol asked as she cleaned her photo lens.

"I think so. She's as ready as she will ever be. You're coming right?"

"Me and hubby wouldn't miss it. We all look forward to great food and splendid company. I want to meet Cameron. I need to see the man who's making you smile," Carol said, winking.

With a flushed grin, Nicole confessed, "He'll be there. Carol, he's a gift to me, you know?"

Carol gave Nicole a puzzled glance. She detected doubt in Nicole's tone. "Honey, you don't sound so sure about that. Is something wrong?"

"During my therapy session, Dr. Williamson and I talked about fear. I shared how things are going with Cameron and me. And I've been having recurring dreams about Tyler. She said the dreams are based on my fear of letting go." Nicole took in a deep breath and then continued. "The dreams are the same. Tyler and I are together in a room. He stands up and looks like he wants to leave the room, but I stop him, asking him to not go."

"Oh, dear," Carol said, walking over to Nicole to take her hands. "I know this is really hard. It's easier to date than be in a relationship after the loss you suffered. You own your emotions. Tell me about Dr. Williamson's perspective on moving on."

Looking down at her feet. Feeling remorseful, Nicole said, "I have to release Tyler. Let him go. The fear is in my subconscious mind. When I release Tyler and the fear I have to love again, I will be free to embrace love with Cameron. He's such a great guy, Carol. When I'm with him, I don't think about Tyler. At all."

"Time. Give yourself time, honey." Carol pulled Nicole into a tight hug. "Are you sure you're ready for Cameron?"

"Yes! I don't want to lose him. I feel things with him I never felt. Even with Tyler. I loved Tyler and thought he was the love of my life. I feel I can love Cameron. In ways I didn't love Tyler. It's possible that's the source of some of my fear. We have electrifying chemistry." Just the thought of last night made Nicole go red in the face.

"Nicole? Are you blushing over Cameron?" Carol said, covering her mouth with a smile.

"I can't help it. Yes. I said it. There."

"Own that feeling, honey. It can lead to something amazing if you let it," Carol offered.

Promising Aubrey to arrive an hour before the opening meant she had to hurry. Aubrey didn't need physical help, having hired a new restaurant staff. Nicole knew Aubrey needed moral support. Luckily, Cameron didn't mind going early, and Aubrey promised she would sit down for ten minutes to meet him.

At 5pm, Cameron rang Nicole's doorbell. She stood behind the door, dressed only in a short satin robe, and opened it for him to come inside.

"I'm almost ready. I just need to slip into my dress, then we can go."

"Hello to you," Cameron said, grabbing Nicole's hand to pull her close to kiss her quickly on the lips. The smell of his cologne waved her away, sucking her into his essence. Nicole stood admiring Cameron for a few seconds, reminded of how drop dead gorgeous he was dressed in a black suit and a black button up, no tie.

"Hey beautiful, you good?" he asked, noticing Nicole staring at him.

"I am now that you're here." Nicole kissed him softly, savoring the scent of him, inhaling deeply.

Reluctantly pulling away from her, Cameron playfully said, "Now, we can't start that. We'll never make it to the opening."

"You're right. Let me get dressed. Help yourself to whatever. Give me ten minutes."

Twenty minutes later, she emerged. "How do I look?" Nicole said, swirling around in a circle, modeling the dress from every angle.

Cameron turned and stopped in his tracks. Nicole stood before him in a blush rose colored long-sleeved, low v-neck, sequin dress that hit just above her knees. His eyes went from her hair, up in a loose bun, to her beautiful face that shimmered like her dress, to her soft, exposed skin. Her strappy heeled sandals laced up her calves, complimenting her toned legs.

"You look absolutely gorgeous, babe. Wow! I'm honored to be your date," Cameron said, feeling grateful to be in her presence.

"I knew you would like this dress." Nicole felt sexy.

"You'll have to stay by my side all night," Cameron said with a joking grin. "I don't trust others with you in this dress."

"Oh, stop. You don't have to worry. I only have eyes for you. And I'm not your date. I'm your girlfriend." Nicole kissed Cameron on his cheek. "Are you ready to go?"

"I'll go anywhere with you, beautiful," he said, flashing his million-dollar smile.

Once they arrived at the restaurant, the valet took Cameron's SUV. He grabbed Nicole's hand as she led the way into the restaurant. Illuminated by a string of white lights, the place had an enchanting ambiance in the evening. The doors stood ajar, the hostess at the entrance, poised to welcome arriving guests.

"Can I help you?" she asked.

"Yes, I'm Nicole, a friend of..."

Before Nicole could say anything else, she saw Aubrey, dressed in her black chef's coat. "They're with me, Stacy. Nicole designed the food photographs on the walls throughout the restaurant." Aubrey approached Nicole and Cameron. "And this handsome gentleman must be Cameron."

Nicole gazed at Cameron with eyes full of sparkle. "Yes, Aubrey, this is Cameron Davis. Cameron, this is Aubrey Carroll."

Cameron held out his hand to shake Aubrey's. "It's a pleasure to finally meet you in person, Aubrey. I've heard so much about you."

"And I've heard so much about you." Aubrey shook hands with Cameron. "Please come sit with me. I only have ten minutes, but I want to make the best of it."

Aubrey led Cameron and Nicole toward the bar to sit at a reserved table for eight. She went behind the bar, poured three glasses of champagne, and carried them to the table.

"Grab a glass," Aubrey directed. "I want to make a toast. To tonight's opening. May it be a success and bring joy to all who attend. May this restaurant be prosperous and be the talk of this city."

"Cheers!" they said in chorus, lifting their glasses to take a sip of the bubbly.

Cameron's eyes scanned the space. "The place looks really great."

"Yes, your girl here helped me so much. We work well together. You know we've been best friends since high school. It was coincidental that we both love food. I cook it. She styles food and writes about it and Carol photographs it."

Nicole saw the puzzled look on Cameron's face at the mention of Carol. "You remember me talking about Carol? She's the photographer I work with. You'll meet her tonight."

Aubrey glanced at Cameron as she took a sip of her champagne. "So, Cameron, you're a firefighter?"

"Yes, I am," he said matter-of-factly, flashing a smile.

"I hear you're somewhat of a celebrity. Did I come across an article or news segment about your heroic act a while back? You saved a grandmother and her grandbaby from a burning building?" Nicole wasn't sure why Aubrey was asking these questions. She knew all about Cameron. Nicole let out a breath and focused on their conversation.

"I was doing my job. My job is to put out fires. The rewarding aspect of the job is occasionally getting to save a life."

Aubrey took another sip of champagne, looked directly into Cameron's eyes and said, "You make my Nicole smile. And for that, I think I love you. She means the world to me, and it's wonderful to see her so happy."

Nicole dropped her mouth to the floor, not believing what Aubrey had just said. She was beginning to feel embarrassed, even though she thought Aubrey was laying it on a little thick.

Suddenly, a warmth spread across Cameron's cheeks, not knowing how many more compliments he could take. "Well, the feeling is mutual."

Nicole's gaze shifted to Cameron and, in that moment, she caught sight of Edward making his way from the back of the restaurant.

"Aubrey? What's Edward doing here?" Nicole asked, now arms crossed across her chest. She saw Cameron's eyes shift to where Edward was walking toward them.

In a hushed voice, Aubrey said, "I didn't want him here, either. The owner hired his company to install the software the restaurant will use for their food orders, cash outs and phone system."

"Well, now, do my eyes deceive me, or do I see Nicole and her new boyfriend?" Edward said, leering at Nicole, licking his bottom lip, then moving his suddenly hardened gaze to Cameron.

"Edward," Nicole said, mouth compressed into a hard line.

"Are you all done back there? I need to check the system," Aubrey asked.

Cameron stood, jaw clenched, walking toward Edward, when he was stopped by Nicole's hand. She then grabbed him around his waist. Leaning up to his ear, she whispered, "He isn't worth your anger. Let it go."

"Yes, I'm done. I'll leave now to pick up my date. I'll see y'all later," Edward announced, a hint of mockery edging his mouth, then walked away.

The three of them remained quiet for a moment. Aubrey spoke first.

"I hope we can spend more time together. If I'm not working, I'm with her, so you have to get used to me," Aubrey said, attempting to cut the tension in the air.

"I look forward to it," Cameron said, face now relaxed, raising his glass to Aubrey.

"Well, beautiful people, I have to get back to the kitchen. Enjoy tonight. You can give me the reviews later." Aubrey stood, hugged Nicole and whispered in her ear, "Girl, you are killing in that dress. You look fantastic. Love you."

Nicole gave Aubrey a squeeze. "Thank you!" Aubrey waved at Cameron and quickly walked to the kitchen.

"She really loves you," Cameron said with emphasis.

"We've been through a lot. We're best friends for a reason. I love her, too. It's beautiful, really." Nicole was proud of her friendship with Aubrey. They had experienced many heartbreaks, life challenges, and sorrow together. She couldn't imagine her life without Aubrey by her side.

"If I see Edward looking at you the way he did a few minutes ago, I'm going to punch him in his fuckin' mouth. Trust me." Nicole saw the rage in Cameron's eyes.

"Let's just sit and enjoy our evening, okay? I'm not thinking about Edward, and you shouldn't either. My eyes are only for you, Cameron Davis." Nicole then interlocked her fingers with his.

Cameron and Nicole sat at the table, sipping on their champagne. The hostess shortly brought over the tasting menus for the evening. Just as they were previewing the menu, Nicole's parents walked toward the table. Cameron and Nicole stood to greet them.

"Nicole, my baby, you look sensational," Walter said, greeting her with a kiss on her cheek.

"Thank you! Mom? Dad?" Nicole grabbed Cameron's hand. "I want you to meet Cameron. Cameron Davis. Cameron, these are my parents, Jeannette and Walter."

"It is very nice to meet you, Mr. and Mrs. Graham," Cameron said, shaking Walter, then Jeannette's hand.

"The pleasure is ours, young man," Walter said, patting Cameron on his shoulder.

"Aren't you handsome?" Jeannette told Cameron and gave her daughter a wink.

"Thank you. Please sit down. Can I get you a beverage of some kind?" Cameron asked.

"I'll take a diet coke," Walter said.

"A glass of white wine for me, please," Jeannette requested.

Squeezing Nicole's hand, Cameron said to the group, "I'll be right back."

Nicole looked at her dad, then her mom, for some kind of feedback.

"Honey, he's dreamy. You look happy," Jeannette said, delighted.

"I am, Mom. I really am," Nicole said, beaming.

Cameron came back with the drinks. Carol and her husband arrived, introducing themselves to Cameron, then greeted Jeannette and Walter with hugs. Levi arrived shortly after Carol, alone. Since Elle, he didn't bring women around his parents.

"You must be Cameron," Levi said, reaching his hand out to him.

"Yes, and you must be Levi, Nicole's brother." The two men shook hands and exchanged a warm smile.

"I like you already, man. You got my sister smiling again," Levi said with affection in his tone.

"I've been hearing that a lot lately," Cameron said, trying not to show the wonder in his face.

Just as they were all seated awaiting their food orders, Edward walked in with an attractive woman on his arm, dressed in a revealing black lace dress and heels. He caught Nicole's eye and gave her a wink before planting a sloppy kiss on his date's mouth.

"Is that show all for you?" Cameron asked.

"Who knows? I don't care. I promise you, we have never dated. He's destined to always be just a friend. And right now, his friend status is shaky." Nicole was so over Edward and his antics.

The restaurant was crowded, and servers were buzzing from table to table, taking orders and delivering food.

The owner of the restaurant spoke to the crowd. "Thank you for coming this evening. I appreciate each one of you for believing in the grand re-opening of this historic establishment. I would like to introduce Aubrey Carroll. She is responsible for the renovation, the new menu, and the delicious food you're enjoying tonight. Working tirelessly, she and her team breathed new life into this place. Please eat, drink, dance, and enjoy your evening."

The crowd stood, applauding the evening. Everyone ate great food, drank free flowing drinks, and danced into the night. Cameron kept to his word, staying close to Nicole. The men who watched her this evening had a lot to bear.

Later that evening, Cameron and Nicole entered her house, exhausted with full stomachs. Cameron spoke, with a hint of sadness in his tone, "Babe, I have to work tomorrow night."

Pouting, Nicole said, "You do?"

Massaging the back of his neck, he said, "Yep. I want to stay tonight, though."

Nicole reached for Cameron, tugging at his belt buckle. "Can you?"

"The way you look tonight, I want to show you how much I want to stay by removing that dress," Cameron said, passionately kissing her and gazing into her eyes. Without saying a word, Nicole took Cameron's hand and led him into her bedroom.

Chapter 24

Cameron

Cameron and Nicole lay sleeping, naked bodies intertwined in a deep sleep, both blissfully exhausted from lovemaking the night before. Cameron awoke to Nicole's sudden movement. Her eyebrows were drawn inward, lips pressed together in a frown. He didn't want to wake her. Curiosity struck him as he wondered about the inner workings of her beautiful mind. Her head swayed back and forth.

"No, please don't go," Nicole said in a low whisper.

Cameron wanted to embrace her and let her know he was there, but he hesitated. Was she dreaming? This was the first time he heard Nicole talk in her sleep. He wanted to hold her close and tell her he was right there and going nowhere. She was safe with him. She continued to toss and turn, her face tightening with frustration.

"Tyler, you can't go. I need you. Please stay with me," Nicole whimpered.

Cameron froze. His entire body went stiff, frozen. Did he hear Nicole call out to another man in her sleep? Who was Tyler? Then he remembered the note he saw in her kitchen. It read to call Tyler's father.

Was Tyler in Nicole's past? Was she seeing Tyler now? Flashbacks of Shannon and the brief notes she left around her house gave Cameron pause. 'Call Derek', one had said. 'Calendar lunch with Derek', another note said. Shannon had cheated on him with Derek. By the end of their relationship, she got really messy and didn't hide what she was doing. Nicole was a good girl. He had to dismiss those thoughts.

Heart frozen, Cameron felt all the feelings he was building for Nicole were in that instant, turning to stone. He felt the ping in his chest. The same ping he felt when he found out Shannon was seeing someone else. This couldn't happen twice. It just couldn't. He was immobilized. He just lay in bed next to Nicole, staring at the ceiling, still not wanting to wake her up. What was he going to do? What would he say when she woke up? A sharp pain gripped Cameron's chest. His face now throbbing from the pain of clenching his teeth. He just lay next to Nicole, unable to move or wake her.

"Good morning, handsome," Nicole said, rubbing sleep from her eyes.

Cameron drew in a deep, harsh breath, then said, "Morning."

"Do you want breakfast?" Nicole asked, moving to make a pot of coffee.

"No, I'm good. I just realized I need to go home and take care of some things." He couldn't bring up what he experienced last night, Nicole's conversation in her sleep. He needed time to process his feelings.

A sudden look of sadness crossed Nicole's face. "Are you joining me at my parents' house for lunch?"

Cameron promised they would spend the day together. "Yes, I'll meet you there if that's okay." It pained him to leave Nicole. He always wanted to be in her orbit, be in her company.

"Sure." Nicole looked at Cameron for a few seconds before sitting on her couch, scrolling through her phone.

Cameron wondered what she was thinking. The happiness seemed to leave her eyes. He was certain she detected the chilliness in his voice. They had an amazing night. Aubrey's opening was a complete success. The event was trending on Instagram based on the notifications on his phone. Everyone posted live shots from the event to their stories. Their night together was the best nightcap. Cameron had to leave, though. He couldn't stay for fear of saying or doing something he would later regret. Being in the comfort of his own home was necessary for him to ponder the events of the previous night. With no explanation and a quick kiss on Nicole's cheek, Cameron was in his car, headed home.

Cameron felt his phone buzz in his pocket as he unlocked his front door. He threw his keys on the counter and pulled out his phone, and saw a text from Nicole.

Nicole - Hey, Cameron! I had a beautiful night with you last night.

He didn't know how he wanted to respond to her text. He had a beautiful night, too. What he didn't expect was Nicole calling out another man's name in her sleep. He ached to be in her arms again. Was everything in his head? Did he hear what he thought he heard? Not wanting to be rude, he typed a response.

Cameron - Hey! Yes, it was an amazing night.

Nicole - You busy?

Cameron - Doing stuff around the house.

Cameron preferred not to discuss this over text. He doubted his ability to have the conversation. Not now. Maybe he was half asleep and didn't hear Nicole call out another man's name. His phone buzzed with another text message.

> **Nicole** - I made quiche. I can share some if you want.

> **Cameron** - Thanks. What time do I meet you today? Can you send me the address?

> **Nicole** - Sure.

To rid himself of negativity, Cameron chose to run and pump iron. He sent one last text before this afternoon.

> **Cameron** - Going to the gym. I'll see you later.

> **Nicole** - Ok. smiley face.

The gym wasn't too crowded. Cameron walked toward his favorite treadmill and hopped on, turning up the speed and incline to increase the intensity of his run. His pace rapidly escalated, mind racing of thoughts of Nicole, his growing feelings, and the thought of her cheating. The rhythmic pounding of his footsteps mirrored the acceleration of his heart rate. His increasing heart rate was a physical outlet for the anger he felt in response to the scene at Nicole's last night. Cameron held firm to his conviction that she wasn't cheating. The best response to this was to talk to Nicole. What made it hard for him to open up and share what he heard? Was it fear? There was something special about his relationship with Nicole. He knew in the depth of his soul that she was the one. He had to own that, but would keep it to himself.

Drenched with sweat from head to toe, Cameron grabbed a towel to wipe off the perspiration before making his way to the weights. He craved the challenge of throwing some heavy weight. He began with barbell curls and overhead presses. Lifting at maximum weight, the exertion of the strained movements acted as a force, pushing out the negative energy he felt in his heart. With determination, Cameron transitioned to the sit-up bench, needing to push with maximum effort to complete one hundred stomach curls. Each repetition served as a deliberate confrontation of his discomfort regarding Nicole being with another man. He concluded his workout with leg presses. With each press he felt the release of the swirling, tumultuous thoughts that occupied his mind. Cameron put the unsettling scene to rest, choosing to continue his relationship with Nicole and not bring up her calling out another man's name. Now, in his mind, nothing had happened.

Chapter 25

Nicole

Nicole arrived at her parents' house to discover a meticulously arranged backyard. Fresh new patio furniture adorned the sheltered patio area, which expanded into the stretch of grass, leaving room for the large flat screen television mounted in the corner. The new brick smoker sat next to the custom made eight seater table, creating a welcoming and stylish outdoor space.

"Wow! This all looks amazing! What made you redecorate?"

"We wanted a revamped aesthetic. Plus, your dad and I enjoy being outside. We have wonderful weather here in southern California. We can have indoor and outdoor living now," Jeannette said.

Nicole sensed Levi approaching her, placing his arm around her shoulder. "Hey, brother."

"Hey, yourself. Where's Cameron?" Levi said, looking around the backyard.

"He'll be here soon." Nicole was hopeful his mood had improved from earlier in the day.

"I like him for you, Nicole," Walter said with an approved nod.

"Yeah, me, too," Nicole said, flashing a laid back smile. She didn't want her parents to detect her genuine worries.

"Did you tell Aubrey to stop by?" Jeannette asked.

"Yes, I did. She'll be here soon."

"How about some music?" Walter suggested.

"I would love some," Nicole said. She needed a distraction from her wandering thoughts.

Walter went to a covered box and clumsily rummaged for a few seconds. Then, out of nowhere, the sound of Frankie Beverly and Maze blared from speakers, strategically placed around the backyard.

"Built-in speakers now? No more speaker box?" Nicole said with a chuckle.

"Absolutely not. This is now your mother's and my dance club," Walter said with a sway of his hips.

Jeannette clapped her hands and began swaying to the music, too. Levi emerged from the kitchen with a tray of assorted meat for the new grill next to the smoker.

"So you're grilling today, huh?" Nicole asked, remembering what happened the last time she was over for a BBQ. Overcooked meat was not what she had in mind for Cameron's first meal with her family.

Walter pounded on his chest confessing, "I'm the best."

"Oh, you got jokes," Nicole said, giving her brother a nudge to join in making fun of their dad.

"Hey, family!" Aubrey came through the backyard carrying a tray of dessert.

"Hey, girl. What do you have there?" Nicole asked, lifting the aluminum foil from the tray Aubrey was holding.

"We had one tray left of the peach cobbler, so I snagged it before someone else did to bring it today. I warmed it up a bit before I came over," Aubrey said with a smile.

"It smells delicious. We have vanilla ice cream in the freezer," Jeannette announced. "You can bring that inside, Aubrey."

Nicole followed her friend and mother to the kitchen. On the counters sat baked beans and sliced vegetables to go on the grill.

"I made potato salad and a pasta salad. I wasn't sure what everyone wanted," Jeannette said.

"Mom, you always overdo it. We appreciate it, though," Nicole said, reaching to give her mother a kiss on her cheek.

"You know I'll take leftovers home, Mom. Don't you worry," Levi said as he brought in the meats that didn't fit on the grill.

"I got you some shrimp for the grill, Nicole. I know how much you love shrimp." Jeannette knew her child.

Like a kid, Nicole showed her excitement by clapping her hands, a burst of joy radiating from her. As she threw her head back in laughter, Nicole noticed Cameron's presence in her peripheral vision. He was outside, greeting Walter, a bouquet of flowers and a bottle of wine in his hands. Walter pointed to the kitchen entryway. The sudden flutter of butterflies in her stomach accompanied a brilliant smile as Cameron entered the kitchen.

"Hello, everyone! Where can I put these?" Cameron asked, holding up a bouquet of marigolds and a bottle of Pinot Noir.

"You can put the wine in the refrigerator, and I'll get a vase for these beautiful flowers. Thank you so much, Cameron. You're so thoughtful," Jeannette said with appreciation.

"You're welcome." Cameron did as he was told, then walked over to Nicole, giving her a big hug and a quick peck on lips.

Cameron then caught Aubrey examining Nicole with a discerning eye. "Aubrey, it's good to see you. Did everything go as planned for the opening?"

"Better than expected, I have to admit," Aubrey responded with a defining glare.

"It was a beautiful evening," Nicole added.

Nicole felt relieved as Cameron seemed to settle in.

"So, Cameron? Nicole tells me you're a firefighter?" Levi asked.

"Yes, I am. I really enjoy the work." Nicole noticed the nervous expression on Cameron's face, sensing his uneasy feeling of Levi's questioning.

"It's a noble profession," Levi said, winking at Nicole. What she didn't understand was why Levi was acting like her father.

"Yes, it is. As a little boy, my grandfather took me to the fire station near our house. It was then I knew what I wanted to be when I grew up." Nicole noticed the glimmer of light in Cameron's eyes when he spoke about his grandfather.

"I have to be honest with you, Cameron. I haven't seen my sister this happy in a while. I contribute her happiness to you being in her life now," Levi complimented.

"Thanks! That's a tremendous compliment," Cameron said, nodding his head.

Levi's smile transformed into a warning glance, signaling a shift in his demeanor. "I like to see my sister happy. I don't like to see her unhappy. Remember that."

"Of course." Cameron nodded. Nicole watched the two men exchanging a knowing look, affirming the unspoken agreement to prioritize her happiness.

"Dinner's ready! Come meet us outside," Walter called out.

The table displayed the BBQ meats, potato salad, baked beans, pasta salad, grilled zucchini, and corn on the cob. The Marigolds sat in the center of the table creating a picture worthy scene. Nicole put down the green salad and sat next to Cameron, grabbing his hand and giving it a squeeze. When their hands touched, a surge of electricity bolted through her body, giving her a sensation of warmth and desire. Cameron turned to look at Nicole, realizing the mutual desire that lingered between them. Jeannette came out with glasses and the wine Cameron brought, interrupting their moment.

Walter stood at the head of the table, scanning his guests. "Thank you all for joining us for dinner this nice afternoon. Nothing means more to us than family. Cameron, you're always invited. Thank you for being so wonderful and putting that beautiful smile back on my baby girl's face. Let's eat!"

After dinner, Aubrey left to close her restaurant and Nicole helped her mom with the cleanup. She was happy Cameron had time to get to know her family and Aubrey. At the end of the night, Levi warmed up and gave Cameron a brotherly handshake before he and Nicole left the house. Outside, Nicole took Cameron's hands and held them in hers.

"Do you want a nightcap and my house?" she asked, gazing at him through her lashes.

"Nightcap? What kind of nightcap?" Cameron said, making an exasperated sound low in his throat.

Holding hands, Nicole took a few steps closer to Cameron. She gazed into his eyes, stood on her tiptoes, drifting her face closer to his. Cameron gave her a slight smile, his eyes burning with desire. She brushed her lips over his, teasing him. Shifting her face to the side, she planted a kiss next to his mouth. She then moved to his lips, kissing him, testing, to see if he would respond to her advances. He followed her lead, kissing her back, until they intertwined their lips in a battle of the tongues. Nicole let go of his hands and put her hands around his neck, drawing him closer. Cameron moved his hands to her waist and pulled her to him until her breasts were against his chest.

"Cameron?" Nicole whispered, her eyes smoldering with lust. "Come home with me?"

He kissed her lips once more, then whispered in her ear, "I got a text saying I don't have to come into work. Yes, I'll go home with you."

By the time Cameron and Nicole reached her driveway, they rushed to her door. Cameron, standing behind Nicole, grabbed her waist, pulling her into his growing bulge, kissing the back of her neck, moving to just below her jawline. Nicole opened the door, causing them both to fall forward into the house. After closing and locking her door, Cameron grabbed her face and kissed her, like he wasn't going to ever let her go. They stayed that way, never unlocking their kiss, walking to her bedroom.

Chapter 26

Cameron

Nicole's movement awakened Cameron. Her head swayed back and forth, tears running down her cheeks, but her eyes were closed. She settled for a few seconds to freeze her body, grabbing the sheets.

"Tyler, please don't go. I need you to stay," Nicole whined.

Instead of just lying there, listening to Nicole having this dream, this time Cameron shook her awake.

"Nicole? Nicole? Nicole, wake up."

Nicole shifted her body to face Cameron. She opened her eyes to find his concerned gaze on hers. "What's wrong?" "You were having a dream. Are you okay?"

Nicole laid in silence for several seconds, seeming to search for the right words to explain what had just happened.

She swallowed, then said, "Yeah, I'm okay."

Cameron couldn't believe this. Nicole called out for Tyler again. Who was Tyler? He didn't have anyone to ask. He didn't know Aubrey well enough to ask her. He was certain he wouldn't be cheated on. Not again.

Nicole reached for Cameron but he pulled away, turning to his side. He was aware Nicole was unsure how to react to the situation. He wanted her to say something. Anything about her dream. Following a few minutes of silence, Cameron rose, collected his clothes, and entered the bathroom. Emerging from the bathroom, he was met with the look of confusion, knowing Nicole wondered why he was already dressed.

"Are you leaving?"

In an edgy tone, Cameron said, "I gotta go."

"Go where? It's 5am." Cameron could hear the panic in her voice.

"I'm going home, Nicole." Cameron could no longer hide his hurt feelings. He needed to leave before he said something he would regret.

"Why, what did I do? Are you upset? Is it something I said?" Nicole got up to search for her robe.

"It's nothing. I just think this is a lot." Cameron couldn't face her. He had to just go. "I need to clear my head, have some space."

"Space?" Nicole stood, arms crossed, jaw tensed.

"Yeah. I'll call you soon," he said, now dressed, heading for the front door.

"Soon? What does that mean, Cameron? You aren't going to even explain what changed?" He could now discern her anger, clear in her expression.

Cameron reached down, gave Nicole a kiss on her cheek, and left. His head was spinning. Again, she uttered his name. Tyler. The question lingered. Who was he to her? Maybe this is what Cameron deserved. Another woman cheating on him. It was punishment for jumping into a relationship too fast. He should have remained single.

By the time Cameron got home, his head throbbed with a combination of hurt and worry, dual emotions creating an overwhelming sensation. Nicole was now a part of him. Why wouldn't he want her in his life?

Cameron lay on his couch, feeling lost and confused. He reached for his phone to check his work schedule when he saw a text message from Nicole.

> **Nicole** - I don't know if I did something or if I have made you upset. If so, please explain to me what I did. I'm sorry.

Cameron set his phone next to him, closed his eyes, and tried to sleep. He dreamed of Nicole's smiles, her laugh, her soft skin, her kisses. His pondering question was why everyone expressed such joy at seeing her smile again. What happened to her smile before he met Nicole? Each time someone said that, Nicole blushed and put her head down. Cameron knew he had to take it as a compliment. He couldn't leave Nicole hanging. He had to respond to her text message.

> **Cameron** - You're fine, Nicole.

Cameron knew he needed to explain himself. He couldn't bring himself to even repeat what he heard. His Nicole, with another man? It made him queasy just thinking about it. His buzzer interrupted his thoughts. Despite the initial thoughts of ignoring the buzzer, his heart insisted otherwise, urging him to answer the person on the other end.

"Hi Cameron, it's me," Nicole said, hand on her hip, hoping Cameron would open the door.

Cameron gave no response and just buzzed Nicole up. When Nicole reached his door, it was ajar. She entered to find him on his couch watching the Sunday news.

"Hi. I got us some coffee and croissants," she said, setting everything on his kitchen counter. He glanced at her from the corner of his eye. Why was she so irresistible? He yearned to pull her into his arms and hold on forever. Cameron beat himself up for not just talking to Nicole.

The only word he could muster was, "Thanks," staring at his television.

Nicole walked over to the couch, sat his cup of coffee in front of him, and took a seat next to him. "Are you okay?"

"I'm fine," Cameron said, unmoved. He could feel her staring at him.

"Well, you don't seem fine." Nicole reached to grab his hand, but he pulled away. Cameron fixed her with a stern and cold gaze, a look that conveyed a sense of severity and disapproval.

"Thanks for the coffee," was all he could say.

"You're welcome. Are we okay?" Nicole asked, concerned in her gaze.

"Sure," Cameron said, although unsure where he stood with Nicole.

"Why did you leave this morning?"

"Nicole, I don't know. We've been moving fast, and I think we should slow things down." He said those words, knowing he didn't mean them. He wanted Nicole every day.

"Cameron, can you even look at me?" Her eyes gave him a puzzled look.

After a sip, Cameron set the coffee on the table. "I just need some space. Can you leave, please?"

With a tremor in her tone, Nicole stood. "Leave? Oh, okay. If you want space, you can have it." Nicole looked back at Cameron, his eyes remained fixed on the television. From the corner of his eye, he noticed tears welling up in her eyes, a silent expression of unspoken emotion.

"Close the door behind you, please," Cameron said in a stark tone. And then she was gone.

For weeks, Cameron busied himself in his work, requesting extra hours to fill the void he felt in his time and heart. He replayed the scene in his house over and over in his mind, each iteration adding to the weight of his thoughts. He needed to apologize to her. For his rudeness, his behavior. He owed Nicole an explanation why he reconsidered, or why he felt they needed space. It took everything in Cameron to not pick up the phone and call her. He had to sort out what he was feeling. He felt hurt and betrayed. He wanted to trust Nicole. She had never given him any indication that she was seeing someone else. Maybe they rushed into things. Was he already in love with Nicole? Was it fear? Fear of getting hurt? Fear of being loved? The entire situation was driving him to the brink of insanity, a relentless turmoil in his mind. Just as Cameron reached for his phone to message Nicole, the station alarms sounded for a call.

Cameron got back to the station and reached for his phone. He needed to see Nicole. He wanted to see her face, see her smile, hold her, kiss her, feel her. Cameron felt that sending a text message was a cowardly method, but he knew he had to contact her without further delay.

> **Cameron** - Hi!

Cameron was surprised to receive an immediate response.

> **Nicole** - Hi!

> **Cameron** - I owe you an apology. I shouldn't have acted like that.

> **Nicole** - Ok?

> **Cameron** - How are you?

> **Nicole** - I'm fine. You?

> **Cameron** - I miss you.

He then sent Nicole a dedication. Missing You by Case.

It took Nicole several minutes to respond.

Nicole - So you went into the 2011 crates to pull that one. LOL.

Nicole - I miss you too.

Cameron - Can I see you?

Nicole - My schedule is pretty busy right now. Cameron? You hurt me, disappearing with no explanation.

Cameron - I know. I need to apologize and make things right.

Nicole - Maybe we can see each other soon.

Cameron - I would like that.

Cameron understood why Nicole wasn't open to seeing him. He acted like an ass and just disappeared. He deserved that. He would do anything for things to go back to the way they were.

Cameron took the hint that now Nicole needed her own space. He had to own the fact that he pushed her away. Luckily, he could pick up extra shifts to keep him busy. To fill his days off, he registered for lessons on how to use his DJ equipment. He would spend more time with the guys. With Myles' wedding coming up, no one asked him questions about Nicole and, for that, he was thankful.

Chapter 27

Nicole

"I don't know why he said he needed space. I thought things were going so well," Nicole explained to Dr. Williamson.

"Do you think he felt the relationship was moving too fast?" she asked.

"Maybe. He did say that. That our relationship was moving fast. I enjoy him, Dr. Williamson. I went on dates since Tyler's death, but he is the first man I have invested in, developing feelings for."

"Have you told Cameron about your feelings? That you may be developing feelings for him?" Dr. Williamson sat, arms crossed, resting on her lap, waiting for Nicole's response.

"I have not. There are still things I need to sort through. Feelings I need to sort through, I mean. Dr. Williamson? The dreams haven't gone away."

"The dreams about Tyler? Yes, you shared them with me during previous sessions."

"Tyler and I are in a room, sitting next to one another. He looks at me, stands and I beg him to stay. He held the doorknob in one dream to open the door. But he stopped. I beg him to stay and he does." With that, Nicole rested her head on the back of Dr. Williamson's couch.

"Please remind me. When did you begin having these dreams?" Dr. Williamson asked, eyes narrowing.

Nicole closed her eyes to think before responding to the questions. "After I started dating Cameron."

"Hmmm. And in these dreams, Tyler is trying to leave, but you stop him?"

"Yes," Nicole said, holding her head down.

"Do you feel you've released your feelings for Tyler? I mean, he will always be in your heart. You'll never forget him. You've made tremendous progress moving on with your life," Dr. Williamson said, studying Nicole's face.

"I thought I released my feelings for him." Nicole understood where Dr. Williamson was going with her questions.

"Sometimes our subconscious mind tells us how we're feeling. It sounds like you may want to move on, but perhaps fear or apprehension is holding you from feeling for Cameron. Did you ever think about the fact that you may be afraid to fall in love again?" With that question, Dr. Williamson wrote notes on her notepad.

Nicole sat still in her chair, arms crossed for a few minutes, looking down at her lap. "Maybe I am scared. I hadn't considered it from that perspective."

"Your homework for this week is to journal how you feel about falling in love again. Consider your emotions towards the idea of falling in love with someone other than Tyler."

"Okay." Nicole was apprehensive about discovering what her thoughts would mean.

"Also, when you have these dreams, I want you to write about what you are feeling as soon as you wake up. First, document the dream's details, then describe your immediate emotions," Dr. Williamson directed.

Nicole replayed her dreams in her head for the first time. Maybe she wanted to release her feelings for Tyler, but was scared. Why did she hold so much fear? Did Cameron feel that fear? Did he know she had these dreams? How could he know? He doesn't know about Tyler. Nicole chose not to share that much information about her last relationship. She didn't want Cameron to feel sorry for her. She didn't want Cameron to judge her. She wanted to be her authentic self with Cameron. Nicole felt she was her true self when they were together. Thinking about Cameron made her heart ache. She missed him. It had been over a month since they last saw one another. The holidays were coming up. Nicole reached for her phone to send him a text message.

> **Nicole** - Hi!

Moments after the text was delivered, Nicole saw the three dots dancing on her screen.

> **Cameron** - Hi!

> **Nicole** - How are you?

> **Cameron** - I'm good. You?

> **Nicole** - I miss you…

She then sent a song for dedication. Paradise by Sade. Several minutes passed before Cameron replied.

> **Cameron** - Thank you for the dedication. Like paradise, huh? I miss you, too.

> **Nicole** - I know you said you wanted space. I hope I'm not bothering you.

Cameron - No, not at all.

Nicole - Good.

A few seconds passed, and neither sent another text. Nicole regretted reaching out. Maybe she should've waited for Cameron to reach out. Then her phone buzzed with another message.

Cameron - Hey, I'm DJing a set at the record store on Friday. Do you want to come?

Nicole - Really? At the record parlor? Are you sure?

Cameron - Yes, I'm sure.

Nicole - Ok. I'll see you on Friday.

Cameron - Looking forward to it.

Given it was Tuesday, Friday seemed so far away. Caught up with her contracted work, Nicole could return to her cookbook. She opened her laptop and pulled up the changes she made to the book's layout. Most cook books began with breakfast, lunch, then dinner recipes. Nicole wanted her book to be different. She shuffled recipes to organize them into days of the week. Sunday brunch followed by a traditional southern Sunday dinner. She designed the recipes from Monday to Friday for easy weeknight cooking. She created a section for the weekend, adding the cocktail recipes, menu ideas for entertaining, and desserts. She reset the layout and sent it to Carol for feedback.

On Thursday night, Nicole woke in a panic. Once again, Nicole found Tyler appearing in her dreams. They sat next to each other in a room.

He squeezed her hand, stood to his feet, looked into her eyes, and gave Nicole a warm smile. Tyler turned and headed towards the door. Hand on the knob, he twisted it, slowly opening it as if to leave, but halted in his tracks by Nicole's unexpected plea to not leave her.

Nicole wouldn't see Dr. Williamson for another week. As instructed, she recalled her dream and wrote out every detail in her notebook she now kept on her nightstand. As Nicole read through each journal entry, a sense of fear crept in, not just fear of letting go, but a deeper fear of abandonment. Did her own fear of letting Tyler go mean she was fearful of being abandoned? Tyler left her. They promised to be in each other's lives forever. Nicole knew deep in her gut, her fears may be affecting her relationship with Cameron. Maybe she was projecting something that conveyed an inability to love Cameron. How could she release the feelings of abandonment? Nicole made a reminder in her notebook to bring up this concern during her next appointment with Dr. Williamson.

On Friday afternoon, Nicole paced her bedroom floor. Anticipating seeing Cameron again, she became a bundle of nerves, her emotions tightly wound with a mix of excitement and apprehension. To calm her nerves, Nicole found solace in keeping busy with chores. After cleaning her house, she filled her refrigerator with groceries and took the time to deep condition her hair. To ensure her hair behaved for the night, Nicole added extra hair product and diffused her curls to add body to them. She dug out her fatigue green jeans with the holes at the knee and a black, fitted ribbed long sleeve t-shirt and black leather booties. To round out her look, Nicole paired the outfit with a black fitted leather jacket. Admiring herself in the full-length mirror, a smile lit up her face at the thought of seeing Cameron. Was he still her boyfriend? He hadn't told her they were no longer exclusive. Putting essential items in her crossbody leather purse, she grabbed her keys, preparing to walk out her door. Right before she could leave, her phone rang with an incoming call. Edward's name scrolled across her screen as it rang.

"Why now?" Nicole voiced before answering the call. "Hello?"

"Hey, Nicole. I know we haven't spoken since the restaurant event. I want to apologize for that. I won't lie. It hurts me to see you with someone else."

In a fiery tone, Nicole said, "Why were you hurt Edward? We are not together. We were never together. You cannot and will not replace Tyler. If we can't just be friends, then there's no need for us to communicate."

"Nicole, I know. It's just, I know Tyler would want me to look out for you. He would want us to be together," Edward pleaded.

"Edward? Do you want us to be together? Like boyfriend and girl-friend?" Nicole couldn't believe she was asking this question to Tyler's cousin.

"Why not? We'd be good together," Edward suggested. "I've been around to console you. Comfort you after Tyler died."

"Yes, you're right. You have supported me, but now it's time to let go. I have." Nicole couldn't believe her words. Had she moved on? Did the dreams about Tyler mean she moved on?

There was silence on the line. Edward then asked, "Are you and this guy serious?"

"On the way to be." With a brief apology, Nicole hung up the call as she rushed out the door.

Nerves fluttered in the pit of her stomach as Nicole got closer to the record store. The call from Edward was disturbing. Her suspicions were correct. He wanted more than friendship. There was no one she wanted but Cameron. The parking lot was packed, as the record store had become a popular hangout spot on Friday nights, drawing a crowd of music enthusiasts and socializers. Luckily, someone was leaving the store, so she waited to slip into the man's spot when he backed out and left the lot. Walking into the store, Nicole noticed a shift in decor. The dance floor was placed near the DJ booth in the back left of the store. This must be what their newsletter advertised. Friday night jams and a groove, she thought it said. The groove meant dancing, judging by the display of patrons swaying to the music, hands up in the air, moving to every beat of the hip hop compilation. Nicole approached the DJ booth and noticed Cameron was already on the turntables. She watched him as he skillfully moved around the equipment, seamlessly blending in the next song, his new mastery of the music clear with each new mix of tunes. His presence mesmerized her. His handsome appearance didn't escape her, captivating her attention, only adding to the mix of emotions, intensifying the feeling of missing him over the past several weeks. Nicole stood staring for at least a minute before Cameron spotted her. With desire in his eyes, Cameron gave Nicole a playful wink, a subtle gesture conveying a shared moment of connection.

Impressed by Cameron's work, Nicole moved over to the corner of the area, so she could enjoy the crowd and watch Cameron. When he played one of her favorite Run DMC songs, Run's House, she couldn't help but sway her hips and put her hands in the air, mouthing every word. Cameron shot a glance at her, pumped his fist, gave her another wink, and continued his set. The crowd's energy escalated as they jumped up and down, caught up in the infectious vibe of the music and lively atmosphere. The dance floor was packed. A smile curled on Nicole's mouth as she admired a couple on the dance floor who appeared to be her parents' age. Another couple dressed in Adidas gear began a top rock move. Was this hip hop 80s night?

"This is my last song of the night. Thank you. Thank you for joining my set. I hope to come back soon," Cameron said with an invigorating smile. The crowd responded by singing the verses to Method Man and Mary J. Blige's All I Need. Nicole got a glimpse of Cameron looking at her mouthing the words of the song. She couldn't help but join in. The song's lyrics had profound significance, echoing the emotions they shared for one another.

"Hey, you," Cameron said as he came up to Nicole and kissed her on her cheek.

"Hey, yourself. You were incredible up there. You've been practicing."

"Yeah, I've had some time on my hands," he said, his words carrying an expression of longing, a look on his face that mirrored the depths of him missing Nicole.

Cameron moved closer to Nicole, brushing his fingers over her hand, then asked, "Do you want to get out of here? I'm starving."

Nicole responded with a beaming look, "Sure."

Exiting the store, a strong, cool breeze swept through their bodies, creating a momentary chill in the air.

"Wow, it's gotten cold," Nicole said, drawing her leather jacket closed in a tight grip. Cameron reached for her, put his arm around her, and pulled her close. Nicole shivered at his simple touch as he drew her in, an instinctive gesture to warm her with his body.

In an alluring tone, Cameron asked, "Where'd you park?"

"I parked in the lot," Nicole said, pointing in the direction of her car.

"Can we take your car? We can get mine later," he suggested.

Nicole and Cameron found a cute little Mediterranean restaurant a block from the record store. Seated in a small, cozy table against the large window, they spent the next hour eating and catching up on how they've been spending their time apart. When they got back to Cameron's car, Nicole stopped him before he exited her car.

Extending her arm, Nicole grasped his hand for a moment, giving it a tender squeeze before speaking. "Cameron, thank you for inviting me tonight."

Cameron stared at their hands for a few seconds before speaking. "It was good to have you here. You look amazing, by the way."

"Thank you."

For several seconds, they sat in Nicole's car gazing into each other's eyes, a shared smile illuminating the space between them.

Cameron nervously asked, "Can I offer you a drink at my place tonight?" as he pressed his lower lip.

Nicole released a deep breath and said, "I think that's a great idea."

Nicole followed Cameron to his place. They walked in silence to his door.

Cameron turned and pulled her into a hug, then said, "Nicole? I really missed you."

Her face laying on his chest, Nicole said, "I really missed you, too."

Hand in hand, they entered Cameron's condo. Nicole removed her jacket and Cameron grabbed two tulip shaped glasses, a bottle of cognac, and poured some liqueur for them both. They clinked their glasses together, then took a sip of the drink. Nicole settled her drink in her hands on her lap. Shocked to watch Cameron down his cognac, Nicole suddenly felt nervous. Without saying a word, Cameron pulled Nicole into an embrace, holding her for a few precious seconds. She inhaled his scent, savoring the moment, not knowing where the night would lead. He slowly pulled away slightly, gazing into Nicole's eyes. He planted one kiss on her face, followed by another and another. Nicole couldn't help but think how good it felt to be in Cameron's arms.

Brushing a kiss near her ear, he then whispered seductively, "Nicole, I care about you a lot. You're still my girlfriend, by the way."

"Really? Cameron? We haven't spoken in weeks. I thought..."

"You thought what? We were over? Nicole Graham, I don't think I'll ever be over you."

Nicole gazed into Cameron's dark eyes, his stare melting her. "Cameron. I need you."

Cameron then covered Nicole's mouth with his, giving her a soft, deep, long kiss. He then grabbed her hand and led Nicole to his bedroom. Their kisses were slow and intentional at first. Without breaking their kisses, they removed their clothes and devoured one another.

Nicole woke up to Cameron snuggling up to her, his nose on the back of her neck. He couldn't see her flashing a sleepy grin as she positioned herself to get even closer. They lay naked, awake, savoring the shared moment of waking up together. Last night was momentous. Cameron made love to Nicole with so much passion and tenderness. He licked, sucked, and caressed her entire body, leaving her spent and in a haze of multiple orgasms.

"Good morning, beautiful," Cameron said, brushing soft kisses on the back of Nicole's neck.

"Good morning to you."

"Are you busy today?" Cameron wondered.

"No, not really. Why?"

"Will you go with me to a bowling party? It's for my friend Myles. He's getting married next week. I'm the best man. It's kind of like a wedding party gathering."

Taking a moment to think, Nicole replied to him. They were together and then they weren't. They didn't speak for weeks. Now, she lay in his bed, the morning after what she could only describe as the best sex ever, if that was possible given sex with Cameron was always amazing. This time, though, there was so much feeling. She felt it and knew he did, too. They both longed for each other. This was unfamiliar to Nicole. She has never longed for anyone. Not even Tyler, until he was gone. Were she and Cameron developing feelings for each other? During their last conversation, he told her things moved quickly, and he needed to sort his feelings. She understood that. She was still his girlfriend? Maybe his invitation was his way of getting them back on track.

Nicole turned her naked body to face him. "If you want me to go, of course I'll go."

"You'll meet my friends," Cameron said, brushing kisses along her neck.

"Okay, I'm good with that. Are you?"

Cameron lifted his head, then nodded, and said, "Then, it's settled. Tonight we'll go bowling."

Chapter 28

Nicole

Hands intertwined, Nicole and Cameron stepped into the bowling alley that was rented for the night based on the decor of bouquets of white and silver balloons scattered throughout. Centered across all aisles hung a banner that read, Congratulations Jessica and Myles. Nicole attempted to push the queasiness she felt about meeting Cameron's friends, focusing on maintaining her composure. They were the first to arrive based on the empty seats. She swallowed hard as Cameron pulled her into him by her waist, as who she presumed to be Myles and Jessica approached them.

"Cameron!" Myles said, giving him a bear hug.

"Hey, man! I want you to meet Nicole. Nicole, this is Myles, the groom."

Nicole wiped her hand on the back of her pants before holding it out to shake Myles' hand. "It's nice to meet you. Congratulations on your upcoming wedding."

"Hey, Nicole, thank you. It's nice to meet you too. Let me introduce you to my soon to be wife. Jessica?"

"Hi, Jessica," Cameron said, giving her a hug. "This is Nicole. Nicole, this is Jessica."

"Hi," they both said in unison.

"Congratulations on your upcoming wedding," Nicole said to Jessica, giving her a genuine smile.

"Thank you. I'm so excited about the wedding and to become his wife," Jessica said, giving Myles a kiss on the cheek.

"You guys look great. I'm excited about next week. But, tonight, we came to play. No holding back," Cameron bolstered.

Rubbing his hands together, Myles said, "Oh, so it's like that, is it? Baby, let's get ready to beat them."

Feeling nervous, Nicole inched closer to Cameron. After all, this was a room full of people she didn't know. She was thankful for his closeness. He reached to give Nicole a kiss on her forehead.

"Ain't y'all cute?" Ryan said, walking up to Nicole and Cameron.

"What's up, man? This is Nicole. Nicole, this is Ryan."

"Hello, Ryan," Nicole said, shaking his hand.

"Hello to you. Man, she's beautiful," Ryan remarked as his eyes traveled over Nicole, offering a compliment through the unspoken language of admiration.

"Yes, she is. Step back," Cameron said, half-joking. They all laughed. The next thing Nicole knew, she was being introduced to Josh and Terrell.

"Your friends seem really nice," Nicole said in a low tone.

"Yeah, they're all good guys. However, Ryan isn't suitable for a setup with anyone. He's definitely a ladies' man. I can't vouch for his behavior," Cameron said with a laugh.

"I caught on to that," Nicole said, chuckling with Cameron.

The place was crowded when they finally started bowling. Buffet tables of slices of cheese and pepperoni pizza, mozzarella sticks, french fries, chicken strips, and sliders along with bottles of assorted beers, sodas, juices, and water aligned the back of the bowling alley. Between bowling sets, people eagerly snacked on food, indulging in spirits to celebrate Jessica and Myles.

Cameron stood in front of Nicole and asked, "Are you having a good time?"

Nicole looked up at Cameron, a sparkle in her eye. She replied, "Yes, I am, actually. The food is good, the company is amazing, and your friends are hilarious."

Delighted, Cameron said, "I'm glad you're here with me."

"I'm glad I'm here, too," Nicole said, staring into Cameron's eyes. He then reached to give Nicole a quick kiss on the lips.

It was Nicole and Cameron's turn to bowl. Although it had been a while, she used to be quite the bowler. She walked to grab her ball, adjusted its weight on her hand, walked forward, moved to roll the ball, and just like that, hit a strike.

"Wow! Baby, I didn't know you could bowl like that," Cameron said, awestruck. Everyone applauded her strike.

"Nicole, wow, that was amazing," Jessica said, giving her a high five.

"Thank you!" Nicole said, taking a bow.

"Man, she's a keeper if she can bowl like that," Ryan said.

"Let's be clear. I know she's a keeper," Cameron gushed.

Cameron went next. He grabbed his ball, adjusted it between his fingers and glided to the line, throwing the ball down the aisle, hitting a strike. It appeared as though he and Nicole intended to bowl two strikes consecutively. Now they were tied with Myles and Jessica. Myles went up and laid eight pins. He missed the last two. Jessica rolled a strike. Cameron and Nicole took the lead with this accomplishment. After about ten minutes, the last turn would decide the game.

"Baby, I know you got this. Can you bowl a strike again?" Cameron asked.

"I think I can." Nicole wasn't sure. She glanced at the people around her, confirming all eyes were on her. She knew Cameron wanted to win. She took her ball, inhaled a deep cleansing breath, and threw it down the aisle. The ball rolled down the lane, destined to strike the left pins. To everyone's dismay, it was another strike.

Releasing a sigh of relief, Nicole rubbed Cameron's back and said, "You're up, babe." He rolled and hit seven pins. He evened the score by hitting the remaining three pins. Myles rolled and only hit three pins. He went again and hit five more pins, leaving two standing. Jessica's turn would decide the game.

"I'll be your husband," Myles announced, his voice carrying to everyone. "Baby, you gotta make this."

Jessica looked over her shoulder, winked at her soon to be husband and said, "I got you, baby."

Jessica rolled her ball and only knocked four pins down. She warmed her hands with her breath, took the ball, and rolled her last bowl of the game. The entire bowling alley went silent. All that could be heard was Drake's music, blaring from the speakers. With a slow motion roll down the lane, the ball knocked down four pins and made the last two on the right wobble. Then, all that was left standing were those two pins. The crowd shouted with sighs and awws.

Cameron looked at Nicole, the both stood up and hugged in their victory.

"This win is amazing," Nicole whispered in Cameron's ear.

"You're amazing," Cameron replied, reaching for Nicole to draw her into a kiss.

"Okay, break it up," Myles said as he walked over to them.

"Even though this party is in our honor, I'm happy you won," Jessica said to Nicole.

Nicole smiled and said, "Thank you!"

Nicole and Cameron ate and drank beer. She did her best to make small talk with Cameron's friends. As the night winded down, she yawned, a consequence of the considerable amount of beer she drank throughout the evening.

"Are you ready to go, beautiful?" Cameron asked, putting his arm around Nicole's shoulder.

Feeling flirtatious, Nicole said, "I'll go anywhere with you, handsome." They said their goodbyes and began the drive to Nicole's house.

At the first red light, Cameron reached over to Nicole and gave her a passionate, deep, but quick kiss. He took her hand in his and brushed little kisses on each knuckle. Nicole gazed at him as he drove, taking her free hand and brushed it over the side of his face. At the next red light, Nicole lifted her body just so she could plant kisses on Cameron's cheek. Her fingers strolled from his knee to his thigh, all the while drawing featherly circles, stopping at his hip. Cameron gasped for air, holding his breath, then exhaled, trying to maintain control of his SUV as he drove. Releasing her hand, he gripped the steering wheel. He sent longing looks of lust her way as she continued to draw little circles, now in his right pocket. She moved her hand out of his pocket, into his waistband, traveling to his belly button. His skin felt hot to the touch, her fingers feeling like rods of heat. Without moving her own eyes from the road, she unbuckled his pants. Cameron's grip on the steering wheel caused his knuckles to flush a deep shade of red. Nicole's hand drew more circles, now below his belly button, moving downward until she felt his hard on. Cameron let out a low moan as she toyed her hand up and down his shaft. Just as they pulled into Nicole's driveway, Cameron parked, turned off the engine, and pulled Nicole close, grabbing her face for a hot, wet, sexy kiss. Their tongues danced in each other's mouth, heavily breathing, causing loud exhales from their noses. Cameron put his hands on Nicole's chest to cup her breasts. He moved his hands to go under her shirt, feeling her hot skin. He pulled away from her lips and kissed her neck, licking her skin, tugging on her ear with her teeth.

Dark eyes dancing with passion, Nicole growled in a soft tone, "Cameron? Please spend the night with me."

Heat rushed his face. He responded by sucking along her jawline, then said, "You don't even have to ask."

Nicole and Cameron rushed out of the car, Cameron's pants close to falling to the ground. Nicole opened her door, stepping in so Cameron could follow behind her. As soon as she closed the door, Cameron reached for her, pulled her close, and kissed her again. He lifted her shirt above her head, unsnapped her bra, and feasted on her breasts. His hands moved to remove her pants as he sprinkled kisses from her breasts to her neck and behind her ear.

"Cameron!" Nicole growled as she crept from her entryway to the living room.

"Lie down," Cameron instructed.

With his clothes now removed, he lifted her legs over his shoulders and kissed the path down to her stomach. He then slid his hands along her thighs until they cupped her ass, bringing her groin against his face. Nicole cried out as he planted kisses on her center, moving to suck her clit. She didn't have an instant to think before he shoved her thighs wider and thrust his index and middle fingers inside her. She moved her hips, riding them, tensing, ready to explode.

"Hold on, baby," Cameron whispered as he removed his fingers and flipped Nicole to her stomach. With a groan, he slipped his hand from her neck down her back to her ass, leaving a heated trail behind his touch. He then drove inside her, thrusting in with deep strokes. Nicole felt all of him, losing control. Cameron reached around to cup her breasts as he pressed himself up against her back. The sound of slapping skin on skin sent Nicole into a frenzy. Her moan was pleasure filled as she gripped Cameron's dick with her pussy. He let out a grunt, feeling Nicole tighten as she reached climax. Cameron's sudden rapid thrusts sent him over the edge as he emptied inside of her. He held Nicole at the hips, both panting. They lay on her living room floor, out of breath, smiling with satisfaction.

Nicole, laughing, exclaimed, "That was fun."

"I'll say," Cameron said, flashing his signature grin. "Can I ask you a question?"

"Sure."

"Will you be my date to Myles and Jessica's wedding next Saturday?"

"Yes. Can I ask you a question?"

"You can ask me anything," Cameron said, pulling Nicole into him, pressing his lips to her cheek.

"Did you mean it when you said I'm still your girlfriend? Are we still exclusive?"

"Nicole, why would you think otherwise?" he asked, now looking into her eyes.

"I know we hit a rough patch. I want to be sure," Nicole said, pulling Cameron closer to her chest.

"You're my girl, Nicole." Cameron cupped her face, giving her a soft brush of his lips on hers.

Satisfied with his words, Nicole pulled away from Cameron to stand. She reached for his hand as he stood, leading him into her bed.

Chapter 29

Nicole

One week later, Nicole walked through the sturdy wooden doors, beckoned with timeless warmth, hinting at the sacred serenity that was within the sanctuary, where Myles and Jessica were to be married. She walked along the aisle closest to the stained glass windows, casting a kaleidoscope of colors as the late afternoon rays of sunlight lit the space with beautiful radiance. The rows of polished pews led Nicole's eyes to the altar, where a soft glow emanated from the flickering candles. Beautiful displays of white hydrangeas spread across the chantry. To have a complete view of the scene, she chose a seat near the front pew. Soft instrumental music played while guests entered the church to find seats. With Cameron being the best man, she wouldn't see him until the reception. It was a beautiful church. Her mind wandered with thoughts of one day getting married herself. She hoped to have a wedding complete with all the fanfare. What mattered most to her was finding a man who would love her through thick and thin, in sickness and in health. She sought a man who possessed the qualities of a good husband, sex appeal, and a good heart. She would marry the man that would promise to hold her heart and cherish it. With her desire for children in mind, this man had to have qualities that would make a fantastic father. A man who enjoyed being around her family and close friends. Her ideal man would be someone who could make her laugh, honor her, and respect the institution of marriage. She wanted a man who was ambitious and career driven. Nicole chuckled to herself, knowing she just described Cameron.

Nicole's thoughts were interrupted when a young boy dressed in a white tuxedo began ringing bells, shouting, "There's gonna be a wedding, there's gonna be a wedding," as he walked down the center aisle. The music shifted to an instrumental version of All of Me as Myles and Cameron walked into the church from the side door, now standing at the altar. Both men were dressed in black tuxedos, tailored to fit their physique. Myles wore a white shirt, white silk vest and white bowtie, while Cameron wore a white shirt with a black tie. Nicole's eyes were fixed on Cameron, standing there looking so handsome at the altar. The music changed again as the bridal party, pair by pair, walked down the aisle and took their assigned spots. Nicole remembered Ryan, Josh, and Terrell. They were all paired with Jessica's bridesmaids. The maid of honor walked alone, greeting guests with her warm smile. The most adorable little baby girl, dressed in a beautiful white dress, sat in a shiny red wagon filled with white rose pedals, being pulled by the same young boy who announced the wedding earlier. Her precious, tiny fingers grabbed a handful of petals and threw them out of the wagon onto the middle aisle. The back of the wagon adorned a sign that read, the bride is coming. The back doors of the church closed and everyone stood to their feet. Make Me Whole by Amel Larrieux began playing as the doors opened. There stood Jessica, with her mom holding one arm and her dad holding the other. She looked stunning in a white gown, with beautifully hand placed lace appliques, a sweetheart neckline and a caged ball gown skirt. Her veil elegantly placed on the crown of her head to accent her long, loose curls. She was stunning. Guests could be heard whispering, "just beautiful," and, "she is breathtaking". With tears of joy in his glossy eyes, Myles descended a few steps from the altar to meet his bride. He shook Jessica's dad's hand and kissed her mom on the cheek, then took his future wife's hand and led her to the altar.

The minister gestured for everyone to take their seats. He began with a brief sermon, sharing the history of marriage and what it means in the eyes of God. A trio then sang Amazing Love. As the song ended, guests were moved to tears, including Nicole. The minister walked Myles and Jessica through their vows before they sealed their marriage with a brief kiss. In pairs, the wedding party walked down the aisle to exit the church. Nicole clapped her hands as each pair headed toward the exit. Cameron spotted her and gave her a wink to acknowledge her presence. His winks always melted her heart.

Nicole drove the ten minutes to the reception and parked. She lay her head back on the headrest of her car, her mind flooded with so many thoughts. It was a beautiful wedding. Myles and Jessica looked so happy and in love. She felt the love between them. Were she and Cameron building that kind of love? They just regained their momentum from their brief period of no contact. Cameron wasn't great at communicating with Nicole. Would this become a major issue in their relationship later on? Was she a good communicator? Were there things she didn't share with him? Of course, there were things she didn't share. Nicole tried to push those thoughts to the back of her mind.

As Nicole walked up the cobblestone walkway to the reception room on the Beverly Hills estate, she got a glimpse of Cameron and the wedding party posing for pictures. His smile was electrifying. He took her breath away. She closed her eyes with a vision of grabbing Cameron and running away with him to keep all to herself when she heard approaching footsteps.

"Nicole?" a woman called out.

"Yes?" Nicole said, turning to face the voice.

"Hello! I'm Patricia Davis, Cameron's mother. I recognized you from the pictures he has on his phone. I hope you don't mind me introducing myself."

"Hello, Ms. Davis. It's nice to meet you. Of course, I don't mind at all."

"I believe we're at the same table. Would you like to go inside?" Ms. Davis asked as she waited for Nicole to walk with her. The two women walked inside the reception room in silence, communicating through their smiles. They stepped into a huge room adorned with wall to wall glass windows, round tables dressed in white tablecloths, beautiful bouquets of white flowers and white china.

"This room is breathtaking, beautiful," Ms. Davis shared, scanning the room.

"It's very glamorous, like a scene from an old Hollywood movie," Nicole responded. The women found their table and sat next to one another.

"Cameron is very fond of you, you know," Ms. Davis admitted.

Before responding, Nicole offered her a warm smile, setting a positive tone for their future interactions. "I'm very fond of him, too."

"He's a good man. It makes me, as his mother, happy to see him happy. I think you make him happy, Nicole," Ms. Davis said, placing her hand on top of Nicoles.

"For what it's worth, Cameron makes me happy, too." She couldn't lie to his mother. Nicole felt the most happy when she was with Cameron.

With an interested gaze, she inquired, "Tell me about your family," inviting a conversation about personal connections and shared histories.

Nicole told Ms. Davis about her parents and brother. She mentioned her parents' store and showed pictures from their Instagram page. Ms. Davis spoke of Cameron, his upbringing, and how his dad would be so proud of him. The two women were engrossed in their conversation when they were interrupted by the start of the music, announcing the wedding party. Side by side, they watched as the wedding party gracefully entered the reception room. Cameron glanced over to their table, an interplay of relief and nervousness seemed to flicker across his expression as he seemed to assess the mood between the two women. Nicole thought it would have been better for Cameron to introduce his mother to her. Nonetheless, they knew each other now, and she adored Ms. Davis.

After the bride and groom's first dance, Cameron was relieved of his duties. He walked over to the table and planted kisses on Nicole's cheek, then his mom's.

"So, what did you both think of the wedding?" Cameron asked, exhaling an exhausted breath.

"Beautiful," they both responded in unison.

Cameron looked at his mother, then Nicole, and said, "I'm happy to see my two favorite women together."

Nicole flashed a blushing expression. "Your mother is lovely, Cameron."

"Nicole and I are going to be great friends." At that moment, she saw the resemblance between Cameron and his mother in their smiles.

"Mom? Would you mind if I danced with Nicole?" Cameron asked, never removing his eyes from her.

Shooing the two with her hand, Ms. Davis said, "You two go ahead. I'll be fine."

Cameron interlocked his hand with Nicole's and led her to the dance floor. Their mood was mellow as they held each other and swayed to the music.

"You look amazing, Nicole," Cameron complimented, admiring her in a sleek print midi dress that flattered all of her curves. His eyes grew dark with desire.

"You look incredibly handsome yourself, Cameron," Nicole replied, meeting his passionate gaze. He then grabbed Nicole's hands and brushed kisses over them. They stayed in each other's arms swaying to the music, as if they were the only ones on the dance floor.

"I'll need a ride to my car, if you don't mind?" Cameron asked.

Nicole snuggled into him, then responded, "Of course." She looked up to Cameron, her eyes capturing his. In the silent exchange of their gazes, the unspoken 'I love you' resonated between them, conveyed through their eyes. Nicole was first to avert her stare. They danced a few more songs before Nicole spent the rest of the evening with Cameron's mom.

"Nicole? It was a pleasure to meet you. I hope to see you soon. I'm going to call it a night. Be safe, my dear." And then she was gone.

With the guests mostly gone, Nicole stood to wait for Cameron in the entryway of the reception room. He snuck up behind Nicole, seizing her waist, pivoting her to face him. "Can I kiss you now?" he asked with great anticipation.

Nicole nodded. Cameron pulled her in and brushed his lips across hers, lightly. He then kissed her deeply. Nicole pulled away.

"Cameron? People are watching us."

Cameron looked around and the few remaining guests busied themselves with one another, paying no attention to them. He shrugged his shoulders and pulled Nicole into a hug, then knelt down to whisper in her ear.

"I'm going to follow you to your house once I get my car. I need to be alone with you, Ms. Graham."

Cheeks now flushed in a rose color, Nicole responded with a smile resting against his face. She then spoke. "I would love that, Mr. Davis."

Once inside Nicole's house, eyes glittered with want, Cameron kissed her lips. This kiss was rushed and hot. He tore away from the kiss to run his tongue over her lips, pinning her to the wall, moving his lips to her neck and into her cleavage. He tore away, glaring down at Nicole, emotions swirling in his eyes, as if unable to share what lay heavy on his heart. Her eyes met his, overwhelmed with emotion for Cameron, rendering her speechless. They held their gaze for several moments. Her mouth opened and shut and opened again, like that of a fish suffocating in air. At that moment, Cameron lifted Nicole's dress over her head, revealing her light gray lace bra and panty set. His voice turned seductive, and she swallowed hard.

"I need you, Nicole," he whispered.

Only able to nod, Cameron kissed her quickly on the lips, moving down her body, stopping at her navel. He knelt down on his knees, lifted her right leg over his shoulder and kissed her center. His fingers traced her hip, then linked inside her panties, pulling them down to reveal her center.

"Gorgeous." He growled as he admired her.

He then licked the wetness between her folds, flickering his tongue across her clit, before diving in.

"Cameron," Nicole called. "I-I—" she whispered, feeling every sensation, rendering her speechless. She tensed as he nibbled on her clit, inserting two fingers inside her, massaging her walls. She let out a soft cry, feeling close. She moaned in agony, wanting to hold on before letting go.

"Come on, baby. I feel you. Let go," Cameron whispered. He dove in for another taste, sucking her clit. With that, Nicole cried Cameron's name, releasing the rush of pleasure only he could bring.

Nicole was awakened in the middle of the night, gasping for air, calling out Tyler's name. Her heart felt as if it would beat its way out of her chest. Hot and sweaty from her dream, she glanced at Cameron, whose back was to her. She was relieved he was asleep. She took several cleansing breaths and reached for the bottled water on her nightstand. The Tyler dreams were happening more frequently now. In the latest dream, Tyler stood up, glanced back at her, unable to leave the room. Nicole closed her eyes trying to remove the image of her and Tyler staring at one another before she woke up. After several minutes, she spooned Cameron and fell asleep.

"Good morning!" Nicole said sleepily.

"Morning," Cameron coldly replied.

Wanting to pull Cameron into an embrace, Nicole reached for him, only to be brushed away. He stood and went into the bathroom, shutting the door behind him. She thought that was very rude. He came out of the bathroom in the sweats he kept in his car and a t-shirt.

"Are you leaving?" Nicole asked, confused.

"Not yet," Cameron said, his jaw clenched and eyes furrowed in deep thought.

"I can make us some breakfast," Nicole offered.

"Sure." His tone was short and cold.

Nicole freshened up and dressed in pajama pants and a tank top. She gathered bacon, eggs, and fruit from the refrigerator. Putting yesterday's bagels in the toaster, she started brewing coffee. She was about to crack eggs into a bowl when Cameron walked into the kitchen holding her ringing phone.

"Hello?"

"Levi? What?"

"What?"

"How bad is it?"

"Was anyone hurt?"

"Are mom and dad okay?"

"I'll be right there."

Chapter 30

Nicole

By the time Nicole arrived at her parents' store, the building structure and all of its contents were burned to the ground. As the firefighters smothered the remaining small ember flames, her parents stood on the sidewalk across the street from the store. Tears ran down Jeannette's face as Walter held her in his arms, staring at the charred reminisce on the ground. Their store, their business, their livelihood, burned to ashes. Nicole was speechless. She stood still, in shock. Levi ran out of his illegally parked SUV towards them, mouth agape, eyes wide, in a shock at the scene before him.

"What happened?" he cried.

"The firefighters are uncertain, but they suspect the store's electrical box," Walter said.

"When will they know for sure?" Nicole weighed, wanting clarity on how this could have happened.

"The investigator is on the way. We'll wait here until they finish the inspection," Walter informed Nicole and Levi.

"Did you call the insurance company?" Nicole inquired.

"We will, honey," Walter said, trying to calm his children. "We will as soon as the inspector gets here."

Nicole and Levi closed the gap between them and their parents, now standing in a family hug, comforting Jeannette. She had dressed and left, barely saying a word to Cameron.

"Cameron!" Nicole said in surprise. She had to call him, needing to get his expertise on the matter. Maybe he could expedite the reports so the insurance company could focus on settling their claim. Nicole questioned how long the store could remain closed. Her parents owned the building so, there was comfort in knowing that the insurance money could help to rebuild and open even stronger than before.

Rather than go home, Nicole went to her parents' house to comfort her mom. The store was her baby. Jeannette birthed the idea of a store, then sketched what she saw in her vision. She researched the industry to settle in on a shop that would thrive. The store had become a viable business in the community, all because of her mother's hard work and dedication. Walter joined her in the store when he retired from the movie studios. Him being a lawyer in contracts and negotiations was the bonus, boosting their business as an industry store to fulfill set needs in the filming studios.

"The store was my home away from home," Jeannette sighed.

"We'll rebuild, baby," Walter said, rubbing circles on Jeannette's back.

"And we'll help," Levi said.

By the time Nicole settled in the guest room of her parents' house, she looked at her phone and realized it was noon. She acknowledged the importance of sleep for everyone, yet still felt the need to reach out to Cameron. She decided to send a text message first.

After several minutes, Cameron replied.

Cameron - Is everything ok?

Nicole - My parents' store burned down.

Cameron - Are your parents ok?

Nicole - Physically, yes. Emotionally, not so much.

Cameron - Is there anything I can do?

Nicole - Maybe you can follow up with the report that's filed with the fire department, maybe help with the insurance follow up?

Cameron - I can do that.

Nicole - Are you still at my house?

Cameron - No, I went home. I took a bagel though.

Nicole - smile emoji

Cameron - Do you want me to come to you?

Nicole - No, I'm good. I just want to be available for my mom.

Cameron - I understand.

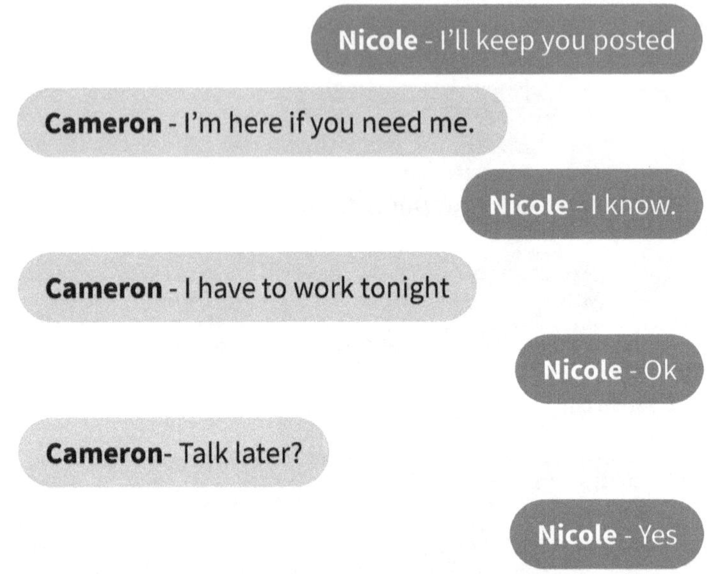

Nicole walked into her parents' kitchen to find her dad sitting at the table drinking a cup of coffee.

"Dad? It'll be okay," Nicole said, walking over to him, placing her hand on his shoulder.

"I know, honey. It will take some time, but we'll rebuild. I have to get your mother to understand that."

"Right now, she's in shock. She'll soon realize that rebuilding can be a blessing in disguise. She can have fun with it." Nicole did her best to console her dad. He would be the one to support her mother when she wasn't around.

Walter stared into space for a few seconds. "I agree. Can you be with her today?"

"Of course," Nicole said, giving her what she thought to be a comforting smile.

After making herself a cup of coffee, Nicole went into her parents' bedroom to find her mother lying down, eyes closed, in a fetal position.

"Mom, are you sleeping?"

"No sweetie, I'm not," Jeannette said, facing the wall opposite Nicole.

"Do you mind if I sit with you?" Nicole asked, sitting at the foot of the bed, shifting her body toward her mom.

"I could use the company," Jeannette replied.

"You know, once everything is settled, you can rebuild," Nicole said hopefully.

"Yes, I plan to. I put so much into the business. Our customers relied on us to furnish or style their sets and scenes."

"And you will do that again. Now even better." Nicole believed in her mom. She was one of the strongest women she knew.

"Do you think Cameron can help with some of the paperwork?" Jeannette asked.

"Yes, I think he can," Nicole said without sharing she had already asked Cameron for his help.

"One step at a time," Jeannette said with a sigh.

"How can I help mom?" Nicole didn't want to be a lug. She wanted to dive in and help with whatever her mom needed.

"Let's wait until the insurance company gives us an update before we make plans for the rebuild."

Nicole moved to the other side of her parents' bed and laid down beside her mom. She embraced her mom and kissed her on her forehead. They held each other until they both fell asleep.

The buzzing of her phone woke Nicole. It was 3pm. She had slept for almost three hours. She quietly left the room with her phone in hand while her mom slept. She opened her phone to see a few missed calls and eleven text messages.

Aubrey - Hey Nicole, I tried to reach you but you didn't answer.

Aubrey - Is everything ok?

Aubrey - Levi called me and told me what happened. I'm coming over with some food at around 5.

Aubrey - Call me when you can, ok?

Edward - Hi!

Edward - I saw the story about your parents' store and the fire. Are you ok?

Edward - I'm here if you need me.

Carol - Let me know if I can do anything to help you and your parents.

Aubrey - Is baked chicken with mushroom risotto and sauteed vegetables good for dinner?

Aubrey - Apple pie for dessert?

Aubrey - Oh and homemade rolls too?

Aubrey had a knack for stepping in and helping. Food was her love language. Realizing she hadn't eaten all day, Nicole couldn't wait until 5pm. She sat for a few minutes thinking about what she assumed were several stories circulating news outlets, given the reporters that were on the scene. She wondered if Cameron saw the story? Even though it had only been a few hours, she missed him. She hungered for his arms to be around her, to comfort her and assure her everything was going to be okay. She wanted to be a pillar of strength for her parents, her mom in particular. Nicole knew she could be the warrior her mom needed, but she needed Cameron. Nicole reached for her phone to send him a text message.

> **Nicole** - Hi!

After about 5 minutes, Nicole got a reply.

> **Cameron** - Hi! How's it going?

> **Nicole** - It's ok

> **Cameron** - Do you need anything?

> **Nicole** - Aubrey's bringing dinner.

> **Cameron** - At least you will eat something

> **Nicole** - I eat

> **Cameron** - Have you eaten today?

> **Nicole** - Ok. No.

> **Cameron** - Can I stop by before I go to the station?

> **Nicole** - I would love to see you.

> **Cameron** - I'll be there in about an hour

Nicole called Aubrey to let her know she was okay and her parents were okay. Levi was sleeping on the living room couch.

"Levi?" Nicole said, softly pushing Levi's shoulder. "Levi?"

Levi opened his eyes to see his sister watching him. "What's up?"

"Aubrey's bringing food in a few minutes. Are you hungry?"

"Yeah, starving." Levi sat up and put his head in his hands. "This is crazy, you know?"

"Yes, I know. They'll rebuild. Mom wants to. And we have to help her," Nicole said, knowing without a doubt Levi would be right there and ready.

Levi looked up at Nicole, then said, "I'm all in."

Nicole sat next to Levi on the couch and put her hands around his waist. He put his head on her shoulder. They stayed like that until they were startled by the doorbell.

"Are Mom and Dad expecting company?" Levi asked, standing to walk toward the door.

"Aubrey is bringing food. Cameron's stopping by before work. Maybe it's him."

Nicole beat Levi to the front door. She opened it to see Edward standing in the doorway, fresh flowers in hand.

"Edward, what are you doing here?" Nicole asked, confused by his presence.

"You didn't respond to my text. I wanted to at least bring your mom some flowers and to offer support," he said, walking through to stand in the entryway.

"That was kind of you, but unnecessary." Nicole didn't understand why Edward was at her parents' house. He had no right to be there. This was a family matter, and he wasn't family.

"I wanted to. Can I come in?" Edward asked, scanning the area.

"You're already in, so sure, I guess." Nicole shut the front door, wondering how Edward's presence was going to make everyone feel. Levi glared at Edward, a flash of temper lightening his eyes.

"What's up, Edward?" Levi asked, walking toward him. Nicole could see Levi's jaws tightening.

"Levi? You good?" Edward questioned the look Levi was giving him.

"Fine!" Levi responded, unmoving of his stance and scowl toward Edward.

Nicole walked between the two men, interrupting Levi's stare down. "Let me take these flowers and put them in some water. I'll let my mom know you're here." Nicole went to her mother's room to announce that Edward was there to show support. She and her mom then walked into the living room to see Levi, Edward, and Cameron standing near the front door.

"Cameron!" Nicole said, running to him, giving him a hug and kiss on the lips.

"Hey, beautiful," he said and hugged her tight, kissing her back and then kissing her cheek.

"Hello, Cameron, and hello to you, Edward," Jeannette said, looking from Edward to Cameron.

"Hello," both men said in unison, Cameron looking at Edward in irritation.

"Edward brought you a bouquet of flowers, Mom. They're in the kitchen," Nicole said to her mother.

"Thank you, Edward. That was kind of you." Jeannette turned to Cameron. "Nicole mentioned you could assist with the paperwork. Is that correct?"

"Of course. I'm working tonight, so I'll check the system when I go in," Cameron said, giving Jeannette a warm smile.

"Thank you, dear. We appreciate anything you can do." Jeannette gave him a smile before going into the kitchen.

The air was thick, and everyone was silent until the doorbell rang again. Nicole opened the door to find Aubrey holding a cake.

"Hello, everyone," she said, giving Nicole a look.

"Do you need help bringing in the food?" Cameron asked, walking toward the door.

Without waiting for an answer, Cameron went out to help Aubrey.

Nicole glared at Edward. "Edward, it was very thoughtful of you to come to support my parents."

"Yeah, man, it was nice of you," Levi spat. "We're about to have a family dinner. You can go now."

Edward gave Levi an icy stare, then turned in Nicole's direction. "Call me if you need anything."

"She's good, man," Cameron blasted as he brought the last load of food in from Aubrey's car.

"Mrs. Graham? Let me know if you need anything. Take care everyone." Edward left without looking at Cameron, Levi, or Nicole.

Nicole held the door open for Edward and watched him walk out. She shut the door behind him, looked around the living room, then proclaimed, "Let's eat. I'm starving."

Chapter 31

Cameron

The scene at Nicole's parents' house left Cameron unsure of what to think. Edward was not only Nicole's friend but also her family's. Levi's complete lack of care for Edward was apparent. He trusted Nicole and knew nothing was going on between them. Edward always showed up unannounced. His male radar was rarely wrong, and it told him Edward liked Nicole. A lot. He may even be in love with her. He could not bear the thought of Nicole being with someone else now. Cameron and Nicole's time together was amazing. What Cameron didn't understand was why Nicole called out another man's name in her sleep. Who was Tyler? He found it difficult to muster the courage to ask her. Deep down, he was afraid of the answer. Flashbacks of Shannon and her cheating made him so angry and sick to his stomach. Nicole had to be different. Cameron's chain of thoughts was broken when his supervisor called him into his office.

"Sir, you wanted to speak with me?" Cameron asked his superior, unsure of what he might want or need from him.

"Yes, please sit down," Captain Gary requested, gesturing for

Cameron to sit in a chair facing him.

Sweat beaded Cameron's brow as he attempted to conceal his anxiousness when he asked, "You're making me a little nervous. What's going on?"

"Cameron, I know you've been working hard and that hard work has not gone unnoticed," Captain Gary shared proudly.

"Thank you, sir!"

"If you didn't know already, you are on a promotion trajectory."

"Yes, sir." Cameron hoped he was, but hearing his captain confirmed his wishes.

"What are your goals, Cameron?" Captain Gary asked, hands clasped on his desk.

"My goal is to ultimately be chief. I know I have a lot of work ahead of me, but that's my goal." Cameron didn't know where this conversation was going, but he was grateful for it.

"As someone who believes in you, I believe you can get there. There are a few promotions you have to earn before becoming chief."

"Yes, sir."

"I've added your name to the short list of potential firefighters to be promoted to engineer. By being on the short list, you must gain more experience and take the exam, etc., but I know you can do it. I want you to shadow Lieutenant Jackson for the next several months." Captain Garey then sat back in his chair, giving Cameron a moment to process what he had just shared.

"And when do I begin shadowing Lieutenant Jackson?" Cameron tried to contain his excitement. He knew this development was sudden and unexpected for someone with his experience.

"On tomorrow's shift. We'll announce it to the staff when you come on duty tomorrow. Can you wait to share the news with the guys?" the captain asked.

"Of course. Thank you, sir!" This was what Cameron was working toward.

"This is well deserved. Keep in mind, you'll have to put in more hours at first," Captain said.

"Yes, sir. I'm good with that." Cameron stood, shook Captain Garey's hand, and left his office. He couldn't wait to share his news. He wasn't promoted yet, but it was in the works. His hard work and dedication was paying off. He immediately pulled out his phone and texted his mother.

Cameron - Mom! You'll never guess what just happened.

Mom - What baby? Are you ok?

Cameron - Yes, I'm so good.

Cameron - I'm on the short list for a promotion to engineer.

Mom - Really? That's wonderful. Congratulations!

Cameron - Thank you! I've been working really hard. It's really early in my career but the dedication is paying off.

Mom - I know you have. You deserve it.

Mom - Where are you?

> **Cameron** - I'm at work.

> **Mom** - Well, we have to celebrate.

> **Cameron** - Yes, I want to. How about dinner with you and Nicole?

> **Mom** - Nicole? Yes. I like her.

> **Cameron** - I like her too, mom.

Cameron entered the spare office, his usual spot to FaceTime Nicole during work hours.

"Come on, Nicole, answer," Cameron said as the call rang.

The phone rang unanswered.

"Come on, baby, I need to talk to you." He tried again, but Nicole didn't answer. Their call wasn't scheduled until 9pm, but he couldn't wait to talk to her. He wondered what she was doing and why her phone wasn't close to her. He hoped everything was ok. He would check on her via text.

> **Cameron** - Nicole? Baby?

> **Cameron** - You good?

Cameron stared at his phone for what seemed like forever. The time on his phone told him only ten minutes had passed. Worry sank in with the realization that Nicole hadn't answered his calls, a sense of unease settling in his stomach. The sounds of sirens shook Cameron from his muddled thoughts.

"Time to go to work," Cameron said, rushing to his cubby to change into his uniform and prepare for the fire he and his guys had to put out.

The guys took their positions on the truck and waited for Captain Garey to give them an update.

"Guys? This is a housing community fire. Possible arson. Several homes are on one street. Some houses may be a total loss. Prepare for family displacement and possible injuries," he said over the radio.

The scene was out-of-control and chaotic when Cameron and the guys arrived. The once warm and communal atmosphere was now one of distress and urgency. The flickering flames raged with erratic intensity. A home across the street from where the station's truck was parked was fully engulfed in flames. Windows shattered, sending shards of glass cascading to the ground and intense heat from the blaze sending a trail of fire onto the grounds of the house next door.

"Nickelson, Perry, let's go," Cameron directed. "Grab the hose. Nickelson, start spraying."

Emergency sirens wailed in the distance as additional trucks were close to help put out multiple home fires. Onlookers, their faces etched with concern and disbelief, gathered at a safe distance, their collective worry palpable in the air. Flames consumed structures in the near vicinity, sending acrid smoke through the air. Firefighters, clad in protective gear, moved with purpose and precision.

"Cameron? You and the guys spread out to get an even spray," Captain Garey commanded.

Nickelson, Perry, and Lieutenant Jackson pointed a steady thrum of water against the structures that were collapsing in front of them. As the guys approached a structure, two children suddenly ran out of the nearby home. Billows of smoke escaped the roof. Cameron knew it was seconds before the home would be fully engulfed.

"You gotta get our parents. They're trapped in the back of the house," yelled a boy who looked to be about twelve years old.

"Captain Garey. Send a unit to our location. We have to go in and search for parents of two kids who just ran out of a home that is about to blow," Cameron requested. "Perry? Nickelson? Let's go through the back and see if we can get the parents out."

The three guys dropped their lines and hustled to the rear of the house. Broken glass riddled the ground.

"Watch your step guys," Perry yelled.

With straight precision, Nickelson and Perry entered the house, Cameron falling behind. "Firefighters on scene. Can you hear us?" Cameron yelled. "Perry, you take this route. Nickelson, go that way," Cameron said, waving his hands in opposite directions for the guys to take for search and rescue. Within seconds, the guys carried a man and woman out.

"Captain Garey! They got them. Send an ambulance," Cameron demanded.

The three of them exited the house and ran to the front. Cameron resumed his line, spraying powerful streams of water in the attempt to reduce the possibility of the home collapsing. With multiple stations on scene, the intensity of the fires diminished, pockets of smoldering embers quelled.

Once back at the station, equipment clean and showered, Cameron checked his phone to find text messages from Nicole.

Nicole - Hi babe! I'm good. I was listening to stories about my mom's favorite clients when you called. I didn't have my phone close.

Nicole - It's passed our scheduled call.

Nicole - Do you want to talk?

Cameron looked at his phone. He pulled up the pictures he had of Nicole. Her smile brought him so much joy. He knew just the sound of her voice would lift his spirits. He scrolled through his phone to dial her number, but before he could push send, the siren went off again.

"Let's go, let's go!" Nickelson yelled, running down the hall. Cameron didn't know how long it would be before he could talk to Nicole.

A week went by without Nicole and Cameron seeing or speaking to each other. They exchanged a few text messages, but that was it. Work kept him too busy to engage in conversation. Upon announcing his new role, he was assigned night shifts for the next two weeks. This meant he would be working through the holidays. Could he get through the holidays without his gift being Nicole? It had been years since he had such a grueling schedule. Rookies had this schedule. His training meant sacrificing free time. Cameron had to talk to or see her. He reached for his phone to send her a text.

Cameron - Hi!

She didn't reply for twenty minutes.

Nicole - Hi!

Cameron - I miss you!

Nicole - You've been at work all these days? I miss you too. When can I see you?

Cameron - Soon I hope. I have been working every day. There is a reason for that, though.

Nicole - Oh? What is it?

Cameron - Good news. On my path to promotion. I'll explain when I see you.

Nicole - And when will that be?

Cameron - I have a split day on Thursday. Can you free up your calendar?

Nicole - I think so.

Cameron - I just need a hug from you

Nicole - Is that all you want?

Cameron - Well, now that you mentioned it. I have a few things in mind that I want us to do.

Nicole - Like what?

Right before Cameron could get sexy, the siren interrupted.

Cameron - Baby, I gotta go on a call. Talk later.

It was noon on Thursday. Cameron had exactly five hours before he had to go back to the station. He didn't even bother to go home first. He went straight to Nicole's house.

"Hi there!" Nicole said, opening the door wearing only a pair of black babydoll shorts and a black tank top, no bra.

Cameron almost rushed her, pushing her back into the house, shutting the door. He took her into his arms and just breathed her in.

"Baby, I don't know if you truly understand how happy I am to see you," Cameron said, holding Nicole in a tight squeeze.

"I can see that, and I can feel it, too," Nicole said as she lifted one leg and gyrated on Cameron's erection.

"I need to take a shower," Cameron said, reluctantly peeling himself away from Nicole.

"Go ahead, the bathroom is all yours."

Still holding Nicole around her waist, he planted small kisses on her face. He then grabbed her chin to meet him and kissed her lips. He kissed her softly, tugging on her lower lip. She then opened her mouth to take his tongue. Their tongues tangoed while he ran his fingers up and down her arms.

Cameron pulled his lips away to whisper into her ear. "Why don't you take a shower with me?"

"Aren't you hungry?" Nicole whispered back.

"Yes, but I would rather we shower together. I can eat later," he said, planting soft kisses along the nape of her neck. Nicole pulled Cameron close to kiss him. This time, she shifted her stance so she could pull him backwards toward the bathroom.

In the intimate confines of the bathroom, the running water provided a soothing backdrop as Nicole and Cameron stepped into the shower. The scent of Nicole's shower gel filled the air as she lathered her loofah bath sponge. Cameron's eyes filled with desire as he took the loofah and lathered Nicole's shoulders, traveling between her breasts, stopping to pull her into a deep, long kiss. The water coursed down their bodies as they stood under the spray, bodies adorned by the glistening rivulets that traced the curves and contours of their skin.

Nicole retrieved her loofah and gently scrubbed Cameron's upper body, paying special attention to his pecs. Hands lathered, she glided them up and down his back, working her way down to his firm ass. She grabbed his ass, pulling him closer. Cameron bent down to wrap his arms behind Nicole's upper thighs and lifted her so she could straddle him. They locked lips, his tongue searching for hers as he deepened the kiss. She pulled away from her kiss, gazing at Cameron. He saw her eyes burning with a craving for him to be inside her.

"Nicole, I want you, now," Cameron barked as he lowered her so his dick was tickling her entrance.

"Yes!" was all Nicole could muster to say. She wiggled herself to take him in. They both hummed at the sensation of Cameron being inside her. His strength supported them as he thrusted inside of her. The shower, a channel that coursed down their intertwined bodies, creating a sanctuary within the confines of the steamy stall. Within seconds, Nicole was biting on Cameron's shoulder as she climaxed. He buried his head into her neck and exploded. Water streamed over them, rinsing the shared heat they had for one another. Nicole dropped her legs and leaned against the tiled wall to catch her breath.

"Wow, that was amazing," Nicole sang, as she reached for her washcloth to clean herself.

"Let me do that," Cameron offered.

"Oh, no. We'll never get out of here," Nicole said, laughing into her hands as they cupped her face.

They both cleaned themselves in the shower and got out, dried off, and dressed in comfy lounge wear.

"I'm going to make us a bite to eat before you have to go, and you can tell me about your news."

Cameron watched Nicole as she grabbed all the ingredients for shrimp tacos. He watched her move around her kitchen to make their lunch. It was at that moment he knew. Cameron Davis was in love with Nicole Graham. There was no other explanation for what he'd been feeling. Maybe if he was honest with her, just as he was now being honest with himself, he could open up. He could talk freely and share how he felt. He was going to tell her. Before he went back to the station. He knew he may be ahead of her in how he felt. He loved her. He was in love with her. Although he felt she loved him, too.

"Would you like something to drink?" Nicole offered, waking Cameron from his thoughts.

"Water is fine. I have to go to work soon." He couldn't say anything else in that very moment.

"What did you want to share with me?" she asked as she added ice and water from the refrigerator to a glass.

Cameron took a deep breath then said, "Before we get into my news, how are your parents? I reviewed the report that was sent to the insurance company."

"Yes, my mom told me she spoke to them the other day. I can't thank you enough for doing that for them."

"It was my pleasure." Cameron took another sip of his water, drawing up the courage to confess his love for Nicole. He watched her chop tomatoes and shred cabbage for their tacos. She pulled a skillet from the lower cabinet, washed the shrimp, then added them to a bowl and tossed them in seasoning. Just as she was going to add some olive oil to the pan, Cameron's phone rang.

"Hello."

"This is Cameron Davis."

"Yes, Patricia Davis is my mother."

"What?"

"Where is she?"

"I'm on my way."

Cameron got up to find his sweatshirt, socks, and shoes.

Cameron fumbled in search of his keys, the urgency heightening, wanting to be by his mother's side. "Baby, I'm so sorry. I have to go. It's my mom."

"Is everything okay?" Nicole asked, a worrying expression on her face.

"I don't know." Cameron could hear the shakiness in his voice.

"Go. I'll see you soon." Cameron gave Nicole a kiss on her cheek and rushed out the door.

Cameron drove into the hospital emergency exit, barely parking, and hurried to reach the emergency room front desk.

"I received a call? About my mother, Patricia Davis?

The receptionist at the front desk glanced at Cameron. "Your name, sir?"

"My name is Cameron Davis. Patricia is my mother."

Pointing, the receptionist showed Cameron the way. "You can go down the hall and to your right. The nurse at the emergency room entrance will direct you to your mother's bed."

When Cameron approached his mother, her eyes were closed, and she appeared to be resting. He couldn't remember the last time his mother was sick. Over the phone, they didn't say it was an accident. The nurse arrived to check on Patricia.

"Oh, hello, you must be Cameron, Patricia's son," the nurse said.

"Yes, I am. Can you explain to me what's going on?" he asked with impatience, wanting answers.

"Your mom passed out here at work. She was at the nurse's station. They said one minute she was awake and alert. The next minute, she was slumped in her chair with her head down. One of her colleagues found her unconscious. The doctors are reviewing her vitals. This may be the onset of hypertension. If the heart is beating hard and the blood pressure is high, blood can stop reaching the brain, eventually causing you to faint."

With Cameron's medical background, he knew he shouldn't be worried. His mom definitely needed to reduce her workload and take a break. When he was younger, she worked many hours to add to the household finances. Now, his mother didn't have to work so hard. She had kept the same pace, even after Cameron graduated college. When he graduated from the fire academy, he told her to reduce her hours and slow down to enjoy life, make new friends, and even date. She wouldn't hear it. She loved her work, and she felt she needed to stay busy.

"What type of care will she need?" Cameron asked the doctor when he entered the room.

"We're keeping her overnight, to observe her behavior, to see if the hypertension has affected her abilities to do simple things. If she can adjust her routine to reduce work, she can go home and rest for about a week or so. We're prescribing medication to control her blood pressure. We'll monitor it during regular doctor visits. She'll also need to keep a log of her pressure readings to ensure the medication is doing its job. We are definitely recommending reduced work hours."

"Okay, I'll make sure she follows the doctor's orders. Thank you." Cameron was grateful the diagnosis wasn't more serious. Glancing at his watch, he realized he had an hour until he had to return to the station.

Uncertain about what to do, Cameron asked the nurse whether he should cancel work or go into the station. "Will she sleep all night?"

"We did give her something to help her sleep. She'll sleep for the next several hours."

"Thank you," Cameron said, grateful his mother's condition wasn't worse. He stepped outside the room to call the station, letting them know he would miss his shift. He thought to call Nicole, but texted. He could do that quietly while he sat with his mom.

Cameron - Hey baby!

Nicole - Hey, how's your mom?

Cameron - She's resting, likely sleeping until the morning.

Nicole - What happened?

Cameron - She was diagnosed with hypertension

Nicole - Do you need me to do anything?

Cameron - No, I'll be here with her.

Nicole - Of course

Cameron - Talk soon.

Two weeks before Christmas, Cameron sat in his condo that he barely saw these days because of his schedule and checking in with his mom. He missed Nicole. He was tired of their only means of communication being text messages. It had been two weeks since he last saw her. Without thinking, Cameron hopped in his car to surprise her. When he pulled up to the driveway, he saw an unfamiliar car parked in front of her house. He stood outside the door waiting for Nicole to answer, only to find Edward answering her door.

"Where's Nicole?" Cameron said coldly.

Leaving the door slightly open, Edward stepped out. "Look, man, I know you two had a thing, but she and I are back together. So you can go."

"Back together? What do you mean? You two are only friends."

"That's what she tells people, but we're together. When she met you, we were on a break. I love her and she loves me. We're back on again, and this time it is for keeps."

Cameron couldn't believe his ears. With this news, he frowned at Edward, turned around and walked back to his car, started the engine, and left.

Chapter 32

Nicole

"Aubrey, I don't know what happened. One minute we're all into each other. The next minute, I don't hear from him. Communication just stopped." Nicole sighed, her heart giving a twist in her chest. "You know I had to explain his absence at Christmas dinner. Levi didn't believe me when I said he was working. You know what it was like for me to bring in the new year alone? Without Cameron? You were there."

"Well?" Aubrey thought for a moment before speaking, as she finished her bite of shrimp caesar salad. "If you want to know, you should just show up where you know he'll be. He can't avoid you if you are right in front of his face."

Nicole said, folding her arms, "I have too much pride for that."

"You're miserable, Nicole. You talk about him all the time. I know you miss him," Aubrey said, tearing off a piece of sourdough bread to butter.

"I miss him. I miss him a lot," Nicole said as she tossed her fork over her half eaten BBQ chicken salad, tears welling in her eyes.

Aubrey put her fork down and watched her best friend struggle to not let a tear drop, masking what was clear. "You love him, don't you?"

A flush stung Nicole's cheeks. "What?"

"You love him? I know what love looks like, Nicole. I know what you look like when you're in love. I haven't seen you in love since Tyler," Aubrey said in a low tone.

Nicole put her hands on her face and sobbed. People around them gave them curious stares. Their server rushed to the table. "Is there something wrong? Can I get you ladies anything?"

"We're fine," Aubrey shared, without taking her gaze away from Nicole. "She just realized she's in love."

"Oh, well, congratulations," the server said, then stepped away from the table.

"I haven't talked to Cameron in weeks, Aubrey. He hasn't tried to call me or anything. Not even during the holidays. Who does that? It's like he just disappeared. I need someone who'll communicate with me, share feelings, and talk when something is wrong."

"I read somewhere that he's up for a promotion. It seems the media loves him, so they're keeping tabs on his career," Aubrey shared.

Nicole looked up from her folded hands. "What? He's up for a promotion?"

"Yeah, I'm sure his schedule has kept him busy with the possibilities of moving up."

With an inquisitive expression, Nicole realized, "That's what he wanted to share with me."

"Huh?" Aubrey said, confused.

"When he was over, he said he wanted to share something with me. We didn't have time to talk because he got the call about his mom," Nicole realized.

"You now have a reason to go see him. You can congratulate him,"

Aubrey suggested.

Nicole bit her lower lip in thought before speaking. "I don't know, Aubrey. I don't want to make a fool of myself. I don't want to seem desperate. It's been weeks."

"How are you desperate? You both agreed to be exclusive. And now he won't even talk to you. No official breakup, nothing," Aubrey rationalized the facts.

"You have a point." Nicole didn't think about it that way. What if she met someone else and wanted to date them? She would want to be sure they were officially broken up.

"I know I do," Aubrey said indignantly.

"I'll think about it." Nicole wasn't sure about just being somewhere Cameron was. That seemed stalkerish.

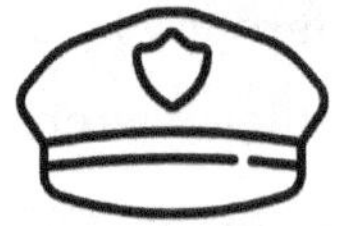

Later that afternoon, Nicole sat in her living room, thinking about her conversation with Aubrey. Maybe Aubrey was right. Maybe she should go see Cameron. Although he ghosted her. No communication, explanation, no reason they hadn't seen each other. No Merry Christmas. No Happy New Year. Feelings of anger overwhelmed her at the audacity of him just disappearing from her life. He left her house the last time they saw each other to go check on his mother. They exchanged text messages for a few weeks. Then communication stopped. No more 'good morning, baby'. No song dedications. Maybe Nicole didn't give him the impression she cared for him, too. Did she reveal her inability to release Tyler? Did Tyler still have a hold on her heart? She had powerful feelings for Cameron. Could there have been some way she could have shown him how much? Envisioning what this could look like, the buzzing of her phone interrupted Nicole's thoughts with an incoming text message.

Edward - Hey, free for dinner?

Nicole sighed, rolling her eyes. She and Edward had gone to the movies. Was that a mistake? She wanted to get out of her house. Everywhere she looked, she saw Cameron's face. Edward was a distraction. Even though he made her angry by just his presence, his presence brought Nicole comfort. A kind of comfort that made her feel she was close to Tyler. But was being close to Tyler what she needed? Tyler may have wanted Edward to take care of her and ensure her safety, but not pursue a romantic relationship. Edward asking her for dinner seemed like he was asking her out on a date. She typed a reply to Edward.

Nicole - Hey, no, I have plans, but thank you.

Edward - Oh?

Nicole - Yes plans.

Edward - Are you ok?

Nicole - I'm fine. I have to go.

Rather than tempt herself to say yes to Edward, Nicole decided to hang out with Levi. She confirmed her plans with a text message.

Nicole - Hey Levi. I'm coming over. I'll bring dinner.

Levi - Sure.

When Nicole pulled up to Levi's house with Chinese takeout, he was standing in his doorway hugging a woman, kissing her neck before giving her a quick kiss on the lips.

"Hey!" Nicole said loudly, hoping to not make their display of affection awkward.

"Hey, Nicole. You remember Suzette?" Levi said, pulling his lady friend by the hand, walking toward her car.

"Yeah, from the restaurant a time back," Nicole said, giving Suzette a warm hug.

"Yes, hi. I was just leaving."

Nicole watched as Suzette gave Levi a kiss on his cheek and walked to her car. She waited until Suzette drove away before speaking.

"So, are you guys a thing?" Nicole asked, watching Suzette's car disappear down the street.

Levi cleared his throat, then said, "She's nice, but nah."

"Then what was she doing here?" Nicole asked, even though she knew the answer.

"Filling time," Levi responded, pulling his sister into a hug, then grabbed the bags of food to carry into the house.

"What does that mean? I know she likes you." Nicole stepped into the house, closing the door behind her.

"She does, and maybe if things were different, she could be my girlfriend, but..." Levi then distracted himself by grabbing plates out of the cabinet, utensils out of the drawers preparing to scoop the delicious fried rice and Mongolian beef waiting to be eaten.

Nicole reached for two bottled waters and asked, "But what, Levi?"

Levi stopped where he stood and looked at his sister. "My heart belongs to Elle. And I will get her back," he said with determination.

"Levi, I get it, but don't you think you should move on?" Nicole pleaded.

Levi inhaled a deep breath, clenched his jaw, then said, "Why? Because Elle says she's engaged? Until she's married, I still have a chance. I have faith that I can win her back, no matter what."

Nicole took a deep breath, then said, "I don't want you to get your hopes up."

"Thank you for wanting to protect me, but I'm a big boy. I can handle it."

Nicole looked at her brother with loving eyes. She had a gut feeling that he would never move on from Elle. Maybe he knew something she didn't. She left the subject alone.

After talking about their parents' store rebuild, Nicole caught Levi up on Cameron.

"You love him, huh?" Levi asked.

"I think so. I'm not sure. Levi? I'm scared," Nicole admitted.

"He's a good guy. I'm not sure what's happening, but there must be a reason." Levi was certain of it.

"I haven't felt like this since Tyler. I know it sounds corny, but it's true. I'm prideful, though. I don't want to reach out to him. He ghosted me." It saddened Nicole to admit this fact out loud.

"Pride can block happiness," Levi said matter-of-factly.

"You have a point." Her little brother giving her advice was new.

"If you don't want to talk to him, you should at least invite him to the store reopening," Levi suggested. "That may open up lines of communication. Maybe one of you will have the guts to take it from there."

"That's an idea. I don't know, Levi." Nicole was hesitant to contact Cameron. She didn't know where she stood.

Levi shrugged his shoulders, then said, "It's just a suggestion."

Levi and Nicole finished their food and scrolled through Netflix, looking for a movie to watch. Snuggled on the new cozy couch with the one man who loved and understood her no matter what, Nicole laid her head on Levi's shoulder as they watched Top Gun–the original. In the end, the movie watched both of them. Nicole woke up to the movie on repeat. She put a blanket over Levi, kissed his cheek, and quietly left to head home.

On the day of the reopening, Nicole busied herself with the finishing touches to her parents' store. Carol took new photos around the new layout for the website, while Aubrey and a staff member prepared food in the back. For the first time in a while, Nicole felt pretty good, dressed in fitted jeans, the store's newly designed t-shirt, and her Adidas, ready to greet customers. She glanced out the window, admiring the beautiful February afternoon, realizing it would have been a good morning for a run.

Invited guests were arriving. Nicole's dad's excitement bubbled up as he turned on the new sound system and programmed his created oldies' playlist. Music blared from the surround sound as people sipped on wine, perusing the store's inventory and relishing in the songs from previous eras. Nicole walked over to get a bottle of water and a turkey slider when she heard Aubrey call her name. "Nicole!"

"I'm right here, what?" she answered, walking in Aubrey's direction.

"Cameron just walked in the door," Aubrey whispered.

Nicole's stomach did a flip-flop just at the mention of Cameron's name. She couldn't bring herself to turn around, fearing that seeing his face would be overwhelming.

Aubrey nudged Nicole forward then said, "Turn around, girl, go greet him."

Nicole inhaled a deep breath and turned around to see him, dressed in khaki colored pants, a white ribbed long sleeve shirt that hugged his muscles and white tennis shoes. He was clean shaved and just beautiful. Nicole saw Cameron glance over to her, giving her a small smile, just as Levi stepped up to him, slapped his hand into Cameron's, and pulled him into a quick hug.

"Glad you could make it, man. Good to see you," Levi said.

"Good to see you, too." Cameron looked back at Nicole and began walking toward her.

"Hi," he said in a low tone.

"Hi," Nicole replied, in a disappearing voice.

A mutual yearning bled through their gaze, both hesitant, caught in a moment of yearning and uncertainty.

Cameron spoke first. "How've you been?"

A smile tugged at Nicole's lips when she spoke. "I have been okay. Busy with this store and my recipe book."

"Really?" A smile on the edge of Cameron's lips.

"Yeah." Nicole was lost for words. She didn't know what to say. She wanted to see this man, and here he was, in front of her, and she had nothing to say.

"How've you been?" Nicole asked.

"Busy with work," Cameron responded.

"Congratulations on making the short list for a promotion," Nicole said, keeping her voice low.

Cameron's voice softened. "Thanks. I wanted to share that with you. I wanted to share something else, but..."

"Aubrey told me. She read it somewhere. I guess the media is still following you and your career after the fire."

"Yeah, they kind of made it a big deal, given the baby incident." Cameron looked down at his feet, then up again into Nicole's eyes.

Nicole met his gaze and said, "It's well deserved. How's your mom?"

"My mom is good. She's been home for a few months, taking time off. She'll go back to work soon, on reduced hours." They stood in silence for a few seconds, unable to tear their eyes away from one another.

Nicole averted Cameron's gaze to Walter and Jeannette dancing around the store. "My parents would love to see you."

"Yeah, I'll speak to them when they stop dancing." They both chuckled.

"I wanted to say congratulations to them for getting the store reopened. Levi told me about the reopening when I ran into him a few days ago," Cameron said, seeming a little hurt. Maybe because Nicole didn't invite him first.

"Levi's just as excited for the store to be open," Nicole said, laughing. "He doesn't have to spend his spare time helping now."

They both let out a chuckle.

"Hey, Cameron," Walter said, giving him a pat on the back.. "Good to see you, young man. How do you like the store?"

"It's great. Really great. Congratulations!" Cameron said, shaking Walter's hand.

"Jeannette, come say hi to Cameron," Walter said, waving Nicole's mom over to them. Jeannette walked over to greet Cameron with a big hug.

"It's so nice to see you. This rebuild exceeded our expectations, didn't it? Don't you love it?" Jeannette said in excitement.

"Yes, it is amazing," Cameron said with a grin.

"Well, enjoy yourself, and thank you for coming," Walter said as he whisked Jeannette away to speak to some movie executives who had just walked through the door. Cameron watched them walk away and turned back to Nicole. He walked closer to her, but stopped when he saw Edward intercept them and greet Nicole with a hug. Cameron's face turned instantly cold and hard.

"Hey, Edward," Nicole said. "You remember Cameron."

"Yes, I remember Cameron," Edward said, holding Nicole at her waist.

Cameron directed his gaze at Edward, then to her, and said, "Nicole, it was nice seeing you. I'm going to go." With that, Cameron walked out of the store.

Chapter 33

Cameron

Seeing Nicole was one of the best and worst things to happen to Cameron. She looked so adorable at the reopening in her store t-shirt and sneakers. He had the desire to pull her into his arms the moment he laid eyes on her, an overwhelming emotion tugging at his heartstrings. The ache of Nicole's absence lingered in his heart. His work schedule, helping his mom recuperate and get used to her new, more restful lifestyle, was Cameron's savior. He would be lying if he said Nicole wasn't a missing piece of his life. He included her in everything. Witnessing her with Edward stoked a fire of anger within him, a visceral reaction to the sight that intensified his emotions. He missed spending the holidays with Nicole. He couldn't see her knowing she was with Edward. His heart shattered at the sight of him holding her at the waist. That moment echoed with the ache in his heart. Nicole was his girl. Was she still his girl? They never talked about a breakup. But Edward said they were together. Were they?

Cameron picked up groceries and drove to his mother's house. She always helped him clear his head and gain perspective.

"Hey, Ma," Cameron stated as he opened the front door, grocery bags in hand.

"Hey, son. I'm in the kitchen." Patricia was washing some dishes when Cameron set the groceries on the kitchen counter and unloaded the items in each bag.

"I'm going to make us some lunch. I'm starving," Patricia said, adding the last dish to the dish rack, pulling the towel from the counter to dry her hands.

"Let me make lunch, Mom," Cameron suggested. He wanted to stay busy to cloud the images from the reopening from his head. He set out the freshly baked, sliced bread and deli sliced turkey with crisp lettuce and provolone cheese. Patricia grabbed plates from the cabinet as Cameron rinsed a tomato to slice. His mother watched his intense expression resting on his face as he made their sandwiches. She opened the bag of chips and poured some on each plate.

"Do you want some lemonade?" Cameron asked, filling two glasses with ice and setting them on the table.

Patricia spoke in a consoling tone. "How have you been, son?"

"Just okay." Cameron couldn't lie to his mother. He knew she would see through his charade.

"Why just okay?" Patricia asked as she took a bite of her sandwich.

"I've been swamped." Lately, work was his go to excuse for being distant.

"How's Nicole?"

Hearing Nicole's name tugged at Cameron's heart. "She's good."

Patricia took a sip of lemonade, set the glass down and put her hand on Cameron's knee. "Are you sure about that?"

"What do you mean, Mom?" Cameron asked as he took a big bite of his sandwich.

Patricia looked straight into her son's eyes as she spoke. "I know you two haven't been seeing each other. Why is that?"

Cameron stopped chewing and asked with a mouth full. "How do you know that?"

"One thing you'll learn: a mother knows her child. I can always tell when you're unhappy."

With a puzzled expression on his face, Cameron asked, "How do you know that?"

"I just know. I knew when you and Shannon were on the outs," Patricia admitted, grabbing a chip and putting it into her mouth.

"What?" Cameron thought he had masked his break up pretty well.

"You shut down. You stop talking," Patricia shared, taking a sip of lemonade.

Anxious, Cameron had to ask, "Mom, how do you know about Nicole?"

"Nicole has been checking on me. She even stopped by a few times to bring me food and one of her friend's cakes."

"Is that where the lemon pound cake came from?" Cameron remembered seeing it the last time he was over.

"Yes, I still have some. I sliced the cake, wrapped individual pieces and placed them in the freezer to enjoy later. You know I can't eat an entire cake."

Cameron's heart sank at the betrayal he felt. "Mom, why didn't you tell me?"

"It's not my place to meddle in your business." Cameron knew his mom always meddled in his business. She was subtle, but she still meddled.

"This would have been the time, Mom." Cameron felt irritation swelling in his chest. He didn't want to be angry with his mom. He knew she meant well.

"Nicole's a nice girl. I really like her. I like her for you. Without each other, both of you are moping in misery. I see it in your face. I see it in how you carry yourself. You walk around with your shoulders drooped. I saw the same in Nicole when I saw her. You both are just stubborn."

"Mom, but—"

"Cameron! I know you. I've watched relationship after relationship over the years, and the worst breakup was with Shannon. You shut down. You've always been a poor communicator, and during the last breakup, it almost ruined you."

"What are you talking about?" Cameron didn't understand where all this was coming from. He knew he could work on communication. But Shannon cheated on him with her now husband.

"I know Shannon cheated on you with her ex-boyfriend. I know they're now married. You never talked about it. I ran into her mother at the mall a time back and we talked. I held my tongue, but got the gist of what happened. That woman is lucky I didn't slap her face when she was done sharing her story. Anyway, the details of that conversation aren't important."

Was Cameron getting the closure he needed to move on from his relationship with Shannon? "Why didn't you ever tell me about this, Mom?"

Patricia shrugged her shoulders. "I figured why bring up old stuff?"

"This was important stuff, Mom. It would have helped me a lot."

"Anyway..."

"I can't believe you kept all of this from me." Cameron was confused now. Did his mother really understand what knowing that information could have done for him?

"Were you ready to listen? When I saw her, you had just started dating

Nicole. Why bring up Shannon when you are beyond smitten with Ms. Graham?"

In a sharp tone, Cameron said, "That was not for you to decide."

"Okay, fine. Now you know. And watch your tone, mister. Moving on, what are you going to do about all of this?" Patricia always had a way of calling her son out, making him face what he was not ready to deal with.

"I'm sorry, Mom. Do about what?" Cameron's head hurt. All he wanted was to finish his lunch.

"Nicole?" Patricia asked, in a cool tempered voice.

"There's nothing to do," Cameron sighed as he covered his face with his hands. "She's moved on."

Patricia, now frowning, said, "Moved on? What does that mean?"

Cameron tried to keep his voice steady when he shared, "She's dating someone new."

"I don't think so, son." Patricia knew better.

Cameron couldn't share the encounter with Edward at Nicole's house. He couldn't replay the scene at the store reopening. Those words wouldn't escape his mouth.

"Son, you have dark circles under your eyes. You have an edge to you that's not friendly. You look sad all the time. You miss that girl."

Cameron said nothing. His mother was right. He missed Nicole so much. Interfering in her new relationship was not something he planned to do. He was not that guy. His feelings were genuine. He thought he loved Shannon, but his love for her was not like the love he felt for Nicole. What he shared with Nicole came down like a summer storm, catching him off guard. In the beginning, it was an unexpected spark, a magnetic pull that drew them closer. He was in uncharted waters, discovering the depth of their connection each day they were together. Cameron thought Nicole felt the same. They never said the words, but he felt it. He loved Nicole. Now, though, he couldn't handle confronting her and being rejected.

It was Saturday, and Cameron was meeting his friends at their spot to watch the game. He needed this distraction, having not sorted through his feelings for Nicole and what to do about them. His friends would consider him crazy for falling in love so fast. He couldn't share that they were no longer together, or that she had moved on. Deep within, he sensed the fragile threads of his composure just thinking about talking about Nicole in front of the guys. He needed to defend himself until he could understand everything.

Cameron walked into the bar to find Myles sitting in their usual spot, alone.

"Hey, Myles, how's it going?" Cameron asked as he slid into the booth.

"Hey, man, long time no see. I know you've been busy with work and that beautiful girl of yours," Myles said with a grin.

Cameron's face collapsed when Myles mentioned Nicole.

"Man, what's up? You kinda look like shit."

Cameron tried to gather his thoughts. "Man, I don't want to talk about it. Not here. Not with the guys coming."

"You two are having problems already?" Myles asked, taking a swig of his beer.

"Something like that," Cameron whispered.

"Well, by the look of you, I say it is pretty bad."

"What's wrong with the way I look?" Cameron asked, giving Myles a nudge.

"You don't have that glimmer in your eye. Your face looks long and sad."

His mom told him the same thing. Now Myles. "We're not seeing each other anymore."

Eyes widened, Myles asked, "What happened?"

"It's a long story. I don't want to talk about it." Cameron put his hands on the table and scanned the bar, looking for who knew what. He needed to divert his attention from Myles' shocked expression.

Myles stared at his friend for an extended moment. Cameron knew Myles would see through him. Ever since the first day of basketball practice, freshman year in college, they became fast friends. He almost knew Cameron better than he knew himself.

"You love her, don't you?" Myles asked.

Cameron just looked at Myles and shrugged his shoulders.

"Man, I know you. You don't have to say the words, but I know you."

Cameron said nothing.

"Whatever it is, go get your girl," Myles urged.

Right as Cameron was about to reply to Myles, Josh, Ryan, and Terrell entered the room together.

"Hey y'all, what's up?" Josh asked.

The guys exchanged handshakes and hugs and called the server over to take their usual order. For the next three hours, Cameron immersed himself into conversation about sports, Ryan's dating escapades, and a new girl Josh was seeing. Cameron played it cool, thankful the guys didn't ask about Nicole.

"So, Myles, how's married life treating you?" Josh asked.

"Man, the best decision ever. When you find the right one, wife her, man. Married life is grand." Myles smiled.

A warm glow emanated from Myles, casting a radiant aura that was impossible to miss. Myles was blissfully happy. Cameron wanted to bask in that radiance. He wanted that with Nicole. He wanted Nicole forever.

How could he tell Nicole how he felt when she was with Edward? He wouldn't survive her rejection.

Cameron felt the urgent need for calm. The storm swirling in his head would soon be lethal. The record parlor was the one place that settled him. He wanted to lose himself in the music. This place was where he first met Nicole, but he could still set aside his emotions and concentrate on discovering new albums to bring home and play. As Cameron flipped through the Miami rap section, he heard the beginning of Anita Baker's Angel. His heart did somersaults as her beautiful voice belted out of the chorus. Cameron gripped the crates and lowered his head. This was a new feeling. He now had an inability to control his thoughts and emotions. He brought his few albums to the counter, paid for them, and left the store. As he walked out, he ran into a man, trying to enter the store.

"I'm sorry about that," Cameron said, holding his hands up to let the guy know he meant no harm. He raced home, put his headphones on and got on his spin table. He placed the new vinyl on the table, letting the bass and beats fill his head, waiting for the perfect moment to blend into the next song. Immersed in each song, Cameron lost himself in the rhythms that surrounded him. His surroundings faded into the background, creating a cocoon of sound that shielded him from the outside world.

Two hours later, Cameron was sweating. As the last notes lingered in the air, he returned to reality. His throat was dry, and his head hurt from being under headphones without a break. He thought of nothing but what he was doing. Cameron imagined being on stage, the crowd bouncing to his tunes, having a good time. He wanted to be in a crowd, dancing, feeling the music in his veins. He closed his eyes, picturing himself floating over the crowd. With that image diminishing, he felt the pain in his heart from missing Nicole, becoming unhinged at the thought of her. Thoughts of Nicole weren't going away. He needed to sleep.

After a shower, and a cup of calming tea Nicole had left for Cameron to drink following a hard shift, he got into his bed. He tossed from one end of his bed to the other, incapable of getting comfortable. He ended up just lying on his back with his arms behind his head, staring up at the ceiling.

Chapter 34

Nicole

Seated at her dining room table, Nicole surrounded herself with the array of book cover samples, each one a visual interpretation of what this book meant to her. What her grandmother meant to her. Floating in thought, her fingers traced the embossed details, eyes wandering over the diverse choices that lay scattered across the table. Memories of Ms. Ely resonated in the background as Nicole wrote and photographed each recipe, the book absorbing the essence of the dedication to her grandmother. In quiet moments of contemplation, it was as if Ms. Ely sat beside her, offering insight and encouragement. Lost in the beauty of possibilities laid out before her, the artistic interpretation of her vision mirrored the soul of her work. Nicole found herself drawn to a particular cover that seemed to encapsulate the very essence of Ms. Ely. The design was a tribute, capturing the essence of the woman who shaped her world. As she gazed at the cover, she could almost hear her grandmother's laughter echoing through generations, the image becoming a portal to the shared stories about food that connected them.

Based on her work as a food stylist, she knew there was an audience for her grandmother's recipes. The younger generations wanted recipes and food like their grandmothers made when they were young. Her audience were people her parents' age who knew good food but didn't have family recipes to pass down to their own children and grandchildren. Her audience were chefs who were driven by a desire to transcend tradition and carve out their own culinary identities, reimagining age-old recipes in modern, innovative ways. It was Nicole's audience for her book that drove her to finish this labor of love. She refused to postpone the launch. She would work tirelessly to get it done.

Nicole pushed herself away from the table after several hours of working, her muscles tense from sitting all day. She checked her phone and only found a message from Edward. As the evening wore on, it became increasingly clear that tonight, above all nights, was not the one she wanted to confront everyone, especially Edward. Her yearning for Cameron lingered in the air, the echoes of her own company feeling more pronounced, accentuating the emptiness of her space that was often occupied by Cameron. The solitude pressed against her. The longing for Cameron created a tender ache, urging her to seek sleep. Nicole wished sleep would bring her solace to the loneliness that lingered in her heart for him.

Nicole walked into her bathroom, stripped off her clothes, and examined herself in the mirror. Dark circles ringed her eyes, likely due to lack of sleep. However, she had lost some weight, but her muscles were toned. Nicole ran her right hand along her left shoulder, softly caressing her skin, drawing feather-like circles over the middle of her neck, slowly moving down between her breasts. Eyes closed, she imagined Cameron touching her. His touch brought relaxation, satisfaction. His touch was warm and sensual, melting her insides whenever he touched her. The ache of missing Cameron manifested in the tender vulnerability of her tears, each one a testament to the depth of connection she had. Nicole's tears carried the tale of her fairytale love, separation, and a pain that only time and the hope of a reunion could mend.

Once in the shower, Nicole let the hot water pound on her back, slowly releasing the tightness she felt in her neck and shoulders. Turning her body to allow the water to stream down the front of her chest and stomach, Nicole grabbed her favorite body sponge and pumped the magnolia scented body wash onto it. Using her hands to lather the body sponge, she brushed small, then large strokes up and down her skin, all the while the water was still streaming down her body. Nicole scrubbed her entire body until the body wash no longer lathered her skin. She then rinsed off and took her oversized plush towel to dry off. In her tired state, she chose a pair of old gray cotton shorts and a tank top to wear. Feeling a slight chill overcome her body, she found one of Cameron's sweatshirts and pulled it over her head and through her arms. It smelled of him. She sniffed his cologne embedded in the fabric and wrapped her arms around herself, dreaming it was Cameron. Each step to Nicole's room carried a weight, as if the air itself held the residue of the emotions she carried. Consumed by thoughts of him, she curled up into a ball on her bed. She lay in that position for a while, envisioning Cameron next to her.

Nicole must have dozed off. The next thing she knew, her phone was ringing. Levi!

"Hello," Nicole said in a low, sleepy voice.

"Hey, sis, are you home? Are you sleeping?"

Nicole yawned into the phone, then said, "Yes, I'm home. I was just taking a nap."

"Are you alone?" Levi asked, wanting to be sure he interrupted nothing.

"Yes, I'm alone. What's up?"

"Checking in. Can I come over?"

"You can come by."

"I'm on my way. And I'm hungry," Levi said with a chuckle.

It was 7:30. Nicole had slept for three hours. She got up and walked into her kitchen. Despite not having been to the store for days, she planned cooking a light meal for her and Levi was a great idea. When she didn't find a combination of ingredients to make a meal, she decided.

"Food delivery it is," Nicole said out loud.

Flipping through her utility drawer, she pulled out some menus from her favorite local restaurants. Knowing she was ordering for her and Levi, she had to keep his tastes in mind. Having a taste for hummus and pita bread with a nice crunchy salad, Nicole decided on the Mediterranean. Now sitting on her living room couch channel surfing for something to watch, she caught a story about firefighters, how hard they work, and the dangers of the job. She knew Cameron's job was dangerous. The risk of equipment malfunction, explosions, structural collapse and burn injuries were on the short list. Overwhelm settled in as Nicole grappled with countless thoughts. She didn't think about how dangerous Cameron's job was. Without warning, a floodgate of emotion within her, tears began streaming down her cheeks, this feeling sudden and unanticipated. Cameron was in danger each time he went on a call. Tyler entered her stream of thoughts, mourning how hazardous his job was. So much so, he was killed while on duty.

Just as Nicole pulled herself together, she heard Levi pull up. Nicole opened the door, then sat back on the couch.

"What's wrong?" Levi asked, rushing to her side.

Overwhelmed with emotion, Nicole couldn't speak. She just pointed to her television.

"What show were you watching?" Levi asked, holding his sister in a tight hug.

"That show. Cameron's job is dangerous," Nicole revealed, wiping her tears on Levi's shirt.

Nicole turned to face her brother, only to fall into his arms again, unable to release him for fear of falling to the floor. Levi hugged her tight until she stopped crying.

"Have you spoken to Cameron?" Levi asked in a whisper.

"No."

"Don't you think you should?"

"No, he has my number, too." Nicole was not going to be the first one to make a move.

"Does he know how you feel?" Levi wanted to support his sister, but he knew she was miserable.

Nicole lacked clarity about her emotions. "How do I feel, Levi?"

"It looks like love to me." Levi pulled away from his sister to look at her.

Nicole rolled her eyes and stepped away from her brother. The doorbell rang.

"I ordered food. Can you get that?" Nicole asked as she ran into the bathroom.

Levi opened the door to find the food sitting by the door.

"What did you order for us?" Levi asked, carrying the food into the kitchen.

"Mediterranean," Nicole yelled from the bathroom.

"Yum! I feel like hummus and pita chips," Levi said, eagerly emptying the bags onto the counter.

Nicole and Levi set their food up on the living room coffee table in front of the turned off television. She caught him up on the progress of her recipe book. Levi made Nicole laugh, feel normal for a short while.

By the time Levi left, Nicole was exhausted. Spending time with Levi always made her feel better. After brushing her teeth and loosening her ponytail, Nicole got into her bed, then reached for her phone to play her calming app. Relishing the sounds of waves on the beach, Nicole closed her eyes and envisioned she was walking along the shore, watching the sand and water bury her feet. Tyler was suddenly walking beside her, not talking, just walking. Nicole reached out to hug him, but he disappeared. She twirled and found herself back in the room, seated on the bed beside Tyler. He smiled at her, rose, walked to the door, and glanced back at Nicole.

"Tyler!" Nicole screamed.

Nicole sat straight up in her bed. Her heavy breathing and damp skin reminded her she had another dream about Tyler. The dreams were becoming uncomfortable now. They used to bring her comfort, but ever since dating Cameron, she felt as if she was cheating on him. Or was she cheating on Tyler? Feeling the weight of stress pressing down on her, Nicole yearned for relief. It was after 4am. Although wide awake, Nicole felt drained. She knew she couldn't fall back asleep. Being too early in the morning to call anyone, Nicole made a cup of coffee, walked into her dining room, surveyed the table filled with Ms. Ely's book materials, and went to work.

Chapter 35

Cameron

Cameron and Nicole hadn't spoken since her parents' reopening. They were not even sending text messages any more. Judging by appearances, she had moved on. Nicole and Edward were together. Cameron couldn't believe this was happening to him. Again! What was wrong with him? What flaw did he possess that caused women to seek solace in another man's embrace? Cameron thought he and Nicole were different. They seemed to both fall hard and fast for one another. They talked about their past relationships, or so he thought. Edward's name was never mentioned. In the end, he knew this wasn't about Edward. Tyler! Who was Tyler? In all fairness, Cameron knew he didn't have a case. He never communicated with Nicole about what he heard, what he was feeling. He didn't give her a chance to argue, share her side of the story. Cameron couldn't stomach any conversation about it. He would get over it. One day. He had to.

After weeks of continuous work, Cameron finally had a day off and wanted to sleep. For many nights, he lay in quiet darkness, haunting flashbacks of Nicole, him kissing her, touching her, feeling her, being close to her, casting a shadow over his attempts to find solace in sleep. Vivid scenes of their past played out in his mind with an almost cinematic quality replaying moments that stirred a complex array of emotions. Reminiscing held power which transported Cameron back to moments he couldn't forget, making the closing of his eyes painful, revealing the battleground where the ghosts of memories waged a war against the peace he needed to rest.

The ringing of his phone broke him off his train of thoughts.

"Hello?"

"Cameron? It's Mom. How are you, baby?"

"Hey, Mom. I'm tired, but good." Cameron could hear the edge in his mother's voice, knowing a request was coming. She wanted him to do something.

"Listen, I'm having some friends over later today. You know, to celebrate me going back to work. It's now April. Time to get my schedule back before the hospital fires me," Patricia said with a laugh. "Anyway, I was hoping you could help me."

"What is it, Mom?" Cameron asked. He just wanted to get some sleep.

"Do you remember the cake Nicole brought me?" Patricia asked.

"Yes, the lemon glazed pound cake?"

"Yes, that's the one. Can you pick one up for me?"

Cameron heard the eagerness in his mother's voice. He couldn't say no to her. "What time are your guests arriving?"

"Two o'clock," Patricia said.

Cameron looked at his watch. It was 10:15 am. "Yeah, Mom, I can get you the cake and bring it over."

Cameron took a shower, dressed in sweats and a t-shirt, and drove to Aubrey's restaurant. Her eatery had become a city favorite. She made good food and great desserts, one being her lemon glazed pound cake.

Cameron felt apprehensive about going there, though. He hadn't seen Aubrey since the reopening of Nicole's parents' store. Given she was Nicole's best friend, he knew she knew everything. What story did Nicole tell? They broke up without conversation. He felt like an ass. His situation could have been different if he had talked to Nicole. Maybe it was all a misunderstanding. Maybe it wasn't how it looked. Edward made it clear they were together, though. You don't put your hand around the waist of a friend. In the scenario in his head, Aubrey wasn't at the restaurant, and Cameron could enter and leave without her awareness.

Walking through the door, the restaurant was busy with customers finishing breakfast, staff getting ready for the lunch rush. He stood in line, scrolling through his phone until he could place his order.

"Cameron?" He looked up to see Aubrey at the edge of the counter.

"Oh, hey, Aubrey!" he said with a nervous edge.

"What are you here to pick up?"

"My mom wants a lemon glazed pound cake."

"Step out of line and come back here. I'll get you one and package it to go."

Cameron stepped out of line, walked around the counter, and followed Aubrey to the kitchen. Cameron, unsure of what to say or do, stuffed his hands into his pockets. What would he say to Nicole's best friend? Aubrey busied herself with getting a pound cake from the rack of cakes, placing it into her custom box that read Aubrey's Favorites. They remained silent as she placed the cake in a bag. The kitchen was loud and bustling with cooks and wait staff. Besides exchanging greetings and gratitude, Cameron had no substantial conversations with Aubrey.

Aubrey handed Cameron his cake, then said, "I'll walk you to your car, Cameron."

"Sure," he said in surprise.

"I'll be right back, Starr. You got it?" Aubrey said to the young woman overseeing the orders to go out.

With a thumbs up, Starr responded, "Yes, ma'am. I got it."

Cameron and Aubrey made their way through the crowd, walked out the door, and headed down the street towards Cameron's parked car.

"Aubrey? Let me pay you for the cake," Cameron muttered.

"Cameron, it's on the house. You don't owe me anything," Aubrey said, point blank.

"Thanks," he said as he put the cake on the floor of his passenger seat.

Hand folded across her chest, Aubrey asked, "Cameron, can we chat a bit?"

A queasy sensation swept over Cameron, causing his stomach to somersault in response to Aubrey's request. The thought of opening up about Nicole to someone so close to her felt like navigating a minefield of emotions and unspoken boundaries. What would he say?

"Sure," he said to Aubrey, his arms across his chest, looking straight into her eyes.

"You know Nicole and I are best friends. We've been close since high school." Aubrey didn't look away from Cameron when she spoke. It was intimidating.

"Yeah, I know."

Aubrey continued, "Nicole knows me, and I know her. I can't let her experience another heartbreak, even if it means she won't be happy knowing I'm talking to you. Not like this."

"Heartbreak?" Cameron asked, perplexed.

"Yes, heartbreak," Aubrey said, with an irritated frown.

"I didn't break Nicole's heart, Aubrey. You know she's with Edward. He made that very clear."

"What?" Aubrey said, eyes wide with confusion. "When did you talk to Edward?"

"Nicole doesn't know this, but I stopped by her house unannounced. When we were still dating. He answered the door. He said they were back together, in love, and I should give them their space."

Aubrey pushed Cameron in the shoulder, mouth agape, then said in a raised voice, "You are lying!"

"I can't make this up," Cameron said, giving Aubrey a side grin.

"Cameron!" Aubrey said, shaking her head.

Cameron was now leaning against his truck, to prevent his knees from giving out and he crashing to the ground. Just the repeat of that conversation made his heart ache.

"First of all, Cameron, you should've communicated this to Nicole. Your lack of communication is another conversation." Aubrey's face was stern. She took a deep breath before continuing. "Cameron, Edward and Nicole are not together. They were never together. Ever! Edward wants them to be together, but they have always been friends, nothing more. He may play like they're dating, but I promise you, they're just friends. They have never been on a date, nothing. I will say, though, Edward has been there for her during tough times. When Tyler died, Edward was a rock for her, helping her get through everything," Aubrey confessed.

Tyler? There was that name again. The name Nicole called out in her sleep. "Who's Tyler?"

Aubrey looked at Cameron, giving him a questioning look. "Nicole didn't tell you about Tyler?"

"No!" Cameron said, giving Aubrey an inquisitive glance.

"Tyler was Nicole's boyfriend. He was a police officer. He was killed on a call. It hit her hard."

Cameron's head now ached at hearing this information. Tyler. The person she called out to in her sleep. "How long ago did he die?"

"It's been about three years since he died."

Cameron's mind was racing with so many thoughts and feelings. "Aubrey, I didn't know."

"Nicole really loves you, you know. I hadn't seen her happy since before Tyler died. She fell for you hard. Now you two don't even talk." Aubrey gave Cameron a garbled look.

"Aubrey, this is all news to me." Cameron closed his eyes tight, then opened them to look at Aubrey.

"Edward is Tyler's cousin. They grew up like brothers. I'm sure Edward felt he owed his cousin to look after Nicole. I think his attachment has gotten crazy, though," Aubrey shared.

"Edward and Tyler, cousins." Cameron was struck dumb at this news. They stood in silence for several seconds. Cameron opened his mouth to say something, but words were not coming out of his mouth.

"Cameron, trust me on this. Nicole is in love with you. She didn't express this to you. Out of fear, or thinking her love for you happened too quickly, and she didn't want to scare you away. I don't think she has even admitted to herself she loves you, but I know my friend."

Jaws clinched in thought, Cameron said, "Aubrey, I love her, too. I've been going crazy not being with her."

"What are you going to do about it?" Aubrey was direct.

Cameron stood in disbelief at what Aubrey just shared. A torrent of emotions consumed his racing thoughts. "Aubrey, I love her. I'm so in love with her. I can't sleep. My stomach is in knots." He felt relieved, letting his feelings out, even to Aubrey. He knew he should be talking to Nicole.

Aubrey looked into Cameron's eyes before speaking. "Then do something."

"Will you help me?" He knew he couldn't get her back without some help.

Aubrey hesitated before speaking. "If I help you, you have to promise to not break her heart again. Communicate. Share feelings. Assume nothing."

Cameron wasn't great at communicating, but he was determined to get Nicole back. He knew he would lose her if he didn't talk. Cameron reached for Aubrey to give her a hug. "You don't know what this means to me."

Holding her hand out, Aubrey demanded, "Give me your phone."

"Why?"

"Just give me your phone." Aubrey stood waiting.

Cameron handed Aubrey his phone. She dialed a number, let it ring, and then hung up.

"That's my number. Gather your thoughts, call me, and I'll help you get Nicole back. You're a good guy, Cameron. I feel it. You need to work on some things, but you make my best friend happy."

Cameron reached for Aubrey again. "Thank you!"

After dropping the cake off to his mom's, Cameron stopped to pick up lunch and raced home to do some research. Edward was not Nicole's boyfriend. They weren't together. What an idiot Cameron had been. Edward likes Nicole, though, loves her. However, Cameron was just as determined to prevent him from having her. He was going to get his girl back.

While eating a sandwich and fries, Cameron got out his laptop. In the search engine, he typed, 'killing of Tyler, on duty cop'. The many articles that appeared amazed him. He clicked on the article with a picture and read the facts. Tyler was on scene, a robbery in progress. He and his partner, Jim Stone, had guns up, searching the commercial building for suspects. Tyler entered an unlit closet. The suspect was lying in wait and shot Tyler in the neck on sight, hitting his jugular vein. Cameron laid back and dropped his head onto his couch. His mind, usually quick to process, faltered in the face of this unexpected turn of events. Expressions of shock painted his face. Being killed in the line of duty is a big deal. It was a testament to the dangers of being a police officer. Being a firefighter was dangerous. Why hadn't Nicole told him about her relationship with Tyler? Was it too painful to share? He couldn't imagine what it was like to lose someone you loved. Not a breakup, but actually someone to die. Nicole had nightmares. Nightmares about him. That had to be why she called out his name in her sleep, waking up startled. Had Cameron said something, would Nicole have disclosed the entire story to him? A deep yearning welled up within him, a primal instinct to seek condolence in a hug. The yearning wasn't just about physical proximity, but a deep-seated desire to be a balm to Nicole's emotional wounds. He would never leave her. He would love her for the rest of his life.

Cameron's schedule was getting back to normal. He was working fewer hours, and he was fine with that. He and Aubrey had exchanged text messages and had a few planning calls. Nicole was upset with Cameron. He ghosted her with no explanation. Winning her back required a lot of effort on his part.

It was Tuesday, and Cameron was working a double shift. He was getting impatient. He wanted to at least talk to Nicole. Even though he was at the station, he kept his phone close. During down time, he would pull it out, stare at Nicole's picture. He wrote countless text messages, only to delete them without sending a word to Nicole. Cameron had to listen to Aubrey. She said to wait and follow her lead. She knew her friend, so he had to trust the process. Cameron knew he couldn't mess this up, so he had no choice but to sit back and wait for Aubrey to give him his cue.

The sound of the siren jilted Cameron to his feet. He dressed for the call and took his place in the truck.

"This is a bad one," Captain Garey said on the radio.

"What's the makeup?" Cameron asked, wanting to prepare for what he was walking into.

"It's a downtown, corporate sky rise building. Fire is in the middle of the building, threatening the foundation of the structure. We will have to move in quickly," Captain Garey warned.

As the piercing wail announced their arrival, Cameron could see other stations were already going in. This type of fire took multiple units. Cameron and his team, clad in their protective gear, rushed toward the imposing corporate skyscraper.

"All hands on deck," Lieutenant Jackson demanded on the radio.

The guys ran toward the building. Inside, the guys navigated through the maze of hallways, guided by the echoes of the alarms and the rising heat. The air was thick, challenging each breath. Captain Garey could be heard through the crackles of communication as he outlined their strategy. They had to combat the flames that raged above with precision and safety. Reaching the fire-stricken area, the guys unleashed powerful streams of water, the arching jets slicing through the smoke and fire. Once the men saw the path ahead, they had no choice but to move forward and reach the other side of the floor.

Cameron called, "Perry? Nickelson? Cover me."

With Cameron taking the lead, he tested the strength of the floor with each step, his guys behind him ready to blast water to put out the raging flames ahead. Cameron took one step, flames rushing toward them.

"Let it rip," he yelled.

It was either the force of the water thrusting Cameron forward or part of the floorboards missing, causing him to step forward and fall out of sight.

"Go!" Nickelson said into the radio. "We need help. Cameron's down."

Chapter 36

Nicole

Nicole closed the document, experiencing a mix of emotions—closure and anticipation of something new. The finalization of her recipe book became a moment of profound significance, a bridge between the realm of imagination and the tangible reality of completed work. This event marked both the completion of her book and the acknowledgment of the strength and dedication required to make her dream a reality. Nicole sat, head resting on the back of the dining room chair, eyes closed, taking cleansing breaths. She would wait to share the news with Aubrey and her family during dinner on Saturday.

Nicole reached for her phone to add an appointment to her calendar when Cameron's mom's name popped up on her screen with an incoming call.

"Hello, Ms. Davis," Nicole greeted.

"Nicole, sweetie, is that you?" Ms. Davis' voice was low, barely recognizable.

"Yes, ma'am, are you okay?" Nicole could hear the cracking of her voice.

"I'm okay, but... but..."

Nicole could hear her sniffles through the phone. "But, what? Ms. Davis?" Nicole's accelerated heartbeat caused her to breathe in through her nose, then letting out air through her mouth.

Voice trembling, Ms. Davis said, "It's Cameron. He was in a work accident."

"What?" Did Nicole hear Ms. Davis correctly? "What do you mean?"

"He was on a call." Ms. Davis now sounding more in control. The fire engulfed a high-rise building. The fire compromised the building's structure. The floor wasn't stable where Cameron was and he fell several floors down."

Nicole felt the blood drain from her face. "Is he okay? What's his condition?"

"He's critical, but stable. He broke several bones. He had some internal bleeding, but we believe surgery corrected that." Ms. Davis sniffed.

Nicole considered Ms. Davis' words. Afraid to ask but knowing she needed to know, Nicole asked, "What does that mean, Ms. Davis?"

"It means he's unconscious, resting, out of surgery, and now we wait."

"Surgery? Is he going to be okay?" Now plagued with erratic possibilities of losing Cameron without reconciling, telling him she was in love with him, Nicole could do nothing but wait for Ms. Davis' response.

"The doctors said his physical strength and health saved him. We still have some challenges ahead. We have to wait," she explained.

"Ms. Davis? I don't know what to say." Nicole at that moment thought she would lose her mind. The man she was in love with was unconscious in the hospital.

"My son loves you, Nicole. He doesn't communicate well, but I know my son," Patricia admitted.

"Ms. Davis, where is he? How are you doing? Can I come to the hospital?" Nicole needed to be close to him.

"I'm okay. I felt you should know. He's at Cedars-Sinai Medical Center."

"Thank you, Ms. Davis. I'll be there soon."

When Nicole arrived at the hospital, she found Ms. Davis in a chair next to Cameron, holding his hand, her head back, eyes closed. She entered the room and stood at the foot of Cameron's bed. He was hooked up to machines, breathing through an oxygen tube. His skin was pale, face unshaven. He looked as if he was sleeping. A heaviness settled into Nicole's legs as she approached the hospital bed. The site of Cameron lying there, confined by sterile white sheets and beeping monitors, cast a shadow over her. She wanted to be a pillar of strength for Cameron and Ms. Davis.

"Nicole? You're here," Ms. Davis said as she tried to stand to embrace her.

"Ms. Davis? Please sit." Nicole walked to Ms. Davis and bent down to hug her. The two women held their embrace in silence, the weight of the circumstances holding them still. Nicole felt the fear in their hug. The uncertainty of Cameron's outcome. They both knew challenges of healing were ahead, doubt becoming a formidable adversary, infiltrating the space where confidence and assurance should live.

"Do you want me to get you some coffee or food?" Nicole knew Ms. Davis had not left Cameron's side.

With a sigh, Ms. Davis replied, "No, not right now."

"Is there anyone I can call for you?" Knowing their family was small,

Nicole still asked.

"No, not right now. It's just Cameron and I, you know. I have notified his friends. They all agreed to stay away until he was awake." Ms. Davis held up her phone, giving it a wave. "I have them in a group text. To give them updates."

Nicole moved over to the empty chair on the other side of the bed. She put her head in her hands and took a deep breath. As Nicole worked to keep her tears in check, there was a poignant vulnerability in her efforts. It wasn't just the physical act of keeping from crying, but the strength required to manage the depth of her emotions. Amongst the familiar, a nuanced blend of recognition and reflection emerged. Tyler was gone by the time she reached the hospital. Cameron was alive, breathing, and returned to life. She knew she had to relish in this and focus her thoughts and prayers on Cameron's healing. She stood, knelt to kiss his forehand, then stroked his cheek with a feathery touch.

"Nicole? Why don't we go get some coffee in the cafeteria, okay?" Ms. Davis gave her a warm smile, reaching for Nicole's hand as they exited Cameron's room.

Ms. Davis got a coffee and a grilled cheese on sourdough bread. Nicole just ordered coffee. They found an empty table towards the back of the cafeteria.

"I don't feel like eating much, but I know I have to. I think this is my first meal of the day," Ms. Davis said as she bit into her sandwich.

"I understand. Keep your strength up. You don't want to make yourself sick. Do you have your blood pressure pill?" Nicole wanted to be sure Ms. Davis took care of herself.

"Yes. I take one pill a day. I took one yesterday." Ms. Davis reached into her purse to pull out a pillbox. She retrieved a pill and swallowed it with a sip of her coffee.

"Nicole? I believe, in my heart, Cameron will be fine. He'll be fine, but it will take some time." Ms. Davis reached across the table and placed her hand over Nicole's.

"I have to believe you, Ms. Davis," Nicole said, giving Ms. Davis' hand a squeeze.

"I know you and Cameron haven't been seeing each other. He cares for you more than you may realize. He would want you to be here."

Nicole stared at her and Ms. Davis' combined hands, finding strength in them, enough to say, "Thank you, Ms. Davis. I want to be here too."

The women sat in silence, no words, just deep in thought. Ms. Davis finished her sandwich, and they both sipped on their cups of coffee.

"Do you mind if I take a break while you're here, dear? There are things I must take care of before I come back later tonight."

"Of course. I'll sit with Cameron." Nicole couldn't imagine doing anything else.

The women said their goodbyes and Nicole headed back upstairs to sit with Cameron. Her heart ached. She missed him. She wished they had been in communication all these months. She couldn't bear to witness him in such a state. Needing to share the news with her family, Nicole pulled out her phone, created a group text with her parents, Levi, and Aubrey, and began moving her fingers to write a message.

Nicole - I'm here with him now. I'll head to you, Mom and Dad, when I leave here. I relieved Ms. Davis for the rest of the day. I'll be here until she comes back for the night.

Nicole - I love you all so much. I'm okay.

Nicole held the phone to her chest, closed her eyes, and sighed. She looked over at Cameron. The room was silent, except for the machines and monitors working their magic to keep Cameron on the road to healing. She took his hand and held it and took him in. He remained handsome and strong, a beautiful man. She didn't understand what happened between them, but she knew she wanted to be near him, to help him through this. Nicole moved the chair closer to the bed. With his hand in hers, she clutched it and laid her head down across his chest to be close to him.

At 7:30, Ms. Davis returned wearing fresh clothes, carrying a lunch bag, an enormous bottle of water, and a coffee mug.

"Nicole, honey? You look exhausted. I'll sit with Cameron. You go home, dear."

Nicole nodded, then asked, "Ms. Davis? Will you call me if anything changes?"

Ms. Davis looked into Nicole's eyes. Seeing the sincerity and hope in them, she responded, "Of course, dear."

Unsure how she drove to her parents' house, Nicole was just glad to be there. Her dad greeted her with a hug, and then her mom.

"Nicole, are you okay?" Jeannette asked, rubbing her back to soothe her.

"Yes, I'm okay. My heart is so heavy, though."

"I know it is," Jeannette said, offering an understanding of what her daughter was going through.

Jeannette knew Nicole had not eaten. "Are you hungry? I can make you some food."

"No, Mom. I'm okay." Nicole didn't feel like eating.

Nicole followed her mom to the kitchen and sat on the stool to watch her mother make some tea.

Walter walked over to Nicole, giving her a kiss on the forehead, then said, "I'll leave you two alone."

Nicole put her head down onto her folded arms, resting on the counter.

Jeannette glanced over at her daughter, then said, "I know what you're thinking."

"What am I thinking, Mom?" Nicole said, head still down.

"You're thinking about Tyler and whether Cameron is going to be okay."

Nicole looked up, studying her mother's face, waiting for her next words.

"Your thoughts revolve around finding a way through this," Jeannette consoled Nicole with her words.

Nicole opened her mouth to speak, but words didn't come out.

"Do you love him, Nicole?" Jeannette asked, already knowing the answer.

"Mom? I know I care for him." Nicole didn't want to admit to her mom she loved Cameron. Despite the complicated emotions stirring within her, she recognized the need to navigate the landscape of her feelings alone.

"Go into the living room. I'll be in with our tea," Jeannette said, giving her daughter a warm and what she hoped to be a comforting smile. Nicole rose from her seat and carried herself to the living room couch.

She gripped the warm mug her mother gave her and took a sip of tea. The warm liquid coated her throat and warmed her insides.

Jeannette sat next to her daughter on the couch and took a sip of her own tea before talking. "Nicole, I'm going to share something with you I never shared with you or Levi."

Nicole glanced at her mom, settled on the couch, sipped her tea, and waited for her mom to speak.

"I must have been about twenty-two when I met Peter. Peter was a handsome man. We met at the bowling alley one Friday night. He was there with his friends. I was there with my friends. By the end of the night, we were all sharing food and bowling together. It was a great time. Peter and I began dating after that night. We were always together. Our families got along." Jeannette looked through the glass doors, appearing to be in thought. Nicole looked at her mom, seeing she was playing this vision out in her head, eyes not blinking.

"Peter and I dated for about a year and a half. We were making plans for marriage. We finished college and were planning our lives together. One Friday night, Peter was at the house. We were watching movies. We both fell asleep on the couch. Waking up around 2:30 am, he kissed me on the cheek, said goodnight, and assured me he would see me the next day."

Nicole was so intrigued. Where was her mother going with this story?

"When tomorrow came, Peter was gone." Jeannette inhaled a deep breath and looked at her clenched hands.

"Where was he?" Nicole didn't understand.

"He was killed in a car accident. Some kids were speeding and ran the light. Peter died instantly on impact when the kids sped through a red light."

Nicole stared at her mom. She wanted to ask so many questions.

"Mom, I had no knowledge of Peter. You never said anything about him."

"I don't share that story. I thought it was important for me to share it now because, like you and Tyler, Peter and I planned to spend the rest of our lives together. I thought I wouldn't love again until I met your father. I didn't express my feelings to him, just as I know you didn't express your feelings to Cameron. I was holding on to Peter. To truly move on, I had to let Peter go. Your dad knew about Peter. I shared our story. He was patient. I knew your dad loved me. It took me a while before I realized I loved him. When I surrendered my love for Peter and let him go, my heart was open and filled with love for your father. I thought Peter was the love of my life. That man in there? Your father? He showed me what love is, what it meant. I know, in my heart, your father is the love of my life. He's my soulmate." Jeannette reached for the tissue hiding in her pocket and wiped fresh tears from her cheeks.

A hush settled around Nicole as she took a deliberate moment of stillness, gathering her thoughts, anchoring herself to the present. When she spoke, the stillness that preceded her words added weight to what she knew in her heart. It was a conscious choice, an acknowledgment that sometimes the most impactful words are delivered not in a rush but in the measured and purposeful cadence of a deliberate statement.

"I think I'm in love with Cameron," Nicole finally admitted.

"Okay. What's holding you back?" Jeannette heard the fear in her daughter's voice.

Nicole looked at her mother, tears now streaming down her face. "Tyler."

Chapter 37

Nicole

Nicole left her parents' house, feeling encumbered with so many sensations. Her muscles ached, and she was tired. She showered, then warmed leftover food from Aubrey's restaurant. She ate in silence, processing what her mother shared. Jeannette experienced the same things as Nicole. Cameron didn't know about Tyler, making it the sole distinction. She didn't share that part of her past relationship. Conversations with Ms. Davis gave an inclination that Cameron didn't share his feelings or past relationships either. Now he was in the hospital, fighting for his life. Nicole could lose him. How would she survive the loss of Cameron?

Now in bed, Nicole hugged one of her pillows and closed her eyes. When she closed her eyes, she only saw Cameron lying in the hospital bed. She turned on her Calm app and tried to fall asleep. Thoughts of her mom and Peter, her parents, and Tyler, made her wonder, what would Tyler want her to do? She began to toss and turn in her sleep. Nicole was in the room. She was always in the same room with Tyler. They were sitting next to one another. Nicole, staring at the hardwood floor, spoke. "Tyler? Living life without you is so hard." Tyler took her hand, but didn't say a word. He squeezed her hand and stood to his feet.

"Tyler, I don't want you to go," Nicole pleaded.

Tyler looked at her, put his hands to his chest, shaped his hands into a heart and gave her a smile.

"I love you, too." Tears falling down Nicole's face, she gave Tyler a caring smile. He gave her one last glance, turned around, opened the door, walked through it, and closed it behind him.

Nicole woke up, looking around her room. "Tyler!" She lay back on her bed, recalling her dream, now crying, sniffling through each tear. She grabbed her chest, kneading the skin on top of her heart. The weight she carried for so long in that spot was gone. Her heart felt free, no longer constricted. What did this mean?

Nicole got up and went to her refrigerator to grab a bottle of water. After taking a few gulps, she sauntered back to her room and sat on her bed. Her phone read 5:35 am. It was early, but Nicole felt she needed to process her dream with her therapist. She sent Dr. Williamson a text requesting a session as soon as possible. To Nicole's surprise, she immediately received a return text inviting her to come into the office at 9am. Unable to go back to sleep, Nicole journaled what she remembered from her dream. She wanted to understand it and knew Dr. Williamson would read her notes.

At 8:55am, Nicole sat in the reception area, waiting to be called into Dr. Williamson's office.

"Nicole, Dr. Williamson will see you now," the receptionist said.

"Thanks!" Nicole walked into the office and sat in her usual comfy chair.

"Hello, dear! How are you? What brings you into my office so urgently?" Dr. Williamson asked.

Nicole took a deep breath and gave Dr. Williamson the update. She shared Cameron's condition, her mother's story, and the details of her dream.

"Nicole? You've been stressed. You've dealt with a lot of traumas in a short period. What I can say is that it seems you've had a breakthrough."

"A breakthrough?" Nicole needed an explanation. What was a breakthrough?

"I want you to think about your previous dreams you've had about Tyler. What was happening in those dreams?" Dr. Williamson waited as Nicole processed her question.

"Well, I've been having dreams about Tyler off and on since he died. They started off as flashback dreams. Once I began dating Cameron, the dreams were more frequent, and the sequence was the same. Tyler and I are in a room, sitting next to one another. We lock eyes, facing each other. He gets up, and I beg him to stay, not wanting him to leave me."

"Okay. You've described some variations of that dream, right?" Dr. Williamson pushed.

"Yes, sometimes he remains seated. Sometimes, he stands up but doesn't leave. In other dreams, he has even gone to the door and grabbed the knob to open it but has never left the room though. Until last night."

Dr. Williamson held her pen to the corner of her mouth, tapping it against her skin, then asked, "Have you ever told Cameron you love him?"

Nicole gave Dr. Williamson a questioning look. "Well, no, I haven't."

"Do you love him, Nicole? Are you in love with Cameron?"

Nicole pondered on the question for several seconds. Remembering Myles' wedding night, the overwhelming feeling of Cameron's presence was in the best way. While they danced, she felt a subtle twinge nestled in the depths of her gut, a quiet, yet unmistakable that love had woven itself into the fabric of her being. That was Cameron. Nicole read Cameron's eyes and knew he felt the same, yet neither of them spoke their truth.

"I think I do. I think I love Cameron." With that, Nicole let out a deep sigh.

Dr. Williamson tilted her head, gave Nicole a warm smile, then asked, "Are you making a statement or asking yourself if you love Cameron?"

It took a few minutes for Nicole to break the silence. She stared down at her feet, looked out the office window, then clasped her hands together.

"I love Cameron." As those words escaped her lips, Nicole felt lighter.

"The dream likely signifies your love for Tyler is now in your past and you have the freedom to love again, someone new. Or in your case. Cameron. Your heart has released the hold it had for Tyler. He left the room and closed the door for a reason."

Nicole now said this with conviction and meaning. "I love Cameron. I'm in love with him."

Nicole left Dr. Williamson with new knowledge. Was the fact that she loved Cameron new? The new revelation was her admission of love for him. The hospital was on the way home from Dr. Williamson's office.

"Hello, Ms. Davis!" Nicole said, walking into Cameron's room.

"Hi Nicole. You look refreshed." Ms. Davis noticed.

"I feel better this morning. Any updates?" She had to know Cameron was getting better.

"Well, not really. Cameron is stable, though. Being unconscious is helping him heal. His unconscious state is him sleeping so he can get better." Ms. Davis then glanced at her son, smiling.

"That's great news," Nicole said, relieved.

"Although last night, his breathing slowed a bit. That raised concern. They gave him something and now his breathing is back to its normal pace."

"Oh?" Nicole said with concern in her tone.

"He'll be fine, Nicole," Ms. Davis said with confidence.

"Ms. Davis? If you don't mind me asking, what was Cameron's last relationship like?" The urge to know about Cameron's past overwhelmed her.

Ms. Davis gave Nicole a warm smile. "He didn't tell you anything, did he?"

"No, ma'am," Nicole answered, returning the smile.

"Shannon and Cameron dated for a couple of years. She was a nice girl, however, well into her and Cameron's relationship, she realized she hadn't gotten over her old boyfriend. They began seeing each other while she and Cameron were still together. She cheated," Ms. Davis said, nodding in agreement with what Nicole's expression revealed.

"Oh, wow! I wasn't expecting to hear that." Maybe that's why Cameron shut down. Did he think she was a cheater?

"Instead of facing the situation, Cameron just stopped talking, communicating. The relationship ended, obviously."

Nicole thought about how Cameron stopped talking to her. She wasn't a cheater. She recalled the last times she saw Cameron. She recalled the scene at her parents' store with Edward. Did Cameron think she cheated on him with Edward? Her dreams! Did Cameron hear her call out Tyler's name?

"Ms. Davis, I can stay with Cameron tonight. I'm here to get an update and let you know I can stay. I can come back at about 8pm. Is that okay?" Nicole needed to be close to Cameron, feel him breathing, and watch over him for the night.

"Yes. That's perfect. I'll go home and get some things done. Sleep in my bed," Ms. Davis said, excitement in her tone to get a full night's rest.

Nicole walked over to hug Ms. Davis and left the hospital to return later that evening.

Nicole parked her car in front of Edward's house. She didn't care that she didn't call first. He was home because his car was in the driveway.

"Hey, Nicole! What do I owe this honor?" Edward said, opening his front door.

"Can I come in?" Nicole said, arms folded across her chest, gathering her words she needed to say to Edward.

Edward opened the door wider so Nicole could walk in.

"Can we sit?" Nicole had to remember, even though she was ready to let Edward go, let go of all the things he did to sabotage her and Cameron's relationship, he was there for her, comforting her during her grieving of Tyler.

Edward held out his hand and let Nicole into his living room. "I was making some lunch. Would you like something to eat?"

"No, thanks. I won't be here long," Nicole said, eager to finish.

Edward walked back into the living room with two bottles of water.

"Edward, we need to talk." Nicole released her arms and rested them at her sides.

"What's on your mind?" Edward asked, sitting back on his couch, crossing his legs.

"You've been my rock since Tyler died. You've held me up when I couldn't stand. You made me laugh when I wanted to cry. You basically took care of me, like family. The hardest thing I've ever done was bid farewell to Tyler. I will admit, your presence was a comfort and a curse. You were a comfort because you reminded me of Tyler. You were a curse when I looked at you and wished you were Tyler, because you remind me so much of him. I wanted you to be him. But you aren't him."

"Why are you telling me all of this? Where's this going?" Edward looked impatient, eager to hear Nicole's next words.

"Edward? You and I never dated, and we never will. I appreciate you taking care of me, watching over me after Tyler died. We're friends. Nothing more," Nicole explained.

Edward looked at Nicole, frowning. He opened his mouth to say something, but the words escaped him.

"I'm moving on with my life. Tyler will forever hold a special place in my heart, but he's gone and will never return."

"This is about Cameron, isn't it?" Edward's face turned from one of understanding to anger.

"Me moving on with my life has nothing to do with Cameron." Nicole wanted Edward to really hear her words and understand what she was trying to convey.

Frowning, Edward admitted, "I told him to leave you alone."

When did Cameron and Edward speak? What did they say to one another? "You what?" Nicole felt heat rise from her chest to her neck and then her face. She was furious.

"Nicole, you know I fell in love with you. I love you not as a sister, but more," Edward admitted.

"You spoke with Cameron? When?" Nicole felt steam was escaping her head, she was so angry.

Edward looked at Nicole, fear in his eyes.

"What did you say, Edward? What did you do?" Nicole asked, already standing.

"That's not important. My conversation with Cameron gives you more time to socialize and hang out with me." Nicole wanted to slap that sly grin off Edward's face.

Nicole's expression transformed into a visage of complete anger, a storm brewing in her eyes and etched across her face. "Edward, you know what? We can't even be friends. I will NEVER date you. I'm ending this friendship. Don't call me, stop by my house, talk to my family, nothing."

"Nicole, you don't mean that, do you? You're just being emotional." Edward now stood, reaching for Nicole's hand.

"Don't touch me. And I'm not being emotional. I'm finally being rational. I'm thinking clearly now." Nicole walked to Edward's door.

"You love him, don't you?" Edward asked, knowing he already knew the answer.

"Yes! I'm in love with Cameron." Nicole gave Edward one last look. "Goodbye, Edward."

"Nicole, wait. Can we talk about this?" Edward followed Nicole out the door, only to stop in the middle of his front yard, realizing there was no stopping her.

Nicole walked to her car, got in, drove away without saying another word. She stopped her car just around the corner from Edward's house and pulled out her phone. She scrolled through her contacts, pulled up Edward's information, blocked his number, then deleted it. She would no longer receive his calls.

Nicole went home, took another shower, changed into leggings and an oversized sweatshirt. She then packed her bag and left, stopping at the florist before heading to the hospital.

"I would like to buy a healing plant. Do you have anything like that?" Nicole asked the woman at the front counter.

"Well, you have a few choices," the woman said, walking over to the refrigerated cabinet filled with different green plants. "This Lemon Lime Prayer plant is one. English Marigold is another one. The orange color can brighten a room. The Spider Plant, Snake Plant, Fiddle Leaf Fig, Ponytail Palm, and Boston Fern are also excellent choices.

"Okay," Nicole said, rubbing her head, deciding on which plant to purchase. "I'll take this one."

Ms. Davis was scrolling through her phone when Nicole entered the room.

"That's a beautiful plant, Nicole," Ms. Davis complimented.

"I thought the room needed something other than machines and monitors." Nicole proudly placed the plant closest to Cameron.

"It's a delicate touch," Ms. Davis said.

"I'm here now, Ms. Davis, ready to stay with Cameron for the night. You can go home now and get some much-needed rest," Nicole urged, feeling eager for some alone time with Cameron, even though he was still asleep.

"If you're sure?" Ms. Davis stood and lifted her arms above her head to stretch her body.

"Yes, please Ms. Davis. Let me stay. It's my pleasure."

"Okay then." Ms. Davis gathered her things, hugged Nicole, and left.

Nicole paused, taking a deep breath, and glanced at Cameron. She grabbed his hand and held it, studied it, and brushed a soft kiss onto it. Tears swelled as Nicole cleared her throat. An overwhelming feeling came over her. Within her heart, she felt nothing but love. In the embrace and admittance of loving Cameron, there was a sense of tranquility and acceptance. Even though the true love of her life, her soulmate, lay in a hospital bed, the world around Nicole seemed to shimmer with a different light, an enduring state of being.

Nicole began whispering. "Cameron? You may not hear me. Unbeknownst to you, I've been through a lot in the past few years. I lost a man I loved with all my heart. After meeting you, you taught me to love differently. You taught me to love stronger, deeper. It was you. You all along. I'm willing to do everything I can to show you how much I love you. My life feels incomplete without you. I crave your presence. We can work out our differences. We can learn to communicate better. You've rescued my heart and shown me the love I want to only experience with you. I want you in my life, forever."

Nicole gazed at Cameron. His body was still. She placed her hand on his chest. Felt his chest move up, then down, in rhythm with his breathing. She brushed her hand alongside his stubbled face. Cameron had to wake up. He had to get better. They had to be together. Begin a life together. She would not lose Cameron. He was strong and healthy. Time would heal him. She knew she would never leave his side. Nicole took out the blank card she bought with the plant and wrote three words.

I love you! - Nicole.

Chapter 38

Cameron

"Cameron, can you hear me? Cameron, can you feel my hand on yours?" Dr. Cortes asked as she nudged his hands.

Cameron could hear the doctor talking to him. When the doctor ran the flash of light across his eyes, he squinted them closed.

"Try to squeeze my hand if you can hear me," Dr. Campbell asked.

Cameron used all of his strength to push on the doctor's hand.

"Yes, that's it. Ms. Davis, he's waking up." Dr. Cortes pulled Cameron's chart and jotted down some notes, looked at her watch, then wrote the time.

"Praise God. Yes, my son. I'm here." Ms. Davis stood, eyes glistening at Cameron.

After several minutes, Cameron opened his eyes.

"Do you feel any pain?" Dr. Cortes asked.

Cameron opened his mouth to speak, unable to make a sound. He nodded instead.

"We can give you something for that. Something that will coat your throat, to allow you to talk. However, we need you to rest." Dr. Campbell took Cameron's vitals while Dr. Cortes stood ready to list them in his chart.

Cameron nodded his head once again.

"Ms. Davis, can we speak to you outside?" Dr. Campbell asked as he and Dr. Cortes exited the room.

Cameron heard his mother and the doctors leave the room. His vision coming into focus, he slowly turned his head to look around the room. He was alone. Unable to move, Cameron lay in his hospital bed, trying to figure out what was going on.

After several minutes, his mom entered the room in tears. Cameron frowned, looking at his mom for answers.

"Cameron. Son, these are tears of joy. You're going to be just fine. Allow yourself ample time for recovery. Be patient and do the work, okay?" Ms. Davis said, grabbing Cameron's hand, kissing his knuckles.

Cameron nodded his head.

"Do you see that nice plant next to you?" Ms. Davis asked, gesturing to the gift Nicole had brought.

Cameron nodded again.

"That's from Nicole. Every day, she's been here with you, checking in and sitting with you while I took care of things at home," Ms. Davis said proudly.

Just the mention of her name made Cameron feel rejuvenated.

"She left you a card. Would you like me to read it?" Ms. Davis asked, beaming.

Cameron could only nod.

Cameron watched his mom walk over to the other side of his bed, pull the card from the stand planted in the soil, and open the envelope.

The look of admiration shown on his mother's face. A sob caught in her throat. She cleared it and read the card. "I love you! - Nicole."

Cameron couldn't believe what he heard. Nicole loved him? Although his memory was a little foggy, he was able to recall his conversation with Aubrey. She agreed on the same point, yet he lacked certainty. They had never spoken those words to one another.

"Son, she's a wonderful girl. And now I hope you have the answer you were looking for," his mother shared.

Cameron nodded again. A smile appeared on his face, a feeling he hadn't experienced in a while.

With the nurse assisting him, Cameron took sips of room temperature water and drank broth. The first sips and spoon full of liquid seemed to scorch his throat. The more he drank, the more tolerant it all became. After finishing his meal, he attempted to speak.

"Mom?" Cameron said in a deep, scratchy tone. "Can you bring me my phone?"

"I kept it charged. Once you woke up, I knew you would want to look through it."

Cameron pushed the button to turn on his phone. Within seconds, it chimed with email, text, and phone messages. All of those notifications had to wait. Cameron wanted to communicate with only one person. He pulled up a picture of him and Nicole, taken at Myles' wedding. His eyes hurt, filled with so much emotion. He typed a text message.

> **Cameron** - Hi! It's me. I'm awake. I would love to see you, but I want to wait. I hope you understand.

After several minutes, Nicole replied.

> **Nicole** - Hi! I'm shouting God's praises. You're awake and on your way to recovery.

Nicole - I want to see you too, but I understand. I'll be here when you're ready.

Cameron - I would call you, but my voice isn't that strong. Texting is easier.

Nicole - I understand.

Nicole - Cameron?

Nicole - I'm so happy you're awake.

Cameron - Me too!

Nicole - Did you see the plant I got you? It's a healing plant.

Cameron - Yes, I look at it like every minute

Nicole - Really?

Cameron - You gave it to me so, yes.

Nicole - Do you need anything?

Cameron - You

Nicole - heart emoji and kissy face emoji

Cameron - I love you.

Nicole - I love you too.

With a few days of rehab and proper nourishment, Cameron regained most of his voice. His firehouse buddies and superiors had come by once they heard he was awake. They saved a copy of the news article that updated the city of his accident and recovery schedule. Although their visit was short, they wanted to convey their thoughts and wish for a quick recovery. It took an exhausting hour to go through all of his messages. Myles, Josh, Ryan, and Terrell sent a gigantic bouquet of balloons and flowers. He knew Jessica had picked it out and added their names.

During the following three weeks, Cameron put in a lot of effort to return to a state of normalcy. Cameron and Nicole communicated via text daily. She updated him on her recipe book, sending pictures and the plans she and Aubrey planned for the launch. He updated Nicole on his grueling rehabilitation and the awful food. Cameron sat up in his hospital bed, feeling more like himself, for the first time since waking up. He could use his voice now, but he liked the freeness of sending messages to Nicole. He reached for his phone to send her a text.

Cameron - Good news! I'm going home tomorrow.

Nicole - Really?

Cameron - Well, not home, but to my mom's house.

Nicole - Awesome news.

Cameron - I feel pretty good about it.

Nicole - Can I visit?

Cameron paused before replying. He wanted to see her beautiful face, smell her, hold her, have her next to him. He knew they had so much to talk about. All he wanted was to return to 100%. Seeing Nicole would be healing for him.

Cameron walked into his childhood house, albeit really slow but he did it. His mom had bought a queen-sized bed for his old room. She knew he would be more comfortable in that size bed compared to the full he used to sleep in.

"Make yourself comfortable, Cameron. I'll get you some lunch."

"Thanks, Ma! The hospital food was awful. I'm ready for some good food. By the way, Nicole texted me. She's bringing us dinner," Cameron shared.

"Oh? Okay. I like her, Cameron," his mother yelled from the kitchen.

"I know, Mom, I know."

With Nicole coming over later, he had to do something about his appearance. After lunch, he took two hours to shower, shave, and put on clean clothes.

"God, I feel better already," Cameron said, looking at himself in the mirror. Now tired, he went to lie on his bed to wait for Nicole.

Cameron awoke to the sound of voices coming from the living room. His mom and Nicole were laughing about something. He slowly moved his feet to the ground while sitting on the bed. He was about to stand when he heard footsteps, growing louder by the second.

"Cameron!"

Cameron turned to find Nicole standing in the doorway of his old room. There she was, the woman he could admit to loving, dressed in black leggings, a long black sweater, her lovely curls in a high bun, wearing little makeup. He almost lost his breath. She was so beautiful. She seemed more beautiful than before his accident.

"Stay seated. I'll come to you," Nicole said as she stepped into Cameron's room, flashing a huge grin. She sat on the edge of his bed.

"Can I hug you?" Nicole asked, moving closer to Cameron.

"Yes, you better," Cameron demanded, flashing his unforgettable smile.

Nicole put her hands around his waist and rested her head on his shoulder. Cameron returned the hug and kissed the top of her head. They stayed in that embrace for several minutes. Grinning, they expressed gratitude for this moment. Nicole was the first to pull away, sitting in silence for a few moments.

"Nicole?" he said. Before he could get her name out of his mouth, she said.

"Cameron?"

They let out a subtle laugh.

"Let me go first." Nicole stared at Cameron. He took her hand.

"I have never been the best communicator. Sharing my thoughts and feelings is hard for me."

Nicole took his hands in hers and gave him her full attention.

"From the first time I set eyes on you, well, at the record store. When I'm at work, I don't pick up on women. I knew you were something special. I was angry at myself for letting you leave the store without getting your phone number. I knew it was fate when I saw you at the awards dinner. Our relationship started strong. Everything was going so well. What I didn't communicate to you was that I suspected you of cheating." Cameron took in a deep breath, relieved he was letting it all out.

Eyebrows raised, Nicole asked, "Cheating?"

"Yes. My last girlfriend cheated and rather than saying anything, I just stepped away from our relationship. For that, she didn't put up a fight to save our relationship and confirmed my suspicions."

"Cameron," Nicole pleaded.

"Please, let me finish. I couldn't have been more stupid. Communication and conversation could have fixed all of my suspicions. Instead, I took the cowardly way out. I made myself miserable."

Nicole held her head down and spoke. "I could have done better." Now looking into Cameron's eyes, she continued. "I didn't tell you about Tyler. Well, I mentioned our relationship, but I didn't tell you he had died. When I saw you in that hospital bed, I was so scared. It scared me that I would lose you."

"I'm not sure if Aubrey told you, but she shared the story about you and Tyler. And she cleared up my suspicions of you and Edward," Cameron admitted.

Nicole lowered her head, shaking it from side to side. "Aubrey did not tell me she spoke to you."

"I stopped by your house a while back. When Edward answered the door, he told me that you two had reconciled and were in love, suggesting that I should keep my distance." Cameron's stomach ached just saying the words.

"What?" It made sense now, Nicole thought, based on her last conversation with Edward.

"I didn't fight for you. I took the easy way out and left without confrontation. That was the worst mistake of my life."

"Edward and I were never together," Nicole pleaded.

"I know that now. Aubrey cleared everything up. I intended to see you after our conversation, but I had the accident."

"Cameron, Tyler, and I were together for a little over two years before his death. We talked about getting married, spending our lives together. I was uncontrollably crushed when he died. My heart hurt in ways I didn't think capable. It took me two years to pull myself together and believe I could find someone new to love me. I went on a few dates, but then I met you. When I was with you, I didn't feel the pain of heartache. I felt love and passion. I felt like you and I were friends and could support one another. I continued to have dreams about Tyler, though," Nicole admitted.

"Is that why you called out his name sometimes in your sleep?" Cameron asked.

Nicole's cheeks flushed. "You knew about that? You said nothing."

"I told you, I'm not the best communicator," Cameron reminded her.

"After you got hurt, seeing you in the hospital bed, I got scared. Seeing you lying there unconscious made me realize I had fallen in love with you. That night, I had a dream about Tyler. My recurring dreams were of us sitting side by side. He never spoke a word. I always called out to him to not leave. He got up and walked toward the door. He touched the doorknob. I always woke up. That night, he rose, walked to the door, glanced back with a smile, and exited, closing the door behind him."

Cameron stared into Nicole's eyes, looking for any remorse or sadness.

Nicole continued, "After two years, the interpretation of my dream in therapy allowed me to finally let him go. I was holding on to him subconsciously. I knew I wanted to be with you, but fear held me back."

Cameron reached for Nicole's face and pulled her close. He spoke into her ear. "It's okay to be scared. I don't wish what you went through on anyone. To think I almost lost you because I refused to talk." Cameron kissed her cheek. He planted kisses along the side of her face. Their lips were so close, but not touching.

"I love you, Nicole Graham," he whispered. He moved in to kiss her on the lips. He wrapped his arms around her to embrace her. They stayed in each other's arms for a while.

"Cameron?" Nicole asked.

"Yeah?"

"I love you."

Chapter 39

Nicole

Nicole saw Cameron every day while he rehabilitated at his mother's house. She brought food from Aubrey's restaurant and from her own kitchen. Cameron began working out, gaining his full strength. In a few weeks, he would be back to work on a light schedule. Helping Cameron heal had given them time to open up and understand one another. They were getting closer. Nicole knew now more than ever that she wanted to be with Cameron, always.

Getting Cameron back to 100% and preparing for the book launch were Nicole's top priorities. In two weeks, her agent, all of her industry contacts, friends and family would celebrate the publishing of her recipe book at her parents' store. Nicole hoped Cameron could make it, but he told her he wasn't sure. She had settled to the fact he wouldn't be there. Aubrey and Nicole selected their favorite recipes from the cookbook, which they could prepare in bite-size portions. She wanted people to mingle, talk business, and buy her books.

A week before the launch, Nicole's dad called with bad news.

"Baby girl, we can't launch your book in the store," Walter shared.

"Dad? Why? What happened?" Devastated, Nicole didn't know what she would do now so close to the launch.

"The plumber mis-installed some pipes," Walter explained. "The existing pipes are on the verge of bursting. We have to find a new place for your launch, honey. We don't want pipes bursting in the middle of everything."

"What am I supposed to do? Everything was planned. Now what?" Nicole didn't want to panic. They had to find another venue to launch her book.

"Call Aubrey. Your mom was in her restaurant this morning and explained what was going on. She said she was on it," Walter said.

Instead of calling, Nicole went to the restaurant. She tried not to panic. She had hundreds of books in her garage. Carol had already blown up the photos of her food. After framing them, Nicole had the photos ready to be placed around the store. Now, what was she going to do?

The restaurant was not too busy. Nicole caught Aubrey in the kitchen, teaching a new sous chef how to season the chicken before frying.

Nicole greeted Aubrey, "Hey, girl!"

"Hey, Nicole. I'll be with you in just a sec. You can go into my office," Aubrey directed.

Nicole sat in Aubrey's office and pulled out her phone to share this news with Cameron via text.

Cameron - Can't we fix it before the launch?

Nicole - My dad says he doesn't want to risk it.

Cameron - What are you going to do?

Nicole - I'm at Aubrey's. My dad said she has it under control.

Cameron - Let me know if I can do anything.

Nicole - I will

Cameron - I love you

Nicole - I love you too.

Nicole and Cameron said 'I love you' every time they said goodbye. She felt so loved by him. Cameron, still healing, made special efforts to talk with Nicole and express his dedication to her. Her dreams of Tyler stopped. She knew now her heart fully belonged to Cameron.

"Hey, girl!" Aubrey said, as she sat down at her desk.

"What can you tell me about my book launch?" Nicole wasted no time getting to the reason for her visit.

"I'm doing fine. Thank you for asking," Aubrey said with a chuckle. "Well, I pulled some strings and got you the record store you like so much."

"What? Really? Who do you know over there?" Nicole couldn't believe Aubrey's connections.

"Girl, you know I know everybody in the city. They either want catering, a restaurant hook up, or both. I called in some favors. The store is closing for the night," Aubrey said, giving Nicole an ear to ear smile.

"I love that store, but they sell records, t-shirts, and music memorabil-ia." Nicole tried to visualize her photographs spread around the record store.

"I know. We're in negotiations to cater food for them on Friday nights. Your book launch is a great way to test some ideas," Aubrey shared.

"If you say it will work." Nicole had her doubts, but she trusted her friend.

"And I have already talked to Carol. She'll be there early to position the pictures of the food. All you have to do is bring your books. The store has tons of tables to style your launch. Levi can help you with that, right?" Aubrey wondered.

"Yeah, he can." Nicole could always count on her brother.

"Then it's all set. You have nothing to worry about," Aubrey said, thumbs up.

The day of the launch, Levi gathered the boxes of books from Nicole's garage.

"You don't have to get to the store until 5pm," Levi instructed.

"What? I have to set up the books. The launch starts at 5:30pm," Nicole reminded Levi.

"I know. Mom said she wanted to do it. As a gift," Levi said, shrugging his shoulders.

"When was she going to tell me?" Nicole was nervous and on edge. She had to trust this arrangement.

Levi gave Nicole an annoyed stare. "I'm telling you."

Nicole gave Levi a concerned look. "I can't do that. I can't let Mom do everything. I'm gonna hurry and get over there."

"Can you allow someone to do something for you, just this once?" Levi pleaded.

"Do I have a choice in the matter?" Nicole pouted at the idea she wouldn't be able to style her tables.

"Relax. The hard part is over. Tonight, all you have to do is show up and sell books. Share stories, taste good food." Levi was right. Nicole needed to relax.

Nicole trusted her mom whole-heartedly. She was certain of her ability to put together an impressive display. Tonight, Nicole wanted to look like a published author. Black was the color for most creative folks, so she pulled her black dress with the bateau neckline and scooped back with three-quarter sleeves. She would wear her black large rimmed classes with her hair slicked in a neat and tidy bun. Black, red-bottom pumps and her large silver necklace would complete the look.

Exiting the shower, Nicole checked the time: 4pm. While applying her makeup, Cameron called.

"Hey, babe," she answered.

"Hey, beautiful."

"I'm getting ready. Why Levi and Mom insist I show up at 5pm is beyond me. Knowing Carol and my mom will make the place look great is the only solace I have in this plan."

"They'll do an amazing job," Cameron said in a consoling tone.

"I wish you were coming."

"Me, too."

"Are you sure you can't come?" Nicole whined.

"Yes, but I know there will be more launches like this. I'll be at all the rest of them," Cameron assured Nicole.

"Will I see you afterwards? I can visit now that you're home."

"I'll see you then," Cameron said.

"Love you." Nicole sighed, resigned to the fact Cameron wouldn't be at the launch.

"I love you more," Cameron said, before ending the call.

Nicole's bun took longer than she planned. She had to search for her special pen she had bought to sign her books before she left the house. Based on the writeups on Instagram, she had a good feeling the turnout was going to be strong. She drove into the parking lot, eyeing the sign above the door that read Closed for Special Event.

That special event was Nicole. Her passion project had come to fruition. She felt immense pride in the hard work she dedicated to the book, knowing that her grandmother's recipes would now be accessible to others. Nicole walked into the store, smooth jazz playing. Despite the event's scheduled start time of 5:30, people were already present at 5:15. She saw Aubrey directing her staff to replenish the food when needed. Her mom was standing at the impeccably designed tables of her book, talking to a few people.

"Nicole! Come meet some people." Her mom gestured.

"Hello, I'm Nicole Graham," she said, greeting people with her warm smile.

"Yes, we know. Your mother has spoken so highly of you. What an achievement, putting your grandmother's recipes into a book. We're looking forward to tasting some of these delicious bites. We're also thinking of linking you with some of the book chains we support," the literary executive suggested.

"That would be amazing. Thank you," Nicole said, reaching to shake the woman's hand.

"Your mom has our contact information. Reach out to us sometime next week, okay?" the executive said.

"I will, and thank you." Nicole couldn't believe the attention she was getting.

Nicole turned to her mom. "The table looks amazing. I couldn't have done this any better myself."

"And where do you think you learned this from?" Jeannette said, smiling.

"You're right," Nicole said, reaching in to hug her mom.

"Miss Graham? We'll give you the mic at 5:30 to say a few words if that's okay," the store owner directed.

"Um, okay." A sudden wave of nerves engulfed Nicole's being. She took a cleansing breath before looking at her phone.

"Not much time to prepare," Nicole said to her mother.

"You've been prepared all your life. You can do this." Jeannette reached for Nicole's hand and gave it a squeeze.

As Nicole looked up, she saw that the store was filled with people. In those few moments, so many people arrived.

"Ladies and gentlemen, thank you for coming," the store owner said, standing at the front of the store. "We're so proud to host this special event. We've never hosted a book launch, especially not for a family recipe book, but there's always a first time. We're so happy you're here. Please let me introduce to you, the woman of the hour, author of this amazing book: Nicole Graham."

Nicole walked to the front of the store with her mic in hand, waving to the folks in the audience she recognized.

"Thank you, thank you so much. First, let me thank all of you for coming tonight. I've been working on this recipe book with passion and love for just over a year. I'm sure many of you have a relative who was an amazing cook. Or at least I hope you have one of those." Nicole paused as laughter blanketed the store. "My grandmother, Ms. Ely, created and chefed every recipe in this book. I feel her spirit shining down on us this evening, in celebration of these recipes that she handed down to me from her own grandmother. These recipes are both delicious and easy to make. Anyone, even the most inexperienced cook, can make them. In honor of her, I present to you, The Love of Family and Recipes that Feed Them."

The room erupted in applause.

"Please enjoy this evening, the food and company. Dance and enjoy yourselves. Thank you again for supporting me, launching this labor of love."

Nicole nodded her head to the applause. She worked her way to the table where she would sell and sign books. Jeannette was by Nicole's side, prepared to collect proceeds of the book sales. Nicole sat down and opened her first book to sign.

"Who do I make this out to?" she asked, smiling at the middle-aged man standing in front of her.

"Make it out to Grandma Betty. She's going to love this," the man said.

"I hope so. Thank you."

While signing a few more books, the shift in music broke Nicole's concentration. Instead of instrumental jazz, she heard the beats of old school hip hop. She scanned the store, searching for the DJ. Nicole froze in her seat. The sight of Cameron at the turntables almost knocked her off her chair.

"Ladies and gentlemen, let's give another round of applause for our talented author, Nicole Graham," he announced over the mic.

Her mouth was open with shock. Nicole looked at her mom, all smiles. "Did you know about this?"

"A mother knows everything," Jeannette said, bobbing her head to the music.

"If I can request Nicole to come to the DJ table please," Cameron said, resting the music on You're All I Need by Method Man and Mary J. Blige. One of their favorites.

To Nicole's surprise, people began dancing. She strolled to the DJ booth, reaching out for Cameron's hand to support her as she walked up the few steps in her high heels.

"What are you doing here? I thought you couldn't make it?" Nicole spoke in Cameron's ear.

"Did you really think I would miss this important night?" Cameron whispered back, giving her a wink.

Nicole reached for Cameron and gave him a huge hug. When she released him, she saw her parents, Levi, Carol, Aubrey, and Cameron's mom, circling around her. Cameron took the mic.

"Ladies and gentlemen, I want to share how important this magnificent woman is to me. We met in this store over a year ago. When I first laid eyes on her, I knew she was the one. She's beautiful, intelligent, has a heart of gold, and she's the love of my life." Cameron put the mic down, got down on one knee, and looked up to see Nicole in tears.

"Nicole Graham? Will you do me the honor of becoming my wife?" Cameron held out a red velvet box he opened to reveal a huge solitaire stone set in white gold.

Nicole wiped her tears, looked around to see her family smiling. Her mom and Ms. Davis were in tears. She turned to him. "Yes! Cameron Davis, I will marry you."

Cameron placed the ring on Nicole's finger, stood, cupped her face, and gave her a tender, passionate kiss.

Levi took the mic and said, "Ladies and gentlemen. We have a newly engaged couple in our presence. Let's give Cameron and Nicole a round of applause and congratulations."

With Etta James' At Last blaring through the entire store, Cameron wiped the joyful tears from Nicole's face, then whispered, "I love you, Nicole Graham." Flashing his million-dollar smile Nicole loves so much.

Epilogue

Aubrey

Nicole stood before her mom, Ms. Davis, and Aubrey in a floor length sheath, white Aldora crepe gown with layers of sheer lace and lace motifs, with a sheer lace bodice, and sheer halter neckline. They stood in awe of how beautiful the dress was and the way it fit Nicole's body. She was stunning. Jeannette's lower lip trembled as she gazed at her daughter with so much pride.

"You will be the most beautiful bride," Aubrey said, covering her mouth with her hands, holding back the surge of emotion, eyes glistening as she looked to the sales woman to ask the important question everyone wanted to learn the answer to.

"Is this your dress?" the consultant asked.

Nicole admired herself, twisting her body to get a view of the dress from every angle.

"Cameron is going to love it," Ms. Davis said. "That is, if you choose this one. What do you think?"

"Can I see this with a veil?" Nicole asked.

The dress consultant left the area to bring back a veil to give Nicole an idea of how she would look on her big day.

"This is the veil the designer assigned to complement the dress." The dress consultant assisted Nicole with her hair, pinning it up to allow the veil to attach properly. "There! Turn so you can see yourself from the front view."

"Oh my God!" Nicole whispered, eyes welling up with tears. She inhaled, then bit her lower lip, hands trembling as she adjusted the veil to cover her bare shoulders.

"There won't be a dry eye in the church if you walk down the aisle in this stunner of a dress," Jeannette said, dabbing her eyes with a tissue. Both she and Ms. Davis now cried tears of joy, embraced, then gripped hands in solidarity.

"Well, Ms. Graham? What do you think?" the dress consultant asked.

Nicole looked at each woman whom she cared for so much. With one last glance in the mirror, she confidently stated, "This is my dress."

Everyone in the general area of where Nicole stood applauded, lifting their hands in a cheer for her exquisite choice.

"I have to make sure I stay fit, knowing the wedding is eight months away," Nicole said, laughing, wiping tears from her eyes.

"No more cake sampling for you," Aubrey said, and everyone laughed. Just as she was about to ask the ladies where they wanted to go for lunch, her phone rang.

"Excuse me, ladies. This is my real estate agent. I'm gonna step outside to take this call. Be right back." Aubrey stepped outside the bridal salon and stood in the warm sun and accepted the call.

"Hello, this is Aubrey Carroll."

"Hello, Aubrey, it's Kate. I have some news for you. About the space next door to your restaurant?"

"Yes! Were you able to secure the property for me?" Aubrey wanted that space to expand her business and open up a bakery to complement her restaurant.

"I asked the agent to hold the offer for ten minutes while I called you. Another bidder is prepared to increase his offer. I wanted to be clear on your budget before I outbid him."

"Another bidder? Where'd he come from?" The thought of being outbid sent a surge of nerves through her, a palpable tension that tightened in the pit of Aubrey's stomach.

"The agent says her client has been seeking space along your block for his restaurant. He's a chef, too. Apparently, he wants to open a fusion type eatery. I don't think his food will compete with yours, but he wants the space next door to Aubrey's Favorites."

"Kate? Outbid him!" Aubrey demanded. "I want that space. I'll worry about my budget later. I'm sure my investors will understand." Aubrey calmed down, knowing that she would get her space, no matter the cost.

"Yes, ma'am. We'll resolve the bidding war shortly. I'll send you a confirmation text to let you know the deal is done." Kate waited for Aubrey's response.

"Thank you. We'll talk soon."

Unbeknownst to Aubrey, her face was red as a lobster when she walked back into the bridal salon.

Nicole, now changed into her regular clothes and at the counter ordering her dress, turned to share a celebratory grin with Aubrey when she recognized her unexpected facial expression.

"What's wrong, Aubrey?" Nicole asked with concern.

Jeannette and Ms. Davis now stood alongside Aubrey, ready to console her.

"That was my real estate agent. Someone is trying to outbid me for the space next door to the restaurant."

"What? How could that be? You said no one else put in a bid and you were the only buyer," Nicole said, confused.

"Well, not anymore. Kate will handle it. I have complete faith in her. She'll text me soon." Aubrey took a deep breath and asked, "So where are we going to have lunch? I'm hungry."

Aubrey was calmer when they arrived at the beachside restaurant for lunch. She still hadn't received a text from Kate, but she was hopeful. Talk of Nicole's upcoming wedding was the distraction she needed.

"So, Aubrey? You're going to cater the food for the wedding, right?" Ms. Davis asked.

"Yes. It's not every day your best friend finds the love of her life and walks down the aisle to marry him. It's my gift to Nicole and Cameron." Aubrey grabs Nicole's hand and squeezed it.

"Aww. You're going to make us all cry, Aubrey," Nicole says, holding back tears.

"It's an honor. I promise." Aubrey reached for the bread basket and grabbed a sourdough roll and placed it on her plate. Just as she dipped her knife into the butter, her phone chimed with an incoming text message.

> **Kate** - It's yours! The realtor will draw up the paperwork and have it ready for signature within 48 hours.

"Yes!" Aubrey yelled, forgetting she was in a public place and restaurant patrons were now staring in her direction.

"What? You got it?" Nicole asked.

"You are sitting with the new owner of the building that will house Aubrey's Favorites Bakery."

All ladies applauded and high-fived each other across the table. Aubrey grabbed her phone to reply to Kate's text.

> **Aubrey** - Great! Thank you for all of your hard work.

> **Aubrey** - Do you know who the other bidder was? The culinary world is kinda small. I may know the chef who's looking for a space.

> **Kate** - His name is Benson Carter. Do you know him?

Aubrey's mouth flew open.

> **Aubrey** - Yes, I think I know him. Anyway, thanks again. See you soon.

"Now what?" Nicole asked.

"Benson Carter is the chef who tried to outbid me." Aubrey frowned at the thought of that man.

"Do we know him? Are we supposed to know who he is? I'm gonna Google him." Nicole reached for her phone and typed in Benson Carter in the search bar. After a few seconds, a list of articles appeared. "He's an established chef." Nicole scrolled and found a picture of him. "Aubrey? Is this him?" Nicole held her phone toward Aubrey, Jeannette, and Ms. Davis so they could check out Mr. Carter.

"Aubrey, he's cute," Ms. Davis said.

"Yes, he's very handsome," Jeannette offered.

"I'm not looking for a date or love connection," Aubrey adamantly said. She sat in silence for several seconds. She thought she rid herself of Benson Carter years ago. Why was he in town and searching for restaurant space on her block? Aubrey couldn't worry about him. Her focus was on Nicole and planning the most fabulous wedding ever. There was no time to think about Mr. Carter.

Acknowledgments

The teenage me is jumping for joy.

Writing a novel is a dream come true. I did it!

To my hubby, my soulmate. I'm forever thankful for you, Darryl, for loving me in life and supporting me in my writing journey.

To my favorite son, Mason. Your commitment and strength inspires me. And you make me laugh.

To my favorite daughter, Maleyni. Your warm, loving hugs feed my soul in more ways than one. Telling me to "lock in" and get it done is always the encouragement I need. And you make me laugh, too.

To Monty, my fur baby, for being my writing partner, sitting at my feet hours on end while I wrote. I'm forever thankful to my family for supporting me along the way.

Special thanks to my mother, Patricia, for your enduring love and FaceTiming me to remind me how fabulous I am for staying committed.

To cousin Devin, for helping me through technology glitches and just listening to me vent.

To cousin Carolyn and Aunt Carrie. Thank you for your prayers and checking in to see if I was still writing.

To my sister, Afkara and brother, Ray. You both motivate me with your wisdom and love. To my core - Katrina, Majela and Rhonda. My life's cheerleaders. Love you forever.

To author and dear friend Linda B. Martins. Thank you for holding me accountable to every word on the page. Without your calls, video chats and text messages, I'm not sure how I would have done it. I'm forever indebted to you.

To my talented author friends; M.A. Cobb, Darcy Embers, Autumn Green, Elle Maldonado, Luna Mason, Riley S. Baron, Simone Monroe, and K.C. Bullen. Your support, advise, and encouragement is unmatched.

To Dee Ahvion, Sara Cortes, and Sheridan Gregory. You took time from your busy schedules to read my story and share your honest thoughts. I am forever grateful.

To Liz Borum, Leondria Brown, and Theresa Asuncion. Just checking in, offering advice and critique, helped me push to the finish line. Thanks a bunch.

To Samantha Matamoros. Muchas Gracias for all your words of encouragement and just being you.

To my editor, Sarah Wentworth at Indie Proofreading. Thank you for advancing my story and answering my many questions. You made this process feel like a cake walk.

To my father and grandfather shining down on me from above. Your brilliant light and heavenly spirits breathe within me and inspire me to create and share happily ever afters.

To you, the reader. Thank you for choosing my story. I hope you enjoyed reading Love to the Rescue.

About the Author

Kat Neil is a hopeless romantic and educator.
After many years as a reader of happily ever afters, she has plopped into the writing chair to craft love stories and main characters that make her swoon. When Kat is not writing, she is reading, shopping, or watching cooking shows.
She is a loving wife and mother to two amazing children.
She resides outside of Los Angeles, California.

Instagram – @katneilauthor
Website – http://katneil.com/